Ralph Trout is the author of four fictional novels, one non-fiction, and one reference book.

The Wreck

Soucouyant – The Caribbean Vampire

Something Fishy

Soon Come

Non-fiction
Road Trip Huautla: The Mushroom Cult

Reference
The Caribbean Home Garden Guide

All titles are available at Amazon.com and Barnes and Noble.

SOON

COME

Divorce
Caribbean Style

By

Ralph Trout

I dedicate this book to two captains. A chance meeting of a pair of Pennsylvania boys over a pool table at an upstairs bar on Back Street in Charlotte Amalie, St. Thomas, in the US Virgins, changed my life for the better. Captain Earl provided me with the opportunity to sail. He also introduced me to Captain Chris, forever with a smile, a joke, kind words, and always willing to help. Earl, the navigator, and Chris, the journalist, together gave me a course to follow.

Cover photo by the author. Thanks to Dr, Claire Hu for her patience in helping a dummy with Photoshop.

INTRODUCTION

Marriage in the twenty-first century is a risky proposition carrying a fifty-fifty chance of success. The split probably isn't amicable, and there probably wouldn't be an even division of assets. Who was at fault? Who provoked the irreconcilable differences requires a legal judgment who gets the lion's share of properties, possessions, and money. The lawyers are always the only true winners in a divorce.

Merging two lives, with distinctly unique identities, isn't easy living in a modern, fast-paced, stressful, and competitive world. Newlyweds are usually carrying a huge load of debt. Add family and cultural traditions, and drug and alcohol abuse; the pressure can be immense. If communications lapse between partners and they can't resist temptation, a slight crack in the marriage union can expand to the width of the Grand Canyon.

To the anxiety of day-to-day life of making ends meet while wearing a smile, add a Caribbean island setting of pearl blue cloudless skies, sparkling crystal-clear seas, waving palm trees, cute tourist girls stretching tight bikinis, and handsome, muscular men. Everyone visiting the islands tries to squeeze out the most sparks during their never-long-enough vacation. Whatever it takes, fun at anyone's expense; get the most bang for your buck.

The axiom that only death and taxes are definite in life must be modified to include change and perspectives. Change always occurs as people grow. Everyone's tastes and interests change as time progresses. Very few people stay the same person as the day they were married. And some partners premeditatedly weren't really who they projected themselves to be at the betrothal. There are clandestine motives for the marriage. In the islands, this often involves immigration issues.

Perspectives will be different between multiple viewers of every occurrence. Everyone sees something that has happened, but each individual, because of previous experiences, catalogs and remembers unique aspects. The courts settle divorce disputes after capable lawyers present alternative perspectives of the same dysfunctional marriage.

Each divorce creates a distinctly unique operations manual depending on the psyches involved, ages, and materialism. If people split early, there's plenty of time to rebuild finances and egos. If the divorce comes late in life and hard-earned savings and investments are lost, tempers often flare.

Getting even, or revenge becomes a prime goal.

Divorce Caribbean style is often fueled by drugs, alcohol, and infidelity. Partners plot against each other. Marriage becomes a game; one partner must win. The sun combined with rum can fuel vengeful personalities.

The war on drugs is not being won, and it continues to threaten stability and democracy not only in the Andes, but throughout the Caribbean as well, where tiny police and military forces are outclassed by the sophisticated equipment in the hands of traffickers passing through the region on the way to their market in this country.
Elliot Abrams

CHAPTER ONE

"What do you really want!?" This phone conversation had already exhausted his patience. "I don't have any more money! You persuaded the courts to give everything to my ex. Now you want more! Hell, you didn't even leave me enough to continue my business. That was stupid on your part, Charles; she could have milked me for bigger money. You and that damned judge crushed me and then shook me by the ankles to get the last penny!"

The floor fan chattered through its rotations while the lawyer droned on. "Yeah, sure, indiscretions, irreconcilable, okay, okay, I'll listen." His ex's attorney had chosen five-thirty on Friday afternoon to demand the biggest part of his meager weekly paycheck.

It was hot. May in St. Thomas could be hot or rainy. This year it had been blistering hot, great for tourists, but bad for the locals who had to hump it every day just to squeeze by.

"Okay, so the bottom line is… you want my money, all my money, every cent. Charles, you and I were friends once, now you really want to dunk me in the shitter. No, no, you want to leave me permanently swimming in the turd bowl." He glanced at his pale blue paycheck, "All $316 for a forty-hour week after Uncle Sam and the USVI get their shares. Buddy, my old friend, your percentage from my wife must have netted you over ten grand; give her some of that if she can't make ends meet." He was beginning to understand how the homeless learned to enjoy their plight after shedding their possessions. "Yeah, yeah, I know, she has expenses. The dog has to eat. That was *my* dog. What about me? It's not like we have kids…"

The run of terrible luck had stretched almost two years for Keith Gardnar. The constant question was how he would dig himself out of this hole. He couldn't remember being more broke. He cradled the phone against his shoulder and drew a glass of water from the kitchen faucet. He frowned as he remembered how a moment of stupid lust had ended his marriage. Almost instantly, he'd lost his house on Skyline Drive, his boat, his truck, his businesses, his finances, and his dog.

"Whoa, get a grip there buddy! Be realistic, I have to eat,

pay rent, and occasionally do my laundry. $316 a week doesn't spread very far. Hey, hey, whoa, whoa, buddy, who's tapping your revenues? Huh? I'm out there planting new fresh water lines five days a week so Maddie can get her hair done to go out to dinner with you." Keith wiped the sweat from his brow, more frustrated than ever. "I really don't think so. St. Thomas is a small island. I don't have to be a psychic to know what's going on. Put it this way, you do what you have to do and I'll do the same. End of conversation!"

Telephones were the great umbilical. All alone, pretending to enjoy the solitude in a sleazy, one-room flat, and the damn phone could still bust balls. The cell slammed into the wall and ended the lawyer's monotone lecture.

"That's it for incoming calls. Screw 'em, they can send a letter. Who else other than creditors or the cops would call?" he asked the walls.

Sandwiched between the steaming, smelly asphalt of the highway and the broiling sun had made him harder. Keith could still pinch an inch, but the intense manual labor of replacing the water lines had slimmed him down. Years as a diver had toned an entirely different set of muscles. Beers, deliciously cold beers, toned his midriff and adjusted his attitude. His calloused hands splashed water and sensitivity onto his face.

"Yeah, a cold beer sounds excellent. I guess it's late to watch the sunset, but a coldie with some conversation would be nice." He surveyed his hovel, entertaining the fantasy of bringing back a tourist honey. The futon was also his bed, depending on if he wanted to sit or recline. He attempted to fold his sheets, mouthing a promise to do laundry tomorrow. The week's trash of leftovers, newspapers, and containers he'd drop along his walk into town. After some masterful broom work, the place sparkled.

Exercise wasn't new to him, but discipline was. He racked off a series of ab crunches and some stretches with deep breathing to ease the stress from the lawyer. Meditation would be staring at the barroom mirror. He sighed; the day was finally beginning to wear away. Even though the shower was smaller than the old telephone booths, the apartment came with city pipe water, a luxury in the tropics, and he could use as much as he wanted. Hell, he was replacing the main pipelines. Freshwater was a by-product of the gas generators that fed electrical current into the tourist trap. Most houses depended on rain on the roof catch stored in a cistern. It was a triumph to stand in a shower in St. Thomas for five minutes. After the conversation with his ex's lawyer, it might take double that to wash all the bullshit away.

The rusted overhead fan couldn't diminish the muggy evening. This side of town seldom got a breeze. That made for a lot of uncomfortable people. It was certain to become more humid as the night wore on. He didn't even have a paperback for company. His below-counter fridge yielded a plastic gallon of store-bought water to quench his thirst. It was one thing to wash with the pipe water, and he knew better than to drink it.

Keith took a twenty and stuck his paycheck in his stash. The faded burgundy polo would be okay at the bar, as long as the lights were dim. He knew it was senseless to lock his sliding glass door, but he did it anyway. Inside was all he had, slim pickings. He hoped that any crack head wouldn't have a pry bar or the strength to use it. Crack had changed the complexion of this once sweet island.

His glued flip flops slapped down the concrete steps. In all his years in the tropics, this was the only time he'd lived in town. The course was west to Goodfella's Bar, where he'd find cute, young waitresses serving cheap beers. What remained of his circle of friends would be there continuing liver damage.

Along the waterfront, the political big wigs with all their wisdom and taxes, had chosen this prime ocean view to house those most stricken by poverty. Keith chuckled and shook his head; it was some of the most expensive real estate anywhere in the world - ninety percent of the tourists passed it more than once during their holiday. It was a dangerous place filled with unhappy people. These were shelters, not homes.

To set it off, the planners had put a beautiful, lighted tennis court opposite on the other side of the street where Keith walked, but nobody in the houses were tennis enthusiasts. No one would play anything during the day's heat. Local teens were shooting hoops at a net-less rim on the converted court. Brown bodies shined with athletic sweat. Elbows and legs flailed amid grunts, groans, and curses. One teenager attempted a LeBron push while another took a Curry turnaround jump.

Keith leaned against the chain-link fence, and thoughts of his own youth irritated him. It had been at least ten years since he'd taken part in any sport other than fishing or diving, and he did those mostly for money. He'd played basketball in high school in West Virginia. His hometown was now more than just miles distant.

The boys he watched were the new Caribbean youth, trained and maimed by the media evolution. They squeaked through hundred-dollar Nike jump shots and wore their bleached and dyed hair braided to salute a favorite celebrity. Their island culture was changing by the second as fresh waves of entertainment spanned the thousand-plus miles; it was received, exaggerated, copied, and sold.

"Heavy thoughts buddy; better keep that to myself. Who cares? It's all somebody else's shit. I got enough of my own," Keith mumbled.

Long dreadlocks swinging, one of the taller players grabbed the rebound and slammed the ball against the fence. He didn't throw it directly at Keith, but the resounding clang delivered the message. "What you want, mon? What you checking us out for?" the most Marley-ish asked, retrieving the basketball. "You looking for something, white man? Something you ain't got, or forgot?" An assured grin reduced the tension, "You ain't a cop, are you?"

The game continued as the West Indians shuffled to both ends of the court with trash-talk that only the players understood. Being watched by an older white man provided extra enjoyment. The island authorities must have finally realized that no one in their right mind would come to this area to play tennis at night, even under the lights. As early as eight, it could be dangerous. Hell, even in the daylight it could be fatal. Maybe not from these players, but across the street, in the projects, they were playing a serious game. It was all about survival.

Three weeks had passed since two Rastas has bounced into him where he worked laying the water line. He hadn't said a word or even looked their way, but they started an argument that had become a fight, but only with him. He didn't have a racial bone in his body, but they did. These hoop-guys could also be dangerous.

"Hey mon, want some shit?" asked a thin, dark man in a tattered orange tank top. "Why you be here if not to buy the shit, mon? White people only want one thing from this street, the shit! The shit!" The man sat cross-legged on the ground rocking back and forth, almost hidden by an oleander bush. The man's body odor outranked the flower's sweet scent.

Keith shrugged and turned his back to the fence. Road dust added to the humid night and haloed the street lights. The bar was a good twenty minutes away. He could swill a few cold ones and get home with a buzz on by ten. That would be pushing the safe hours of this street. Forget the cost of a taxi. A walk and a talk would do him some good. It seemed danger was everywhere since crack had become king.

Dreads shouted again as Keith moved away, "What you want, mon? Why you checking us out?"

His digital watch lit to 8:23. The game continued, but it wasn't good enough to hold his attention. Nothing was that good anymore. The last six months had turned his world upside down. He was feeling old. Everything was feeling old. Maybe he'd been on this saltwater rock too long. And again, by routine, he headed to a bar he'd frequented for decades. Almost everything in his life was too usual. He was a regular guy, getting up early, going to work, coming home exhausted. He laughed; lately, life had thrown some serious curves.

Whistling, humming his musical efforts occasionally merged into a verse of the Dead's *'I Will Survive.'* Across the street, a stereo boomed an unchanging baseline beat. Keith grinned as he thought it sounded like the theme from *Jaws*. His mood was improving.

Cars and taxis passed in a continuous flow. The wind wasn't enough to move the palms overhead. The sky was charcoal, not a crisp black, starry night, yet out to the west over Hassel Island and to the south, he could see some vague constellations.

Trudging almost to the first intersection, he turned to see the last cruise ship pulling away from the dock. The bright lights reflected the white exterior, sending the message of profits to the store owners in Charlotte Amalie.

"That not your boat, huh?" A woman's voice startled Keith. It was Spanish scented and accented. "You not be cruising, maybe you want to be?"

She could have been fourteen or twenty-four with red-skin, maybe from the DR, with a head of blossoming braids. In her one-piece African print shift, she was a sweetheart. "What's up my friend?" Closer, she smelled sweet, like frangipani. "What can I do for you tonight? Or with you, maybe, huh?"

She reached out and grabbed his arm. "You have muscles, I like that. I got good rock and good sensi. We could party if you have enough money."

"That's the sorry part, sister." He put his arms around her, pulled her close to inhale her youth, and whispered, "I would love to take you up on that. It might kill me one way or the other, but I'd probably die with a smile. Too bad, babe, these times my wallet's slim."

She reached down and tugged his crotch. "Yeah, I know what you mean." She broke the embrace and disappeared toward the basketball court.

He never heard it coming. Something hit him across his shoulder blades. Keith's body crumpled, flattened into the dirt along the sidewalk. Two pairs of arms grabbed him and dragged him into the shadows. Without a word, a series of sharp kicks pummeled his body. There was no way he could rally to fight or escape. The first blow had winded him; he was unable to shout or even curl into a fetal ball. Stretched out in the darkness between the highway and the water, he was at his attackers' mercy.

A body landed on his back with the knees pressing on his shoulders. Keith's head was jerked back by his ponytail. He struggled to get a few breaths. A knife snapped open. He felt the tip pressed to the soft skin of his cheek. Hands rummaged through his pockets, grabbed his money and his watch. The knife took a short, bloody trail from his cheek to his jaw.

"Mi amigo, escúhame (*listen*), you can still hear me before we put you out? Yo, yo, yo! Word is you ripped off some brothers. You gotta pay your tab one way or the other, whitey." A foot slammed into Keith's shoulder.

"We won't kill you now," the voice heckled. "This time is a warning. The man who sent us only asks nice once. Pay, plus interest, or we cut you. Next time, gringo," another foot slammed into his side, "have more money." With the last parting shot at his ribs, the attackers vanished.

Keith realized that the shit had just gotten deeper. He didn't owe anybody. Debt was something he didn't believe in. He may not have wanted to pay his ex-wife what the court demanded, but other than that he didn't remember owing anyone more than a beer.

Slowly, he reached his knees. Still winded and aching, he struggled to pull himself up against a palm trunk. Keith felt his body to see if anything was broken. Each breath ached his midriff. He circled his jaw and gingerly touched the scrapes on his face. The knife cut didn't feel very deep. The guy had been a pro and the knife very sharp, like a razor. With a bit of spit on his shirt, he wiped his face. He checked his teeth and none wobbled more than usual. Even though he couldn't straighten upright, he was in one piece. He was alive and probably not maimed for life. They taken his Timex and his drinking money.

He was still alive, and that's what counted. At least

that's what Keith told himself over and over. It had taken only five minutes. He could easily be dead, and it probably wouldn't have felt any worse.

"Next time, huh?" Keith rubbed his jaw and with agonizing lurches staggered to the sidewalk. He'd only walked two blocks from his harbor front studio dump to the basketball court. Now it felt like two miles. Each step became a measured thought. There was no money for hospitals or explanations for the police. He hadn't even gotten a glimpse of his attackers.

Finally, on the concrete stairs to his apartment, Keith rested using the pipe railing for support. Out of habit, he glanced at his now watch-less forearm. They'd beat his ass, taken a thirty-dollar watch, and an Andy Jackson. What debt? His wife? No, she couldn't possibly hate him that much. That's what she always said, anyway. Disgusted, not hated. Maybe they had mistaken him for someone else. All white guys look alike. He was confused.

The front street rumbled with incessant traffic. No heavy players were in sight. No cops or good Samaritans to assist him tonight. This had been well planned; he realized the girl must have been the bait. They might have been watching his place. These were not good thoughts. St. Thomas was a small rock with many people who kept their eyes and ears open. His infidelity created great gossip. There might have been a few people who considered Keith an asshole, but that wasn't a life-threatening offense.

He was wheezing and coughing badly, sounding like a chugging locomotive, as he mounted the last three steps to his tiny patio. So much for the element of surprise, the sliding door gaped open. His apartment was dark, but someone had done fast work. With a painful groan, he raised his right arm and flicked on the light.

The rainbow emitted from the overhead bulb didn't end at a pot of gold. Almost everything he owned was piled in a heap of destruction. His small TV was shattered with the smashed clock radio on a pile of his clothes. They'd soaked everything with a quart of white oil paint he'd bought to do the kitchen. What little food he'd had topped the pile like sprinkles. The room reeked of fresh urine.

He found an unbroken glass and drank from the kitchen faucet. Righting the only chair, he sat and contemplated his evening. Who was behind this? He'd made some enemies in his twenty years on the island. Over the past nine months, karma had continually bitten him on the ass.

This could be the tipping point - all he could take. The finger on the signpost was pointing either down the road or down island, but definitely out of St. Thomas. Out, for certain and pronto. Whoever was trying to make his life even more miserable was doing an excellent job.

Everything was imploding; Keith was close to breaking. All of his social circle were four-digit people, thousandaires. When he'd slipped into bankruptcy, most of his good buddies became strangers. He mused, "Must be the trickle-down effect. Nothing but shit is trickling to me and nothing but rotten luck is trickling out."

It was like that Jimmy Buffett song, '*I Used to Have Money.*' Keith previously had several bank accounts, but his wife's attorney had discovered them all. He wiped his face with his torn polo and struggled out of
the chair to the bathroom to survey his injuries. He shut the sliding door, propped a mop handle in the track, and pulled the shabby, sun-bleached drapes.

After rummaging through the mess, he found a kitchen knife, hoping his attackers would return and give just enough notice. They had violated his life. Neither his home nor this island was safe. He shut off the light and stumbled to the bathroom. Its single bulb couldn't wasn't visible from the street with the door shut.

Keith stripped in the narrow space between the shower and the toilet. Every bend and twist caused sharp pains. He bumped the towel bar and jerked his attention to the face in the mirror. A golf ball-sized lump graced his forehead, crowning what would become two black eyes. He gently washed the scrapes on his cheeks and turned to glimpse the damage to his back. An almost perfect straight-line bruise signified that a board had tattooed his shoulder blades.

Welts decorated his chest and thighs. The shock to his nervous system was diminishing as deep, sharp pains increased. He gulped three Advil from the medicine cabinet and slipped down to lie on the cool concrete floor. Keith again assessed his situation. Who had he pissed off so badly? There was always the chance of being mugged, but the combination of the attack and his house ransacked wasn't a Coincidence, but a message. Why? Who?

The towel rod offered support for a lift, but it pulled off the wall, dumping Keith into the shower stall with an excruciating thud. The dribbling water wiped the sweat from his face. A few minutes of the cold spray didn't work wonders.

Naked and wet, he carefully maneuvered into the main room. At the kitchen window, he wiggled the lower wooden sill free. Beneath the wood was an empty concrete block. It was Keith's safe deposit box. His stiff fingers retrieved his passport and his gold Tag Heuer watch. It was his only luxury that had survived the divorce.

He thumbed his bankroll. "A grand total of three hundred and forty, plus my paycheck; where's that gonna get me? I could fly to the States. What then? I'd be starving among an enormous crowd of unknown faces." He pondered, "Maybe it would be better to head down island until this thing passes. Far down island, like St. Vincent or St. Lucia. Hell, St. Vincent is like Jurassic Park. Yeah, I better go somewhere that speaks English, like Antigua, Dominica, or Grenada."

"What luck, stinking fucking luck!" He slammed his fist onto the stainless kitchen counter. He shivered with pain from the impact. "I finally get a job that pays enough to afford this shithole, clear my head, and these toughs run me off…"

Staring at the few possessions that had escaped damage, "Won't be getting my security deposit back. Nothing to sell, nothing to store, little to pack." Keith opened the closet and at the back of the shelf found a faded green duffle. He packed what he could find that they hadn't completely ruined. A pair of shorts, two T-shirts, an old diver's light, his penknife, and a shaving kit had survived. By some grace, his raincoat, hat, with his good sunglasses were hanging in the closet and okay. Everything got a good rinsing, even though his muscles ached, hopeful about squeezing out the smell of his attackers.

The rain slicker stuffed inside his duffle bag became his pillow and a beach towel was his blanket on the floor. Tomorrow, he was out of there. Cash his check, buy a few things, and get the fuck out of Dodge. Twenty- plus years on St. Thomas had been good, but now that was history. His wife had kept his name, boat, house, and dog. He was sure his story would become one of the many local tales of how a man meets his fate among the islands.

You know why divorces are so expensive?
Because they're worth it.
Willie Nelson

CHAPTER TWO

Morning is the prime time in the tropics, early, before it gets heated by father sun. The earlier the better. That morning, Keith awakened and reached for more pills to soothe his aches. Gulping some water, "Yeah, every morning starts a fresh day. No, I'm not buying into that, but today is the getaway."

Showered and packed, Keith was out the door by 6:15. He turned and glanced over his shoulder. "No, goddamn it, this hadn't been a fit place to live, probably my all-time worst!" He suffered a painful shiver up his spine as he stood. "What's next for me now?"

He shook his head and took a deep breath. "Survival, that's what this next part is about. I coasted for a few excellent years. Payback can be a bitch. But I will get by and this will have been my lowest point. What say, Mr. Good Luck? You ready to chase away my blues? Find me my next woman? That's what caused my problems, but I'm not ready to be a monk. Maybe a rich, slightly older, wealthy widow could set me straight. Yeah, that's exactly what I need, someone to take care of me."

Keith blew a kiss to his flat and headed to the marina. The first order was to get his paycheck cashed and then find a ride to somewhere else.

Banks weren't open on Saturday; it would have to be a store. The docks had a good chandlery. He knew the owner, Adil, could cut a favor, plus he would know which boats were leaving. Yeah, Adil and the dockmaster would know who was going where.

The public docks weren't busy that early. Keith checked out the ads for crew on the marina's office window. No boat needed him. They wanted kids, especially kids who could cook wearing bikinis or less. He'd have to ask around to learn intended destinations. Intended, because Keith knew shit always happened.

A few other boatie dregs were waiting for the food store to open, needing the tobacco or beer. No one looked as though they wanted deodorant or toothpaste.

Adil was from Lebanon and another of the characters who seem to migrate to marinas. He'd been a fixture for over a decade, had a spectacular munchies and wine selection, not to mention the best deli on the island.

"Buddy, Adil," Keith presented his hand to the proprietor when the doors unlocked. He didn't shake it.

"What you want? Buy something; you look like a strong cup of coffee would do you good. What you need, Mr. Keith?" Adil seemed unconcerned and kept busy walking the aisles. "Speak now, what you want? You looking poorly, Mr. Keith."

"I've had better mornings. Say... ah, Adil, could you cash my paycheck?"

"I don't like to cash third-party checks. Risky." "It's from the road company. They're solid."

"But are you?" Adil glared. "Buy about forty dollars of stuff and I'll cash it."

"Man, that's a lot. Okay, okay." Keith didn't know what he would do with the supplies and then reasoned, "Can I leave the stuff here for a few hours? I'll be pulling out on a boat." He said it with self-assurance. A crewman bearing groceries had a better chance of catching a ride.

Forty bucks filled four plastic bags with tasty cheese, biscuits, cold cuts, and tins of tuna for whenever he finally got off the boat. Now, his fate depended on who'd carry him somewhere distant. He didn't need any weekend explorers.

Shuffling through the docks with a coffee and a croissant, he inquired for either passage and/or work. In the middle of Dock B, Keith got a nibble on a ride headed to Dominica. That'd be fine. Some guy was carrying drums of gear oil down to a drilling company. The boat was a tugboat named 'The Mule.' Keith found the small tug on the fuel dock.

"Lucky for you, they had a few other yachts to fuel, or we'd have been gone." The skipper-owner was a rotund man with 50s wavy hair. "I'm Tom. Pay you a buck twenty a day, also unloading. Two, four-hour watches a day. You capable? Can you get your stuff, pronto? Hey, you're on your own when you get there. Understand?"

"Absolutely understood. Thanks for the job. Be back in minutes. Got some groceries. Got a cold box?" Keith asked.

"Bring 'em. We'll find somewhere to pack them, but they'll probably get eaten. I'm a sandwich man on crossings." His hands rubbed his girth. "And some soup at nights. You can work a pot and a pan?"

"Let me see your passport. Wow, are you worried we're gonna sink? Keeping your papers and money in a Ziploc, what's up with that?"

"Organized, just a habit I got into years ago on my own boats. Fell overboard with one blue book. Since then I keep it and my money sealed and in my front pocket."

"Yeah, had my own papers thieved a few times. Okay, it's up to date. Someone after you? Cops?" Tom queried.

"No, just took a beating, as you can see. Decided it's time for a vacation. That's all."

"Whatever. Get your stuff on the hustle. Two days with a broadside sea. You ain't a puker, are ya? Look like you've had a few sea miles. Get your stuff."

Keith returned in fifteen minutes; Tom was filling the starboard tanks. The other mate, who looked to be a local, was tending all the lines, making certain he secured the barrels on the aft deck. They pointed Keith to a bunk behind the steering station.

'The Mule' wasn't spacious. The galley separated the steering station from the bunks. Off to the port side was the head. Everything looked in good order. He could feel the diesels under the floor, probably twelve cylinders. He checked for the life raft and preservers and felt safe enough to get paid to travel.

Tom did the introductions. "Sam, and you are Keith, right? The rules are, no drugs on board, toss them if you have 'em; toss them in the sea now. No drinking aboard. If that's a problem, leave. No DT's at sea. Four-hour watches, got your own bunks, so no hot sheets. Make your food or, what's your name, yeah, Keith, will cook something. Should be there in two days. Mule makes ten knots, twelve in the calm. On your watch, absolutely no reading, listening to music, none of those phone videos. Pay attention to the radar and check everything, pressures, and levels. I'll take you around the first time."

He held a composition book. "Write down everything that happens on your watch and sign your name. Give me your passports again." Captain Tom filled out the Coast Guard and customs forms. It was another hour before he got his port clearance.

Two pleasant days at sea worked wonders on Keith. The stiff sea breeze reduced some bruises and the blueness faded. He'd have liked to hit a new island without bearing scars from the last one. Maybe rosy cheeks would help. He laughed to himself.

The Mule made Dominica in fifty uneventful hours. It wasn't the first time Keith had viewed the island from the sea, yet it always inspired him to think it was still part of the old Caribbean. It was one of the least touched by the expansion of tourism. Once the tug tied to the dock, Tom kept the job moving by begging the crane operator to remain and swing the barrels onto the concrete slab.

The Caribbean

"Here's your pay. Could use a man like you, but you know, things are kind of slow. We'll be pulling out early. I want to get back; not loading anything from here. If you want to ride back, I can let you sleep in a berth, but the work's not steady. Usually hang at Red Hook Marina."

"Thanks, but no thanks. Maybe another time," They shook hands and Keith continued, "Sort of promised myself a vacation from St. T. Just roust me or I'll hear the engines. All my stuff's together, so it'll only take me minutes. Don't see any reason to freshen up for Monday morning in Portsmouth, do you?"

"Don't know and don't care. I like this island all right, but it creeps me out with it so quiet at night, and damn is it dark. Seems it gets darker here than on any other island. Probably the clouds? If you are up to it, I'll buy a few rounds at the nearest watering hole."

"Yeah, that'd work," Keith agreed. They shuffled off down the street, exchanging tales.

The tug's 12 cylinders cranked to life at five. The few beers had led to rum. Tom would have been a great skipper to work for and a decent friend to have, but no, it was too dangerous. If he hadn't learned from one ass whooping, then he deserved what came next. Duffle on his shoulder, Keith shook hands and hit the dock. When the boat was ready, he threw the dock lines to Sam, waved goodbye, and enjoyed watching the small tug disappear to the horizon. There went his first chance at a job.

Work, and more work. Yeah, that's what would have to happen soon. Keith was no stranger to work, but it wasn't his friend either. There wasn't much he couldn't do or hadn't already done. He was good at construction and working boats. Diving with the tourists had been his latest venture. A few of those divers got the special tour. It was one of those specials that had been irreconcilable.

Didn't matter if he had to pound nails, stroke a paintbrush, or pull a fishnet. He was optimistic; by evening, he'd have a job and a place to live. Wasn't going to be easy, he smiled to himself, but he could do it. This was a new island and it wouldn't be the same shit. He might not get a white-collar job, and that would be good because he didn't have a white shirt. He only hoped his next bedroom had a roof.

"It will work out. It always does," Keith smirked. "I still got most of the food I brought, so it'll be dinner under the stars, at the least, tuna and crackers." He didn't have much, but he had this thing about food. He enjoyed having it around, primitive belly security. The few tins weighted his duffle.

He stood on the Portsmouth Government Dock, surveyed the blue sea to the west, and turned to view the lush green mountains that rose into the pillow clouds. It was a beautiful, peaceful vision of an island that still existed without sucking blood from tourists.

"Lost it all, for what? Love?!" Keith snickered, "Love stinks! Bah." He spat and stared into the clear water. "What do I love now? I only miss my dog. What do I even value besides my health? They say health is the real wealth." He laughed out loud, still confused about how it happened. Months of craziness had passed, and none of it made any sense.

Years before coming to the islands, he'd worked for a wealthy Russian real estate developer who continually muttered, "There, but for the grace of God, go I." Now, Keith fully understood; he had fallen out of grace and got tossed out of his St. Thomas Eden.

In his teens, Keith realized that stateside winters were too uncomfortable. Decided it was a waste of money to have two or three separate sets of clothes for the different seasons. That had been his rationale; it was always easier to get cool if you're hot than to get warm if you're cold. He remembered the homeless in the northern states fighting for a place on a warm street grate.

Here, in the tropics, he'd get by; he was down, but not out. He'd survive. Good old Keith would pull himself up and keep on trucking. Lady Luck was just dodging him for the moment. She'd better show up soon.

"The sooner the better," he muttered as he took a deep breath. "Better hurry 'cause I'm homeless. You hear me? Homeless!"

Keith was standing on the only dock that served Portsmouth. The sound of an outboard shook him from his private thoughts. A lone fisherman in an open boat motored toward the dock. The guy had probably hauled his fish traps and wanted to sell his catch. The concrete span was slowly showing some signs of activity early, but by eight, vendors and buyers were scrambling for deals.

Not bustling and not quite a city, Portsmouth still needed everything. The dock was their supply line. From fresh fish to a pickup truck, it all arrived by boat. Farmers brought their produce to the boats that traded with other islands. The French resorts to the north and south in the
Caribbean chain needed fresh vegetables, and they liked the low prices of the Dominican farmers. The incoming boats brought the local merchants' trade goods.

The fisherman tossed Keith his bowline. "What you want, boss?" The black man in a faded blue work shirt asked. "You want some fish? Be awhile 'for I get them cleaned." It was English, but the local accent almost obscured everything except 'boss.'

"I'm looking for work," Keith replied. "I need a job."

"What can you do for a black man like me? What? You want to work for me? Hah!"

"I don't much care if you're purple; I just need to get a few bucks in my pocket. I'm sure you know how that is."

"You want to clean these fish? Hah! Clean them, scale them, all for twenty EC."

Twenty EC was about eight US, and in these parts, it would stretch through some simple days and non-drinking nights. It looked to be about two big buckets of reef fish and some king mackerel caught trolling.

"What you say 'bout this work?" The boatman asked again.

"Okay, no big deal," Keith answered as he estimated the job should take him about an hour. Not a bad wage for where he was. He thought, as he always did, it never really was about how much money you made, it was about how much time it took to make it. If you made fifty grand working fifty weeks a year, eight dull hours a day plus the commute, wasn't it better to make half as much in half the time; relax and enjoy life? Never the money, always the time. Twenty local dollars was more than most of the islanders would make that day.

"Yeah, give me a knife and a board."

"You really want the work? It'll make you stink like fish."

"That's all right. I need the cash and you need the fish cleaned."

The fisherman passed Keith the tools, then reclined and lit a stubby cigar. "I got to say it is always mighty nice to watch a white man work at a dirty job." The fisherman was probably about the same age as Keith, but the sea and sun had weathered him. Dominicans are a handsome people with the African genetics mixed with the original islanders, the Carib Indians. His black face was round with cheerful eyes wrapped with long, graying sideburns. "Yeah, it ain't often I get to see this, 'specially in Portsmouth. First time I ever had a white man working for me. This must be a good omen. Shit, I never think I've seen a white person work on this dock."

Keith stripped to his bathing suit, as it was a dirty, smelly job. He only had two changes of clothes and no laundry soap. Done correctly, the scales and fish guts wouldn't get all over him, but afterward, it required a mandatory swim-scrub.

"You want me to save the guts and gills for your trap bait?" Keith asked.

"White man, you know about that, huh? You must have pulled some traps. You don't talk like a Frenchie. You don't look like a stranger from work, though. Wow, sure got some bruises. Who put those licks on you? Let me see your hands."

It was all part of the show, so the others milling around the dock could see the fisherman had found a helper. He stood out. The dark, purple splotches marked the broad shoulders and torso of Keith's tanned, five-ten frame. His hands were considerably smaller than the black pair that turned his palms up.

The fisherman looked down and said, "These hands have worked hard, but you know the lines in your hands tell more of your story than the scrapes. You been all around, had some bad times, but it says there will be good times again. You see this line here on your right hand?"

Keith politely nodded.

"Yeah man, it says you going to be okay. Soon as you clean all those damn fish. Yeah, that's what it says. Hah!" The fisherman laughed until he coughed. "Yeah, soon as you clean all those fish you gonna be all right, hah!" He reclined on a coil of anchor rope, "Relaxing ain't a awful thing, if you got the time for it. And the heart. Me, I got the time and the heart. I hear there are people in New York and London who can't relax. Imagine that."

"I don't think I'll be relaxing for a while. I need work. You know anything permanent around here or in Roseau?" Keith remarked, carefully watching as he scraped to be certain he missed his hands and only got the fish.

"White man, me, I make my money. You want fish, or pig, or banana, or frog, I got them. It will be tough for you to find work because you gonna want money, and we got very little money now. I can look at you and tell you had money for a while and got used to having it. Right? But here you gotta work for the same as what we work for, right? People happy with three, four dollars a day. Can you live on that? I don't think so. You could make more money... if you had a product, but then you'd have bigger problems 'cause you illegal. Best for you to be quiet. Know what I mean?"

"Looks like I'll have to. If you could have this done cheaper, why hire me?"

"You heard what I said; I like to see a white man get smelly and dirty while I sitting here. You was here already looking for work and I didn't have to find you. So, you just keep cleaning those fish."

The dock became crowded with dozens of people walking around to see what was for sale. Trucks were arriving, and the loading and unloading became a sideshow. Keith's tanned frame in his skimpy, purple bathing suit drew leering glances. He worked at it, humming something out of tune until he'd scraped the last fish. The fisherman had been snoring for half an hour, his head resting against the bow of his boat. Keith grabbed a five-gallon bucket and a scrub brush from the boat's stern and cleaned the dock where he'd worked and then himself. The noise of the bucket splashing water woke the fisherman.

"Ain't much past nine and you done cleaned them all. You do like work. Me, I'd have been scraping them 'til noon, if I had to do it."

Keith stretched out on the already warm concrete to dry off. Three traders approached the dock with noisy engines. He sat up and surveyed the scene. Portsmouth Bay was an extinct volcano crater. Behind the narrow beach were the cloud-capped, dark green hills the locals called mountains. They weren't high mountains, only low clouds. Dotted along the coconut lined beach were houses and a few boats. The few tall buildings signified guest houses or stores. The day was cloudless, with enough sun. It was the usual tropical scene.

"You got my twenty, boss? I'm about ready to roll," Keith requested.

"No, I have to sell the fish first. I'm no bank. Don't worry none 'cause as you see I got the only fish here so far.
They'll go fast. See me later. Don't look like you, or me is going anywhere."

"Okay, later, but I want my money. Understand; I don't work for free unless we're friends, and we're not friends yet. Have my money when I get back and we might be."

One of the noisy boats threw a line that Keith grabbed and wrapped it to a cleat. That led to a morning of unloading cases of canned goods and sodas from Trinidad and then loading sacks of coffee and bunches of green plantains. For that, the captain paid him thirty EC. It wasn't yet lunchtime, but his stomach was grumbling, so he grabbed the ripest banana he saw. The boat captain graciously sliced off a few big plantains and a piece of sugar cane.

The labor was hard, and it punished different muscles than when he'd been digging ditches back in St. Thomas. The bruises still ached when he had time to think about it. He returned to the fisherman and got his pay, plus a nice fish for his dinner.

"Well, thank you, but at the moment, I don't have anywhere to cook unless over an open fire. I've got to find a room with a kitchen or I'll be buying all my cooked food."

The fisherman gave a deep sigh and said, "You come by here later, 'bout dark when I head up the mountain. I have a place you can have for cheap, maybe, unless you find something else between now and then. Leave the fish."

Maybe grace was returning, Keith thought. He felt like Dorian Gray before they destroy the portrait. He had taken so much for granted. "Yeah, buddy, I'll be here."

The walk into town restored his smile. Lunch first. He found a bakery and enjoyed his tinned tuna on a hard roll with added sunshine.

Portsmouth had only slight litter. It was a lot cleaner than Charlotte Amalie in St. Thomas. Then again, there were about a thousand times fewer people traveling through Dominica. On this lush island, tin cans became cups and plastic bottles hauled water home. It seemed everyone took pride in their front yards. Chickens clucked and dogs scratched as Keith walked along the main road.

It was a long afternoon of plodding the dusty streets of Portsmouth unsuccessfully seeking work and lodging. A few hours later he wandered back to the dock and found the fisherman asleep on the same coil of rope surrounded by empty beer bottles.

"Yo, my new friend, is your offer still good for a place to stay the night?" Keith posed.

The man stretched and yawned. "Oh, you back, whitey? Sure man, everything's good. Nice job. No complaints. Got a nice place to stay, but it's a walk from here, a bit. You good at walking… walking steep roads?"

"As there's no bus or train, I guess we're walking. You leaving your boat here overnight?" Keith asked.

"Sure enough. Nobody fucks with this fisherman 'cause they know they can end up fish bait. I love to catch fish off thieves. You ain't no thief, are you? Likely I take you back to my place and you rob me. Hah! White men been robbing the black man forever and ever."

He slapped Keith on his sore shoulders as they started off together. "Especially here in the heat. Whites like to get the blackie here. Sell him some shit, but otherwise just steal his money. Dominica is still the home of the Caribs and they were the first to get theifed by the whites. They like whipped dogs now. Nah, you ain't no thief. You got other problems, right?"

"Maybe, but my business is getting a place to stay and something to work at. That's my only business. You say your business is fishing and farming. Maybe we can help each other out, but 'til then, my business is my own. You know what I mean, buddy?"

"I know… I know," the fisherman croaked as they walked off past Main Street and turned onto a road leading out of town. The rough cement track looped up the mountain to the east. At a tall mango tree, they took a left on a muddy path that, in better times, might have been a road. Now, the ruts and high center ridge made it impossible for most vehicles. At present, four-wheel drives, canvas shoes, or rubber boots were the best means of transport, if you had them. Most traversed it with bare feet or flip-flop sandals.

The sun had slipped into the ocean and only a vermillion glow provided light. Keith knew that the overhanging clouds meant no moon and probably a drizzle.

The fisherman was at least six feet and burly. It was evident he'd worked hard through his years. His silhouette was all that Keith followed, occasionally stumbling as he lost his sandal in a mud hole. It was warm for a walk, but then it was always warm. Sweat drained into his eyes.

He was used to climbing hills, but the beating had him aching. He was training himself to only think about today and tomorrow, not about yesterday. Life could be a roller coaster ride, Keith smiled, but that's what kept it interesting. It was that feeling in your gut as you screamed into the dip, whether the car would fly off the rails or the chain would catch and drag it back up the track. Yep, he needed to get back on track.

"We climbing to the top?" Keith asked.

"I know you white folks like views and my place has that. See most of God's harbor from up there," the fisherman pointed. "Hah, this ain't much of a walk for you, is it?"

"No, it's just dark and the left side of this donkey path seems to disappear straight down. I need you to keep talking so I can follow. No offense, but you're about as black as the night. How long you lived up here?"

"Yeah man, almost fifty years ago God put me in this paradise. I got my place ten years before Hurricanes Luis and Marilyn tore the hell out of this island. I spent most of two years putting my parents' and brothers' places back together. My place wasn't hit that hard, but the bananas, they was gone for years. The whole island had to start over. But we made it. The island shook it off like a dog does fleas. Here, this is my path."

"Watch yourself, whitey, my eyes are better accustomed to the dark than yours. See, that's where home is."

Keith looked up from watching his feet to see a yellow glow suspended about a hundred yards straight up. His back was soaked and sweat dripped from his nose. He felt he'd walked at least five miles and most of it uphill.

Something bounded down the path. Keith grabbed a sapling and held on to keep his footing.

"Watch out for the goats, white man. I just opened the gate and they like to roam at night. I'll bet you don't have much left in you for night roaming, hah!"

"Nope, you're right," Keith wheezed. "Be careful of the steps."

Keith could make out another person's shape in the yellow light visible in a doorway. The night was so dark the light seemed to hover from nowhere. Keith laughed; this was nowhere.

"Mammy, come meet our visitor. We got a white man come home by us tonight. He needs work and figured we could use a bit of help around the yard, huh?"

The woman didn't answer and retreated before Keith reached the doorway. The house was clapboard, and the light was a railroad type kerosene wick lantern. He wiped his forehead and said hello. The woman didn't turn, instead grunted some amenity as she busied herself stirring a pot above a blue propane flame.

"Yeah, this is home, whitey. This is my woman, Sara. Sara, say hello. This is the first time we ever had a white man visit. Hah! Yeah, visit for dinner. Say, whitey, what's your name? I am Carl. You can call me anything you want because there's no one else on this side of the hill, so I'll have to answer. Hah! Sara answers to me." He grabbed a bottle from a shelf. "A sip of the devil before we eat. So, what's your name?"

"Whitey isn't so bad, but my given name is Keith. It makes no difference what you call me. We know I'm the only white man on this mountain." Both laughed.

The fisherman passed the bottle and Keith slugged at the rum. "Is there some water nearby, that walk sweated me out?"

"There's a bucket by the door." He threw a porcelain cup, "Dip your fill. Sara, we gonna eat soon?"

Keith drank and returned to the table. The woman brought the food, and he saw she appeared young, but mature. She wore a red print dress that went well below her knees. The lantern silhouetted her developed breasts and thighs.

Carl, the fisherman, glanced at Keith staring at Sara. "Yeah, I know what you think." His muscular arm stretched around the woman's waist as she set an extra plate on the table. "She's wife number three. First two I buried. Sickness got one, and the second died having a child. I got two boys, but they don't like it here anymore. They want to be clean of this island, so they's in St. Maarten, making money. Hah! Money, money. Money comes and money goes, but the land is the home. Hah!" He grabbed the rum bottle again, "Eat whitey. Sara, sit." He pulled her to the closest chair.

Keith quickly cleaned his plate of rice, beans, and boiled bananas. "Could I have another drink of your rum?"

The bottle passed, and he mixed a splash with water. Keith stretched out in a creaky wooden chair. "Thank you, Sara." She didn't move.

"Don't thank her, thank me, whitey. Sara cooks what I bring her. Here, we all work hard to live. Tomorrow, listen, Sara, Whitey is donating his fish, a nice snapper, and some plantains."

Sara rose, cleared the table, and then retired to a bed in the room's corner, curled, facing the wall, fully dressed.

"So, Carl," calling the fisherman by name for the first time, "what kind of work do you have for me?"

"Well, whitey, tomorrow is work time. Right now is sleep

time. I got a place out back for you to spend the night." Carl took another swig from the rum bottle, burped, and pushed himself away from the table. "Follow me," he said, grabbing a blanket of sorts from a chair against the wall.

He carefully followed his new benefactor down the steps into the darkest of nights. Even though the lantern had been adequate light inside the house, it had adjusted Keith's eyes so it was impossible to see anything on the outside. It could have been that, the long walk, or the bit of rum that caused him to stumble.

"Hah, whitey, too much rum, Hah! Here's your bed."

From what Keith could discern, it was a small shed, open to the front, maybe just a roof on poles. It had a wood floor, and that was some consolation.

"Hah whitey, if you feel something crawling on you let it crawl. If it's moving, it won't bite. Hah, I ain't telling you nothing you don't already know, right, white man?"

"Thank you very much for your hospitality, Carl," Keith muttered. "Goodnight and sleep well."

"You too, and tell me again in the morning how thankful you are. Hah!" The black man turned and headed toward the yellow lamplight. In a few minutes, all was darkness.

He pulled his tired body onto the platform and covered with the blanket. The mosquitoes were already buzzing. He looked at the sky, or rather, in the sky's direction. Was there really a star poking through? Fall from grace, huh? This was about as far as a man could fall unless they imprisoned him. Maybe he was in his own prison? He tucked in his knees and covered his head with the shabby blanket. Hopefully, the rum and exertions would let him fall into a deep, never-never land sleep. As he lay there feeling the warmth of his breath inside the blanket, he heard a cry from inside the house.

There was nowhere to go but everywhere,
so just keep on rolling under the stars.
Jack Kerouac

CHAPTER THREE

Keith shook free from the blanket. A small lizard had fallen onto his cheek, rescuing him from the end of a nightmare. The morning hadn't made an appearance yet. The charcoal sky had no hint of blue. His bladder signaled. He was awake and didn't want to be.

"One good piss and I'll lay down again until the roosters start."

Relief came with another drizzle from the sky. Keith guessed it had rained three times during the brief night. The shed wasn't a palace, but only a shelter… of sorts. Things had to get better.

Carl worked him for three days, basically for meals and a place to crash. Neither were bonus points. After stretching new chicken wire to keep everything out of the garden, Keith had leveled three new garden terraces on the front hillside, hauled the fish traps, and again cleaned the fish. 'Helped' wasn't accurate; he'd done it all except drive the boat and sell the fish. He had spent no money except for a bottle of Bacardi. That was to further cement his friendship with his host. Carl liked to sip a bit in the evening.

Today he'd have time to fix up his sleeping quarters. He required a couple more days to contemplate his next move. Carl liked to have him around, but getting paid for his efforts was something else. Rice, beans, and fish were Keith's meals of choice, but as payment for stacking hundreds of rocks as terrace walls, it was low, real low, rock-bottom low. The fishing had to be profitable, but Carl wasn't sharing.

The house was typical weathered wood, basic bush West Indian, and never had paint or trim. A cement floor rather than wood or dirt signified it wasn't poor-poor. Twenty-by-twenty, one room with windows on each side and two more straddled the front door. On pleasant weather days, Sara cooked outside. A table held a two-burner propane stove. The dishwasher was a tin basin. Chairs were at the table or on the porch, a piece of thick foam made for Carl's bed in the corner. No electricity or running water. They didn't expect guests. Keith realized Carl was cutting him a break.

The back door opened to a dirt yard cut out of the steep hillside. On the slope, someone had leveled the dirt for shelves, and several bottles and cans rested, sprouting various hedges and flowers. A few coconuts sat starting to grow roots. Sara tended these using the wastewater that was collected after cleaning the kitchen wares.

About fifty feet higher up the hill was a stream with a convenient, deep hole for bathing and washing clothes. Carl had set a PVC pipe for a shower and had planted two fiberglass wash tubs easily filled from the stream. Wash hung from a line stretched between a tree and the house.

Another pipeline brought water from the small waterfall to a barrel beside the house. Not having to carry water was as close to luxury as this hillside offered. Carl swore he was the first house along the stream. No one was polluting upstream, and the water was cool and sweet.

Keith's sleeping shack was south of the house, slightly lower on the slope. He didn't ask what purpose the small shack had originally served. It felt like a two-person coffin; probably had been a packing crate. After the previous day's fishing trip, at the hardware he'd purchased enough screen mesh to seal his area and the main house's unshuttered openings. Tonight, he'd spray insecticide before dinner; the smell would wear off and not choke him. All he wanted was to have an uninterrupted night's sleep. With an extra Bacardi, it might be a sound sleep.

He muttered, "I haven't had over four hours of sleep at a clip in over six months. Maybe once all this drama-trauma settles down, I'll enjoy some serious sack time. It used to be great, feeling groggy when the alarm went off. Now, I'm awake waiting for Mr. Sun."

The plague of insects around the house was maddening. Moving rocks to build the terraces, he'd killed two scorpions and four centipedes. He decided the bite of either wouldn't kill him, but a trip to a third-world clinic might. It was almost impossible to clean the entire living area of everything that attracted bugs. The house had been here for decades, and the garbage dump wasn't very far.

Sara kept to herself, busy with her chores. Keith had yet to hear her speak. Her eyes had never met his. If he was outside, she stayed indoors. If he neared, she moved away. If he needed something, Carl was always handy.

After he completed the new terraces, Sara planted some

of her flowering shrubs. She seemed happiest when she was working in her garden. Keith watched everything to understand his place in all of it. There were no problems, only quiet, but the house wasn't a 'friendly' place. Even though this was nowhere, it was better than no place. And he was out of sight. It wouldn't be smart to hang out around town. Even though he had broken no laws, he knew eventually he would have to answer questions either unofficially or officially. Things weren't so bad. On the hill, he could sip a rum waiting for the green flash, when the hot red sun sank into the cool blue ocean. He always had goats for company.

The gray morning could have been fog. Grabbing a paperback, he headed for the latrine. It was far in the bush, behind the house. He slapped mosquitoes along the path. The shanty was the basic four-by-four, one- seater; the type used for centuries. The paperback wasn't for reading in the low light. In two days, he'd used chapter one of *The Firm*. A good book, but something in Sara's cooking made him overly attentive to his bowels. The wooden bench held his attention for twenty minutes.

"Yo, whitey, you plan to be in there all day? I've got to pay some dues back to the land," Carl bellowed.

"I'll be right out." There went pages 19 and 21. He groaned as he straightened. Maybe a quick bath in the stream would set him right.

Carl was waiting, arms crossed, bareback, and barefoot. "I'm telling you; I don't like to wait to shit in my own shitter. You hear me, eh?" He said as he sat down and didn't bother to shut the door.

"What do you got for me to do today, Carl?" Keith was dancing and rubbing to keep away the hungry, swarming skeeters. Red streaks from the dead ones pocked his legs.

"I'm taking some young piggies to the market in Roseau. I meet my ride on the main road at seven. Ain't enough room for you to go along. I could use some help getting down the hill. Bananas with pigs are kind of hard to handle. You want to do something today? Maybe you clean out the chicken and pig pens? No big deal. You could wait a day 'cause I'd like to see how you looking after it. Hah!" Carl rose from his wooden throne, stretching with his pants around his ankles.

"I'll get to it before the sun gets too high. Where do you want the waste? I'd like to walk into town today and see if there are any traders that need help loading or unloading. I need to make some money."

"How much money you need? What you need money for

anyway, 'cept an old-age pillow? Keep your white ass here. Dominica is all right. You don't see that? I owe you for the fish yesterday. Fifty sounds fair. I made five hundred and change."

Walking to the water barrel, Carl farted so loudly that the chickens scattered. He filled a five-gallon bucket and dumped it over his head. "I'm awake! Sara, you better have the coffee hot. I got to get out of here to meet the trucker."

Keith sat on the lowest porch step as Carl entered the house, banging the screen door. The brown dog slowly moved toward Keith, wary of a slap, but hoping for kind attention or a breakfast morsel. The dogs, pigs, and chickens all ate the same and in hard times, one could become food for the others. Sara slopped them from the same pail every night after dinner. They got the few table leftovers with rotting fruits and vegetables. He thought feeding pigs and chickens with mangos probably made them tasty.

Same as his master, the brown dog's farts doomed any affection. A raised hand and the dog retreated onto a barren patch of dirt under the porch it claimed as its own.

"Coffee, whitey?" came from inside the house. "On this island, we like our coffee just like our women, strong and black. Hah! You heard that before, right?"

Again, Sara's back was to him as he reached for the blue steel pot. Keith added sugar.

"Statesiders want their stuff sweet. Life can't be too sweet for them. We like it bitter, as it's meant to be. Bitter, huh, Sara? Bitter?" Carl ranted. "Whitey, you better hurry them four bunches of plantains down the trail. I'll follow as soon as I catch the pigs. If a man in a yellow dump truck comes by, stop him. Hah! He'll stop anyway at the sight of a white man carrying bananas."

He dumped the bunches of green plantains into the bed of the dump truck. Carl grabbed the sideboard, stepped on top of the rear tires, and vaulted up. Keith handed him two squealing piglets wrapped in a burlap sack.

"You clean those animal pens, whitey. Okay? Real good and clean. Hah!" Carl boasted, so the truck driver would know he had a white man working for him, cleaning up pig shit. It would be the town gossip. "Try not to get any of that sheet on you, whitey. Hah! I'll see you tomorrow."

"Yeah," Keith waved. "Tomorrow."

"Probably 'bout dark." The truck ground gears as it started off. "See you, whitey."

Keith thought about walking directly into Portsmouth or

waiting until the next morning when it was cooler for such a hike. He couldn't v i e w the dock from the house, so he didn't know if any boats had arrived. He'd made the walk to Portsmouth twice in the last three days. The return to the house wasn't that bad in the daylight. He reasoned it would probably be better to get the distasteful task of cleaning the pens out of the way, and then he could feel that he sang, or 'shoveled shit' for his supper. He climbed the path back to the house.

Down to his purple Speedo again, he grabbed a square shovel and the dirty five-gallon slop bucket and mucked up a lot of pig and chicken shit during the next four hot, smelly hours. Keith filled the noxious bucket and lugged it to one of the newly created terraces at least a hundred meters below the house. The breeze blew down the mountain, so it didn't smell bad at the porch. With his deck shoes oozing black slime, he headed to the stream. He grabbed a scrub brush and a bar of blue soap from the laundry tub.

Off came his shoes as he sat on a streamside rock. He scrubbed each shoe inside and out, then between each toe, and every area of his body he could reach. A dip in the cool stream and he worked at his hair and ears. Peering between spread fingers at a movement, he saw Sara watching from the backyard. As their eyes caught, she
turned and headed into the house.

Sundried and half-dressed, Keith enjoyed a paperback on the front steps. He glanced and saw Sara hanging the wash. She'd been watching him. He closed the book and moved toward her, fearing she might run away like a spooked animal.

"Excuse me, Sara, if you need help with anything, please let me know." She didn't look around the big, blue work shirt she pinned to the line. "Well, you don't talk much. I just made the offer."

"Okay," Sara said distinctly, "Okay."

At dusk, she said one word through the front door, "Dinner."

Keith washed his hands and wetly padded his sun-bleached locks.

He buttoned his shirt and went inside. The house was spotless and arranged slightly different. No wonder he hadn't seen her all afternoon. Dinner was callaloo, a crab-based vegetable stew, with good cornbread. Sara sat in her usual place, stared at her food and quietly ate. He didn't want to stare at h e r , but there was no other distraction. She wore a dress he hadn't seen before and must have bathed as she combed her hair in a different way.

"This soup is very good, and the bread's delicious," he said.

After a minute of silence came, "Okay," without raising her head. Keith rested in his chair, chewing a square of the yellow bread.

Was she dumb, or shy, or both? He lifted the bottle of rum from the shelf and added a bit to his water. "That was a horrible job cleaning those pens today," he remarked mostly to himself. He sipped while watching her. The two sat in silence, listening to the crickets and frogs outside.

"Where you from?" she whispered.

He straightened in the chair and said just as quietly, "The last place was St. Thomas."

Sara held her face in her hands so her fingers were like blinders to keep her from seeing him. "It the same as here, there?" she asked.

"Not quite. Dominica is prettier, but quiet. Less busy and that's good." He refilled his glass and thought to offer her some. "Would you like some rum with your water?"

Still not looking, "Don't know; never had it. Don't think I'm supposed to drink alcohol. Don't think I should be talking to you. You are the first person I ever met from someplace else."

"What about Carl's sons, don't they come back home?"

"This ain't their home no more." She reached for the rum bottle, bringing it to her nose. "I see what this does to Carl. Little makes him nice; a lot makes him mean." She tipped the bottle and slightly clouded her water.

Sara sipped and winced, but she seemed to relax. "What's it like, St. Thomas?"

"It's a lot like the States. It has all the bad things: traffic jams, drugs, crime, and political crooks. It's pretty, like here, but imagine having lots of people on this hillside."

Sara sipped more, holding the glass between both her hands. She posed so her profile was visible in the glow of twilight. The girl had a high forehead; he hadn't noticed when her hair covered it, but her nose and lips were sleek. Her skin was flawless. She finished her glass in unison with Keith. He refilled both.

Still staring straight ahead, she said, "What you doing here? You a criminal or something?"

"Let's say I'm an unhappy guy trying to smile again. I must work someplace. Here I can afford to live, and by luck I found Carl."

"Luck, you consider what you was cleaning today as luck?" She turned slightly toward him. "Cleaning after swine, that makes you happy?"

"I like it here. This hillside, that box I sleep in, is all that I got. Without that, I'm in terrible shape. So, I smile and do what I got to do."

"I do what I got to do, but I can't smile anymore. We both got the same thing, nothing." After taking another sip, she looked directly at him for the first time. "You've had better, I'm sure. Me, I knows nothing else. This hillside is my life. I go to town, maybe six times a year, if Carl lets me. He brings everything here. I know about nothing."

"How long have you been married to Carl?" The conversation increased tempo. He poured another short one, adding water. Sara took the bottle and poured a half-inch in her glass. Sipping the straight amber liquor, she finally seemed to relax. Keith grabbed the bottle and screwed the cap on. He realized he may have let the devil out and placed it back on the shelf. He didn't want a hangover and wasn't sure how the fisherman would take to him getting his young wife drunk for the first time. It was too late for that last consideration.

"We ain't married. Everyone here knows. You ever see anybody visit? No, 'cause we ain't married." She paused. "I'm his daughter. That shock you? You're the first person I ever had to tell."

"Oh," was all Keith could mutter. Yep, the devil had crawled out.

Quiet again overtook the house. The frogs croaked, and the crickets chirped. The dark orange of the sunset beyond the porch seemed to pulse.

"That shock you?" she whispered. "We don't talk. Carl talks. We don't do, he does." She looked at Keith with tearing eyes. "I can't ever leave. You found someplace in my no-place."

There was no reply. Keith had overturned a rock that had started an avalanche. It was scary. His only refuge had eroded, and he knew it was his fault.

"Tonight, I talk with a white man for the first time. I talk and you get quiet." Sara leaned toward him. "What you think 'bout me? Think I'm crazy, or stupid to stay here? Where can I go? The boys in St. Maarten don't want me. I am a problem for them. Those two had me like a woman when I was just a child.

Now, they don't want to see me. They got their own women. I'm just their little sister by another mother. My mama died when I was just seven. She buried over there by the stream. I have been the only woman on this farm since then."

Keith reached for the Bacardi again. "Look, this is none of my business. No offense meant, but I don't know you, Sara, and I really don't know Carl. So, why'd you want to tell me all this?" He poured an inch of the eighty-proof liquid. Sara reached for the bottle, but Keith grabbed it. "I think you've had enough for a first-time drinker. I really don't need more problems." He reached for the matches and lit the hanging lantern.

"Problems, problems, problems!" she screamed. "All I have is problems. No one wants to hear them. I want things, things that ain't here. I want to be clean from this place." She covered her face with her hands and wiped away the tears that were just starting. She yelled, "I know no one. You come here from somewhere. I want to be somewhere else. I'm trying to tell you what it's like here for me, but you don't want to listen. No one wants to listen. What can I do?" She put her head on her arms and folded to the table.

Keith slugged his rum and pushed back his chair. It was early, with the last shreds of dusk still glimmering. He knew he shouldn't have offered the rum. It was his fault for opening the floodgates. Should he stay and try to console, or should he talk with the dog?

He stood and walked around the table to where she was. He lifted her hair and massaged her slender brown neck. Sara shivered, but didn't raise her head.

"What you thinking, white man? What you think 'bout me? You think I'm good or I'm bad?"

"I'm thinking you could be lucky. It could be worse. Life everywhere isn't easy these days. I know nothing about you and Carl, and I really don't want to. I think you're young and pretty and lucky to be up here on this hillside when the world out there is crazy."

"Lucky? Me? I'm wondering how that can be..." She lifted her head and straightened, wiping her eyes, "Lucky me, huh?" Sara stood and faced him. She was his height and the stare from her brown eyes penetrated his.

Suddenly, it was silent, car-wreck quiet. "Young and pretty. I will be old and ugly and have missed my life up here." She reached out and touched his face. "You know you are the first man who doesn't scare me? I scare you, don't I?"

"You're right, Sara. Look, I got to go. I don't think Carl

would like this. I'm sorry if I upset you. You are pretty and I'm sure everything will be all right."

"What? You going out to your box, white man? I see no one forever; stay and talk to me about other places." She grabbed his hand and led him to the porch where they both sat on the edge dangling their feet. "Talk about America. Everyone's rich there. Sometimes I read the old newspapers Carl brings. Everyone has a car and lots of clothes. And they eat at restaurants. Have you been to Miami and New York?" She held Keith's hand so he couldn't leave, swinging her legs like a younger girl.

Keith had that feeling in his chest: the rum and poor judgment flexed the paranoia he'd carried for months. The girl knew she had his attention. He couldn't be rude and wander off to sleep.

"Sara, how old are you, really?"

"I'm ten and nine. You really think I'm pretty?"

"Yeah, you're pretty enough, all right. The States would be hard for a girl like you. Life is much faster there. Too fast for you, I think. New York has no color; everything is gray or black. And it is dirty. Not the *good* dirty like you get working in the garden, but dirty like the latrine. Stuff in the air you breathe eats you up inside 'til it makes you crazy. Dominica is pretty with all types of colors and flowers. Why do you think the statesiders come here? Because they miss the bright colors, the sun, clean water, and air. And they want to feel safe for a week or two."

Keith didn't really feel safe any longer. He had started a fire that was burning another bridge. It frightened him that the girl had opened up and started talking; talking to him, and maybe talking to Carl. What would she tell him about this conversation? "Sara, no matter how bad you think this hillside is, it can always be worse. This is better than in many places."

Sara's rough hands never let go of Keith's arm. She reclined on the porch, pulling him with her. "You got women in the States? You got k i d s ?"

"I used to have a wife, but that ended."

"She die?" She rolled toward him and looked him over.

"I wish she had, but we're divorced."

"I thought men always need women." Her voice didn't sound sad, "I never had to need a man. Sometimes I feel like I need a woman. Carl don't take me around other women much. Don't take me around anyone much. I can't understand why he lets you here with me? Guess he thinks you, a white man, would have no use for me," she said, leaning over him. Her young breasts were visible. "You got any use for me?" She put her hand on his leg.

"Hey, Sara, uh, I haven't been with many women lately, so don't play around."

She didn't stop, but moved her hand higher. She leaned further and sloppily kissed him. His blood was boiling like he was in his teens again, scared enough to run, horny enough to stay.

"Carl doesn't need to know about things." She kissed him again and unbuttoned her dress. Her young breasts shook free from the opening. "Show me what it's like to be with whites. I know it got to be better." She pulled the dress over her head, revealing a supple brown body. Her perspiration made her glow under the lantern light. She coiled her legs and pulled off his shirt.

Keith knew himself too well. Again, he was floating in a barrel on the Niagara approaching the falls, giving into desires that could only mean trouble down the road. He couldn't win now, but hell, why not finish the game? At least play out a few hands. She'd drank her rum and now wanted to sample a white man's lust. Her taut skin and long, hard nipples tantalized him. It was a no-brainer and his little head was famous for having no brains. Now she was naked, on top of him. He felt her hands in *that* place. His barrel just went over the falls.

Women can be a devilish sort, bending wills and challenging the staunchest of characters. Lust can make a pure soul falter. The best of men can have the best of women, then almost out of nowhere, suddenly lust destroys their paradise. It has been happening since there were snakes in apple trees. When you think you have exactly what you want, something comes along and tests your reserve of willpower. Tempted with unknown pleasures, but with known consequences, it's the roulette of the loins.

As Keith rolled in his sleep, his arm felt something unfamiliar. That jump-started his memory of the previous evening's events. Sara had it her way. It had been good, great, but now it was time for the guilt and the fear of Carl's return. Keith looked at the girl's bronze back and high, rounded buttocks and knew why he'd risked his situation.

He stared at the planked roof. "If women are like wine, I can definitely say I prefer Nouveau Beaujolais over the aged port." Keith laughed to himself as he pulled himself upright. Shaking his head, "Every time I do this, I know it's crazy, but I do it anyway."

Sara stirred and snaked her arm around his leg. He knew he was about to be crazy again. How was a teenage girl going to handle this? Too late to consider that.

Keith bathed as Sara scrubbed laundry. She was smiling, maybe too noticeably happy. More than a week ago Keith was happy to be back on the high seas, away from the monumental problems caused by the women in his life. He'd found some solace and perhaps lost it again for the same damn reasons. The cool stream water swirled around him as he pondered his next move. He'd lost his home and possessions for similar indiscretions. Almost lost it all and was back at it again… a definite repeat offender with no conscience or common sense below the navel. Never had common sense when it came to women, probably never would. He laughed.

At forty, he felt he was still handsome, but the years had taken their toll. Was he still able to catch a woman's glance? Keith cared about his physique, and most of the worst habits had become less frequent. Rum was still a problem, but he considered his current consumption as a self-prescribed sedative so he could sleep. Always a hard worker, he was muscular with a deep tan. A bit of a paunch had formed long before this shit hit the fan in St. Thomas. The hard labor that followed his fall had reshaped his arms, legs, and midriff. His hands were hard again, callused from shoveling. He felt good, but the fear of escaping youth kept Keith seeking reinforcement.

His wife had been fifteen-years younger, and that difference had been pure vitality. She was a bushy-haired beauty from South America, and that's probably where she now was with the entire divorce settlement. Keith thought it had been a lousy decree on the judge's part. West Indian culture was supposed to be a male-dominated society with a realistic understanding of marital infidelity. With usual luck, his case drew a visiting stateside judge whose daughter had recently divorced.

He'd shot twenty years of hard work to hell for a few minutes of pleasure with a cutie from a dive charter. She had come on to him after a few rum punches. Christa had been dark-skinned with the long legs his wife didn't have. Keith had been unfaithful only a few times during their five-year marriage, but he felt that 'slight' infidelity kept it interesting. It wasn't like he had a mistress or even the same woman on the side for months. He liked women and didn't believe a bit of variety could hurt.

Christa had said what he wanted to hear, and then Keith was giving her a ride from the marina. Drink some more liquor, more glances at a pair of long, slender legs, big jugs with a smile. Wham bam, and after some serious sack time, he'd be on his way home. It was then his run of miserable luck began. He'd forgotten to mention he was married. Somehow, as she kissed him goodbye after two hours of adult mischief, the boyfriend she'd neglected to mention arrived. Somehow, the usually invisible police were for once Johnnies-on-the spot. After the usual boyfriend-girlfriend slaps and punches, the boys in blue arrested everyone.

Madelena, Keith's wife, never permitted him to provide an excuse or to return to their home on Skyline Drive. Her brother, Carlos, dropped off three suitcases of clothes at the hotel and assured he could kiss his ass goodbye if he even called home. Madelena was distraught; Carlos explained in heavily Spanish-accented English. So distraught, she would make Keith pay for his infidelity. This wasn't the first time, and there was always the possibility of HIV. Carlos made it clear this problem went beyond the marriage; it was a personal insult. In Colombia, they would have whipped Keith, or worse, for sullying their name and reputation. The family, upper-class merchants, had been against the marriage.

She looked sad sitting in court. Her eyes were darker than usual, with no sparkle. She said nothing to Keith and left directly after the uncontested hearing. Caught with his pants down, with two police, Christa, and her boyfriend ready to provide evidence; why fight it? Losing was bad, but paying big legal bills in a losing cause was worse. It never seemed possible that he would lose everything by a stroke of a judge's pen. After a psychiatrist testified how much anguish he'd caused his now ex-wife, and an accountant, detailed expenses and incomes, Keith was down the tube. A simple, lustful indiscretion had reduced the businessman to a common laborer.

Where would last night's carelessness with Sara lead? Finished bathing, Keith worked at building another terrace. He'd considered walking to Portsmouth but stuck close to hear what Sara would say. If Carl found out and there was a scene, he'd rather it be on this hillside than conspicuous in the village. No matter, he knew he had to leave. Carl would eventually find out, and in true West Indian tradition, he would want to fight. It would be easier to run away ahead of the fracas.

About a hundred rocks into the terrace wall, Carl appeared. "So, white boy, how's things been? All still safe?" Carl was carrying two sacks, one over each shoulder. Keith grabbed one and lugged it to the porch.

"Things are okay. I'm going into Portsmouth tomorrow.

Figured you'd need some help when you got back. I started another terrace. Got the pens cleaned yesterday."

"Sara, come out here," Carl shouted. "Yes, it smells a hell of a lot better now that all that pig shit is somewhere else. Sara!"

She appeared in the doorway, looking as sad as the day Carl had left.

"I brought you some material for a new dress and you can make some shirts for me. You like it?" Carl lifted the folded material.

Sara leaned over the porch railing and touched the material. She simply said, "Thank you."

"Later, you'll thank me proper; now I'ze hungry. White man, you hungry?"

Keith ate some beans and rice while Carl told of his good fortune in Roseau. The pigs brought more money than expected, while the plantains brought less. Tomorrow, the plan was to haul fish traps and sell in Portsmouth.

The rest of the day passed without incident. Sara regressed to her submissive character. As the sun set in ten shades of purple, the two men sipped Bacardi like old friends.

Travel makes one modest.
You see what a tiny place you occupy in the world.
Gustave Flaubert

CHAPTER FOUR

The day at sea was invigorating; so bright that the sun and its reflection off the water burned Keith's skin. The sea's visibility probably went down sixty feet. Soft coral plumes and purple fans were displayed as the fishermen toiled with ropes and winches. Schools of blue wrasse and red squirrelfish darted in unison as soon as the fish traps rose off the bottom. Eighty pounds of reef fish later, the boat returned to the government pier.

Keith hurried, cleaned the fish, and was off to assist the unloading of two traders. One was a true banana boat unloading drums of petrol from the aft deck before filling every available space with green bananas. It was a wooden diesel-sailer, probably built in Bequia. The trader boat had seen better days, but was still seaworthy. The white hull revealed rusting fasteners and could have used scraping, repacking, and finishing with fresh paint. That wouldn't happen unless there was a new owner. Traders worked their boats until they broke, sank, or were sold to upgrade to a better vessel.

This one, the Alita Dee, ran the island route between Puerto Rico and Dominica. In two days, it would return to San Juan. The Detroit diesel needed some gaskets replaced and the fuel filters changed. Puerto Rico sounded better to Keith and arranged a trade of mechanics for passage. His current pocket-sized nest egg amounted close to eight hundred US. Not bad for a few weeks of labor. He could locate an el-cheapo place in Old San Juan or on the west coast. Then find some work until the next move.

Dominica was nice, but it was time to go. Keith figured if he quickly left before Carl discovered his woman had shared her favors, he could always return. If he stayed, Carl would eventually find out because Keith knew himself too well. If he stayed, he'd have Sara again.

The captain of the Alita was Renaldo. A true seafarer, Renaldo spoke Puerto Rican Spanish, Martiniquan Creole-French, Caribbean patois, and the Queen's English. A gentleman captain of sorts, he didn't do greasy engine work. His crew, Ramon from St. Lucia, Moteman of the Dominican Republic, and PR Jesus, weren't capable of doing it either. The Alita's mechanic was on holiday and rather than pay a local, Keith filled in.

The diesel looked to be in relatively good condition, but everything needed a proper tightening. The hour meter read it had run for about ten years. Keith knew his way around most engines. Oil was seeping out of many gaskets. With a few spanners and an adjustable wrench, he finished the job and cultivated some new friends.

The engine compartment had its own peculiar smell, as most do. The Alita's was a mixture of hot petrol, saltwater, and soap from the washroom, combined with the sweet smell of rotten fruit. Keith checked, cleaned, and tightened as he moved around the old blue motor. Three hours and two local Kubuli beers later, he was again topside of the fifty-footer cleaning his nails with his pocketknife. To further cement his crew position on the trader, he offered a dinner of fresh trap fish from his share of the early morning labor.

A greasy Keith rocked the fishing boat and woke Carl. After the typical Caribbean wrangling and bickering, Keith grabbed a few parrotfish. The Alita accepted Carl with another beer and Ramon began an afternoon meal on the gas grill.

"Dese fishes good? We won't get sick, eh?" Ramon asked, referring to ciguatera, a tropical fish poison.

"Nah mon, my fish okay. Just make sure you cook them right. Free fish to you is the very best fish. I hope I enjoy your work on them," Carl snorted. To Keith, he said, "So you's done with Portsmouth and Carl?

Gonna take off with this bunch to Puerto Rico? Me think you not like it here, right? You not like Portsmouth, white man? Ha! Lots to like here, you just need to look longer."

"Well, Carl, I'm moving on, but I can always return. This place is beautiful, but I need to make some more money and see some people."

"Yes, I think you need to see some woman-type peoples. Ha! You guys got some of them PR women at home for this white man? He needs some heat."

Jesús, the youngest crew member, replied, "Si mister, mucho women in San Juan. We got everything, cheap living, cheap houses, cheap loving." He smiled, revealing two gold teeth framed by a thin mustache and a trimmed goatee. "Yes sir, Puerto Rico is a beautiful place."

"Yes, you got it all up there in PR. You got thieves and killers.

Yes, you all got too many people," Carl answered.

"Hey, black man, I hope you ain't saying all Puerto Ricans are thieves? 'Cause if so, we got a problem. My family is all good Catholics. So, watch what you say about my home."

"Me-son, chill out. This crime thing ain't about Puerto Rico. I didn't mean nothing except it is the nature of man to be bad if the numbers are big. You got a hell of a lot of people; some of them are gonna be unhappy with what they don't get. Build a big hotel and more sooner than later, there's gots to be a few that want more than they gots. You's young, take a look around me-son. That's the way it is." Carl reclined against a bunch of green plantains and pulled his salt-stained cap down over his eyes. "Wake me when them fish ready."

Keith helped Jesús rig an old windsurfer that traveled on the roof of the pilothouse. "We found this floating off Guadeloupe a few months ago. We always find things, even small boats. Makes me wonder what happened to the people on them."

Jesús carefully stepped on the old, flat board. "I had one of these when I first came to St. Thomas in the early 80s," Keith remarked. The memories of peaceful moments many years before brought a grin. He had trained his first black Lab to ride along. Could his life ever be that happy again? With a bit of breeze, Jesús sailed off to the south side of the harbor. Keith kicked Carl's feet. "Fish smells done. You can spare some fish money to buy some beers?"

"Whitey, here's your share," Carl unfolded a wad of paper money. "You want to buy them beer, that's on you. I gave them the damn fish they cooking. Right? Man, you want these guys to be your friend bad. I'm already your friend and I don't see you buying me beers. Hah! Yes, I feel you could buy their friendship with beers. Hah!"

The dock smelled of fried fish. Ramon had made a good Caribbean lunch with tostones: fried plantains. Keith ate with true hunger while Carl fingered the greasy fish. Captain Renaldo poured his beer into a mug and ate from a ceramic bowl. Everyone else ate off old newspapers. Jesús returned in time to get the last fish.

It was evening as the two men made their way back to the homestead. The afternoon meal and the beers had made them sluggish. Carl bathed in the stream while Keith packed his few belongings. The Alita was leaving after they loaded the bananas.

"So white man, tomorrow you'll be gone and I need to find the next helper. Sort of got used to you and really liked the way you work. Sure I can't talk you into staying?" Carl spouted with a mouthful of rice. "I can't believe you gonna leave a place as nice as this. Hah! Yes, what more you want besides a woman? Ha! Look, I'ze got a woman." Carl stretched an arm around Sara and pulled her close, "She don't talk much, but cooks good and feels good. Ha!"

"I agree, Carl, you got it all here and I'm not kidding. I envy you for your life and Sara here. I know it's everything you need. I'm an old dog and not ready to relax here, not just now, anyway. I need more options." For a moment, Sara met Keith's eyes. "I don't know what to do with myself, but I feel I need to get more cash, and cash doesn't come easy here."

"You right white man. But what you need will be here for you when you get done with what shit you going through now. Ain't none of my business 'bout your life, but we's half-assed friends for all that you has helped me with. Right? Ha! Half-assed friends. So, when you need to be here, you can come on back. I'm tired and gonna sleep." Carl rose and they shook hands. "You should be on your way early, white man. See you again, I hope."

Carl rolled onto the bed, fully clothed, and was soon snoring. Sara cleared the table and turned her back as Keith closed the screen door before heading to his shelter. Sleep came quickly. He awoke to a tug on his ankle. It was Sara.

"You leaving without a goodbye to me?" Sara whispered. "You my first white man. I like white men now. You love me good and held me. I'll miss you." She ran her hand up his bare leg.

"Whoa, Sara, Carl's here and I don't want any trouble."
"Won't be no trouble, no trouble at all." Her hand held his attention. "Carl had me already, so he is gonna sleep sound. I tired him out. Now, I'll do the same with you." She pulled off her dress; the moonlight outlined her dark body. With a grin, Keith resigned himself to her quiet pleasures. When she finished with him, after a kiss, he dozed.

Still dark, Keith trudged to the dock. The morning mist spiraled in the yellow light of the single streetlight. The glassy water reflected without a swirl. The Alita Dee was silent. Keith stretched out on the damp cement of the pier to await the crew. The sun slowly emerged over the mountains. As the minutes passed, the sky brightened to crimson.

"Pretty strange sunrise. Pretty, but strange," he thought. As he watched, the sky became even deeper red until the wisps of clouds were burgundy. Finally, the orange of a typical sunrise outlined the summits of Dominica's mountains.

Jesús staggered from the wheelhouse to pee. "you know

this sky is a sign, amigo. The red means something? You hear of any weather, amigo?"

It had been a while since Keith had thought about the weather. During his yachting days in St. Thomas, it had always been important. Once on shore, the weather is a roof and walls. In the Caribbean, the climate is usually good, but if it decides to blow, it can blow damn hard. Then, it's the wrong time to be out on the water.

The great God Huracan can rule your destiny. Hell, it can totally blow you away. Keith had experienced eight ballbuster storms while traveling in Hawaii, Central America, and the Caribbean. Eight was enough. The worst were Marilyn, Irma, and Maria. The destructive power of nature was incredible. The government and the people during the storm's aftermath could be just as violent.

"No buddy, I haven't been near a radio in weeks. Switch on the VHF. We should get something from Roseau or Ft. de France."

"Amigo," Jesús cleared his throat and spit into the still air, "Amigo, this boat has many things that do not work. Our VHF quit off Guadeloupe on our way here. There has been little time to work on it. I'll bet you are good at fixing things like that. Man, I don't know," spitting over the side again, "I never see a sunrise like that. You?"

"Not quite. Remind me to check out the radio after the crew's awake." Keith pulled the brim of his ball cap lower and dozed off listening to the crows from the early morning roosters.

The tropical heat woke him. The skipper and Jesús were smoking on the foredeck. Someone was brewing coffee and frying bacon in the small galley. Those smells were the best alarm clock. After he rubbed his eyes, Keith surveyed the Alita for seaworthiness. The lack of a radio made him wince, but loose wires or a bad ground could kill any electronics in the salty, humid climate. She had a small fiberglass dinghy for a lifeboat, no electronics. No depth sounder, no radar, no navigation except a compass and a sextant. They would follow the island chain north and be in sight of land, except for one day when they would turn east. The Alita looked solid and had a good engine. He'd seen two bilge pumps when he was working on the diesel. They mounted a flare gun in the pilothouse. That was it as far as emergency equipment.

"Hey Capt, made this trip many times?" Keith inquired.

"About two hundred. You worried I'll get lost?"

"No, just making small talk. Just thinking. Jesús tell you about the sky this morning?"

"Yes. I've seen that sky before. The first time I saw a big red before the sun, we hit waterspouts around the Virgins. Back then, my captain remarked about it. The other times it was red, nothing happened. Turned out to be beautiful days."

"Do you want some help with the radio?"

"Yes, I think the problem is the connection with the antenna at the mast. We'll get to it after breakfast."

By the time the Alita pulled away from the dock, the day was beautiful with wispy clouds hanging in a sky only a few shades lighter than the ocean. Keith stripped the radio's antenna wire for a new connection and taped it in place. The news and weather out of Guadeloupe shed no worries. The diesel droned steadily, pushing the Alita motored past the north point of Dominica, the Saints, and Guadeloupe. They cruised through the day and starry night to St. Maarten where they'd refuel.

Another Saint island that was not one of Keith's favorites, St. Maarten was as busy as the US Virgins, with too many people and tight traffic. But it had casinos. The crew enjoyed a night ashore before finishing the journey.

Captain Renaldo knew how to keep sailors content. They could have taken a straight course from Dominica to PR, but that would have been a battering, taking the rolling sea sideways on the beam. Cruising north, they stayed in the protected lee of the chain and then, they would turn west after fueling. The Alita would have the sea pushing her home.

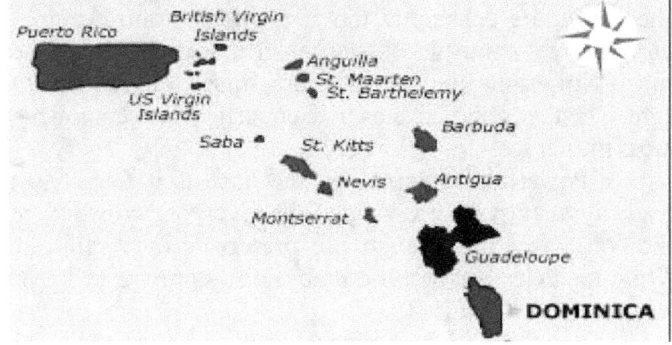

Dominica to Puerto Rico

Keith loved casinos. It wasn't the gambling, but it was watching the gamblers that intrigued him. People were optimistic while facing the grim reality of loss. His motto, like so many others, was 'only lose so much.' Eventually, everyone loses to the house. The winners were usually stupid and kept playing, always hoping to win more. Very few won more, very few. Keith took another card that pushed his hand to nineteen.

He retired to the boat with thirty extra dollars and a few complimentary beers on his breath. The last aboard, his bunk was a folded tarp in the pilothouse. The next morning was cooler as they topped off the tanks in Phillipsburg. It was a normal procedure to check and re-tighten all the lines that secured the bananas on deck. They cinched the empty diesel drums until they groaned. The Alita gracefully rode a westerly breeze away from the Dutch Island.

At noon, the breeze increased and became wind. The Alita had pulled out of sight of the islands. Puerto Rico was a day away. Late in the afternoon, the sea increased to five-foot waves. No one cared about the change since the elements were helping to push the Alita to her destination. A small sail would have been a bonus on this run. When the sun dropped ahead of them, lightning snaked across the eastern sky.

"1001, 1002, 1003...," Bang! Thunder crashed. "That puts the storm about six miles off our stern," Keith reasoned. "Hmm, early in the year for this freaky-shit weather." Renaldo permitted him to scan the radio dial for info. The rusty old box didn't have a weather channel, and every frequency's static seemed just out of reach. About nine, Jesús' boom box picked up a BVI station that had some news. By then, the Alita Dee could have been forecasting the weather.

There's nothing as frightening as a storm at sea after dark. The decks are constantly moving, pitching and heaving. One wrong move, a misplaced step or grip, can end with a serious injury. Noises, the kind heard before, squeaks and squeals, are all right. The thuds and crashes that emanate from unknown places stress the nerves.

Powerful winds rocked the boat as it fought to make headway against the growing swells. Everyone crowded into the pilothouse wearing orange life preservers over rain slickers. White knuckles gripped the grab rails, straining to keep from being tossed and bruised.

Renaldo fought the wheel as the sea pushed the Alita to the north. "Loco dioses... loco dioses (*crazy gods*)!"

Waves began crashing over the stern. At first, it was one in ten; then every wave rose over the rear rail and pounded the empty drums. The Alita rolled and bounced through the deep troughs. Her hull groaned with the corkscrew twists and turns of the stormy sea. The bilge pumps labored continuously.

Keith and the other crew members had endured worse storms, or at least that's what their stories told above the constant hum of the diesel.

Renaldo had been in one during his time in the Royal Navy while in the Philippines. The missile frigate had snapped one of its anchors in Manila Harbor, but luckily the other held in the face of a hundred-plus typhoon wind. Somehow the stories didn't relieve Keith's fears for the wooden, fifty-foot boat he was now in.

A loud crash signaled the drums had sprung free and were bouncing around the aft deck. They screeched and echoed between the claps of thunder. One fifty-gallon tin rode the crest of a wave and smashed into the rear of the pilothouse, clipping off the small mast that held the antenna. It hit with such force that the wooden wall split at two seams.

There was nothing the crew could do except huddle, shudder, and wait. The wheel had a mind of its own. Renaldo felt as if he was arm wrestling with the Terminator. Keith grabbed the pegged ends while the captain surveyed the damage.

Without an antenna, the radio was useless, only receiving the salty spray from the crack in the rear wall. Jesús cowered in the corner, pitting his body against the starboard door. He stared directly ahead into the darkness, hoping to see some lights. Visibility was about an inch beyond the windshield. With rain sheeting on winds blowing fifty, clouds hiding the moon, and constant wave spray, Keith knew they were invisible if another boat should cross their path.

Jesús began reciting prayers. He told that he'd been on a small fishing boat that had hit a reef. His uncle had drowned; they never recovered his body. That was the worst he could imagine, lost at sea and never buried. Not the best topic for the moment. Superstition was if you were lost at sea, you were shark bait for eternity in the afterlife.

The story was interrupted when a bunch of bananas slammed and cracked one of the front pilothouse windows. "Sheet, the wrapping nets must be loose," Renaldo winced. "This is no good... this weather is no fucking good. Now, all our cargo is floating away!"

The storm surrounded the crew with little protection. Even

with hoods up, the rain soaked them. Everyone knew they were in danger, yet no one spoke. Their money from this trip was now drifting in the sea. Their lives depended on the boat. Seamanship had little to do with their present circumstances. The courage of the group was all-important. It would be foolish, if not deadly, to wander on deck in an attempt to save the remaining bananas.

Keith piled his weight on the wheel against the force of the sea. The compass read they were on a north-northwest heading, but no one knew where they were or where they would finish. He estimated they would be looking at the British Virgins in the morning… if they survived these seas. The wind had switched directions, now coming at them from the west. This new force rocked the boat like it was a hobby horse. In the glow of the only 12-volt overhead lamp, each man's face displayed the same thing: fear… serious fear.

Sailors go to sea knowing their lives always hang in the balance of Mother Ocean. Same as miners digging deep into the earth, there is always the fear of an explosion or a cave in. Sailors know when it is time just to hang on… and pray. The Alita's crew were hanging, hoping for a brief respite that would permit a survey of the damage, but it didn't come.

It was difficult to recognize, but the engine sounded like it was losing power. The tachometer showed the RPMs were falling while gauges showed the engine's temperature was rising.

"Renaldo!" Keith yelled, "We've got a problem with the diesel. Losing power. Here, take the wheel and I'll go below and check the filters."

Renaldo eased off the throttles. If the engine died, he doubted they would get it restarted in these seas. Keith's flashlight showed the engine room awash. He carefully moved by grabbing the overhead deck supports to reach the position of the aft bilge pump. Gingerly, he braced his body. Once he cleared the pump's strainer of trash, the water level in the bilge drained rapidly. His light showed some water seeping between the boards, but the Alita Dee was holding together. The fuel filters that protected the engine from sucking in water were clean. Since there were no other tell-tale signs of engine problems, it could only mean that something had wrapped the propeller.

Crawling back up to the pilothouse, he asked Renaldo to put the boat in neutral. The RPMs shot back up. It had to be the prop.

"Si, we must have snagged a banana net or one of the tie lines. We're really pulling some great cards tonight," Renaldo replied.

Ramon, who had been silent for hours, asked, "What do we do now? Should we try to cut it? Man, it is blowing like hell out there. What you want us to do, Cap?"

"Boys, we don't have many options." Renaldo had to shouted to compete with the wind, "We got to continue as we are and hope that whatever is binding the prop will not overheat and blow the engine. Maybe it will fix itself. I hate to cut back on the throttle, but I have to. Or... one of you could go over the side and cut it free. That would be crazy, suicide, so let's just keep our fingers crossed and keep praying. Our God better smile on us."

Ramon and Jesús chanted holy verses in unison while pressed against the rear port-side corner of the small wheelhouse. Renaldo and Keith fought the wheel and stared into the wet blackness. Moteman remained silent, braced, catching the spray from the cracked rear wall and the front window.

"We could fashion a sea anchor to slow us through these waves," Renaldo suggested. "We need to slow down and steady the Alita. Without more power, we're just rolling with the seas. Don't worry, we'll get through this. We are just kind of fucked at the moment."

A blinding sliver of lightning hit the water not far in front of them. Thunder was instantaneous. The storm was directly on them. Trying to be optimistic, it had to pass, but how many more hours of rough seas could they take?

"Yeah, well, let's keep this canoe in neutral for a bit to cool down the diesel. No one looks too excited to hop into the sea in this damn storm," Keith observed.

"I could ask no one to go over the side in these conditions. Really! However, when it calms, even a bit, we will need to free the shaft."

"Your idea of a sea anchor is good and might work since the sea isn't so much following anymore, but coming at us from off the beam. Then again, that will be more shit to get tangled in the prop. Maybe if we get some stability, I'll dive in and do some slicing. But the sea anchor appears to be our best chance. With the bow already listing to port, I can tie a long line on the net of bananas on the foredeck and let it out. I'll need some help. You must spin her quick, as soon as I release it. Otherwise, we'll take a wave broadside and that could make us all swimmers."

"What do you think, Renaldo? I've been on lots of passages with you. Do you think a net of bananas dragging in the sea will help? This is a big blow. Think the Alita has enough cojones?" Ramon asked.

"This boat, she is strong, but if we get hit with a bigger

wave, well, I don't know. A big one could break one of her ribs; then we are in deeper shit. The sea anchor is a chance. The storm could end any time; who knows? The anchor is better than nothing," the captain explained.

Keith shrugged and switched on his flashlight.

"Okay, we do that now. Watch out, you children," Moteman directed to Ramon and Jesús. "We need to keep this old girl afloat, so we will be safe, mañana."

The two crew, nestled on the floor of the pilothouse, moved away from the door to permit the other two to pass.

Keith's watch showed ten-fifteen. "Skip, try to keep her stern to the sea. Stern to and try keeping your flashlights on us. Hopefully, you'll be able to see us through this rain. I'll cut the net loose and then Moteman, when I blink my light, you come out and help me push it over the side. No sense in both of us out there in this blow any longer than we have to be. Got me? Three blinks and work your way down the high side and we'll flip the net load over the port side."

He pulled the drawstrings on his hood tight and put his shades into his jacket pocket. Squinting was the only protection for his eyes from both the wind-driven rain and salt spray. There wouldn't be anything to see in the darkness. He carefully moved by the sense of touch.

Keith lunged out the door with it banging behind him and he found a grab rail just as a huge wave pitched the Alita. He realized how crazy this was. He'd been on this boat for only a few days and was now caught in a gale. In a pitch-black night, he was out on the deck throwing bananas into the sea. Every time he thought it couldn't possibly get worse, it did. Damn, his luck had to change.

The Alita rolled to port after she crested every wave. The decks were awash as Keith pressed his back against the pilothouse and slowly crept toward the bow. His hands sought solid grips as he struggled to move forward against the raw elements of the wind, rain, and heaving sea. Every wave broke and rocked him.

He clutched the cargo boom. As his feet slid, his hands snagged one line that prevented the boom from swinging and he thudded to the wet deck, but held on. Slowly rising, he pulled himself along the boom to the mast. They had the entire deck packed with bananas at the beginning of the voyage. Now it was almost empty. The dull beam of his flashlight showed the only remaining cargo was green bunches wrapped in a thick net between the mast and the bow.

The load shifted with every lurch of the boat. Hand over

hand, he crawled closer. His light revealed all the lines were slack except for the starboard tie-down, now stretched taut. Keith leaped onto the pile.

Straining, he pulled himself along the netting, sure of each handhold. He sliced the two lines on the port side. Drenched, face down, he crawled to the starboard cleat. He realized what a monumental task this would be. A man could carry two bunches of bananas at most. This net contained twenty or more. It would take some coordination with Renaldo at the wheel and Moteman's help to flip it over the side. He undid the wraps on the cleat, and the load shifted more to port.

The rope on the bow cleat remained. Keith loosened it and made his way back to the mast. Carefully, he got a few wraps around the mast that secured the load of bananas. Cautiously moving back along the boom, he found his way to the pilothouse.

"Thank the Holy Mother. You made it back," Ramon exclaimed. "We could barely see your light. She blessed you to keep you safe and not washed away."

"Ramon, you couldn't see shit huddled in the corner," the captain spoke.

"No last rites yet, gents, but we got some problems. All the weight is on the starboard lines because we're listing to port. Should have considered that before I went out there," Keith reasoned. "Skip, put the old Alita through the motions to get gravity to help. I figure if you throw the wheel to port... hard, the bow will swing and dip. With the inertia, Moteman and me can get the heavy net over the port rail. As we let out the restraining line, we gotta be careful; it could get tangled in the prop, or worse, wrapped around one of us. Then we're in deeper shit, or dead.

Maybe we ought to leave well enough alone and ride it out?"

"I could dip the bow to port, but only for a few minutes in this sea. I don't think we'll capsize, but it'll be dangerous. I'm hearing more creaks from the old girl than usual. Ramon, get off your ass and check the bilge," Renaldo ordered. "Look American, come close. These are common crew, not really a seaworthy bunch. Moteman is brave. Be careful, he hasn't been in anything like this before."

"I'm really careful about me. If he stays with me, we can do this. You sure he won't lose his head?"

"This kind of experience can change a man." Renaldo shook Keith's hand as Ramon climbed out of the engine room. "Be careful. Ramon, you keep an eye on them. Jesús, get your ass up here and help. Quit moaning!" The captain gripped Moteman by the shoulder, "Hold on tight at every step."

The two exited and instantly a roller broke against the side of the boat and the spray slammed them against the pilothouse. Moteman slipped, but held on as the next wave washed his feet out from under him. He cried, "Jesus and Mary, this is more than I expected." They huddled together and slowly picked their way to the pile of bananas at the bow. Moteman stayed close and prayed so loud that the angels could hear him over the gale.

"Moteman, pay attention!" Keith barked. "Once the pile slips further to port, push, and let go once it starts to go over. Get the hell out of the way if it slides back against you."

With one arm holding securely to boom, Keith slacked the line. He blinked his light to the pilothouse. It was seconds before the Alita dipped and the pile began to slide. The two deckhands struggled with the netted load while gripping the rail. Trying to secure their footing was impossible. It took a few desperate minutes before enough bunches pulled the rest into the sea.

Satisfied that he'd done as good a job as possible in these conditions, Keith shined his beam on Moteman and found the youth clinging to the mast. His light also showed the line securing the net was still slack because the netted bananas hadn't drifted far enough away from the boat. The surging sea had trapped the net-wrapped bunches in a whirlpool. With a deafening roar, an enormous wave broke over the port bow.

Keith had his weight braced on the high, starboard side and the sudden impact threw him off balance. Flailing, he slid and bounced against the starboard rail. Frantic, Keith grabbed for anything to stop his momentum. The immense power and weight of the wave picked up his body and catapulted him over the side. Wet blackness enveloped him headfirst. Common sense thrust his arms out to protect his face.

After smashing into the sea, the life preserver twisted his frame to bring his head up. Gasping, Keith gulped seawater. The first move was to find his flashlight still attached to the lanyard around his wrist. He frantically waved it to signal the Alita, but realized no one would ever see him in the darkness. His own survival became the immediate issue. The boat could be his savior, but was more likely to crush or stun him. If it ran over him, the prop would slice and dice.

Grabbing a trailing line might save or tangle and strangle. Too much to think about, Keith kicked into the darkness. Another glance and the dim 12-volt light of the boat had disappeared, swallowed by the raging sea. Breathing and holding it seemed better than huffing and puffing, constantly inhaling saltwater, coughing and swallowing more salt. Somehow, in the tumbling waves, the preserver kept his head above water. Feet first, with his hands shielding his head, he floated. Surfing down some waves, Keith felt the brunt while tumbling through others.

There was every reason to be frantic. The immediate issue was about staying alive in the raging storm. Again, things had taken a turn for the worse. Maybe this was the end... of his terrible luck. He forced his mind to relax; no matter the imminent danger, he needed to regulate his breathing to slow his heart rate.

Damn right he was frightened, but this was not the time to lose control and have wild thoughts of terror. He struggled to keep his wits. This was an intense ordeal and maybe a few prayers would help. Only the Lord's Prayer came to mind. Deliver me from evil; he grinned, almost convinced the sea was too rough for sharks. They were probably waiting down in the deep. Yeah, they'd be hungry when it calmed. Yes, he was swimming in God's power and glory.

The freak out part ebbed, and wet sloshing solitude took over. The boat had disappeared. Maybe no one saw him go over the side. Nah, Moteman would have at least looked and called for him. There was no light; everything was black like being locked in a closet, a soaked, bouncing closet. Swimming constantly, he maneuvered to keep his back against the force of the sea, so that his face was occasionally above the water.

His spine arched to let him breathe. He hoped no debris was floating that could clobber his head. Irrationally confident, he kept a constant grin. Back when he'd had his diving business, there'd been many times he popped up far from the boat, and he persevered by swimming on his back and thinking only good thoughts. Once that despair shit crept in, doom and gloom were victorious.

In an instant, something sparked his nervous system and his mind came out of the stupor of shock. All of his senses hit peak performance. Keith was in fit condition and an experienced swimmer; he had enough meat on his bones and could handle the exercise and probably endure for days.

"Okay, give me your best shot!" he struggled to shout. "I promise I'll survive, repent, or anything you fucking want. Jesus, give me a fucking break!"

"I will pull through this one, you'll see." Keith shook his fist. "This is another test." Struggling to mouth the words without gulping more water, "I figure tonight I'm gonna come face-to-face with the high and mighty. This will make me stronger than ever. You hear me, stronger! I'm tough, I'm fucking tough! All the other shit you've put me through is all minor league compared to this. But I'll do it, you hear me? I'll live through this!"

He stretched and rolled his head and laughed into the blackness at the absurdity of his life. He was struggling to survive; for what? He'd lost everything, even the small shit; it was all on the boat. What a sick joke his life had become. Homeless, yet not penniless because he checked and still had his money and passport in a Ziploc snapped in the pocket of his shorts. Maybe a shark would choke on it tomorrow after the sea settled.

"I have no idea where I am except floating in the Caribbean. St. Maarten is back there somewhere," Keith pondered. "But this blow could have pushed us far off course; this could be the Atlantic. If that's the case, we would have passed north of Anegada. I figure a day, two days, well, a half-day out of St. Maarten... with any luck... yeah, like I've HAD any luck... oh, fuck me. Hopefully, when the sun comes up, I'll see the British Virgins. St. Croix would be too far to the south, but who the fuck knows? I'm at the mercy of your winds and currents."

Suddenly, he spun around in the water. Something brushed his leg beneath the surface. He immediately tucked into a ball, but then it bumped against his side. His arms thrashed, trying to scare whatever it was away. All his mind envisioned were jaws... jaws crammed with sharp teeth. His fingers felt a cord, and his stiff hand followed it until he felt the webbing of a net. It was a fight as the rough sea stretched them apart. A few more grabs and Keith discovered bananas. It was a net that slid off the Alita.

Carefully, he maneuvered through the battering waves and crawled onto the wrapped bunches. "Thank you, thank you. Not a bad raft. Not a great raft, but I'm fucking out of the water." In the pitch black, he stretched to find the edges, but decided that his best option was to just hang on. It rode best if he kept his legs tucked up and snagged in the net like stirrups. In the blackness, it felt like his body was above the water, but sloshing between the waves made it difficult to tell.

It was great to have something to hang on to. Once he wrapped arms and legs were through the net, it was time to relax and ride out the storm. He'd tried white water rafting a few times, and this was similar. He had to be careful not to get too wrapped in the net if a wave flipped it over. Stretched out, with hand and footholds, he surfed the pliable fruit bundle through the stormy sea.

Unless a lightning bolt flashed, he had zero vision. The soundtrack was the howling wind, booming thunder, and the crash of the rollers. Counting the seconds between the rise and fall of his banana raft, Keith estimated the distance between the crests to be about twenty feet. That wasn't so bad. Any shorter and he'd be taking a worse battering. The banana raft wiggled and contorted as it slid through the whitecaps and down into the troughs. All he could do was hang on... and be thankful.

The Alita had disappeared. Maybe she'd sunk, not being able to turn with the prop wrapped. He knew they wouldn't look for anyone in this storm, and definitely not the new guy who went overboard. A search would be too dangerous, and losing one man over the side would put more fear into the already scared-shitless crew. They didn't even know where they were. If the sextant wasn't smashed, the captain could shoot the sunrise.

Chances were, they'd take a compass heading north. Hopefully, the sea hadn't pushed them around Anegada, or worse, onto the extensive reefs. With no radio, Renaldo might make a report whenever they found land; then again, maybe not. A missing person's report meant a lot of paperwork and questions. It was doubtful any of the crew knew his last name; he was just some white guy they picked up in Dominica. Both the banana boat, Alita, and the banana raft wallowed at the mercy of the sea, waiting for the sun. Keith sighed, knowing that again he was alone.

We drown our doubts in dry champagne
and soothe our souls with fine cocaine.
I don't know why I even care,
we get so high and get nowhere.
Billy Joel

CHAPTER FIVE

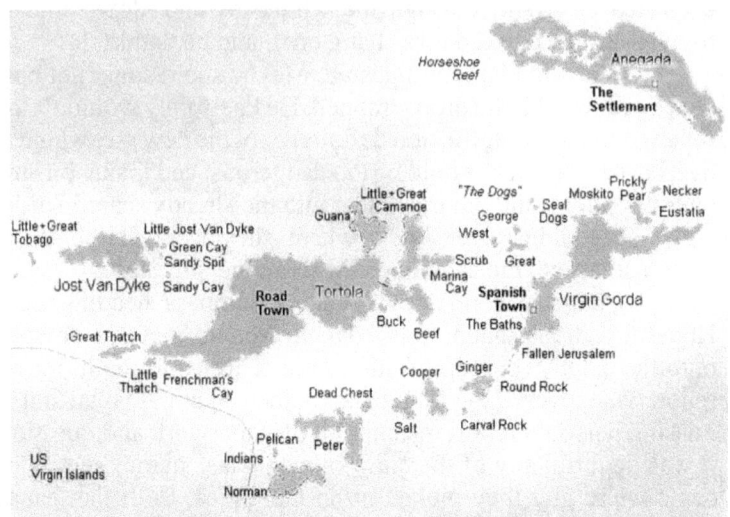

British Virgin Islands

Time doesn't exist in darkness. Humans learn that dark means sleep and awake in daylight. Keith kept his eyes shut to protect against the saltwater spray. He dozed a few times, probably only minutes. A splash would always roust him.

The sky became gray. There was no horizon as the raft slid off wave tips. The sea and the wind seemed to be slightly calmer. Keith could see the dimensions of his raft and it was bigger than expected, about eight-by-eight. He guessed there were a few bunches below the surface that kept his body about a foot out of the water. The green poly net looked new and was wrapped tight around the bananas. He wondered which of the crew had cinched the nets to the Alita's cleats. Their fault had been his savior.

It would become a mess if the net loosened before he made landfall. Keith chuckled as he could see himself floating with a bunch under each arm. It felt good to see a bit of humor in his situation. He figured he was floating on a food supply that could last several weeks.

For the first time, it was calm enough to roll onto his back and look up into the sky that was just beginning to clear. "Believe me, I am thankful. I have no idea what you've saved me for, but I am thankful for these extra moments. You know I'm tough, but without this raft, I don't think I'd still be floating out there face up. Scary to come that close... so, thank you. Can't say what's coming, but you stepped in just in the nick of time." Holding onto the rungs of the net, Keith carefully moved into a kneeling position. "Not much out there to see."

His Tag wristwatch proved worth the expense. It had taken the beating and read six-fifteen on May 10th. A white slicker, polo shirt, and shorts with his pocket full of fun and ID were all of his possessions. His flashlight survived by the lanyard around his wrist and still worked.

Checking his pockets, it surprised him to locate his extra sunglasses wrapped in his ball cap. They would come in handy when the sun started to beat. In another coat pocket, he discovered a small tube of sunscreen. He squeezed out a small glob on his nose and lips.

Another pocket had his folding knife, which immediately severed two green bananas for breakfast. He puckered as they weren't close to being ripe, but swallowed after a good chew. Thirst was critical, and the peels offered some liquid. Keith had read many books on shipwreck survivors and knew his raft would soon become a floating ecosystem that attracted fish. Every account explained that dolphin fish were the first to appear. The thought of raw fish forced a look into the deep.

At eight, the sky was again bright blue. The storm had moved on, but it would be hours before the sea flattened out. The sound of a plane far above twisted him around. Other than using his glasses as reflectors, he had no chance of signaling in daylight. What he needed was a mirror; waving his arms was fruitless to an airliner. Maybe the Coast Guard would send a plane out if they reported him. "Well, I'm still in the air traffic routes." He let out a deep sigh and ate another banana. "One thing, I'll have my potassium quota for life."

The afternoon brought nothing except the scorching sun. Coiled under his jacket, Keith was soaked with sweat. It was hot, and he reasoned that perspiration might deplete even more water. A dip in the sea cooled him off for a few hours. Then the temperature dropped with the sun. The night had stars, but no lights from land or boats. Satellites and planes passed high overhead.

His small flashlight might signal a passing boat if the watch wasn't dozing, but there was no traffic. If he was lucky, a ship might pass a half-mile away. In daylight, the crew would hustle around the deck or rack out in the shade. At night, a watch was mandatory. All that shit about ships passing in the night was true. He'd done lots of night watches on passages through the islands, and any lights helped keep you awake by breaking the boredom. Four-hour watches were usual and being caught sleeping meant punishment... or a collision.

Finally, he felt secure enough on his own banana boat to relax, curled under the raincoat. Dreams came of his mother's farm in West Virginia. Everyone from the small family was there, dressed as they'd just returned from church. Dad was feeding the dogs, and mom was cooking in a frilly apron. He could hear his grandmother's melting southern accent.

The aroma of roasted venison came from the fireplace. This was a typical Sunday dinner. Keith was lying on the shag rug watching an NFL game on the tube. It was cold there. The windows were frosted. His mother entered with a plate of food.

The dream stopped when Keith's hand slipped off the raft into the sea and he jump-started awake. He'd slept for a few hours, sat up, and scanned the horizon. The sea had flattened to a moon-shimmering gloss, reflecting a zillion stars.

"Would have been wise to learn a few more constellations," he talked just to hear something. "Guess I'll have plenty of time to name my own star clusters. A floater's guide to the night sky; I can see it now.

There's lucky doobie, that's kitty, and over there, the mighty mouse. Could make this a home study course. Just buy this book... better make it waterproof... and float around the Caribbean."

A satellite hurtled across the heavens. He figured it was moving west to east because he was drifting the opposite. The waves and current should come out of the east. "Maybe it is a spy satellite looking for drugs, and maybe they'll spot me." He used his flashlight to signal an SOS. "Anything is worth a chance."

He'd read about a guy that had drifted in the Atlantic for more than a hundred days and survived. Another couple in the Pacific whose sailboat was sunk by a whale were passed by seven boats. He'd catch freshwater in the hood of his jacket. Hell, he was resourceful and laughed loudly; let the lawyer try to find him for more alimony.

The night passed with no significant events, but it had been beautiful with a necessary rest. Exhausted, Keith slept until awakened by the heat. Later that day, he scavenged a board floating close to his raft.

Using pieces of the rope that had secured the net onboard the Alita, he fastened a mast. More pieces of line laced his jacket to form a better water catch when it rained. Something higher above the water a boat might see, or a place for a tired gull to sit. The task kept him occupied until he had consumed another dozen bananas, been regular, and tired enough to pass out.

"What would I enjoy today, a walk around the raft, a swim around the raft, a few exercises?" Keith chatted to hear something other than the wind and the waves lapping at the bananas. The raft had become remarkably comfortable. If he reclined in just the right position, he didn't get wet. Since the storm had blown away all the weather, there'd been no rain. During his two days of drifting, he had seen no squalls on the horizons. This was one of the few times he prayed for rain.

Optimism was still working, and he needed to keep his mind occupied, like trying to remember the names of everyone in his small high school class. His thoughts drifted to his marriage and the house he'd built on the St. Thomas north side. He'd bought an acre, and that permitted him to call it an estate. Thoughts took him through every room. It was built strong and had lasted through two vicious hurricanes, but hadn't survived his stupidity.

He had squeezed the money from his diving business. If it could be done in the water, Keith did it: fishing, salvage, moorings, tours… everything. Slow, tedious work scouring boat bottoms, working up from private yachts to inter-island ferries and freighters. Underwater surveys found artifacts and huge clipper ship anchors he sold as moorings.

Hurricane Marilyn was his first big payday. He'd raised eight yachts days after the storm to prevent further damage. The insurance companies were glad to pay ten grand each, ten percent of the appraised value. Other people's terrible luck had been his profit. Who was profiting from *his* awful luck now?

A few careful stretches got the cramps out of his muscles. Keith felt good for his situation, almost limber. He swam a few times a day, always wary of predators. "The drift diet plan: lose weight and get the tan of your life." He laughed. "Women pay through the nose to lose weight and here I am getting thinner and trimmer on my floating potassium fruit raft." He'd shed all his clothes, tying them to the makeshift mast to save them from rotting, hoped he'd need them again.

It was two in the afternoon. Was it good or bad that the days were passing quickly? His thoughts of St. Thomas and his prior life resumed.

His wife... he laughed aloud. He remembered meeting her and being in awe of her beauty. Her almond eyes captured his attention. They'd met at a party for traveling teachers. In other years those parties had paid off with romantic interludes with some very exotic women. He'd met a Moroccan language teacher who had taught him a novel version of French. She was looking for a US passport attached to a husband who could afford her. The French lessons were great, but not *that* great.

Madelena ... he remembered her standing with a group of women where none were svelte. She had caught his eye with an inviting smile. Only five-five, she had long dark brown hair and a luscious bust. After an introduction and several cocktails, she accompanied him home. On his veranda, with the moon reflecting off the beautiful bay, they consummated. She never left the house again, except to bring her luggage.

The new woman had cared for him with a South American style. Back rubs, candlelight dinners on the patio, and a voracious appetite for sex that matched his kept Keith wrapped in her mystique. Seven months later, they were engaged. Her history was brief. She had been born in Santa Marta, Colombia, polished her English. Her family had sent her to the States to get an education and hopefully, a husband. He'd met none of the family, except her brother, and imagined them to be prosperous. Daddy was supposed to be an import-export specialist back home. She told of uncles that had fabulous horse farms and fruit plantations. Someday they'd visit. Brother Carlos was a player who fancied older women. He'd followed Maddy to the islands after she'd married.

In the old days, when risks seemed less mortal, Keith had sailed to Barranquilla to buy Colombia's national products of pot and blow to pay his way through college. He'd begun as a naïve deckhand on a Caribbean vacation that stretched a blue water sail farther to meet a mother ship off the Florida coast. A high school buddy had moved to Florida and scraped enough money to purchase a small sloop. After that, Spring Break had meant a chance for tropical sun, hopefully hotter women, and a chance for some adventure. He took to sailing and never once got seasick. He also enjoyed the thrill of smuggling.

Pot was the only commodity during his early college years. It seemed so easy, so innocent. It only took two weeks to make enough money to pay for a year's tuition; five days down, a few hanging around, and the trip back. Pot, ganja, bud, grass, Vitamin M, whatever you called it, had a huge mark-up. The sloop's owner had it all set up with some Colombian buddies he'd met in Miami. Buy impressive stuff for thirty a kilo and sell it for two-fifty a pound. Not much in expenses, and they only carried what fit in the on-deck life raft container. Laced with talc and readily visible, no one would try to open it because the expected life raft would automatically inflate. Those were times before fiber optics that c o u l d sneak a peek almost anywhere.

Madelena never learned that Keith knew the seamier areas of Cartagena and Santa Marta. The runs increased to four times a year with his first forty-eight-foot sailboat. Fast money goes as fast as it comes, and bank accounts are tattletales. They'd smoked together a few times, but everything was low key. It was difficult to trust anyone. She hadn't wanted to risk her visa and teaching position, yet permitted his indulgence.

"A joint would go good about now," Keith hacked and spit, chewing the moisture from a banana peel. "Yeah, that's all I need is a case of ganja dry-mouth." The sunscreen offered some protection, but his lips were parched. It could have been worse. He raised his aching body using the mast; nothing in sight. Foot tall waves pushed the banana raft slowly toward another brilliant red sunset.

Sleep came with fitful dreams of his past. The quarter moon was high in the sky when a splash startled Keith. He rubbed his eyes. Was it dolphins or sharks? Another splash, followed by a few more, not big, loud splashes like something was leaping or a whale breaching, but something was breaking the calm water. His flashlight didn't penetrate very far, and the moonlight showed little. Straining, he could hear a series of splashes that sounded more as if water was washing against something. For a second, he thought he'd seen a light. The washing sounds were getting nearer. He turned his flashlight's beam into the water and could see the sand and coral bottom about twenty feet below.

Excited, Keith waited for the morning as if he were a child on Christmas Eve. The raft's movement had stopped, and his light showed it had lodged on a tall coral head. Smiling again, he scanned the heavens and saw two shooting stars. "Thank you, I don't know where I am, but at least it is a shallow reef, and that means there is an island somewhere close. I don't know of any reefs in the middle of nowhere. Hell, a few hours ago the downside of this was I'd end up looking like a banana." He laughed out loud. "No known cannibals still around, only a few pirates, and I'd probably know 'em." He almost giggled, "I wonder where the fuck I am?"

Sleep came again.

CHAPTER SIX

"He's out of your life. That's what you wanted, and that's what you got. Very few people get their wishes fulfilled."

"In a way, I loved him. Our times together were good, most of them."

"Little sister, you only love two things, yourself and money. Mierda! Don't bullshit yourself and don't bullshit me."

"Carlos, por qué siempre haces que las cosas suenen tan feas? (*Why do you always make things sound so ugly?*) Keith gave me a good life. Not as good as it can and will be, but it was good. St. Thomas has been very good to me and to you. Think realistically about it: where else could I have done so well? Back home in Colombia, I'd be wearing an apron and dragging a string of pequeños niños (*little children*)."

The attractive woman reclined on a wicker couch, sipping white wine. Her brother was lying on the tile floor. They shared the bottle. "Maybe... being a mother wouldn't be so bad."

"Madelena, in most people's eyes, you are a mother. Una muy mala madre (*a really big, bad mother.*)" Carlos laughed loudly, "Keithy would probably vote you Mother of the Year." He laughed again, his wiry, long hair shaking the constraints of his ponytail. Dark, tanned with raven black hair, his slight six-foot frame cut a handsome presence.

"Yes, I imagine there are those who take my ex's side. Too bad," she chuckled and shrugged her shoulders. "Perspective is everything. Often, I wonder what our parents think of us. You are thirty and never had a real job, even though you have a master's degree in finance. And the family's generosity paid for that. Me," she snickered, "I'm divorced at twenty-six and own an estate on a tropical island. And... I've given you a yacht to live on. Are we spoiled?"

"Madelena, you are a spoiled woman, so very Americanized... and it's only a fishing boat." Pointing his finger, "But you are a strong, manipulative, spoiled woman, just as the Americanas. An exquisite, spoiled woman. A woman who took

what she wanted and now financially secure in her radiant youth."
They touched glasses in a toast. "You know the world is yours."

"Ours. It would have been ours, Carlos, anyway.
Working with Uncle Piedra is doing well. In another year we will
be millionaires, close shop, and be off this island. You must admit
my plan worked. You didn't agree at the beginning," she rubbed
the side of his face, "always impulsive."

"Yes, your cover story is suitable... good enough for
now. Since you've divorced Keith, you can show some money.
We have upgraded my rude existence from living in a ratty studio
on Water Island, but Keith's boat isn't exactly luxury. It will do
for the time being." He laughed as he rose to grab a beer. "Yes,
here's to your generosity, sister. I could hope for no one better to
share a bloodline."

The royal blue Atlantic glistened through the glass doors.
She lit a cigarette and inhaled deeply. "What do we do now, little
brother? Keith will return; you know that. He's not a man to give
all this up without a few tugs. After he stops feeling sorry for
himself, he'll start scheming. And he will scheme about us. He's
been out of here a few months; you and I know he'll get pissed
off, irrational, and come at me, Carlos, at me."

"You always develop a conscience after a few drinks.
Next, you'll be crying, slurring your words. Sister, you are not
sorry. You are not capable of that emotion. Stop it!" Carlos
shouted, "Who cares what that asshole does? He'll end up in jail
if he's lucky, disappear if he's not. Why have all our talks always
grown to value judgments on poor Keith? Fuck him! Too fucking
bad that you didn't have this remorse before you scammed
everything he owned. Yes, too fucking bad!"

"It's just that... well, maybe... I don't know. It would
piss us off, but it will enrage him. I know he'll try to get even.
Maybe we should cash out. I've got a believable story. I'm so
distraught over my divorce, I sell everything and move. This
place has too many awful memories. If we take a rock bottom
price, we can still make plenty."

Carlos looked up from the floor and fished a thin cigar
from his shirt pocket. "You're right about Keith, but he's broke,
no money. I paid to have his ass beaten. We ruined him. He's
homeless, what can he do? Oh, he'll be back, but I bet as a liver-
ailing rummy with a sad story. I don't see him as a threat. I really
don't. No money, no home; it's difficult to get tough when you're
over forty in those circumstances."

She crushed her cigarette. "He'll do what he has to. He
always does."

"Sister, if I got him one whipping, I can get him another. And there are legal ways…"

"And there's crazy, loco ways. You're saying he'd be crazy or stupid to return, and I'm saying he will return and be crazy."

"Crazy men disappear the same as the sane ones." Carlos stared at his sister. "And fewer people ask questions about them." He flicked off the ash, and the liquor talked, "We've built a market, the culmination of a project that began before Keith. Marrying him wasn't my fault. You knew you were complete opposites. I let you make your own mistakes."

His voice increased. "You never listen to me. The marriage could never have lasted, but you craved the blue passport, the identity, inclusion into the island clique. Madelena, it's not guilt you're feeling, instead, the hunger of greed. Our profit will triple next year. Everything is set. Three or four more deliveries and we can put people in place to run things. I am close to being very comfortable; no one will stand in my way."

She sat quietly, staring at the sea view.

"Hermana, estás escuchando? (*Sister are you listening?*)" he roared and clapped his hands. "Especially that low life, cheating ex-husband."

Before daybreak, the rising swell of the sea awakened Keith. As the wind increased with the tide, it dislodged his fruit raft from the coral. He hoped he was inside a reef and not again floating free. Nothing was in sight.

On his back, devouring another banana, he glimpsed the first red that ushered in another day on the sea. He hoped it was his last and he would find land. His back ached from the sharp tips of the green bananas. He yawned and stretched. "Better these than all the other options. Wonder what happened to the Alita? I hope they made it. I've been floating for three days; my tired ass is sunburned and constipated from all these green bananas. That's what I could really use, a fucking, cold green Heineken. Even adrift, those guys should have made land or been rescued by another boat. By now, someone should be searching for me."

His laugh was dry and ended with a cough. "Three days after being washed overboard from a boat without a radio. Do they believe that I survived that storm? They didn't have a clue about our position when I took a swim. Now, where am I?"

As the day brightened, no land appeared. He could see the white sand bottom and to the east was the reef the raft had dragged over. A dive confirmed the bottom was a shallow twenty feet. Crazy thoughts flooded his brain. Was he dead, and this was his eternity? The kid on the boat told about his uncle lost at sea to float forever. Had he discovered some uncharted reef? There might be a fortune in gold below on a sunken galleon. Without some drinking water soon, he'd be joining its sailors in their watery grave. Water was the key. He wasn't getting enough from the peels.

Another banana and then he saw the clouds; clouds that hopefully meant land was ahead. The raft slowly drifted toward them.

His tan was now deep brown and complete except for the bright red cheeks of his ass. Keith's lips were cracked and swollen with sun sores. Scratches on his ankles and lower back were infected and tender from the constant abrasion of the net combined with the saltwater. His knees and elbows ached.

"Life is a bitch, you hear that?" His voice rasped, "Life... life, everything happens to me. Damn it, anyway." Laughter cackled in his dry throat, "Me, who am I to deserve this? Kill me or save me, stop this torture. I keep playing on and on with shitty cards, but I have no control, no control at all. Shit, I don't have enough moisture in me to cry."

"I lost it all, or what I thought was all when I left St. Thomas. I lost more, leaving Dominica. Now I'm at death's door... and damn straight, there's nothing left to lose." Wearily he raised his arms to the sun, "You're cooking my ass! Jesus, why don't you want to finish me off? You've taken everything. Where the hell does this reef end? To the north or south? There must be a spit of sand here somewhere. Come on, cut me a break." Keith held the mast with one arm and raised the other, shaking his fist. "Look at me; I can't take much more of this punishment shit."

Even with his sunglasses, the sun's intense glare made it difficult to survey the horizon. Keith decided that the landfall had to be to the south. The clouds cleared and he could discern a hazy green line... and maybe coconut trees. These trees could be his salvation. His instant elation was short as he noticed the current was pushing the raft to the north. The ribbon of land was at least a few miles away. He knew he couldn't paddle the raft or swim that far.

As he was intently watching the horizon, the raft caught another coral head. Keith staggered and fell into the sea. It felt good, but he was almost too weak to appreciate it.

He stood on the coral head and clung to the raft. "I've got to make a commitment. No doubt; I'm not going much farther with this raft. It was a blessing, but now I've got to decide what comes next. I can see the island; with all the current, it's just a tease. There must be fishermen out here somewhere."

The current ripped the raft's netting as it loosened from the coral. A few banana bunches separated, and the raft became less stable. He pulled himself up once again to check the horizon and he could see a hump. "The island to the south must be Virgin Gorda and I'm stuck in Horseshoe Reef, east of Anegada. Yeah, that's what it has to be. No other island has a reef this big. No wonder I can't see anything to the north. Ana-fucking-gada has only twenty-eight feet of elevation. No fishermen because of the moratorium on even anchoring here. My dumb luck, I wash up where it is illegal to be."

He coughed a laugh. "Fuck me, stuck inside a reef where no one comes to dive or fish. I'm stuck in the third-largest barrier reef in the world. Maybe one of the jet prop commuters out of Tortola will see me. That's a slim chance, buddy."

Virgin Gorda was too far to swim. He knew the reef could be three miles thick, with coral heads as big as city blocks. The heads would make the current crazy and continually snag the raft. Twenty miles to Gorda or three to who knows where?

With his remaining strength and ingenuity, Keith lashed two bunches together as a combination hammock-water wings. It supported him as he lay between them and kicked. Exhausted, he pushed for a last chance.

He rattled to himself, "A hundred and fifty people live over there. I can make it. May is the end of the tourist season. Most of them diving the shallow wrecks off the west. My luck, it's too early for marlin fishermen." Finally, he reached a spot shallow enough to stand and pull the raft. The more bananas he ate, the less flotation. It was the only food. Keith knew there weren't any options, either find land or he'd drown.

The sun was scorching when he finally saw the first coconut palm. A half-hour of exhausting wading through sharp coral, he collapsed on the beach of his salvation. The day had burnt away the clouds, and he knew he was on the east point of Anegada, no mistake. During his chartering days, he had spent a lot of nights at the Bitter End Resort watching this reef. He croaked, "Wish I was there now, sucking down cold Fosters."

Crawling around, he found a few brown coconuts, and with his remaining strength, pounded the thick husks with a stone until he got to the nut. Keith carefully cracked the shell and languished as he savored the coconut water, his first real liquid in a week. He scraped the inside to get the soft jelly. "Thank you, thank you. This is the best thing I could have hoped for." Even the soft coconut meat was hard to swallow, but he choked it down. The moisture slowly softened his throat. Three more nuts followed before he burped and leaned back against the palm, protected from the intense sun by the shade of the branches.

"Well, I made it all right," sticking his hand between his shorts and his belly, "Lost a few pounds, but got a great tan." A genuine belly laugh brought on a series of loud belches before he succumbed to needed sleep.

It was cool in the dark. His watch read four, meaning he'd slept twelve hours. Slightly rejuvenated, he knew he must rehydrate and cleaned more coconuts. The tree trunk helped him pull himself up from the sand, and in the distance, he saw lights out on the reef.

"Boats! It's finally my lucky day! No way I'd walk across this island trying to find a house or village." Keith had been to Anegada many times by boat and plane. It was inhospitable terrain filled with thorn bushes and scorpions, all in rough, treacherous coral. In his condition, it was impenetrable.

Stumbling on weak legs, he found a stick for a cane. He hobbled to the closest point to where the boats were anchored, a few hundred meters offshore. "These guys must know the reef, or they're in deep shit. No matter, they have water and a radio. They can't leave in the dark and I can't pick my way out there. We'll both be here in the morning." Chilled, he huddled in his jacket until he dozed off.

A few hours later, the boats were visible. One was a big catamaran, at least forty feet. Tied along its side was a stretched-out speed boat, like a Cigarette or a Formula. Keith figured the powerboat was probably customs or immigration busting the cat for being in a protected area.

"Now, I'm ready to be rescued. Hell, there might even be a made- for-TV movie in this." His laugh was less hoarse after two more coconuts. He took stock of his situation before approaching the boats. His salt- drenched clothes had survived with his ball cap and raincoat. His Leatherman was on his belt, money and passport were in his pocket.

"That's meager, if there ever were meager belongings. I've still got about eight Ben Franklins and some change. Even if I have to buy passage." He looked at his gaunt, burnt reflection in the sea. "Nah, no one will refuse me. Not the way I look. No faking here. Guess I'd better risk a swim out to these guys before they up anchor and I lose my chance at a ride and maybe a meal. Wonder what they've been doing out there for so long? Must be good skippers to get in there, day or night."

The banana water wings were now more brown than green, but still floating. Keith used them as support when it got too deep to wade. Consciously and with more energy, he kept watching for sharks. "Yeah, the way my luck's been going, you'd stick my rescue out there and get me nailed by a hammerhead on the way. I know God has a weird sense of humor, and I'm the current object of the joke. The sharks are thick up here, especially the reef sharks. This is a scary place, the Serengeti of the Caribbean." He paddled for thirty minutes until he reached the quiet boats.

"That's odd," he thought. "Anchored out in the middle of nowhere and not a sound." Then the implications of the speedboat with radar finally struck. "Man, this could be a drug deal. Shit, my rescue could come to a quick end." He stopped paddling and quietly swam.

The catamaran was actually a trimaran named Shameer out of Delaware. The powerboat was about thirty feet with two three-hundred horse outboards. Its charcoal gray, nameless hull contrasted with the sparkling white tri. He swam to the dive ladder of the sailboat.

"Ahoy, anyone about?" A Boston Whaler, probably the sailboat's tender, was tied to the stern. The crew could be snorkeling. "Seems like someone should be aboard. Ahoy, I'm a man in distress." After a minute with no response, Keith pulled himself on deck and into the cockpit. An Igloo cooler rewarded his efforts with an array of beverages. Beer and sodas could wait as he gulped down a few bottles of water. He finally relaxed on soft cushions under the shade of the canvas canopy. Nobody was around. He grabbed an orange soda and sat back, feeling good he'd finally been saved.

Thirst quenched with another soda, hunger became the issue. "I'd hate for them to find me below on a stranger's boat. That could ruin my welcome when they return. I know this will sound a bit too fantastic, but I tied the banana bunches to the dive ladder. That's got to substantiate my story." Keith clapped his hands together. "I'll hear either a boat or people approaching. I'm certain they wouldn't begrudge a shipwrecked sailor a few morsels from their galley."

He leaned into the hatch and gazed upon a spacious salon. At the far end was a counter that separated the galley. Feebly,

Keith descended the stairway. The galley fridge was a dream. He stuffed cheeses and cold cuts into his mouth. Swallows were hard, and he almost choked, but gulps of cold milk helped push it down.

"Some luck, huh?" He gulped more milk, soothed his throat and stomach. "I was almost dying a few hours ago, and now I'm sitting in the lap of luxury." He looked upward. "Whoever's in charge, you cut it close this time. I figure I owe someone, because from here on, it's borrowed time." He burped loudly. "Yeah, from here on, I'm a changed man. Changed for the better."

The fridge yielded some grapes and from the freezer; he gulped some ice cream until he almost had a brain freeze spasm. "Maybe I died, and this is my heaven? Damn, I never thought ice cream could taste so good. For once, I'm a lucky guy. Damn straight, I'm happy eating ice cream and that's better than fish chomping my tired old ass."

He sat at the small navigation table and checked out the electronics. GPS, radar, an SSB - single-sideband transmitter, two VHF radios, a multitude of switches and alarms for many of the yacht's functions. A cell phone hung from a rack that held several charts. One was unrolled on the desktop that detailed a passage from Panama, island hopping to Anegada.

"Gee, I guess you can do anything with a GPS, autopilot, and decent weather." Keith made himself comfortable on the salon's soft cushions. A full belly brought on the first relaxed sleep he'd had in weeks.

She didn't know what to do with herself on these free summer days, exercises in the morning, followed by a jog through the neighborhood. Now an affluent divorcee, Madelena was in demand by several eligible bachelors and reckless husbands.

"Little sister, you are naturally beautiful, yet you work so hard and then stay home where no one can see you. I am your only date." Carlos laughed. "People will get weird ideas about us. You shun people when we go out. You aren't embarrassed about Keithy, are you?"

"Carlos," she gasped between leg raises. "I am worried. It helps me burn off nervous energy by working my body. I can't gain weight now. It would be too easy. For someone like you who can eat anything, drink all night, and stay slim, this seems hard. I love to sweat."

"Right, sister, there are at least a dozen men who would make you sweat and you would feel better with their attention. Maybe that's what you need? How about it? Have you been getting any sex-o since you tossed Keith out, or are you just sitting around feeling horny?" Carlos chuckled and lit a cigarette. His brunette sister looked especially hot in her leotard. The scent of sweat added to the allure. Sister or not, Madelena was beautiful.

"Yes, what you do is good, seriously," Carlos added. "The image you project of the shocked wife who got all the marbles when hubby lost his, is perfect. Time and money will heal that. Everyone will sympathize with you. Smart, very smart."

"Carlos, our friends have not returned from their errand? With this great weather, they should have been back last night. I'm concerned. Could they get lost?" She grabbed a towel and wiped her face.

"Many things can contribute to a delay of a few hours. There is no reason to worry. You know he will eventually call. He'll be here today.Our friend is very trustworthy."

"Everyone's trustworthy until the right amount of money enters the equation." She stood in front of the wall mirror, checking her shape. "You don't think he got confused? Everything's been so confused lately. We gave him explicit directions. Maybe he just forgot?" She reached into her brother's shirt pocket and grabbed a cigarette and lighter. "We need this to go right; no more problems. My stress level is through the roof."

Carlos' arms encircled her as she viewed them in the mirror. He was taller, but the family resemblance stood out: hair color, face shape, eyes. He squeezed her tight and brought his hands to her breasts. "Sister, maybe you need some deep stress relief, brotherly love... Don't worry, be positive. This kind of thing always has some slight problems. All we can do is wait and be patient. Besides, sister, we are very insulated. It would be very difficult for our friend to implicate us, even if he chose. What would be his gain? Our intermediaries would quickly silence him. He will do the right thing, you'll see. Just have faith."

Madelena turned in his arms and buried her face in his shoulder. "You are right. But if you hear anything, call me. And if you want to give me some brotherly love, start with a neck rub." She bit his shoulder, "Remember, call me if you hear anything."

"Of course, sister." He massaged her taut neck muscles.

When bad luck begins, it doesn't come in sprinkles but showers.
Mark Twain

CHAPTER SEVEN

Keith woke with a gasp, trying to discern where he was. He smiled as he remembered finding the yacht. He stretched and rubbed the life back into his arms and legs and climbed the ladder up to the cockpit of the trimaran.

The sun was about to hit the western horizon. His nap had been about six hours. His energy was returning. Keith rinsed with the deck hose. The ice had almost melted from the cooler, but the beer was still cold. The sweet Corona tasted better than the finest champagne. Sipping, he sat back to scope out his present situation. He'd found a refuge, but it appeared to be a ghost ship. Two ghost ships, including the go-fast boat tied to the side.

"Damn strange, these boats are out here all alone." Opening another beer, he walked to the port side and checked the speed boat to discover it was an official Cigarette. "What the hell? There is absolutely no reason for two abandoned boats anchored inside the Anegada reef. This is some weird shit. Damn, the last three weeks have been world-class weird. This is another candle on the cake of my screwed-up life. Who would leave boats like these? Hmm…" he laughed, "maybe UFOs abducted them."

"Guess I could call Tortola radio or the Coasties, but this is so fucking strange, I could find myself tied into even crazier shit than I am now." Going below, he returned to the salon's couch and tried to reason it through. "Not a doubt, no one would leave a yacht like this unattended for a day unless there were foul doings. Best I'm not involved. Hate to be found below decks, but then it doesn't seem like anyone will be around. Let's see who owns the Shemeer from Delaware."

The navigation table lifted, but no pertinent papers were among the electronic manuals and cruising guides. He'd found the cellphone, considered, and then rejected making a call. Keith opened the starboard hatch. The door yielded after a good yank with a sticking sound. It had a watertight seal. "These multihulls are always thinking about keeping water out. They go too damn fast and the glass is too thin. Pretty classy layout." The bed was made, with no clothes or personal items in the lockers.

The port side hatch yielded an exact mirror image. "Well, I've either discovered another twenty-first century Mary Celeste or at any moment, Rod Serling will boom out an introduction to the…" Keith trailed off as he opened the forecastle hatch and found several sail bags, lines, and lots of yacht hardware strewn about the floor. Other racks on the side of the cabin held various hand and power tools.

"Everything's top-shelf. Not a piece of lint anywhere. Only things out of place are these sail bags dumped on the floor."

Turning and retracing his steps to the stern, he glanced around the salon, feeling he'd missed something. The stern hatches led to spotless engines and generators. Lubricants and spare filters were organized in racks on the walls.

One last hatch led to the stern cabin. The sealed door gave way to a graphic scene of modern business gone sour. Keith didn't move and stared into the cabin. It must have been for the captain and crew since it had two berths. Frozen in dark pools were three men and one woman. Sprawled on the starboard bed was the bikini woman. She lay between two men collapsed who appeared to be Latinos wearing white guayabera shirts with black pants. One was maybe forty, with heavy black hair graying at the temples. They'd shot him in the belly, soaking the sheets with blood. The younger Latino was in his twenties and wouldn't celebrate another birthday. He had taken a bullet in the face. The right eye was gone. His left hand clutched a shiny Glock.

After several hard swallows, Keith carefully stretched to the closest victim and removed the younger man's billfold. A Puerto Rico driver's license was the only ID. The woman may have jumped at them, been pulled, or pushed. She might have given cover to the other white guy. Her bikini showed a heart shot through her ample left breast. She was about thirty, usual boatie: deep tan, sun-bleached blond hair, adorned with trinkets. She looked familiar, but after a while, all boat women look alike.

The last unlucky male must have been the surfer-dude captain. Long hair, deep tan, crumpled on the floor, still holding his small pistol. He must have been an accurate shot to get the other two before getting his, high in the gut. Keith leaned over to see if his shorts had a wallet. As he rolled the man over, a sigh escaped. Checking, he found the pulse was very faint. "You poor fucker, no way anyone could help you now. Maybe if I had been more of a snoop when I came aboard… but what type of shit did you get messed up in?"

The man's body had hidden an aluminum briefcase. "Jesus Christ!" Keith exclaimed opening it to reveal stacks of hundred-dollar bills. "Assholes, killing each other over drugs, no doubt." He moved with the money back into the salon and began a serious search of every cabinet and locker. The cash had only been there to purchase some merchandise. Under the bed in the port cabin, there was a sliding panel that revealed what looked like a water tank. It took a few minutes, but inside there were at least twenty kilos of white powder.

Keith stuck his knife into one package and tasted. It was coke. "Really, this was worth dying over? Live by the sword and all that dumb shit. Every smart ass thinks it can't happen to them. Fucking assholes, bloodying up a sweet boat like this. When you finally get a yacht, why would you continue to hustle?" He knew the answer: pure greed.

"There's always got to be a winner, and I guess that would be me." He got another beer before he removed and counted the parcels of cocaine. Thirty plastic-wrapped bundles. That made sixty-six pounds of the drug. Should have been a mega payday, probably over a million US. Keith smiled because he knew people who knew people who could get him that kind of dough for this shit. The cash counted out to three hundred and fifty thousand.

"Not a bad hand for a luckless son of a bitch like me." The word 'luckless' echoed inside the cabin. "Man, this shit could get me into all sorts of good and bad. I wonder who had what? Were the two with the greasy black hair the rippers or the rippees? I'd guess they were the buyers and decided they wanted it for free."

He gulped the beer. "And the Romeo and Juliet duo must have been ready. Looks like it must have been love if she'd tried to save him and took one herself. Yeah, you are, no, were, the American entrepreneurs."

He sat on the salon couch with the money and the drugs stacked between his legs. Sipping another beer, he considered his position. Call the Coast Guard. He wasn't involved. That wouldn't be hard to prove if the banana boat, Alita Dee, had made it to a port. There wasn't another soul in the world who could give him an alibi for the last week. If the Alita had sunk, then no one could verify his story.

They would charge him with four counts of murder. He could leave the boat just as it is and someone would find the mess in the next couple of days. Or he could help himself to the cash and blow and start a new life. That would have its problems, but a million-plus could solve most of them. "I think I'll choose door number three, Monty. The only thing I have to worry about is leaving traces. Forensics aren't great down here, but they'll thoroughly inspect this scene. If they can't prove I was here, then

I got the winning lotto ticket."

With paper towels and spray cleaner, he scoured the cabins, everywhere he might have touched. Doorknobs, handles, fridge, cooler, freezer, charts, soda, and beer bottles were all wiped or tossed. During the cleaning, he planned his escape. His thoughts passed to the poor soul, who would not recover. Even his sudden change of luck couldn't obscure such a painful, lingering death. But that's what it was; no one could save him.

Even if he'd found him when he first came aboard, the boat ride to Gorda would have killed him. Twice, Keith wiped through the entire yacht. The absence of prints might alarm some big city policemen, but in these latitudes, few would care.

He removed all his treasures to the cockpit. He bagged all the trash. "It is a tough job," he smirked, "this boat cleaning... but damn, it pays well."

It was a moonless ten when Keith crawled aboard the Cigarette to hunt for any clues about the four inside the trimaran. The speedboat's dark gray hull vanished in the night. He had shut off the yacht's mast light and was careful with his flashlight. He did not want to attract attention.

Fumbling through the speedboat's cabin, he found the usual stuff: a few charts, sandwiches in a cooler, and fuel receipts from a marina in St. Thomas, bathing suits, and towels. Looks like they were planning to go for a swim. On deck, inspecting the helm, Keith found another aluminum briefcase, almost hidden between the hull and the captain's thickly padded chair. Inside were two machine pistols with extra clips and another cell phone.

In the darkness, the boat yielded only one identification. His head jerked when he read that the dead, fat Latino was DEA. What the fuck was going on out here? Couldn't have been a bust with only two agents. The place should have been swarming with back up. This was a rip-off. Show the cash, kill, and grab the goods. The DEA boys zeroed their overhead and probably knew every disreputable dealer who would love to make brownie points selling the dancing dust.

Keith knew he wouldn't be around to inspect it in the daylight. The Feds added another element of fear. Sitting in the captain's chair, he formulated his plan. Weighing the risks versus the gain, if he took the loot and ran. His only alibi would be found adrift from the storm, floating. His two-bunch life raft was tied to the stern. There's no way anyone looking as bad as he did, could have pulled off anything like this.

Keith's mind whirled. This was a gift, the last chance to get the fuck over and become a winner again. He'd have fresh bucks for a fresh start. If he floated on the bananas for another day, some cruisers might find him.

"Can't take a chance of being found anywhere around here. This place will be red hot. I got drugs, money, and guns, two boats, the Whaler, and my bananas. What the hell can I do? I can't blow this chance."

"If I take any of these big boats, I'll incriminate myself. If I'm caught with anything from here, I'm fucked. With my luck, if I float again, a shark will hit me. I can't fuck around much longer because someone's got to be expecting these dead heads. Guess the best bet is to play pirate and hide these valuables until I can return. The best place to hide it is on Anegada; that's not far away. The best rescue place is Virgin Gorda's east end. Few people living out there. I hide it here, buried under thorny bushes on a sandy rock with only a couple hundred people who don't wander around. But how in the hell do I get to Virgin Gorda?"

"The Whaler looks like it could serve me well. I could drive it over to the far end, throw the bananas in, and then drift ashore on the Alita's cargo. That should answer all the questions."

He checked the boats again for evidence and curled on the salon couch.

The insulation taped over the bedroom window slightly muffled the loud hum of the kitchen fan from the restaurant across the alley. Downtown Charlotte Amalie usually has a sea breeze. But three streets from the waterfront with closed windows, it was difficult to sleep past six in the morning. The second floor, small, one-bedroom looked over a nineteenth-century courtyard. The building had once been horse stables for the Danish. Surrounding the perimeter were seventeen similar units. Tourists, locals, and offices paid the rent.

Dale stretched and padded the streaked white floor to the tiny bathroom. His slim, six-foot frame leaned against the wall as he relieved the morning pressure. He heard a toilet flush on the other side of the wall. Running only a trickle of water, he rubbed his hands and splashed some on his face, patted down his full beard and bushy hair. He returned to bed to plan his day as the room temperature rose with the sun.

He'd been released from jail three years before, but he still lived the routine. It wasn't as though he was so habitual; he just felt good waking with a clear head every morning. His breakfast was always the same: a bowl of high-fiber cereal and black coffee before starting a hectic day as the maintenance man for the building's realtor. Pushing sixty, Dale appeared forty-five with his brown hair showing no signs of gray. Not an extra pound, his Levi's hung loosely. He pulled on his traditional white T- shirt and stuffed a red handkerchief into his rear pocket. He arched his fingers and scraped his nails through his hair to rejuvenate his scalp before he walked out the door.

Even though most days in St. Thomas were squinting bright, Dale never wore sunglasses. His time in the Marines had taught him to bear up 'to old man sol' as he liked to said. He never drank cold beverages and never had ice as it was too much of a shock to the nervous system. In the rear of his old Renault, he kept a case of Pepsi, never Coke, only Pepsi.

The rusted, sun-roofed Renault had seen better days, but who hadn't. It sufficed, climbing the steep hills from the sea level town to the outlying apartments and condos that required attention. Seven days a week there were toilets that didn't flush, gutters that leaked, clogged sinks, and ripped screens. The old white car with splotches of yellow primer was his office, shop, and a toolbox. At the turn of a key, the car purred to life and sped off to another day of tight, hot traffic. He'd traverse the length and width of the island from rental units to hardware stores.

This grind hadn't been the life he'd planned. He'd been a career soldier for twenty years. Dale had received a hands-on education of warfare, munitions, and general killing. By the time they discharged him at thirty-seven, he'd seen Europe, Africa, and the armpits of the Middle East. His hard body and keen senses hadn't dimmed. That's what had kept him alive, while others had bought the farm. No one ever described Dale as dull or lazy. The Service had taught him French and Spanish.

Within ten years of separating from the Army, Dale had amassed a small fortune with discreet powder runs back and forth from Caracas. Then everything folded into another tropical drama. One client ratted him out. The ensuing legal moves consumed his savings, his beach house, boat, and car. Everything went quickly downhill. The prison at Eglin Air Force Base taught him patience. A loner, Dale worked in the commissary and did his stint as easy as possible. The guilty verdict cost him five years, his wife of two years, and his infant son. When the VI legal system incarcerated him in Florida, his family also returned to the mainland. They didn't visit Dale.

Time for the first Marlboro of the day. With a deep inhale, Dale didn't care he'd been diagnosed with emphysema. It was his only vice, and nobody lived forever. The Renault pulled into a space near the realtor's office. He arrived every morning to get his daily list of duties and make his presence known to the boss, George. One more puff, then he squashed the butt and slid open the office's glass door.

"Well hello, Dale, here's a list of things that need to be done in your typical, efficient manner." The receptionist was a twenty-something, husky West Indian, proud of her dreadlocks. Dale got the feeling she was pressuring him with George so her hubby could slide in as the repairman. She held the list as he tried to pick it up. "Don't you ever tire of constantly dealing with the hassles and the tenants? How come you never tried to become a sales agent?"

"Thanks for your concern, Martha," he snatched the list. "I enjoy doing minor jobs that I can finish in one or two days. Since most of the tenants work days, I seldom see anyone. It's always something different; some are puzzles. Each job is just like human nature, completely different. Me, a sales agent? Never."

"Speaking of completely different human nature, George wants to speak with you. Just go right in."

Dale liked the man who signed his checks. George had amassed a fortune in island real estate and had taken Dale under his wing. He realized how hard Dale worked and fed him jobs that kept him continually busy. His one-man maintenance department kept costs down. It was important to keep him happy and in the stable. Pot-bellied and in his forties, George dressed the part of a beachcomber; loud print shirts, shorts, and sandals were his uniforms. Outdoors, he always wore a straw hat. Years ago, he'd buddied up with a few wealthy investors and built a mall and several housing developments. Management, for a percentage, was his present cash cow.

"Yes, Dale, come on in." The boss offered a cup of coffee as he poured his own, "How's everything going? Are things close with the east- end renovation? I've got it rented next month."

"It'll be done," Dale sighed as he sipped the coffee. He knew he'd have to work nights this week to finish on time. Sometimes the job had its pressures.

"Look, Dale, I know you could use some help. It's got to be tough meeting the demands of all the tenants and sticking to my schedule."

Dale was waiting for George to mention Martha's husband.

"My son is home from college and could use some work.

Actually, he needs to learn about work. His pay won't cut into yours and," George laughed, "it'll help keep you both out of trouble. Hell, you could use a sidekick, somebody to talk to when you are humping. I can't see why you enjoy such a monastic life. My kid will loosen you up and can do all the heavy work. You know Neal, I'm hoping you can teach him some useful knowledge and he can take some burdens from your shoulders."

Dale knew Neal. He was a spoiled kid with soft hands and a softer head. "You're the boss, George. Whatever you say is okay by me." He took another sip of coffee. "When does he start?"

"Hoping you can use him tomorrow. I thought he could finish painting the east-end house. You set him up, get him started, and then you can go about your other duties. Pick him up here tomorrow. I'm sure you'll get along."

Dale turned and headed to the door. "Everything else okay, Dale?" George asked. "Maybe you should take a week off once you get Neal acquainted with everything."

"Yeah, maybe," Dale left. Once sitting in the Renault, he pounded the steering wheel with his open palms. "Damn, damn, damn it all. The last thing I need is some chump kid to wet nurse. A screw-up who'll talk my ears off, won't do a fucking thing, and still collect a check. Nothing I can do about it. If I buck George, then I'm looking for another job."

The workload was big, but because it was a tourist area, everything was seasonal. He needed help in December and January. Now, it is almost June, the slowest time of the year when even the traffic was bearable. The old Renault edged onto the main road as he lit another cigarette.

"I might as well start looking for the next gig. I'm getting kind of old for this, anyway." He grabbed the list and checked what he needed to do. "Shit, it will take me all day just to get ready for this kid."

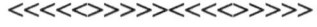

The eastern sky was just becoming gray as Keith loaded three suitcases into the Whaler. Then he returned and wiped anything he may have touched on his exit. With the two banana bunches pulled aboard the twelve-foot runabout; next stop was Anegada. Carefully dodging the coral heads, he pulled the boat onto the beach. The plan was to hide the cases and head out to sea without being witnessed by a fisherman or an airplane. He had no idea if anybody was now searching for either of the boats, but eventually, someone would be. Keith hoped it would be later... much later.

Just over the rise from the beach where he'd sucked the coconuts was a pile of coral rocks. Everywhere was dense, thorny bush. He was counting on the thorns to keep out visitors until it was safe enough for his return. Once he moved the rocks, Keith scraped a pocket in the sand and stashed the three cases. Money, drugs, guns, and phones, everything necessary to be a bandit, went into the hole. He took the added precaution of disabling both phones. He removed the sims and batteries. Not much except technology had changed since the days of the pirates, he thought as he pulled the last rock back into place. Those damn phones could be tracked, but he reasoned they might be useful later. Dead branches covered the rock pile and wiped his footprints.

It was well after daybreak. Before he started the outboard, he searched the horizon for potential witnesses. Once he was away from the beach, he didn't care if anyone saw the dinghy, as long as they hadn't seen him stash the goods. He slowly negotiated the reef and took a sweeping course to the south. As the sun climbed, he checked the time: seven-fifteen. If he hadn't forgotten any incriminating evidence on the boat, he was a millionaire. That was pure exhilaration.

After drinking his fill and eating, he still looked ragged. Must have lost at least twenty pounds floating for a week. His spirit was rejuvenated, but the sores and scrapes were still vivid. The bananas were his own proof to verify his tragedy. Had he forgotten anything, a clue, it could mean his doom?

If someone was watching over him, the Alita Dee would have survived the storm and could substantiate his story to the BVI authorities. The outboard slid along the waves heading east of Virgin Gorda. The mists in Gorda Sound were still visible when he passed. The Whaler rode low in the water and another boat would have to be very close to see it among the waves.

By eight, Keith estimated he was in position for the current to push him toward the big island. Shifting into neutral, he tossed his banana bunch raft into the sea. Then he lashed the outboard to send her on a southeast course. It took a lot of nerve; he kept thinking of the stash. It was tough for him to leave a perfectly good boat and remount his nearly rotten fruit raft. He wiped the interior of the dinghy, the engine, and the rub rail. He couldn't take a chance on any fingerprints. If they found the dinghy, probably no one would look for an owner. Little runabouts like this one were expensive and coveted in the islands. If it washed ashore, the sea and rocks would quickly splinter it.

Flipping the motor into gear, Keith jumped into the sea. The Whaler churned into the distance. Waves broke over the banana bunch water wings, sparking his attention to the landmass about a mile away. With wind and current, he should be there in two hours. Stretched out between the two bunches and refreshed, he kicked to help move things along.

The sea and the wind increased. Keith knew there were several private homes and two big resorts on Gorda's east end where he could find help. For years, Gorda Sound had been on his charter route. A few of his old sailing buddies might be anchored there. "Today is the last day of this shit," he thought, "and I'm over and done with it, finally over." It would be high tide and green grass again.

The bananas drifted to the rocky south shore, farther west than Keith had hoped. The waves crashed onto a shoreline strewn with enormous boulders. Carefully staying beyond the edge of the surf, he kicked and maneuvered the raft into a slight breakwater behind the largest rock. The raft had to be saved for evidence of his story. Even without finding the murders and the money, surviving six days at sea floating on bananas was unbelievable.

With his limited strength, he pulled the raft above what he could see was the high-water mark. He wedged it as best he could. Finally, exhaustion overcame him, and he sat in the rock's shadow. As a final toast to the Gods who had helped him, Keith ate one more banana and took a well-deserved nap.

He awakened to a cool evening, found a suitable staff among the driftwood, and trudged along the rocky shore. It was slow moving, calculating every step, but the finality of this sour episode drove him on. Finally, he met the low saddle of the hills and saw a path. It led to a resort where he startled the lounging guests at happy hour. Their 'New York, hello' elicited a feeble wave from the ragged man as he collapsed. One guest splashed some of his vodka tonic on the survivor as another ran for help. Keith licked the vodka from his parched lips and passed out.

I was making frequent use of cocaine at that time. I had been the first to recommend the use of cocaine, in 1885, and this recommendation brought serious reproaches down on me.

Sigmund Freud

CHAPTER EIGHT

It was one o'clock and baking hot along the waterfront in Charlotte Amalie. The line of cars from the post office to the bank wasn't moving; neither was the breeze.

Carlos glanced at the Suzuki jeep in the next lane. The driver was a cute blonde in her early twenties. Her white cotton shirt soaked in sweat, revealed everything. As he adjusted his smile, the driver returned his look.

"Hot, huh?" she spoke, snapped her gum. "That's why I live here. It isn't for the great roads. What about you? Any cooler with a roof?" "Not too bad. Must be an accident for it to be this slow."

"Only thing slower than this is the way the authorities respond. Probably someone just chatting and blocking the street. Locals love to do it. Know what I mean?" She leaned from the jeep toward Carlos' pickup, giving him an enjoyable view of her cleavage. "My name's Elizabeth." She reached into a cooler behind her seat and offered a beer. "I'm heading to Morning Star Beach for some rays before I go to work. These beers make the day go better. Know what I mean?"

"Thanks." He stretched to grab the Heineken. "I'm Carlos. Where do you work? I'll stop by and return the beer."

Traffic crawled forward. "Pillsbury Sounds at the east end. I'm there 'til eleven. See ya!"

The traffic edged onward. Carlos was in the left lane to turn toward Frenchtown. He was already late for his appointment, but the sweet blonde had considerably brightened his day. His product was late. Josef, whom he was meeting, didn't care to hear excuses for tardiness.

"Fuck 'em, if I care. This town never has a parking space." Finally, one appeared. With a quick check of his appearance in the rear-view mirror, Carlos headed for the white-painted bar.

"Closer to two than one," Josef grumbled, slapping his fleshy arm around Carlos' thin waist. "Jeez, you feel like you could use a meal or two or three." Josef didn't need any extra meals. As the owner of Casablanca, he always took advantage of the delicious meals. He had a fiftyish paunch that stretched his black jersey so tight his navel was visible. Nothing in his attire clashed. It was all black and shiny, from pants to shoes. "So, amigo, what's up? My people want some of your friends' merchandise. I hope it has arrived."

He squeezed Carlos tighter. The younger man freed himself from the grip. "Something happened with the boat. It's running late. You know how these things are. A slight delay on one end, there will still be a lot of money on the other."

"I've got some serious dough invested, amigo. The shit better get here soon."

"Sure, sure, so what else is going on? Why'd you drag me into the afternoon heat? I could have told you about the late shit on the phone, except we don't talk about 'the shit' over the phone." He'd forgotten the beer was in his hand and his gestures splashed the floor.

"Amigo, what is it? You got a beer buzz going this early?" Josef waved at a server. "Yo, Stevie, bring my friend another beer. He's washing our floors with this one. No, Carlos, I thought you'd like to hear that your brother-in-law Keith was shipwrecked.'

"What? He drowned?"

"Close, I guess. There was a supply captain in here from the Bitter End Resort in Gorda. Said a white guy from St. Thomas washed up on their eastern shore looking like death. He's getting nursed back to health," he slapped Carlos' shoulder. "That poor bastard's luck is only bad."

Carlos hooted as he grabbed the beer. "Better him than me. I wonder how it happened. Didn't even know he'd left this rock. I hope he makes it."

"You lie," the fat man laughed. "After all the shit you put him through after the divorce, you hoped he was feeding the fish. If that poor fuck ever realizes how you stacked the deck against him, he'll come looking for you."

"Let him. Yes, my big friend, I got no compassion for Keith. He fucked around on my sister and I fucked him around. You helped, amigo. I seem to remember you engineered a beating he took at the construction site. You did it as a friendly gesture. I appreciated the help, really."

"Yeah, those two Rastas really laid a tattoo on his scrawny ass. Personally, I never liked the dude, too cocky, self-assured. He was always so damned arrogant. Yeah, you and I are friends." Josef toasted Carlos, touching beers, "But the shit better get here quick, if we're going to stay that way."

"Soon come, man, soon come. Look, I really got to go. You'll hear the minute I do. Serious." He shook the lazy hand. "Soon as I hear, you hear."

<<<<◇>>>><<<◇>>>>

"Hello, are you feeling all right?"

Keith felt his arm being tugged. He awakened suddenly and looked around with confused eyes. Slowly, he focused on the two men and a woman. Intravenous tubes were attached to his arms. The room was pale green with thin Venetian blinds that made crazy shadows on the walls with the bright sun. He had no clue where he was.

"Hello, Mr. Gardnar, I'm Dr. Hodge. You staggered into this hotel after being washed up on a beach near here. Here is Virgin Gorda. You must have quite a story to tell. You're a very lucky man to have survived floating the Anegada Passage." The doctor was a West Indian in his graying years, with English grammar as impeccable as his attire. "What do you remember?"

The doctor introduced the attractive woman, "This lady is Gail Archer. She manages this hotel, Gorda Creek Resort. They have been generous in offering you a room; it's the slow season. Still very commendable. This hotel, the management, and every guest hopes you will have a quick rehabilitation."

Keith said nothing, but extended his hand to the petite lady with red hair.

"We were worried about you, Mr. Gardnar. You've slept for almost two days. It must have been a harrowing experience at sea," she almost curtsied. Something smelled good, either her perfume or the flowers packing his room. "Take your time recuperating. You are the most interesting item that has happened on this end of the island in years." She turned and left.

"Yes, you are interesting. Just how you floated with those banana bunches must be quite the story. I'm Inspector Prescott of Her Majesty's Royal Detectives assigned to these British Virgin Islands." He was a solid six-footer, impeccably dressed in a white shirt with blue slacks. His well- polished black shoes jolted Keith to memories of the two dead Puerto Ricans out on the reef. A robust, sandy mustache that virtually hid his mouth separated the inspector's thin, white face. "You can talk, can't you?"

Keith tried to swallow, weakly stretched, grabbed some water from the table, and coughed. Then he meekly croaked, "Yes, how do you know my name?"

"It seems you are such an expert sailor you kept your personal effects were in a plastic bag buttoned in your pants' pocket." The inspector dumped a manila envelope onto a chair. "Passport, sunglasses, wristwatch, knife, belt, money. Seems you were prepared for the worst... and got it."

"It was a horrible storm. What day is it?"

"Tuesday, May eighteenth," the doctor answered.

"You chipper enough to tell your story? Whatever you remember?" The police officer twisted his gold pen and scribbled on a legal tablet.

He pulled himself up in bed and relaxed against a pillow. Keith unfolded his tale from boarding the trader in Dominica, the storm, and drifting for days on a banana raft. In the new and improved version, he didn't remember washing up on Virgin Gorda. The inspector filled five pages with notes.

"You drifted from St. Maarten to Gorda after falling overboard from an inter-island trader named the Alita Dee. You made a raft from some banana bunches, which you ate for six days. Remarkable. You certainly are a lucky bloke to be here in the lap of luxury instead of plying St. Peter with the lies of a pious life." He had a jolly laugh.

The interview exhausted Keith. "That's about it, officer. Guess it wasn't my time yet."

"Well," the doctor asked, "is there anyone you would like us to inform concerning your safe appearance?"

"Hmm?" He mumbled, "No, no one really. I'll make my way back to St. Thomas as soon as I feel fit to travel. Only have a few buddies there who'll have to buy a few rounds to hear my story."

"If I have any more questions, I'll have them ready when I return with this," Inspector Prescott said, waving Keith's passport as he headed out the door. "Harrowing experience, really, get your rest."

Dr. Hodge remained and checked Keith's pulse. "That is quite an account, my dear fellow. I've got you on some antibiotics and plasma. You need to replenish your liquids. The experience has you seriously dehydrated. You have a slight infection on your ankles and elbows, but the salve the nurse will apply should remedy it. I'll return in a few days and pull these tubes. By then you should feel almost chipper. Please be careful when you get out of bed. It might be best to call for Gail to lend you some support. Your legs might not be up to it yet. Get some sleep and say some thankful prayers for your safe return."

The blinds rattled with the rotation of the overhead fan. At this moment, life wasn't so bad, considering he'd just escaped the jaws of a watery Hell. Everything was wonderful. It didn't matter that the resort's hospitality was because of his notoriety. His survival made him a real-life hero. The redhead walked by his door and winked. Keith wondered about her bedside manner.

His sunburn and cracked lips hurt when he smiled, but his outcome a deserved one. "All's well, that ends well." He plumped his pillows and settled into the bed. His thoughts drifted to the boats out on the reef. Had they been discovered? How long would it take to regain enough strength to return for his stash?

The limey cop seemed genuine, not playing him along. Probably knew nothing about the boats, not yet anyway. But he was the first white policeman Keith had ever seen in the BVI. Must be on some special assignment or maybe a tropical perk for exemplary duty. Probably not, as regular Brits hated the sun and heat. They loved their rain and kidney pies. Yeah, he'd have to play it cool for a while. There was too much at stake. He lay back and watched the fan.

No wind made the day seem hotter than usual. Keith could see the flat blue sea from the window with twenty-plus sailboats lulled at anchor. It was rare to be this hot at seven in the morning. The lizards didn't stray from the shade and the dogs lay on the cool cement.

The yellow drapes moved to the 'ra-ta-ra-ta' of the ceiling fan. Vacationers didn't want to sleep and miss a minute of the tropical paradise. Maybe other rooms had more shade. This one was gratis.

"Geez, it would be nice to sleep until noon." Keith rubbed his eyes and his watch read 7:15. His last three days had consisted only of rest. They removed the IVs. Sleeping days away felt good. His optimism had returned. Three naps, after breakfast, after lunch, and after dinner added to fourteen hours of sleep. Stretching, he yawned and smiled. "Today is one more lucky day for the new me on the life-extension, extra innings program."

Sitting on the edge of the bed, he ran through the possible ways he could spend the day. The throaty roar of a big inboard shook Keith's pondering mind. "I guess I'd better look for work. That seems to be the best alibi."

He stood, almost stable, and checked his physique in the mirror. "Not too bad, on the thin side," he laughed, "no hint of a gut anymore. Got to say, it wasn't the best weight-loss program." He ran his fingers through his sun-bleached hair. "Forty-something surfer boy... yeah, I like that. Might help me out to score some young chiquitas." He loudly clapped his hands and carefully stepped into the shower.

"Mr. Gardnar, did you want something? I thought you were

calling?" It was Ms. Archer, the manager.

It felt sexy, him in the shower with the translucent door. He had the water running, but accustomed to only a quick rinse, he exited wrapped in a towel.

"Mr. Gardnar, I see, um, I see you have recovered. Feel better?"

"Much better, thank you. Great, considering. I can't thank you enough for your kindness and generosity for letting me stay here. Please excuse me while I shave? What can I do for you?"

"Oh, nothing really. I am so glad you are making a rapid recovery. I had thought you'd be with us longer." She watched as he lathered his face. "The doctor will return in a few days to give you another look." She brushed her red hair back and pulled it into a ponytail. She looked every bit of the prim-and-proper manager in her pale blue polo and knee-length, dark blue shorts.

Washing the final bit of soap from his face, "Well, Ms. Archer, there must be something I can do for you. It feels nice to have someone worried about me. It's been some time since anyone even had good thoughts about me."

"Oh, you're exaggerating. I'm sure you have friends. I am thinking good thoughts about you… uh, rather, concerning your recovery." She looked down, padding her shorts' pockets, perhaps blushing, "Yes, I'm thinking. In fact, everyone here at the resort is hoping you'd make a complete recovery from your ordeal. Ah, since you are up and around, do you think you have enough stamina to have dinner with me tonight? I mean, if you're too tired, I'd understand. Or, we could have dinner in here, your room? If it's not unnerving, I'd love to hear your tale of how you survived. If you don't want to, that's okay. It is just that you are so lucky to be alive, the banana raft and everything."

"Yeah," he almost whispered, "I'm very lucky. I'd be happy to tell you all the details. But I've been falling asleep around nine."

"Good. We'll eat early, and I promise to do everything to keep you awake."

"Deal."

"Think you can manage by yourself to the beach bar around six? If not, I'll come and wheel you out." She squeezed his hand as she left. "I really am glad you pulled through and are looking so much better."

As her shapely butt moved down the hall, Keith wondered exactly how glad she really was. "I think I could show her some serious appreciation." He dropped his towel and scratched at his groin. "Genuine appreciation might be just what the doctor ordered."

"Got to start thinking about a job, decide what would be the easiest, most unlikely work that I can do as a front until I can go back. Lots of details to figure out." Keith reclined on the bed with his fingers clasped behind his head and stared at the boats anchored in the bay. "Boats, I guess it would be easy to get work as every boat has lots of things broken. I can putz around sitting on my investment. Maybe scrape a few bottoms, and maybe get lucky and scrape Ms. Archer's."

Drugs, sex, rock and roll, speed, weed, birth control,
life's a bitch and then you die,
snort some coke and let's get high.
Ricky Pal

CHAPTER NINE

"We're fucked, mucho fucked! Our friend has disappeared with the product and the money. Damn it, Carlos, where the hell is he?!"

"Madelena, take a chill pill. Can't find him or the boat anywhere. I've called every marina, anywhere he could have refueled, and no one has seen the cat. They can't all be working together and lying. Shit like this happens. Risk, that's why the profit is mucho. This is just a setback. I'm sure it'll all work out. He radioed when he left Anguilla. Everything was on track, but that was two weeks ago."

"Setback... take a chill pill, Madelena, just a setback, Madelena. Shit happens, Madelena. Hey brother, I've got some news for you. We owe a quarter of a million for the product and we lost another three-fifty. And you say chill?! Carlos, that is not small change. And no profit. If our friends down south don't believe our story about the disappearance, then we are really F-U-C-K-E-D! Entiendes?!"

"It's a lot; mucho dinero, sister. I can't believe Andre and Cecilia would rip us off. Sure, this will upset Uncle Piedra, but we'll eat the loss. It could always be worse, much worse." Carlos was in the white bathrobe he'd taken from the Miami Hilton. He drank black coffee and puffed heavily on the thin cigar. The sparkling view of the string of northern cays and the Atlantic didn't lift his mood. "Damn, though, I thought we'd found the perfect couriers. Fifty grand a run. Never look in the briefcases, and just spend a month having a vacation between South America and h e r e. I can't believe they would rip us off. I mean, they know our people as well as we do. They know the consequences. So, where does that leave us? Looking for a villain in a world of fucking thieves!"

Madelena pulled at her hair until it strained at the roots of her widow's peak. Lack of sleep had darkened her eyes. "It's got to be those lousy 'Ricans!"

"It's like this, sister; no one knows what we do, right? The shit must turn up somewhere unless Andre grew balls and sailed it to the States. He should know our network has ears everywhere. No matter, if a big supply arrives in the US or

Europe, we'll hear about it. Thirty keys of pure shit isn't a move for a small timer. So, we play it cool and keep listening, but first, you must tell Uncle Piedra."

"Me, tell him the shit didn't make it? You want me to be the messenger of terrible news? Why not you, handsome and brave brother?!" She lit a cigarette and inhaled deeply. "All right, I'll pass the word along and also get them to check. I still hope it turns up. I'll talk with Piedra about getting another load on my smile. But we don't have anybody to transport it. You check out the Ponce Boys. Have they been calling, wondering where it is, or do they already know?"

"Louie called and said they're dry and when I asked about their boat, he got quiet. Scary. For thirty keys, a lot of heads could roll. Fucking Louie said the pickup boat was good, and he knew the men well. He knows this is no-fool-around shit. I'll eat his heart if he took us off." In frustration, Carlos slammed his fist into the wall.

"Darling sister," he grabbed her around the waist and pulled her to him. She crumpled exhausted into his arms. "It must turn up. Even if they sank, the other boat would have returned. It's as simple as that." He squeezed her tighter. "It is a big setback, but we're still ahead."

"I want to be done with this," Madelena said into his shoulder. "I knew the downside when we began, but this mystery is unbearable. If we were certain it was a bust or a ripoff, then I'd know to handle it. But not being certain of anything makes the loss worse."

They broke the embrace and sat staring out at the deep blue Atlantic. The world was silent except for a slight breeze rustling the leaves of the flamboyant tree. Madelena sipped her coffee while Carlos arranged his agenda for the day. "We must think positive. We cannot let the tension show. Sister, you do your aggressive aerobics and I'll be working at the restaurant tonight." He pulled her close and kissed her forehead.

A sigh of exasperation escaped as she grasped his hand. "Okay, I'll call Piedra from an outside line and continue as if nothing has happened. Uncle will do what's necessary."

Across the turquoise bay, three mega cruise ships rested at the long concrete dock. It was another sweltering afternoon in Charlotte Amalie. The sun reflected on the white buildings with red roofs that shared the hillside with green coconut palms and scarlet flamboyant trees. The view had changed little in the last century, except for the many automobiles.

They constructed the plain brick buildings with English-arched doorways and intricate French iron grillwork to withstand the attacks of rival nations, pirates, storms, and fires. During the 1800s, the town almost burned to the ground three times. These masonry walls, interior courtyards, timbered rafters, and brick-lined doorways reduced danger. Today, those same doors and gates protected the inhabitants. Thirty years ago, residents never locked their doors, yet now they lived in fear.

West Indians didn't bring cocaine to their islands. Continental vacationers introduced the powerful drug, trying to extend their few tropical nights while reducing the moral virtues of the local women. Marijuana, pot, ganja, had always been the drug of choice for the tropics. Burn a big fatty on the beach and jam to some reggae. Anyone could grow ganja in their backyard and finance a new car with a cultivated quarter acre. There was no harm in grass.

During the eighties, cocaine moved to the movie screen and desire for the new culture of fast money spread through the islands. A young man with an E-ticket spirit, unable to get his GED, could buy the entire school from the bottom of a bag of white powder. If he just sold the product without doing it, he could become wealthy, if he didn't get killed. The gold jewelry and fancy clothes didn't fool anyone, but the same as the high; the lifestyle doesn't last long.

"Yeah, yeah, yeah, yeah, you hear? It's like I saying, mon. I... I need a little burn. Come on, mon, Just a hit, okay?" It was difficult to calculate his age. He could have been a hard twenty or a miserable forty. It was obvious he hadn't bathed recently. His nappy hair stuck out in unkempt clumps. The stretched T-shirt he wore had once been white. Now the dirt had almost hidden the Old Milwaukee Beer logo on the back. The checkered food-service pants were pulled high above his waist and tightened with a black vinyl belt, revealing dirty, calloused bare feet. "Come on, mon. Please?"

"That 'please' shit ain't gonna get your dirty ass nothing. Ramble your raggedy, smelly carcass down the road. Pay for the shit or fly!" The dealer was in his teens, short and muscular. His clothes were from the top shelf, all name brands. He raised his expensive shades and stared at the beggar. "My man, don't crowd me." He pinched his nostrils. "Yo, yo, your tired ass is drawing flies. Buzz off with 'em." The dealer grabbed the bum by his arm and dragged him away from the doorway that was his headquarters.

"My friend, you know me. I buying the shit from you every day. Why you got to be so rude to me? Just a whiff and I… I can finish work. Yes, I can finish work. Yeah, yeah, that's it. I can finish work and then I'll get right back here and pay you, I swear," the street man extended his dirty hand, palm up.

With a resounding slap, the dealer plastered the bum's hand with his own, pulled him forward as he swung around and kicked him in the butt. The bum bounced off the curb amid a few mumbled curses and straggled down the street toward the center of town.

The dealer wiped his hands with a silk handkerchief and then brushed off the brick doorway threshold that was his office desk. In front of the eighteenth-century building, he sold twenty-first-century euphoria in the form of crystals… magic crystals. Eddie didn't need the magic himself. Even at eighteen, he'd seen all the evil magic: friends in jail, the hospital, or dead. Friends he couldn't acknowledge any longer because the drug trapped them in that hideous adult never-never land. Never lend them money. Never give them a chance to steal anything. He'd seen buddies from his school days wallow in the gutter after succumbing to the wicked magic of crack cocaine.

But he was Eddie, on top of his game, on top of the world. His pockets were filled with product and money. He was short but handsome with the clothes and women to go with it all. But Eddie was still on the street hustling, waiting to make it big. Someday, he'd make the score of a lifetime, breakaway, and finish with all this shit. That was if he didn't get ripped off or murdered. His pocket piece, a small Beretta, was half of his insurance policy. Money was the other half.

More money was walking toward him. From the left, a West Indian gentleman was striding up the street. At his side was an obviously continental woman with bottle-blonde hair.

"Yo, my man Edwardo," slapping palms, "How goes it with you today, my brother?" Releasing her arm, the gentleman bowed and introduced her to Eddie. "This here is Janet. She comes from that peachy state, Georgia."

"Janet, hmm," Eddie took a step back to scan her, rubbing his jaw. "I'd say from first appearances, 'Juicy' Janet, and what I'm not seeing is probably very juicy." Everyone laughed. "I'm Eddie the third. The third is for the three 'E's': entertaining, everything, every time at your service," He followed, bending in a sweeping bow.

At thirty-plus, she was younger than her escort by ten years. What she'd stuffed into her bikini was stark pale. Days at the beach had sunburned everything else red. Shiny blond and pleasingly overweight, Janet was a head-turner. Big breasts stretched the elastic of her skimpy tube top. Her nipples were highlights. The matching shorts left even less to the imagination. In a drawl, she replied, "I know I'll be very pleased to meet you, Eddie."

"Sweetheart, you sure will," Eddie grabbed her left breast and softly fondled. "You sure will." He tried to move his hand to her perfect ass, but she grabbed it.

Janet kissed his cheek and nipped his ear with a light growl. "Yes, but I'm with Alfred. Catch you later this week. Can I get your number?"

"Nah, girl, I'm not into phones. You want to reach me, see me here. I work ten-to-six. My partners work the other times. See me here."

"I'll be in touch." Janet rubbed Eddie's groin. "See ya."

Alfred leaned to Eddie's ear with his request while Janet rattled on, "Oh, we've seen the town, but this is just my second day of a weeklong, well-needed vacation. Plenty of beach sleeps after late, late nights closing the bars, are to come" She moved Eddie's wandering hand to the outside of her thigh. "I'm hoping you can show me more. Wouldn't that be nice?"

"Al, you better be careful with this woman. She gonna eat you up; I can tell. Maybe I ought to protect you and take her with me?" Eddie pulled his hand from Janet's and reached into his baggy front pocket to retrieve a small vial. He extended his hand to Alfred again.

Alfred smiled, "She'll be all right with me for now, but we'll be back. Thank you, Eddie."

"See you soon," Janet giggled, sauntering back into the sun.

Eddie watched the taut white shorts wiggle away. As they were almost out of sight, Eddie's insurance policy approached.

"What you want, mon?" Eddie replied in street West Indian. He shoved his hands into his pockets, arching his shoulders and back. "It can't be time yet, Michael."

The insurance man wore a powder-blue suit over a pale yellow guayabera shirt. The emphasis was cheap. Everything was tight. The shirt's pearly buttons were ready to pop and sweat-stained between the shoulder blades. His scuffed shoes were black, contrasting the white socks. Bald except for a thin mustache and a tuft of forehead hair, the insurance man stood an unimpressive five-foot-four. What caught the eye was a snub-nose 38 in a belt holster.

"Yeah, well, you know why I'm here. Rent, me-son. Rent. We rent you this doorstep." He laughed, "Yeah, I'm the property manager and I need this month's rent. How's your plumbing? Enough hot water or you want more?" He smiled, "Yeah, Eddie, we know you are doing all kinds of business. What I guarantee, if you want, we can get you another place with more hot water, but I don't think you'd like the view. Lots of bars can block the scenery."

"Spare the narco-comedy. I ain't making that kind of dough. I wish. What we talkin' here? Same as last month and the month before?

"Yeah, Eddie, it's the same this month, but when it's season and we need you to move farther down the street. You know, with the tourists and everything. We'll figure out a location that will work for you. That's three-fifty."

"Man, three-fucking-fifty! Man, I ain't ever gonna get my Beemer with this kind of overhead. Don't be moving my ass to someone else's turf. Talk to Big Man, boss of my posse. I'm paying you civil-fucking-servants for protection, so, protect my territory." He passed the money discreetly.

"We are protecting, me-son. You'd better listen; shit about to happen. The federals are checking 'tings around here like never before. The word is a major player got ripped off and two agents were left drawing flies. Things will get cool again, but for now, keep a low profile.

"Yeah, well, give me a head's up, insurance man. Things kinda dried up on the street. Word is supply's slowed. But nobody dead."

"That's why you pay for that information. That information protects you. We at the station trust you, son. You clean, Eddie. From an all right family, you keep a low profile. So, we like that. You start partying hard, being noticed, then we'll tighten up on you. But now, you're doing what we like, making us money."

Michael grabbed Eddie by the arm and shook his hand. "Pleasure doing business. Keep up the good work," he laughed.

"Mudda-skunt, narc," Eddie muttered as his protection strode off toward the municipal building. "Someday I'm gonna bust a cap in his Northside Frenchie's white ass. Mudda-fucka, poor taste son of a bitch."

He straightened his clothes and wiped off the stoop again, lighting a cigarette before more business came to call.

<<<<<◇>>>><<<<◇>>>>

"Charles, I'm considering selling the house. Everything here has such bad memories for me now." She stubbed out her cigarette, exhaling as she looked to her lawyer.

"Now, now, Maddy, I know the recent year has been traumatic, but you're working through it quite well. I really wish you wouldn't smoke in my office." He rose from behind his desk. "You look the best I've ever seen you. You'll find direction soon and if you want companionship, I'm always available." Charles Detrich Esquire was super-sized, spreading three hundred-plus pounds over a six-foot frame. With his beard almost the shade of his tanned face, he resembled a teddy bear.

With elegant finesse, he gently squeezed her hands. "What about sailing with me on Sunday? Get you out of the house and into the sun and the waves."

"I don't know, Charles," she sighed. "I'd like to, but I just haven't been feeling well lately. Nerves, I guess. I think I must beg out. But please draw up the papers for a sales agent agreement on the house. You have the deed and drawings. Send the agreement by for my signature as soon as possible. I might take off for a vacation. I'm feeling impulsive."

"I think it's a mistake to sell. You own that piece, free and clear. Leave and rent it. I'll manage it for you and you're guaranteed an income." Charles sank back into his mahogany tufted, red leather chair.

"No, I want to be clear of this place. Gone forever." She fidgeted, crossing and uncrossing her dark, shapely legs. "Have a market analysis done and price it at ten thousand under and be prepared to drop another ten. I need a fresh start somewhere else. I will begin to look soon, Charles."

"I'm very sorry to hear that. You seem so definite; I wish I could offer you to stay and enjoy life with me."

"No Charles, I'm thankful for your attention and for being such a sympathetic friend, but I need to erase the past. Everywhere I go, I remember Keith. He hurt me terribly." Madelena rose and paced in front of the desk. Her brushed dark hair drifted in curly rivulets over the white cotton sundress. "You helped me more than anyone, Charles. I'm certain you can understand my position. Please try."

The lawyer rose and hugged her, almost obscuring her with his bulk. "I'll miss you, Maddie. We should finish the paperwork by Friday."

She gathered her purse and left. Outside the air cooled

office, it was a sweltering one o'clock. The Law Clinic office off of Norre Gade was in a masonry courtyard framed by huge royal palms. Just beyond was fast-paced Back Street with tourists trying to find a rare bargain and settling for cheap liquor. Her black Miata was parked in the public lot only a block away. She turned toward Bluebeard's Hotel, two blocks farther on the hill.

Bluebeard's was originally a fort built in the late 1600s. That's what she needed, a fort to protect her. Carlos had promised to pay off the shipment's investors that morning to the tune of over a hundred grand. They still had over a quarter of a million, unless Uncle Piedra called in HIS debt. She had the house and Keith's trawler-work boat. That should be enough cash, but she needed to stay alive to spend it. Perhaps she'd been too greedy, moved too fast? Everything was crazy now. She could feel the pressure.

She took a stool at the bar and ordered a salad with a martini. It was that kind of day. To her, it sounded like Carlos had been threatened. It was time to go. A sip of cool, tangy vodka, with the bright view, inflated her dipping mood. St. Thomas was beautiful. Massive cruise ships, surrounded by taxis and buses, docked on the far side of the bay at The West Indian Company Dock. Below, gaudy sightseers packed the waterfront street. Two more streets farther was the private school where she'd taught Spanish grammar and literature. Educated in the States, Maddy had only a slight accent. She ordered her second martini as the salad arrived.

Food no longer interested Madelena. She only ate out of necessity and constantly smoked. She chewed on her fingertips rather than her nails. Her weight had dropped four pounds since their product had disappeared and the four deaths had been confirmed. Sleep was precious. Her uncle had been supportive, for the moment. Perhaps his superiors would apply pressure. Then, family ties wouldn't mean much.

Everything had been running so smoothly; now it was all turmoil. They'd lost the shipment. It wasn't like a bust where it had been confiscated; it'd just vanished. The uncertainty of what had happened was agonizing. She lit another Marlboro Light, inhaling deeply. Were her activities known by the police? Had she ruined her divorced-schoolteacher character and now become a wanted drug dealer? The uncertainty gnawed at her.

Madelena wondered if the blacks and the Puerto Ricans knew about her. Had Carlos been discreet? She'd been careful never to get involved with those characters. Who could comprehend their way of life? Her part had been to secure the connection with Uncle Piedra and hand- carry the first seven loads from various vacation islands to St. Thomas. She'd enjoyed the brief holidays and returned with snowy assets in her luggage. That had created their stake.

Carlos knew the people to dump it on, and she'd withdrawn from the picture. Keith had come along at the right time to give her more of an identity on the island other than just a Colombian woman. She'd made certain Keith had no connections with the police, good or bad. Th poor chump never looked and never asked. Maddy had played her part well, to the nines. She always was short on funds, and he handed her cash with a smile. Her faked affection had totally fooled Keith.

Madelena inhaled deeply and flicked the cigarette butt into the purple bougainvillea bushes below. Loudly, she sucked the olive off the cute red cocktail sword. Her Rolex sparkled almost three.

"Well, well, Maddy, one more martini? A long lunch today? Say, do you still teach at the private school?" Ellie, the afternoon bartender, had met Madelena through various island boyfriends who knew Keith. "You look like you could use one on me."

"The last one, definitely. I have to drive. Thanks, El, I'm burned out these days. Ah, life has to calm down eventually, but another Stoli can't hurt. This is all you're doing these days?"

"Yeah, doesn't do much for the self-image, but it pays the bills since that asshole Lenny left to take a boat delivery to San Diego. Men, they're all bastards."

She finished shaking the mixture and filled two glasses. Taking one, Ellie passed the other to Maddy. "Here's to us poor, helpless fems."

The glasses clinked, and they sipped, staring out to the harbor. Maddy bounded up onto the window ledge, pushing her white dress up, revealing her tanned thighs. She wiggled into a comfortable posture, pulling the dress even higher. "Yeah, we are the helpless sex. I get helped less and less." She laughed loudly and took another sip. "Had I stayed in South America, by now I'd be big and stretched from having babies."

Madelena thrust her belly out in a drunken, pregnant posture. "Really, can you see me fat and full of babies?"

"Well Maddy, you just had one rotten man in Keith." Ellie turned to make another batch of martinis for them. "Keithy disappeared, huh? I heard something about a shipwreck or some BS." She twisted open the shaker. "Here, help me finish this."

"Old Keithy, you know, I miss him. He was so easy. I

knew what to expect from the moment he got up every morning. You could set the world clock on him, him and that dumb dog of his. Two of a kind. Sex, that's what kept their clocks wound. But he wasn't nearly as bad as the fucking liars who are trying to get me in the sack now that I've got all of Keithy's shit through the divorce. His friends call me a parasite and then try to bed me. Men! Ellie, I'm out of here soon. I can't take much more of this small-rock mentality."

"Ah, Maddy, you just need a little help to regain your sense of humor. Let these assholes wine and dine you. Hell, you think I work here for the lousy ten bucks an hour plus tips? Me, I meet a good-looking guy every other day that thinks he will get a ride on an America's paradise bartender for only dinner and a few drinks. They are my entertainment factor!" She flung her white-shirted arms apart as if giving a benediction. "Amuse me assholes!"

"Oh, they are amusing. I laugh myself to sleep most nights. Predictable, cheap, self-serving assholes. You're right to take advantage of them before they get the chance to do it to you. I'm good at that. I watched my mother let my father have his mistresses and his other toys. My brother tries the same shit. I see him go into the heat-seeking missile act. My brother!" Maddy sounded jealous, "My brother is just a dick. His conscience is nonexistent when it comes to anybody else. Probably even me."

"What's Carlos doing these days?" the bartender asked as she wiped the bar top. "Is he still here? I haven't seen him out in a long while."

"Oh, Carlos isn't out too much anymore." Maddy chuckled, "These days, you have to look hard to find him."

"Yeah, your brother is really the dark-eyed lady killer. Don't worry, once you get back into the spirit of the chase, you'll be the belle of the ball, wherever you are." Ellie grabbed Maddy's hand. "One day, soon, you'll just wake up and you'll be finished with all this divorce stuff."

Maddy again laughed loudly. "I certainly hope not. I worked hard for this." She drained her glass and then threw it out the window and almost went with it. "I deserve everything. Everything! Keith and Carlos, my father, they all deserve nothing." She spat on the red tile floor. "Men should be collared like dogs and led around by their dicks."

"Cool it, honey, you're a little loud. This job isn't much, but it's something I like." Ellie extended a helping arm to get Maddy safely off the window ledge.

"What are you doing? Trying for a feel, too? What are

you, a fucking dyke? Get your hands off me! I'm all right. In fact, this is the best I've felt in a long time. I don't need your help or anyone! I'm in charge." She pointed her finger spitefully, "You work for them. I work for me. Got that?" Maddy pulled thirty dollars from her small waist bag. "That's all the tip I have for you." She spun around, attracting stares from the patrons.

The drug culture has shaped at least one major change since the Sixties; It became the basis for overloading our prisons.
Jimmy Carter

CHAPTER TEN

Fourteen years ago, Fred and Caroline had honeymooned in St. Thomas. They'd hired a cabbie named Stout to give them the island tour. Stouty's old Ford coupe had climbed the winding hills from town each day to take them to distant beaches. Caroline loved the expanse of white sand and palm trees at the east end on Bluebeard's Beach. Fred favored Sapphire Bay because of the nearby restaurant with the spectacular grilled snapper. Stouty guided them with quiet smiles. After an evening of rum tasting and limbo at Lord Rumbottoms, they conceived their first son. They never told him why they named him Thomas.

That was 2004, not that long ago. Fifteen years and twenty pounds later, they'd returned on a second honeymoon. Fred's first thought was the traffic. "My God, what has the tourism done to such a quaint island? Carol, it's like we're back home. All the people... I don't remember it like this!" A successful exec at Midwest Insurance, he was tanned from walleye fishing on the lake, but looked his years. The Cleveland Indians maroon ball cap told where home was.

"Oh, darling, everything changes. And this is probably for the better. Think of all the jobs it's created." She sat in a terraced park on Government Hill overlooking the harbor. A flat-brimmed straw hat hid her graying curls. Carol's face and complexion were Mia Farrow, but her frame was more Dolly Parton. "Honey, it's still so beautiful. I love you for bringing me on this cruise. I feel kind of bad though, only spending one afternoon on our favorite island."

Well, I thought we'd widen our horizons. Puerto Rico, St. Maarten, and St. Barths. I can't wait to see you in one of those tiny French one-piece bikinis."

"Oh, you!" She wagged her finger at him and they rose from the wrought-iron bench. They headed up the hill to see the incredible view from Blackbeard's Tower. She led the way. "You know, my big butt would practically swallow one of those tiny triangles."

Fred raised his eyes from watching his footing to view his wife's madras posterior. "I don't think it's that big, Carol."

As they reached another landing to catch their breath, a

scrawny arm stretched from the shadow of an arched patio doorway. "Spare a dollar, mon? I need to eat bad."

Fred couldn't see the face that belonged to the arm. He probably wouldn't want to. Fred's business was in downtown Cleveland. Homeless beggars were a way of life. It was also a way of compassion. He knew he'd been lucky with a beautiful, loving wife and two great sons. He always had a dollar if it could help someone less fortunate.

As Fred reached and unfolded his wallet, the dirty man snatched the billfold from his unsuspecting hands. It was so quick: Carol didn't see it happen. To make his escape, the beggar threw a shoulder into Fred. She turned as her husband lost his balance and tumbled to the patio below.

"Fred! Fred, oh my God! Fred! Help! Help!" She watched from ten feet above as a rivulet of blood trailed from beneath Fred's head. Caroline fainted and tumbled down the flight of steps, unconscious.

The two tourists lay motionless as three high school-age boys approached. "Check dis out, bro. Dis white cheese is out cold."

"Yo, dere's anudda down there and he's blooding big time." All three appeared clean-cut, in school uniforms, carrying books. The tallest of the three took over. He felt for a pulse from the woman. "She's alive. John- John, check the udduh."

The taller boy dumped out the contents of Caroline's shoulder bag grabbing anything valuable. He then turned his attention to her jewelry. With a jerk, he had her necklace and gold chain.

The third boy watched as a lookout while the other declared Fred a goner. "No wallet, but I got his passport and watch." With a pull, he took Fred's St. Christopher medal. "He ain't gonna need no saint now!"

The three took off running down the stairs. They headed for the bench behind the green Legislature Building. Almost out of breath, they high-fived at the tourists' deadly luck.

"What we got from dat white woman, Charlie?"

"Well, I got one Seiko, two diamond rings, two chains, and an emerald, one-eighty in green, and three good plastics, plus I-fucking-D."

"Yeah, like we know some old white bitch that looks like her and wants to pass the cards."

"Yo, you're an ass, mon. We sell dis shit quick."

"Things gonna be hot. That was an accident, but it could look like murder. Like we robbed 'em dead."

"Didn't rob 'em and didn't make 'em dead. Got it?"

"No difference, but we don't want to have this shit around." "I'll take it to my brother. I know he can dump it among the Dominicans."

The sound of sirens interrupted the tall boy.

Ambulances and squad cars sped to the crime scene, but then everyone stopped. They had to walk either up or down the steps to the murder scene, which was already attracting a flock of onlookers. The EMTs loaded Caroline onto a stretcher and sped to the nearby hospital. Forensics and the coroner worked over Fred, seeking any clues before pulling the zipper on the black bag.

Wiping the sweat from their faces, the last of the police hiked up the steps from Main Street. The two men had risen through the ranks by education and determination. The opportunities for tainted money that constantly surrounded the police force had not attracted the two. Meyers and Faulkner were the M&M brothers to their peers. The cases the boss gave them never seemed to lead anywhere.

Thomas 'Hit Man' Meyers was thirty-eight. In great physical shape, he'd once floored a rowdy bar patron that had taken the first swing, becoming 'Hit Man.' He had graduated from Howard University with a degree in criminology. He was the first college degree on the force. That brought with it a stigma from the outside world. It was impossible for Meyers to become one of them. They wouldn't let him. Hit Man had accepted none of the 'offered' bonus programs. He knew what was happening, but kept his head down.

It wasn't his business. Meyers' job was research. Find out the impossible, and he seldom did.

Miles Faulkner had eaten one too many saltfish patés. At five-foot- ten, he weighed 220. The walk up the steps had crashed his respiratory system. Miles didn't have a nickname. He didn't need one. His trademark was his well-worn straw hat. Miles was also a college boy, but his chosen field had been marine biology. When he realized how little biologists were paid, he opted for the job with the most overtime.

Faulkner's work was his life. He had cajoled Meyers into being a solid friend. It seemed movie-like action surrounded them; rapes, robberies, and murders. They solved a few simple, low profile cases, but the big action remained on the periphery.

Sure, they solved some: a robbery, a blatant suicide, and maybe a crime of passion. But the genuine mysteries seldom got solved.

Clues disappeared, or forensics created new ones. All the West Indian perps looked alike to continentals, so most descriptions were worthless. Few wanted to get involved. A lot of victims just packed up and left the island with their testimonies.

"Man, oh man, what kinds of animals do we have on this rock?" Lt. Detective Meyers asked his partner. Both had been born in a different time in the Caribbean, a time of peace, tranquility, even love. The only thing to fear had been late summer storms and sharks. Now, they could predict the weather, but not the land sharks.

"Me, I don't know who would want to do this to people like these? What you got for us Shine Head?"

The bald coroner's assistant was just zipping the bag on Fred. "Well, could have been pushed or fell? Woman's incoherent, so we'll have to wait. But they've been robbed."

Faulkner pointed to two blue-shirted patrolmen. "Canvas the neighborhood. Somebody probably saw or heard something, if they aren't too afraid to talk. You other two search in the bushes, trash cans, anywhere someone might dump a purse. Be careful, we need the prints, if there are any. Be comprehensive." He knew they didn't know what he meant, but it sounded good, something he'd heard in a Clint Eastwood movie.

"The Commissioner will have to put in some long hours to get this solved. High season is almost on us. If this story hits the stateside papers, it will kill business. What do you think Tom, murder?"

"That's what I think it is, but it will save a lot of like a lot of time if it reads like an accident, say a fall after a heart attack. But what did the woman see? Christ, until she wakes up, or their prints come back, we don't even know who the hell they are! Where do you wanna start?"

"The jewelry has to surface somewhere. Shit, what am I saying? We don't even know what to look for!"

"Someone who has money when he shouldn't is a start. This type of shit is a desperation act: drugs, crack, or a gang initiation. We got to be really lucky to get close to this one. Come on; let's see if anyone saw anything at Blackbeard's. Miles, you look like you could do with some liquid refreshment."

<<<<<◇>>><<<◇>>>

Four streets east, the ragged bum sought Eddie's relief. He was carrying a bottle of rum in a paper bag. "M-m-m-my friend, I-I would like to do some business with you." Pointing a bent finger, "An-and I got money now." He reached into his soiled pants and retrieved four folded twenties. "Give me it all; you hear! I worked hard for this money." Becoming belligerent, "Now give me the stuff!"

"Chill! Quiet, if you expect to get my product. Show some respect, ragman. Where you working for this kind of money? Huh? You ain't nothing 'cept a lift-and-carry mother fucker."

"Give me the shit! I got the m-m-m-money. What I need is the rock!" The bum took a loud gulp of the rum, dragging his forearm across his mouth. "I ain't just no back, mon, I can work, brother, I got skills, I can work."

"Here's four bottles. If you do it all, you'll be one strung-out mother." Eddie said, taking the money, "Look, tell you what, I'll give you the quantity discount if you take the twenty and get a bath and some clothes. Get something to eat. You too rough, mon. Don't blow all that hard-earned dough here and now."

"I doing what I want." He gulped more rum and shook his fist in the air. "Tonight, I feel good. Tonight!"

It's not called cocaine or coke any more.
It's now referred to as Crack Classic.
Jay Leno

CHAPTER ELEVEN

Spanish Town, Virgin Gorda, is a quaint, quiet West Indian village located west of the big Virgin's hump, at the other end from where Keith had come ashore. A quarter-mile past the village are the Baths, the island's principle tourist attraction, a natural wonder of gigantic boulders piled haphazardly, creating a myriad of pools filled with refreshing tranquil seawater.

Centuries ago, Spanish Town residents had a lucrative business luring ships onto Anegada Reef at night with false lights from huge bonfires on the uninhabited island. Captains thought they were sailing into a safe harbor; Anegada had no silhouette. In the morning, locals, known as 'wreckers,' plundered the ships lodged on the reef. Those were the old days when almost everyone took a shot at profiting from piracy.

The village's harbor now entertained a term-charter sailing community with one of the best boatyards in the northern Caribbean. Keith had no problem finding work in the yard. It was hard, hot labor. Boat work gets you sunburned, usually covered with toxic fiberglass or bottom paint, and it fills the air with noxious smells. The chocked yachts are in dry-dock and workers and crew must crawl up and down ladders. With the mega power yachts, they might have to scale three stories.

Everything on boats can cause wounds. They bruise, tear, cut, scrape, and puncture flesh. Repairs bite and can suck bank accounts dry. Nothing comes cheap on yachts. Boats are high maintenance and just like with women, a facelift can be a necessary expense.

It was hard work, but it was a suitable cover for Keith. They'd discovered the boats and bodies out on the reef two days after he washed up. Three weeks, and as many interrogations later, the BVI police granted him a special visa-work permit, undoubtedly because of his unique and famous circumstances.

Now he could find a job. They wanted to watch him, and he wouldn't mind being watched, knowing that his future trust fund was buried twenty miles north. That's the way old-time pirates worked, and why there are so many stories of buried treasure. Someone got caught or killed and the loot remained hidden. Keith had no intention of either getting snuffed or jailed. The briefcases were his dreams, but there was always the nightmarish reality of four murder charges.

The shocker was that the two Puerto Ricans were being

heralded as DEA agents murdered in a supposed sting operation. The sting part never happened, except they got stung. He'd thought about the scenario and couldn't figure it out. The money wasn't enough to buy that much coke. It had to have been the bait. The agents must have been working with the catamaran, otherwise, how would they have known where the meet was?

Lots of questions didn't add up, and Keith knew more of the facts than anyone. The DEA was trying to rip off the dealers, keeping the dope and money for their own profit. Since they'd been Feds, boats, planes, and helicopters were everywhere. They questioned every fisherman, sailboat, private and commercial pilot.

He was being questioned again for the fourth time. Keith's story was always the same. Hell, he'd told it over and over to reporters, locals, and tourists. He'd tell it to whoever would listen. It varied slightly, depending on how many drinks they were buying.

Keith hadn't become paranoid, but sensible. Bath and Turtle Marina Restaurant was his haunt a few nights a week to socialize with other boaties. He had a room down a side road toward the Baths. Working for a week, most of his strength had returned. No one seemed to be able to find Renaldo or the Alita Dee. If anyone could substantiate his story, the ordeal should be over, and he would breathe easier.

"Seems they found a Whaler dinghy washed up on the south side of St. John in the US Virgins with a name sounding like it could belong to the trimaran, Mr. Gardnar. How it got from Anegada Reef to St. John is a good question." Agent-In-Charge Jeffers was a solidly built black man.

Keith couldn't put a tag on his accent. "One thought is the perps used the Whaler as an escape, sweeping north of the Horseshoe Reef to the east. Then, after meeting another boat, the incriminating Whaler was set adrift. However, they rigged the outboard to hold the motor in a straight direction. It ran until drained of gas. So, Mr. Gardnar, did you see or hear any boats out there the morning before you washed up?"

"Mr. Jeffers, I'd been floating for days. My attention was to every sight and sound for the hope of rescue. But, I was exhausted, on my last legs, so to say. I'd have seen a big ship or a yacht, but a small Whaler, maybe not."

"Let's go through it again. You were washed overboard the night of May 10th and you drifted for six days. You wash up on a barren part of this island in good shape and walk to a hotel. I consider that an astounding feat of human endurance, Mr.

Gardnar, you're a strong man. I again congratulate you. The doctor said you didn't even seem malnourished."

"Lots of bananas, Agent Jeffers, lots of bananas," Keith laughed, but it wasn't contagious. He scanned the other two Hispanic agents for a glint of a smile. "Yeah, personally, I don't think I'll ever enjoy another, but bananas are what got me through."

One agent moved and leaned closer. "Mr. Gardnar, we aren't really concerned with your likes and dislikes. They murdered two fellow agents near here, one was my brother," pointing at a chart of the British Virgins, "and you know more than what you're telling."

"Guys, I saw nothing. Sorry for your loss. Tell you what; you float around for about a week and I'll expect a report. Okay? You got the murderers, right? That's what the paper said."

"No, not quite. We hold back information pertinent to the crime. We know more than we put in the papers."

Jeffers slammed his palm down on the desk. "We know things and you know things. It's odd there's no record of this Alita Dee trader-boat you were on. A Dominica entry stamp on your passport, but you can't really prove where you were, Mr. Gardnar. And you are one prepared mother. After more than a week floating on fucking bananas, you wash up with raincoat, shoes, sunglasses, hat, and clothes plus your money and ID. What the fuck are you, a Boy Scout? You're so meticulous, but you forgot to get an exit stamp from St. Maarten. You know that's a crime?"

"Yeah, well, so is jaywalking. Listen, you know how things are with inter-island trading boats; they're always in transit. We fueled in St. Maarten and headed out the next morning too early to get an unnecessary stamp. You fellows keep looking for the Alita. I'm certain she's registered in Puerto Rico. For now, and always, gentlemen, all I know is what I've told you. Now may I go?"

Jeffers rose from behind the desk and moved closer to Keith. "You and I are about the same age. I'm working on my career and you're painting boat bottoms. I just lost two confederates, close friends. If it turns out you had anything to do with it, one more bottom painter won't be missed. Copy? Get out of here."

"Copy." Keith sighed as he slowly walked from the cramped office out into another brilliant tropical day. Just enough breeze to keep it from sweltering. Without sunglasses, the glare would have been a killer. It was almost noon. He'd been with the agents for over two hours. How long would it take for this to cool down? Only patience would pay off, but with all that dough lying out there while he was busting his ass doing boat work, it was agonizing.

"Yo, bro, it's lunchtime. Where you going?" Leroi was another yard worker, a slim, muscular West Indian. His only aims of life were to stay high and own a boat. At twenty-five, he was content with a small ganja patch and a twelve-foot inflatable. "Yo, bro, you want to burn one with me? Make the afternoon go better, mon."

"Nah, but thanks... got those Feds looking up my ass for who knows why. I better keep my act clean. Besides, I need the cash." Keith couldn't really trust anyone or let down his guard. It would be that way for a long time. The end of his labors was so near. He headed back into the office to punch the clock.

It was almost the end of the day when Keith returned to the work shed. Leroi was resting out on one of the long benches.

"What they have you doing, bro? I been stroking more of that Trinidad Blue bottom paint. Hot fucking day, mon, hot fucking day. Shit drying as fast as I put it on."

"I've been installing some electronics. Say, buddy, you wouldn't have half a joint you could spare? I feel like sneaking off and watching the sunset. Catching a buzz. Could use a bit of relaxation."

"No problem. No problem at all. What say I go with you? Fact is, I know how we can get to the Baths if you're afraid of being seen."

"Fuck'em! Let's go."

By six, they were perched on the last western boulder stretching away from the Baths. All the round granite rocks looked like enormous dinosaur eggs in the evening's yellow light. Keith propped himself against one boulder while sitting on another. To the west, the silhouette of Ginger Island shone just south of the glowing rocks at Fallen Jerusalem. Leroi passed him the spliff. Keith inhaled deeply.

"Not bad shit you got there, Leroi. Not bad at all. Been a while since I've been stoned, but this shit is sweet stuff. Yeah, I can tell. Pretty evening, huh?"

"Yeah, mon, beautiful."

"Say, Leroi, you ever think about selling your boat, the inflatable?" "Sure, mon. You know how it is, everything for sale if the price is right. That's got a one-year-old, twenty-five horse. It runs great. But I need to get me something better. I wanna be able to haul fish traps, take tourists on day trips. Got to get away from this boatyard. Why you want to buy it?"

"Who knows, maybe? I'm getting kind of bored just staying here. Ain't a whole hell of a lot to do. Know what I mean? I was thinking, with your boat I could do some cruising around on calm days. You got two gas tanks, right? It would help me relax."

"We'll talk. Let's watch the sun's show now."

The shadows of a half dozen islands merged to black as the sky filled with layers of gold and red. A brilliant light lit up the sky above Beef Island as a shuttle plane was about to land. Everything so far away was suddenly so close.

Everything was right around the next bend. Soon come.

"So, where were we? You were telling me about life back home in Tulsa, right?" Carlos was trying to be attentive to the waitress he'd met in traffic. "Being a majorette?"

"Oh yeah! I really had a blast going to all the school functions and wearing that cute little uniform. Tulsa's like, ah, you know, not really that much going on. Really, that's why I came here."

He pulled her close and kissed her lightly. "I think you made the right decision."

"Hell, I didn't want to get married to one of those oil field monkeys and live in a tiny trailer on a ranch, raising kids. Once I caught a whiff of that, I was out of there. Radical. You're from South America? Born with a dynamite tan and me, I lay there and broil, and this is all that I have." Elizabeth pulled the waist of her shorts down to show the scant tan line and her thong. "You know, if my bod could get as dark as my hair went blonde, I'd look great." She primped in the mirror behind the bar, tossing her long blonde curls.

Carlos wasn't that deep in thought; he felt her fingertip-size nipples rubbing his arm as she wheeled to service a table. He lit a Dunhill and studied her khaki behind, conveniently displayed in his direction. Tall, almost six-foot, Elizabeth would have been turning heads on Malibu or Huntington Beach. Her natural beauty was out of place in these islands. She was still soft everywhere, not just where it was profitable. He could teach her, if he made the time.

"I'll make time." He stubbed out the long butt and turned so he could watch her parade throughout the bar.

Carlos lit another cigarette as the barmaid poured another

wine spritzer. He'd been smoking and drinking too much since the shipment disappeared. The news of the trimaran found in the BVI ended all hope of getting the product or the money. His two mules and two Puerto Ricans were dead. The heat was intense from all directions. The PR boys were DEA riding the thin rail between the law and the dealers. They had always been a problem, as they could steal and deal without fear. These two had a side job as couriers for San Juan's biggest importer. They were to buy only a part of the load. It bothered him because it would never be clear if the DEA were rip-offs on their own or following orders.

Uncle Piedra was making inquiries. If a quantity appeared anywhere from an unknown source, he offered a big reward for the info. Carlos had enough money to pay back the investors on this deal. He'd lost three hundred large. Paying out the other one-seventy- five was a sickening bite. To stay alive and keep people loyal, he had to pay it back. His uncle was putting another shipment together.

"Oh, Elizabeth," Carlos smiled, "How are you at back rubs?"

"I've been rated as great." She rubbed his back. "I get off at eleven. Want to find out?"

"Wait for me." He kissed the cheek she presented and walked to the parking lot. A white Escalade squealed to a stop, blocking him.

"What?!"

"What yourself!" shouted dreadlocks from the passenger seat. "Where you been? Big Man Rashad is looking for you and either some tall green or some shiny white. If he don't get either, you gonna be one dead Spico. Rashad doesn't want me to shoot you this time." The dread turned and leaned back. "What do you think, partner?"

The rear door opened and an older dreadlock stepped to the pavement. "Carlos, my friend, excuse my bodyguard. He enjoys blood too much."

"Look, Rashad, I know I haven't talked about our problem. It seems the shipment got jacked. I'll return your capital when the banks open Monday. Sorry for the inconvenience, but I wasn't certain; I had to wait. I found out yesterday the couriers were murdered, and the goods vanished. You know, amigo, shit like that happens with this product."

"Yes, my friend, shit happens. I operate so I don't get shit on me. Make sure it don't happen to you, amigo. Answer your fucking phone! That's why everyone has a cell, to keep fucking in touch!" He moved to get into the car but turned and curled his trigger finger, "Yes, be cool so no shit happens to you."

The white Escalade made a tight circle, squealing tires, and throwing up a cloud of dust as it vanished. Carlos exhaled a long breath of relief and leaned trembling against his car.

The Caribbean is exceptionally beautiful on a calm night. Skies gleamed with a myriad of brilliant dots. The sea offered a haze of slight phosphorescence on the wave tips. A chill permeated the night an hour before dawn.

His newly purchased dinghy was on the west side of Mosquito Island, where Keith had spent the night. He'd successfully escaped everyone's attention to return to Anegada to claim his treasure. Over two months had passed since he'd washed up. His now 'expert touch' had cleaned and painted thirty-two boat bottoms. That was about thirty-one too many. All the horrible smells of drying algae, tinned bottom paint, and mineral spirits brought on nauseous headaches.

The fumes might have caused the headaches, but it could have been the attention he received from the local and federal police. The DEA had a courtesy agreement with the British authorities to locate any clues in the quadruple murder case. Everyone knew it wasn't a murder since a gossipy Tortola police officer had received the ballistic tests' fax. There'd been no outside intruder. The powder burns were accurate and coincided with the scenario. They had shot each other. The only problem was they were prolonging the investigation until they found a fall guy. Keith hoped he wasn't being tailored for the part by the Prescott of the Yard.

Word had leaked, the money was marked, but that may have been to discourage the thieves. It would have been a better strategy if they'd said nothing; let everybody think the money was safe and let it get spent. But it looked bad if it wasn't marked and the two dead agents were attempting to make a legitimate, but illegal, drug buy. Eager for an early start, he'd spent the night in the breeze on the small island. He had fifteen gallons in three gas tanks to feed the inflatable, which Keith estimated to be a tank more than enough for the journey. To break down or run out of fuel with the money, guns, and drugs would mean curtains.

At five-thirty, an orange glow began to his right. The plan was to get there, uncover the loot, wait until dark, and return without a problem. The Johnson twenty-five purred on the first pull. It was calm before dawn; flat, late July seas. No weather, as expected. The trip to the east end of Anegada took about an hour. It was another half hour picking through the reef to the sandy spot near the cash. He pulled the motor off his dinghy and lugged it into the underbrush. Paranoia and common sense predicted that if he was being watched by the authorities, they'd scout for him by plane.

It was almost nine when he finished camouflaging his dinghy. Keith walked inland to the pile of dead gray coral that hid his future. A grunt of satisfaction escaped when he saw the outline of the first aluminum briefcase. He pulled the three clear and sat back after opening all of them. The guns were in excellent condition, but they could implicate him in the murders. Even if the guns had never been registered, somewhere the serial numbers were recorded. But a Mac 10 and two 9mm pistols could come in handy. He fondled the Beretta that had done in the DEA agents, decided not to bring it, and dumped it back in the hole.

Keith didn't expect a shootout, but the amount of white dust would attract some very crazy people. Dangerous people had lost a lot of money. He kissed the machine gun because he knew the mentality of coke dealers and users. What he had was pure rock. He dug his knife into one of the tape-wrapped bundles. The white flakes on the stainless blade reflected the morning sun like an opal's pinkish glow. A taste instantly numbed his tongue.

Smiling, he opened the last case, and stacks of Ben Franklins smiled back. This was his immediate liquid wealth. The bills weren't new. Keith held them up to the sun and didn't see any extra markings. Before he spent any, he'd hold a few under the black lights at the village disco. It didn't matter because he wasn't in any hurry to spend it. His aim was to stay alive and out of jail.

Pulling out the bills, Keith found a cell phone wrapped in one stack. "What's this?" he muttered and tried to turn it on. The weeks of no use probably had killed the battery. "Good thing someone wasn't smart enough to track this phone. I'll take you back and give you a charge. Then I'll find out who answers."

He carefully packed everything into two watertight shoulder bags and then reburied the empty cases after wiping all fingerprints. Evening came and Keith carefully picked his way through the reef. It was difficult to see the coral heads among the shadows late in the day. One wrong move and he could lose the prop and his future. An hour later, he was motoring toward his landmark, Big George Dog Rock. He gathered his bearings and his nerve to return to Spanish Town. It was Sunday night and the town should be in the bars after the weekly cricket match.

Motoring to the Baths, he clamored over the rocks under a moonless sky until he'd found the three plastic five-gallon buckets he's buried days earlier. This was Keith's second stash. Everything should be safe there until he could inconspicuously quit his job. He buried the buckets about two feet deep. He'd taken the precaution to remove the metal handles in case some tourist was metal detecting for lost jewelry. As a final precaution, he rolled a hundred-plus pound rock to cover them.

Back in the dinghy, Keith silently drifted about a mile until he was well west of Virgin Gorda, almost parallel with Round Rock. He lay between the inflated cylinders staring up at the stars, considering his future possibilities. The loot was definitely within his grasp, and that meant he had to be even more cautious. This drift should disguise his route if anyone saw him return. The motor purred to life when he felt the distance was correct, and he steered back to the dock in the yacht harbor.

Spanish town was quiet as he walked back to his room near the boatyard. As he neared, he saw the red glow of a cigarette in the shadows. It was Prescott.

"Nice tropical Sunday, wasn't it Mr. Gardnar? Hope I didn't startle you. I'm just out for my nightly constitutional stroll. You know how it is, sitting behind a desk getting squat. How did you spend your day off? Relaxing, I hope."

"Well… howdy, Inspector, I took advantage of the calm seas and went west to a little lagoon on the south side of Ginger Island. I'm just beginning to feel up to snuff again. Decided it was time to take a lazy day and try to decide where my life is heading. I won't be content painting yacht bottoms for much longer."

Keith unlocked the door to his room at the rear of the boatyard's machine shop. "Don't get me wrong, I'm happy to have a job. Hell, I'm thrilled to have survived, to still be sucking in air and squeezing out shit."

"I must say, you have a different handle on the local lingo," Prescott commented.

"Hey, you must know my story. My luck was not great the last year." Keith looked over his shoulder as he pulled the light switch. "You want to come in, or I can stay outside with you, if you feel the need for conversation?"

Prescott leaned into the dimly lit room. The walls were bare plywood except for a bikini calendar girl. The light was a hanging bulb shrouded by a wicker basket. The furniture was a military cot with a small fridge. Beneath the only window, a white table fan sat on what could have been a sea chest. A few clothes hung over a wire stretched across one corner.

"Yes, I know it is a meager existence, but it's free. A few people feel sorry for me. I'm trying to put back a little money so I can move on."

"Say, Gardnar, you wouldn't have a cold beer, would you? I wouldn't mind a chat. Beautiful night. Missing the wife and children in Birmingham."

The fridge revealed only a gallon of water. "Sorry, only water, inspector. I try not to drink alcohol. Gets me into too much trouble."

"Water then. Where is Ginger Island? There are so many islands among the British Virgins, and I've only touched Tortola and Gorda."

"Ginger's six miles west, between Round Rock and Cooper. I used to captain sail charters, so I know most of the islands like the back of my hand. It's nice when the water is flat. The lagoon is open to the south, teeming with life, and quiet. I'm tired of hearing the boat lift, grinders, and compressors rattling all day." Keith handed the Englishman a plastic cup and poured.

"I find it much quieter than in London. These islands are nice, a bit too warm, and much too slow. You're just returning now? Isn't it too dark for navigating?"

"What is this, twenty questions, Prescott? I said, I know these waters, and I finally relaxed and fell asleep on the beach. Something about the pleasant sound of a calm surf. Probably would have slept all night except for the bugs," Keith replied, irritated. "The no-see-ums and mosquitoes swarmed because I was the only meat on that rock."

Prescott swatted his arm, either in belief or mockery. "Nasty little devils. I gather they can give a man a fever quite like malaria. Gardnar, I'll be frank with you; this place, the people, the insects, and the heat are getting to me. I miss the cool fog of the Queen's flatlands, a decent beef broil, and my family. Do you have any relatives here?"

"Just an ex-wife and an ex-dog. I miss the dog. You know all that from my dossier. Let's cut to it, okay? You're checking up on me, so you can stop the nice-nice shit. It's late and they'll be hauling boats in the morning at eight. I don't mind some friendly conversation, because all I've got now is my calendar girl. And she doesn't have much to say. If you want to play Columbo, do it somewhere else."

"Columbo?"

"An American TV detective who tries to put his suspects

at ease before he cuffs them. He hopes they slip up."

"Oh, Mr. Gardnar, I don't think you'll slip up, or rather, I've changed my mind about you. Truthfully, the Yard doesn't consider you a potential suspect any longer and never really did. Your American boys are a different story, though. The Drug Enforcement gentlemen want a body in the worst way to close their case, for public relations, I surmise. No, I never thought you were capable of floating all that distance with drugs and money. The reason I came by was to inform you that your banana boat, the Alita Dee, was discovered in Ponce, Puerto Rico undergoing extensive repairs. The captain related your exact story to the authorities. He said you were washed overboard a few hours out of St. Maarten on the night of the ninth of May, seven days before you were found here. Everything checks out. The DEA may still attempt to mount a case against you." The inspector sipped his water. "But I will try to save them embarrassment and wasted time by solidifying your alibi."

"That would be excellent, inspector. I apologize if I came off rude, but I've been interrogated one too many times. The US guys put genuine fear into me. After the life and death shit of floating around, all I want is some peace and quiet. Not getting much peace and no quiet. You read all the time about the guys who the DEA railroad into jail just to close a case. The guys are corrupt, and everyone in the islands knows it. Christ, I couldn't afford an experienced divorce lawyer, let alone one for a murder case. That's great; the Alita made it. I truly thought they'd sunk."

"Yes, according to our information, they also drifted more than a week before being sighted and towed into Ponce. All four of the crew survived. Seems they weren't going to report you as lost. A visiting customs agent noticed the vessel's name from a newspaper report of your rescue. Once approached, the captain praised the Virgin Mary that you had been so miraculously saved. It is amazing, isn't it?"

"You'll never know how good this makes me feel. Now that it's been proven, I want to sell my story to some tabloid and make some money." Keith slid down the wall until he sat on the dirt. "Yahoo, yahoo! Looks like I might get out of here sooner than I thought. Getting damn tired of eating canned beans, cold canned beans."

"I'm glad I could brighten your spirits, Mr. Gardnar." The inspector returned his glass to Keith. "I'll be going. Take care, Mr. Gardnar, stay out of trouble. You are a famous man around this sleepy island. I'm certain things will turn around for you. Tomorrow, if you want, come by my office and you can fax your fellows on the Alita."

"Hell no, they weren't even going to report me lost. I'll fax them my ass!" He extended his hand to the Brit, "Thanks for the help, Prescott. And I hope they transfer you back to your beloved England soon. Come by again, anytime. As you can see, chances are, you won't be interrupting anything." Keith closed the door, switched on the fan, and relaxed toward sleep with a grin.

I've never had a problem with drugs.
I've had problems with the police.
Keith Richards

CHAPTER TWELVE

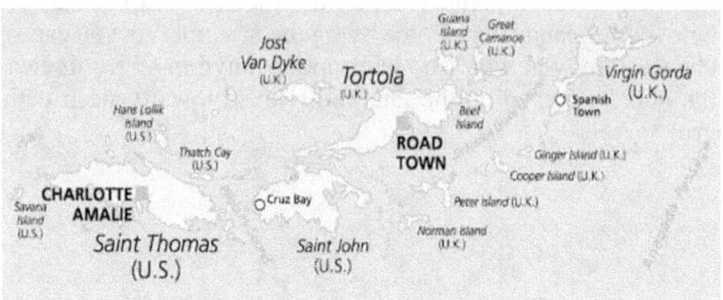

British and US Virgin Islands

Everything happens when the time is right is the adage. Once the Alita supported Keith's alibi, he started making plans. The cash looked good, but the white powder would return a bigger sum, only if he could safely move it. Not a dummy to that business, he knew people would wait for a load to surface and then grab the seller and the goods. It was all food for great thoughts while he continued to clean boats.

After another month, Keith gave his notice. Constantly wary, he made preparations. He dragged two concrete blocks close to the buried stash buckets. The plan was to tie the waterproof bags to the blocks and stay in the deepest part of Drakes Channel on his return. If he felt challenged or threatened, he'd dump it over the side. The trip wouldn't be a straight shot. He'd need to refuel. With a bit of engineering, he stuffed his few clothes in with the stash and fashioned the blocks to look like an anchor. On top, he laid his mask and fins like he was snorkeling.

On the next new moon night, he slipped away at dusk, making Road Town, Tortola by morning. He tied his inflatable to the fuel dock and slept until they opened.

"Hey, ain't you Keith? Member me?"

Keith opened his eyes to a bearded, tanned face leaning over the dock. After a long yawn, "Can't say I recognize you, partner."

"Oh, shoot, must be the beard and longer hair. I'm Johnny; you called me Long John. I crewed for you years back." The man pointed to the ketch tied at the dock. "Now I'm a skipper. They call me Tortola Johnny now. Hey, heard a yarn about how you got washed overboard, floated on bananas. If that's true, you're looking good."

"Where'd you hear that?"

"Oh, all around the docks in St. T. You know how shipwreck gossip flies through the bars. And you were a well-known hombre," John replied.

"Not so much now, buddy. Yeah, hit a bad piece of weather and got washed overboard. Like the song, down to rock bottom again."

"Yeah," John sang the lyrics, "Just a few friends, time to go fishing again. You'll be okay. Going back to St. T? People there will help you get back on your feet. If you want some work, I can always use a hand. Hell, you could take a charter or two and I'll sleep in the hammock."

"Thanks, might take you up on that, John. I'm sort of at ends now. Say, you know Dale, real slim white guy, a few years older than us?"

"Yeah, I know Dale, always a big head of hair." He fluffed his own hair, "Look at me talking, back in the day we called him Fuzzy. Saw him not that long ago. Think he's living above the old Danish stables on Vesta Gade, behind the library. Why?"

"No reason, except he always knew where to find work."

"Yep," John's voice dropped. "He always had excellent blow, until he did that stretch. Like you, never figured he'd come back to St. T."

"Why shouldn't I come back?" That annoyed Keith. "Everyone comes back. St. Thomas is the only half-assed home I've got. I figure might go into house painting, if Dale can fix me up."

"Ah, thought a guy like you would find work around the docks. Hell, you know most everybody. Maybe last week, Wednesday or Thursday, I saw Dale at Goodfellas. You used to belly up there, didn't you? Anyway, he was looking sad, saying it was about time to move on. Something about working with the boss's kid. I didn't pay much attention. We split a couple of rounds." John looked into the dinghy, "Planning on some skin diving?"

"Be baking by the time I hit Coral Bay. Thought a swim might be good. Never know what you can find," Keith replied. Optimistically, if successful, he wouldn't be looking for work ever again. If he failed, he'd either be worm or fish food, or getting three squares under a government roof. "By chance, you don't have a number to contact Dale?"

John rubbed his bearded jaw in thought. "No, sorry, no reason to. Always bump into him. He said he's living behind the public library. It'd be easy to find him. Just like you, everyone knows Dale."

"Okay," Keith climbed onto the dock. "Thanks."

"So, where you headed? In Coral Bay, check out Frenchtown Lucy at her bar. She and Dale was always close. She'll probably have his number. You must know her?"

Keith had forgotten so many faces, but the island moniker rang a bell. "Yeah, Frenchtown Lucy... she has her own bar now?"

"Yep, ain't America's enterprise great? Nice tits and ass with a wild reputation are good for business."

A clang of metal announced the fuel dock was open and ended the conversation. In less than an hour, Keith had fueled and cleared immigration in the BVI and was underway to the most eastern point in the US: Coral Bay, St. John. Landfall was always in eyesight throughout the Virgins. The seas were bumpy in the channel, and the inflatable rolled with the waves until he rounded the southern point of East End and motored into the flat water of the bay.

The Virgin Islands have beautiful waters from the drier, western Spanish Virgins that begin just east of Puerto Rico, through the US Virgins and all the way to desolate Anegada in the British islands. St. John is the most luscious of all. It stays status quo because the Rockefeller family bought a huge chunk and donated it to remain virtually undeveloped as a national park.

Coral Bay could be considered the last outpost of the hippie counterculture in the Americas. The image of tropical isolation was just that, only an image. Within hours, traveling by buses, ferries, and planes, any destination was reachable. With enough loot, hanging in Coral Bay was one of the most desirable habitats in the US. Long-haired, rainbow tie-dyed attired, self-appointed gypsies gravitated, and Keith knew many. Recent years had attracted the nouveau-tech-rich. The cost of living had risen, but so had the price of labor. It was big bucks to live at the edge of paradise.

The dinghy ride had been pleasant, and he'd considered many versions of the same plan; sell the goods and disappear. If he kept his wits, it would take a few years to run through the cash. The burner phone could play an important part. Keith kept wary of any official-looking watercraft, but in the anonymous gray dinghy, he felt invisible. It could have been any yacht's tender. If he'd have been in a larger boat, he might have drawn some attention. Smuggling was still a big industry in Coral Bay. Someone had to feed the habits. He had the stuff, but no desire to hustle it in small pieces.

During the hot, bouncy dinghy ride, water had quenched Keith's thirst. It was now well past beer o'clock. Tying to a small dock, he entered a bar where he could keep a close eye on his inflatable. Two chilled Heinekens solved one immediate problem. Next, where to spend the night? Continue to St. Thomas, or stay on St. John? He needed to find somewhere to crash. He couldn't remember the last time he'd seen Lucy. Had they parted as friends? He grabbed the duffel, threw it over his shoulder, and trudged off, the same as sailors had for centuries.

Loose Lucy's was an open-air bar. The roof shaded the patrons and the beer coolers. It was getting close to happy hour and regulars were straggling in. Memories of happier days were saturating Keith's mood, forcing a wide grin. Yes, they'd parted as friends, good, intimate friends.

Lucy came to the islands to escape the harsh Wisconsin winters. Starting as a bartender in Frenchtown, her always-stretched-to-the-limit halter tops and shorts, plus a quick wit and willing smile, soon built a clientele. Two robberies and a rape drove her to a much safer St. John. Insurance and lawsuits against her landlord, who'd never secured her apartment, provided the down payment on the saloon.

Except for a few gray hairs and slight laugh lines, not much had changed with Lucy. "A Heinie, please," Keith asked.

Lucy didn't look up from her crossword puzzle. She reached into the cooler, flicked off the cap, and mechanically handed it. Keith pushed the three bucks and grabbed her hand.

"Hey," Lucy grunted. Then, after looking up, said in a sweeter tone, "Hey! I don't fucking believe it." She swung over the bar to hug Keith. "I haven't seen you in a long while. Things okay?" They kissed cheeks. "Heard you had some sour luck a while back; then I heard you survived a shipwreck or some typical Keith shit."

"Yeah," he mumbled and swigged the beer.

"So, what have you been up to? Got to be two or three years since you drank at my place."

"Maddy knew we had a history, so rather than create problems…"

"Yeah, I heard you created one big, fucking problem."

"Marriage tanked. I couldn't keep it in my pants. Shoulda, coulda, woulda known better, and I'd still have my house, business, boat, and my dog. Thinking with the little swollen head has always been a problem."

Lucy walked around the bar and hugged Keith and gave

a yank on his crotch. "Oh, you don't need to tell me. I remember!" Another tug, "Boy, do I remember. It's good to see you. You were really shipwrecked?"

"Not so long of a story, but I'd rather tell it to you in private."

"In private, huh? Well, we could arrange that later... much later. Julio's making the fixings for Taco Tuesday. The place will be jumping tonight. You still sip tequila?" She pulled him close, "Maybe we could do some dancing tonight?"

"Me and Vitamin T, that's gonna be the title of my biography, and the downfall of a good man. Maybe some horizontal bopping later? I'd like to check if I've fully recovered."

"Some never change. You might give yourself a bit too much credit with that 'good man' shit." Lucy giggled and spun around to the bar and grabbed two shot glasses and the Jose Cuervo. "This is on me." They clinked glasses, swilled the liquor, leaned, and kissed. "Yes, I'm really glad to see you, Keith. For a while, since I heard about the wreck and recovery, I've been thinking about you and the old days. We had a little thing back then."

Keith reached and tweaked one of Lucy's very visible nipples. "Sweetheart, there was never anything little about you. We had a great thing, but I was stupid. Both of us spinning in different directions; all the stuff that makes up the lyrics for the old songs. Look, ah, I know this is awkward, but I need a place to crash tonight. Left Gorda before daybreak, sort of tuckered. I need a shower to wash off the salt spray."

Lucy sighed and sternly looked him in the eye. "After all these years, you think you can just float in and be a bed warmer?" Her mouth wrinkled into a smile, "Of course." She tossed him a key. "Drag your old ass and your bag up the stairs over there. You're in luck. I'm not getting any regular pounding lately. But clean up, nap, and get back down here. You won't sleep long 'cause the music will blare 'round eight. I want some company and socializing. We close up 'bout ten, and then we can swap stories."

A loud guitar riff rousted a freshly bathed Keith. It was a dark eight-thirty, and the floor vibrated from the music. He'd hid his duffels behind the couch where he'd napped. Peeking from the stairs, off-season regulars packed Lucy's looking for a cheap meal and cheaper thrills. He sat on the top step considering his approach; he vaguely recognized a few. There would probably be questions he didn't care to answer. Invisibility was what he wanted, but as a three-plus decade local, that was impossible.

Some handshakes, hugs, more free drinks flowed mostly for being a survivor. Keith realized how far his story had spread. No one seemed threatening, but he couldn't elude his wary nature. A few younger cuties snuggled up for a combined selfie: he'd look and Lucy would give a knowing nod and wink. They herded the few stragglers out of the saloon by eleven as Lucy helped lock the gates.

"Well, well, well, how 'bout a Lucy's closing time special? You want me to make you one, Julio?" She got an affirmative. "Making money here, almost at the end of the US. People like it and I can't complain. Feels safer than St. T, but I take no more chances." She pulled a revolver from under the counter. "It goes where I go."

"Whoa, darling, those things frighten me. Feel you need protection tonight?"

"No," She leaned and gave a wet kiss and laughed, "You're gonna need protection. I figure it's a sore subject, so I'll get it out quick. Saw your wife and her brother over here a week ago. I was coming from my boat and saw them walking the docks. No hi, bye, or why. Make you feel any better, Maddy isn't looking good. Both were chain-smoking. Her brother's cute, but he gives me the creepers. Looks at you with criminal eyes. Know what I mean?"

He sipped the drink. "Wow! I can see why this is the last call."

Keith remembered locking his dinghy to the stern of Lucy's boat, but after that everything was hazy. His head ached as he looked at luscious Lucy enveloped in the sheets. The half bottle of tequila coupled with poor judgment ushered the rough morning. He reached under the sheets, located her junction, and tickled her awake.

"What... what are you doing?" She cooed, "Nice alarm, practiced touch." She pulled him down. "Better not be a false alarm."

They uncoupled. It remained a rough morning, but one of the few good rough mornings he could recently remember.

"You gonna stick around for a few days, or is this one of Keith's famous hit and runs?" Lucy asked as she nuzzled his neck.

"Two aspirins, nurse. Truth is, I don't know what I'm doing. Like to get in touch with Dale in St. T; you got his number? Looking for work; figured he always has some iron in the fire."

Lucy yawned and stretched. "Could be some work for you here, if you want to continue taking care of my needs." She poked him in his ribs, "My boat, Starlet, and the place could use a handyman, and last night you were plenty handy. I have Dale's number. Didn't think you'd be in any hurry to return to the scene of your crimes."

"No hurry," Keith kissed her. "No hurry at all, but I'm making plans. I'm certain I'm not staying on that rock. It is a good place to make fast money, but there are people who don't like me there."

"Sweetie, there's one person here who likes you. This is the most relaxed I've felt in weeks. You know your way around my plumbing." She laughed, "Stay for a few days and I'll see if I can coax 'ole Dale over to Coral Bay. Meanwhile, you can fix a few things here and there." Pointing to her boat and herself, "Make yourself useful for room and board."

He interrupted her, "Don't say it. I know; no one rides for free." He grabbed her and pulled her down to the bed.

Two days and numerous repairs later, Keith was stroking a paintbrush as Dale's Renault pulled into Coral Bay. "Wow, after all the stories I heard about Keith Gardnar, you don't seem any the worse for wear and tear. Looking good buddy, slim and trim." The two men hugged. "Back with Lucy or is she just keeping you busy?" Dale teased.

"Been a while buddy, just playing the cards I'm dealt." He pulled his pants away from his midriff. "Been on the banana diet, but don't recommend it unless as a last resort."

"From what I've heard, they stacked the deck against you."

"Let's get some beers. I'm looking for gainful employment."

"Me too. Times are tough for old cowboys like us. The Caribbean has changed mucho from the old days and we're getting long in the tooth. Since my free, government-mandated vacation, I've been on the straight and narrow, no fun at all. Hasn't been bad, but nothing to write home about, just treading water." He laughed, "From your shipwreck story, I guess you know all about treading water."

They touched bottles as Lucy approached and kissed Dale. "What are you old dogs up to?" She rustled Keith's hair. "This hound's learned a few new tricks. What do you think; I can tame him to curl up at my feet? Maybe his wild streak is gone?"

Keith's arm encircled her thighs and as he pulled, she slid into his lap. "Just like the old days, sipping brews at Johnny Harms. Doesn't seem so long ago."

"It was! I drifted into the Virgins in '98. Twenty-plus years, first it was fun, then penance, now fun again." Lucy continued, "Turned out okay... in the long run."

"The jury is still out deciding on my outcome," Dale queued.

Lucy laughed and prodded his shoulder. "I thought the jury already had its say. Hey, we all had our ups and downs..."

"Mine lasted for five long ones," Dale answered. "Don't know if there is any bouncing back or just bouncing my head against the wall. Times are tough for the entrepreneur who has nothing to entrepreneur. I've painted too many walls since they released me." Lucy subtly murmured the words to *Please Release Me* as he continued. "Sort of tough looking at the sea and feeling landlocked."

"Ah," Lucy smooched Keith's cheek and leaned over and squeezed Dale's hand. "Things will get better, and I've got to get back to work. Coral Bay isn't so bad. You both should consider a move here. All the rich millennials need shit done around their houses and all are inept or lazy. Money to be made, boys... money to be made." She clapped her hands and returned behind the bar.

Keith carried two fresh beers to the table and nudged Dale. "Let's take a walk over to the old battery. I always like to look at the cannons. Think about those guys from Europe dressed in hot wool uniforms, coming to these unknown islands."

As they tramped through the prickly scrub, Dale said, "Not so unknown now. Popular, damn expensive, and getting more dangerous by the day. Did you know that the Virgins had the highest per capita murder rate of the entire US in 2016? Probably the highest unsolved murder rate as well. The local police have a hard time solving a suicide."

They laughed and Keith added, "Those dumbo police are what kept us in business, back in the day. Dumbo and Bribe Bo!"

"Man, do I hate to hear that 'back in the day' shit. 'Back in the day' my ass. The risks were worth it. Hmm, I lost my house, wife, family, five years, and all my money. You, huh, about the same, so now what? Go to church and pray for a new day?"

They stopped in the shade and Keith looked around; Dale produced a joint. "Not bad stuff. Been keeping to myself. Remember Josef? He's the only one I trust to get me any herb. Crack is everywhere. Seems even the locals have given up on weed."

They passed it and Keith asked, "You ever think about trying it one more time? You know, one run, one big score, and disappear?"

"Hell yeah, I think about it constantly, but don't have any cash. Nobody gives anything on credit. Dreams, buddy, only dreams."

"But would you? Would you if the opportunity was there? Prison put the fear of God into you?"

"Hell, Eglin Air Force Base, where they had me, was almost as good as any resort." He flexed his arms, "I did the weights and even got good at playing tennis. Met some powerful dogs in there." He sucked hard on the joint, "I was in the commissary. Everyone had to deal with me."

"Can't get any of those guys to front some cash?"
"Nah, I was a tadpole to them. We'd shoot the shit, tell tales, but when the gate opened for them, those guys wouldn't remember my name. That's how it goes." Dale straddled one of the old rusty cannons. "Thought about asking my boss for a loan, but he's treated me sweet. Got a roof and got me that Cadillac I'm driving."

"The Renault isn't yours? I think it is a perfect island ride. Must be economical."

"Fuck you and your gas mileage. Georgie pays for all the gas, and I work it off. It struggles up the mountains, but better than walking."

"Ya got that right. I'm clean of everything. Lucky they left my shoes. But suppose you could get some good dancing dust, a quantity, think you could move it?"

"Keith, what you got cooking? Buddy, my circle is small and I keep it that way. How much are you talking about? An ounce?"

"Keys."

"Wow, I can try. But you know that shit brings out the crazy and the violent. What's the price?"

"Reasonable. Say a grand under the usual price. But this friend wants to move the lot, one time, one buyer."

"What are we talking about?"

"Future freedom. Dale, you are the only one I can trust. I met a guy just before I was washed overboard. The guys on the banana boat weren't moving bananas." He spun the lie.

"Ricans? Can't trust those guys."

"Really? Who can you trust with making your dreams come true? Me, I trust you… or you wouldn't be here. I know you did all the time because you wouldn't rat. And you?"

"Hell, Keith, I guess I gotta trust you. We've known each other for a quarter of a century. When you put it that way, it sounds almost safe. But nothing is safe around the dancing dust. Now, down to the nitty-gritty, how much can we make off it? Enough to retire, I hope?"

"One way or the other, we retire or it retires us. Mention nothing around Lucy or anyone. You and I pulled off some shit and I feel we could do it again, only one more time again. We really have to think this one through, but it also must be quick. We split fifty-fifty. Lots of getaway dough. You in?"

They walked around the old stone fort. Keith finally saw what he'd been looking for. "Depends how crazy a scheme it is. 50-50? Where you getting it for free? Where do we got to go to get it? You know the people? I ain't going into no barrio in PR."

"We get it here. Don't worry where it comes from. You don't meet anyone on the buying side and I don't want to meet anyone on the selling side. I get it, you dump it."

"How much you talking about?"

"Fifty pounds, maybe more."

"Holy shit! That's a load!"

"Yes, sir, like I said, one hit and hi-ho Silver! Away! You think you know a big enough player?"

"I said, I only trust Josef. We know the locals got their sources, and I won't walk up to one of the Rasta families. That would be suicide to mention that quantity. You don't want to sell it slow?"

"Personally, I think that would be suicide. What do you think it brings now? Say pure, never whacked?"

"Maybe 15K a pound would be reasonable." Dale rubbed his eyes and drew a long breath, "I don't know; I really don't. The most I ever moved was five keys, and that was six, no, seven years ago. You try the goods?"

"I tasted what they had, but I stopped that shit a long time ago."

"Well, partner, now it's all about crack. They can take an ounce of pure and make four to six ounces of rock. I got to think about this. Hmm, fifty-fifty on fifty pounds. That's almost four hundred large. Take me forever to put that much back by painting apartments. What's the next move?"

"You talk to Josef or whoever you feel good about. I don't need to say, don't mention me."

"This will take extreme planning… extreme. We got to do the deal, get the cash, and not kill or be killed. Then escape to somewhere nice where the cash will provide a decent life. I gotta drop at least half of mine on the wife for her and the boy. Take out a double indemnity policy, just in case."

"Aren't you the optimist? You and I have been around the block so many times we've worn a rut in the street. We can plan this. Double indemnity, huh? You think about this type of thing a lot?"

"You're the guy who brought up the subject. Yeah, I think about protecting what's left of the family. She left. Can't blame her. I guess I was a poor influence. After the kid was born, I should have stopped. She's in Atlanta now with her family. Got restraining orders on me."

"About time for another coldie. You need more info?"

"You got more info?" Keith shook his head. "I didn't think so. You gonna hang out here or what?" He patted Keith on the back as they walked. "For a shipwrecked guy, you're coming out of this okay. No more hassles with the wife?"

"That's done. Think I'll stay over here until I hear from you."

The two old friends drained a few more greenies before Dale left to catch the last ferry. Keith had found his temporary stash in the old battery. There was a pile of rubble where part of an inside wall had collapsed. It would suffice to cover the bricks of coke and the guns. The money he'd keep close by.

"Where you been hiding?" Lucy asked.

"Not used to beer in the afternoon; took an unplanned nap. Passed out under the almond tree."

She teased him with a beer. "Sure I didn't tire you out? Damn, what'd you do to get so dusty? Roll around having a bad dream?"

"Maybe it was a good dream, one of the best. Just sprawled out. Feels good to relax again." Keith smiled and squeezed her ass, "And, felt good to end my celibacy."

On the ferry, Dale weighed Keith's proposition. He knew trust existed between them, and they both needed a chance to reclaim their freedom. That chance could also end their freedom. Dealing with the white shit could also end their lives. He was no stranger to risk, reward, and punishment.

Watching the blue Caribbean, he assessed his situation, and it wasn't much different from Keith's. They were both divorced and had lost almost everything. He chuckled to himself, considering his incarceration equaled being shipwrecked. Closing in on sixty, many options had closed. His present life was worth living, but it was every bit of drudgery. He knew this chance could make it better, but also could damn certain make it worse.

In the old days, the coke business hadn't been so crazy. They'd made money and knew the dancing dust had ruined the lives of those too weak to control it. He shrugged; that was the way with all drugs: moderation. The new version, crack, was incredibly addictive. He'd tried it once. The resulting paranoia had not been pleasant. He nodded to the sunset. His conscience could handle the curse inflicted on the community. It was one shot and go. The rationalization was easy; if they didn't sell it, somebody else would. The odds were better than buying a lottery ticket. The risks were obvious. It would take some serious planning.

No reason to hesitate; he drove directly to Josef's Casablanca Bar in Frenchtown. It was a pub on the fishing dock that catered to locals and tourists. Josef was an institution. He always had dope and had never been busted, paying off the police while keeping a low profile. Everyone knew him, and he knew everyone. "Jo around?"

"In his office," replied the shapely young bartender pointing to the corner table.

"Long time, no see. How's tricks, Dale? Bring me a beer," Josef ordered. "So, what brings you back to the docks? You've been out of sight for weeks. I figured you ended your socializing days." They hugged. "Keeping busy?"

"Yeah, still stroking a brush, doing apartment maintenance." He sat, sipped the beer, and scanned the bar. "This was always one of the nicest places on the rock. You've done well."

"Hungry? The kitchen's still open. What brings you around?"

"Um, can you break away? Thought we could take a stroll."

Jo fidgeted, "If you need a loan, no problem as long as it doesn't break my back."

"No, no loan. Just a private chat."

They walked along the waterfront. "Privacy has been always one of your concerns. Dale, you never wasted time, straight to business."

"Yeah, and I still got pinched."

"Should have bought the local insurance policy. For me,

it's just another cost of doing business. Now the costs are always inflating. Everyone's got their hands out. The policy lets you know if outside agents are watching and tells the local bandits to stay away. The crazies are worrisome. So, this privacy... you moving something?"

"Maybe," Dale paused and looked around, "What's the deal these days on blow? Think anyone would be interested? What's it paying?"

"Pain and misery! Same as always. Didn't expect to hear about that shit from you. People are always looking for a money maker. What do you have? An ounce of maybe 40%, and that's considered good, is going for about a grand and a half. For tourists and locals, they can put another whack on it."

"Geez, that's rotgut."

"Yeah, that's because there's not much around. For months now, they're stretching it thinner and thinner. I know a few who are looking and can handle a quantity. How much you got?" Jo pulled out a joint and motioned to sit at a concrete bench. "This is some of Northside skunk, not too bad."

Dale took a hit and coughed, "Wow, that shit explodes in your lungs. I've got a reliable source, fifty keys." He pulled on the joint. "Wants to move it."

It was Jo's turn to cough. "Holy Hell! Fifty?! Must be a stranger. Only a few family operations rule this island's supply; you should know that. What's the deal?"

"Boat broke down, can't make it to the States. Be a bargain for the right player. Met these guys doing time in Florida. Shit's pure. No taste available 'cause they don't want to pull it out from hiding until. What do you think they can get for an el-bee?"

The harbor lights held Jo's stare; he took the last pull and flicked the roach into the sea. "If it's pure, and I don't mean to doubt you, but how many times have we heard that? If it's pure, probably get 18 to 20 a pound. Those guys can put a quarter whack on it and so can the next buyer."

"How about you sell it for 18 and for the effort you get one off the top as commission? I'll get a taste they can test. You know these guys good? Don't want any cowboy bullshit."

"Hey, come on, we know what comes free with the white stuff. Yeah, they've been moving some quantity. Something happened to the last load, delayed, disappeared, or some shit. Not much on the street, aren't you listening? I said it's been dry for months. All I can do is ask."

"It doesn't leave my sight. I pay your commission when

the deal's done." They shook hands. "Jo, I trust you. This is my ticket to get off the rat race merry-go-round. We'll make a chunk of change, just middling. This must be careful - careful."

"Okay. Understood. I'll make a few calls. How do I get hold of you?"

"I'll come by. This won't be a quickie. Take me a bit to put my hands on it. These guys are super paranoid."

"Dale, we've known each other for a lot of years. We both know what can happen. My people don't play. Take that to heart."

"Done and done." Dale walked off.

Josef worked his cell, "Carlos, see me ASAP."

Cocaine is God's way of telling you,
you're making too much money.
Robin Williams

CHAPTER THIRTEEN

Every day, Keith took a leisurely stroll and checked where he'd hidden his cache of modern treasure. Late one afternoon, certain no one was around, he retrieved the cell phone he'd found on the DEA speed boat. He inconspicuously charged it at Lucy's place after pulling the sim. It was a burner, and he copied the only number. In case it was being tracked, he wrapped it in aluminum foil.

Lucy was keeping him busy at both ends of the day. During the day, he was sorting out various problems with her bar and boat, and at night, he was soothing her other problems. It worked well for Keith; he kept busy while his mind fashioned a plan of action. Couldn't be too hasty concerning what was in the works.

"Hey sweetie," Lucy cooed. "What you been up to? Haven't seen you today."

He kissed her. "Well, if you really want to know, last night I took care of your bottom and today I scraped and scrubbed all the algae off your boat's bottom. Lady, that thing had an underwater forest growing."

She laughed and hugged him. "Might keep you around. Nothing like a man who looks for things that need fixing. You have my place near perfection and now you have started on my boat." She kept him in a hug. "May I ask what your intentions are?"

"Thinking maybe we could go for a sail. Lucy, you bust ass. Maybe take a day sail or an overnighter. Try to remember why we live here."

"Shit, I thought after all that floating around, you'd be finished with boats." She wrinkled her nose and squeezed him, "Baby, that sounds sweet. When?"

"You're the boss. We both know my schedule is open. Your ketch, Starlet, I got her ready. Throw together some beers and snacks, we're good to go. My treat for your lovely hospitality. Say, anchor at the Willie T. That old barge is still in the Bight on Peter Island, isn't it? Get buzzed on Pusser's Painkillers."

Lucy stretched and pulled his lips closer. "What happened to the old Keith? I like the new guy, a lot!"

"Keith, Version 2020." He replied, "Started the next chapter and now I can see everything, perfect vision. Living and loving in the moment." A deep sigh escaped as he pulled Lucy closer. "Yeah girl, now every little thing, every minute is precious."

Three hours and seven tacks brought Road Town, Tortola. Once cleared in, Lucy headed to a favorite local art shop and deli while Keith kept busy checking Starlet's rigging.

Once alone, Keith brought out the two cell phones from Anegada. The phones were disposables and had been off for months. He'd copied the only one number on each. He would record the calls by placing the two phones together. He walked to the far end of the main dock where small boats were being loaded with deliveries for a few of the outlying resorts. One was loading cases of liquor.

"Where are you heading with that much booze?" he inquired. The dark boatman replied, "Peter Island, boss."

Keith walked farther down the dock and stared at the phones, knowing the calls would probably cause problems, but would provide answers to the 'who.' "Guess I've been afraid of what I'm gonna hear. Better to know whose stuff I got. It's a small world around these islands."

With a handkerchief wrapped around the phone, he pushed the key on the first cell.

"Who is this?" The Spanish accented reply was immediate. "You know who this is? Answer me, damn it. Do you work for the people? How did you get this phone? You killed my brother. I'll kill you, motherfucker!"

Using a combination of bad French and down island patois, Keith slowly responded, searching for the correct words. "Wait, mon ami, relax. Settle down, relax. I found the goods. No kill no one. You buy from me, sell, make a fortune. Think it over. I'll call when I am ready."

"It's all fucking stolen! Not buying anything!"

"Mon ami, you want this, you must pay. You think it over..." Keith paused, listening, "I will call again." He switched off the phone, carefully wiped it clean.

If the other end was competent, it had been a long enough chat that they had a trace. Brother, huh? That rang a bell. He slid the phone into one of the liquor cases being loaded onto the transport.

Walking into the public restroom on the docks, he tried

the Nokia. It rang ten times before a vaguely familiar voice answered. "Amigo… who is this? Who is this? What do you want? Where did you find the cell?"

Again, with the same handkerchief and accent, Keith replied, "Have your shit. Want it back?"

"What?"

"Mucho drogas."

"Who are you? You can't sell it."

"Mira, you're gonna pay half a million."

"No way, you are one fucking loco amigo. That shit is mine; if you didn't know, well, you got the fucking phone."

"Okay, there're others. Thought you would want it. Called you first."

"Wait. 500 is loca!"

"No señor, supply dried up. It's worth more now. You work the magic, amigo. Think it over. I've got your number. Make it happen." Again, he wiped the phone clean and stashed it between the bathroom's rafters. Keith was shaking as he rinsed his face and glanced in the mirror.

"Well, well, both are beaners, one with a dead brother. That sounds about right. A familiar voice, yeah, the second sounded familiar. I wonder? Lots of familiar voices, lots of beaners. All are probably 'Ricans.'"

Deep in thought, trying to add up the new clues, Lucy caught his eye as she waved from a table at a waterfront pub.

"Hey boy," she kissed him, "What's got you frowning? Something wrong with Starlet?"

"Nah, just thinking. Sometimes…"

"Sometimes shit; you need a beer, probably several. Don't forget this is a prescribed holiday. Doctor's orders, no bitching, no frowning or scowling, only smiles and sweet words."

Then their day took a dive. "Hi, I'm Christa, your server. I don't believe it! Keith!"

He slowly nodded.

"You know each other?" Lucy asked.

"Yep, this lady was my major indiscretion. Better make that two beers and two shots of Cuervo, each."

The waitress nervously rattled, "I am so sorry. Let me get you a round." She left for the bar.

"That's who cost you everything? Darling, she is cute, but what were you thinking?"

"I wasn't thinking. Let's get out of here. I'm not thirsty anymore." He moved to stand, but Lucy pulled him to his chair.

"What's done is done. Look, the other day you said this is your new version, so get rid of all the old shit. Flush it away."

The waitress returned, "These are on me. That's the least I can do."

"From what I just heard, it looks like you've done enough," Lucy said.

"Oh, yeah, kind of… never expected it to turn out so bad for you. You know, I thought it was some a prank. Then I heard…."

Lucy tuned in. "Prank, what do you mean?"

Christa bent over and it was obvious she had no bra. Keith avoided her tatas by turning his head. "Sit down girl, or he'll start slobbering over your tits!" Lucy barked as she threw down a shot of tequila. "What prank?"

"Your friend, the Colombian, Carlos, thought it was funny. He got me for your birthday present. I never thought much about it 'til afterward. Needed the money. Back then I had a problem, an expensive problem," The waitress held their attention.

Keith nervously swigged his beer.

Christa continued on almost nonstop, "Yeah, well, I was between jobs and met him at Magens Bay. He hooked me up with some blow to play you along. The other dude was the same thing: supposed to be my husband, boyfriend, or something. Never saw him before or after."

She rubbed Keith's arm. "You're cute and the diving thing was cool. I figured what the hell, some afternoon delight. Then the other guy shows up, making a big argument. And it gets mean… with punches. I'm new and don't know shit. The police were right there, I mean immediate, like they were waiting. Me and the guy walk, but I guess you went through the wringer."

"Slow down," Keith grabbed her wrists, "You're said it was all planned by Carlos, my brother-in-law?

"Oh… I didn't know he was related to you. I thought it was me screwing you; like I said, I was a birthday present. Now I've cleaned up my act. Got into a program. I'm thankful to see you, get a chance to say I'm sorry. That's step number two."

"You stupid fucking bitch," Keith muttered, rose, and turned. In a calmer voice, "Wasn't your fault, you were just the right bait." He walked outside.

"Honey," Lucy threw some money at her, "I better never see you again. Your little joke nearly ruined a good man, a very good man. You're just another coke whore. I know everyone in the Virgins and, believe me, everyone will know what you did. I don't care if you're dancing on the twelve fucking steps, if I were you, I'd be looking for another bar job very, very far from here." She gulped another shot and grabbed the beers as she left.

Keith was standing on the edge of the waterfront, just staring. As Lucy approached, "Can you fucking believe it? They set me up. What the fuck did I do to deserve that?" He took one beer from her and drained it. "Yeah, baby, I'm pretty fucking dumb, about as dumb as they get. Wow, I never saw that coming. Let's go someplace else and have more drinks."

"If that works for you, it works for me," she said, grasping his arm. "Remember what I said about it all being flushed away now?"

"Not quite, Carlos, and all this, wow! Got to think about this, reason it out." He winked, "Drinks always help me think. Come on, pretty woman, I'm already in a better mood. A liquid lunch and then we set sail?"

"Works for me."

Suddenly, a siren screamed, and all heads turned toward the mouth of the harbor. The go-fast boat Keith had encountered tied to the catamaran in Anegada was plowing toward the dock, wailing an alarm. It rode its own wake to the pier and slid broadside as men leaped out.

"Damn, it's not Friday the 13th is it?" he thought out loud. "No, baby, what's wrong? You know that boat?"

He took a deep breath, thinking about everything. Christa had put it all in a fresh and irritating perspective.

"Fuck it, nothing to worry about, just the noise." She tried to drag him away, but he continued to watch the activity on the dock. Even from the distance, Keith could see a stocky black man; the silhouette resembled Agent Jeffers, marching along the dock holding some electronic device. That man directed the other men to one of the cargo transports where Keith had stashed the phone. They ordered the crew off the boat. It was obvious it was being searched.

"You're right," he kissed her hard, "as always. Fuck it, forget it, flushed out. Yep, all my old shit's flushed out. Let's go." Keith grabbed Lucy's hand and twirled her around. "Food, booze, and fun. Been an enlightening day, woman, very enlightening."

"Looks like someone's getting busted," she said as they walked off.

"Who cares, as long as it's not us."

<<<<<◇>>>><<<◇>>>>

It was another beautiful day throughout the Virgins. Dale was honoring his commitment to finish another of George's rentals. After the meetings with both Keith and Josef, he could finally see a speck of light at the end of his tunnel. But he was still stroking a brush and turning wrenches while babysitting Neal, the boss's son.

"Ah, Dale, how come we can't have music on the job? I know my father wouldn't care, and it's proven that listening to music increases productivity."

"Listen," Dale whispered.

"To what? I don't hear anything."

"Neal, that's the point. Quiet. Sweet quiet is what best motivates me, alone with my thoughts."

"Want to share those thoughts? I mean, we could chat. I saw a great program on TV last evening…"

He interrupted Neal. "I don't watch TV and I'm not very talkative. The birds, the rustle of the palms, that's my favorite music." His present dreams of regaining financial security and his freedom filled Dale's thoughts.

A car crunching the gravel of the rental's driveway broke the quiet. "See, if you'd have been rocking out, we'd never have heard the car. These days can't be too careful. Stay here; I'll go see who it is. Probably someone to view the apartment."

Two men were in an open jeep. "You Dale?" The big West Indian driver asked. "Appreciate a word with you."

Dale didn't approach, and then he saw the passenger had a pistol leveled at him. "Amigo, I know you're thinking about making a run. Don't do it," the thin man said with a slight Spanish accent. "We just want to talk. You got time for that, don't you? Make time!"

"Sure, sure, but put that away. Nothing here to steal."

"Steal? Dale, do we look like thieves?" The Latino laughed as he approached with the pistol still aimed. The big man pulled a cutlass from behind the seat and joined them. "You misunderstood. I think you stole something from me and I want it returned."

"Got the wrong guy."

The obvious Hispanic laughed again. "Isn't that what they all say? Call me Don, like Don Juan, and this big hombre is called Hook, because once he grabs someone, they seldom get loose. Dale, are you still thinking about running? It would be better to think about what I'm asking. A mutual friend says you have a quantity of merchandise for sale."

"Fellows," Dale put up his hands, "Fellows, let's take this conversation away from the house." Now he wished music was blaring. Neal would be all eyes and ears. "Not sure what you're asking?"

"I'm not asking," the Latin nodded to the black man, who smacked Dale hard in the shoulder with the broadside of the cutlass. Dale folded to the ground. "No, it's more like I'm demanding the return of something of mine you have. We could play around out here and you would get bloody. You better just agree."

"Seriously, I don't know what you're talking about."

"Last time I hit you with the flat side of the blade," the big West Indian demonstrated against the palm of his hand. "This time it could be the sharp edge. Better tell the man what he wants to know rather than this gets messy." He chopped a branch off the hedge for effect.

"You talked to Josef?" Dale replied. "Right."

"Can't be your stuff 'cause guys I know brought it up and their boat's broke. Asked me to move it since they don't know anyone. They were carrying it to New Orleans, I think. But I don't have it. They just asked me to move it."

The big West Indian cleaved off a bigger branch with one whack of the cutlass.

"Guys, I'm just the messenger. Met them in prison in Florida. We'd all been in the same business and stayed in touch. They'd passed through a few times in the past, said hello and gave me a taste. I'm clean now, done with it. Look, I'm a house painter, but they're jammed up. Figured I'd make a few extra bucks."

"Where are they?" the Latino asked.

"Don't know, honest. Consider the type of business; they didn't invite me. Just like you, they dropped in, told me the deal. Then I went to Josef. Me, I'm out of touch. I'm only the messenger."

The slim one pushed the gun into Dale's belly. "I don't believe you. But I know who sells the product, my competitors. Josef said you were out of business for many years and then show up with a load. Me, I don't believe in coincidences. Months ago, a load of mine went missing. Now you got mucho. See what I'm talking about? Me lost, you got. Just return it. No problem."

"I would if I could. I don't have any way to contact the other guys. I told them it would take about a week to set up the buyers. They said for me to make the connections and they'd meet me. Honest, I thought you were them."

"Hmm, when you say honest, I think the opposite. You could move that much? How much did they have?"

"Fifty keys."

"How much you planned to make?"

I don't know. Hell, I'm stroking a brush and driving a piece of shit car. I'm not a dealer anymore, just trying to scrape a little off the top. A grand a key would have been nice. It tasted like quality."

"You tried it?"

"Sure. Then I went to Jo. He figured we could each make a grand. He has the customers; I have the product."

"Had! I want it! It has to be my load that disappeared. You do not want to fuck with us. Thieves find a painful end," Slim nodded to Big.

In a blink, the West Indian connected the broadside of the cutlass with Dale's lower back, pushing him to the ground. The Latino kicked him in the side.

"Okay, here's what's gonna happen. I do not believe any of this honest story you are telling. I do believe you don't have it, because I checked with your office and they said you took no time off this year. You didn't steal my load, but you know who did. I want it returned. Entiende? I'll give you ten large to set up the meeting."

"Okay, I'll try."

Another kick jolted Dale's body. "Try won't make it, amigo. It's important you understand. Do it and we stay friends. You do not want Hook or me to be your enemy. We don't have enemies. They disappear."

"Okay."

"You set it up fast and tell Josef. He knows my contact. See, isn't this better than a very bloody alternative? Josef said you are a solid guy. This is your chance to prove it, make some points and I'll give you the opportunity to make some scratch, besides the ten."

They left and minutes later, Neal helped Dale up from the dirt. "Who were they? I saw the gun, or I'd have come down. I've got a brown belt, you know. Martial arts teach you to know when to wait. Dad told me you'd had an interesting past. Looks like you have a dangerous present."

"Shut up, just shut up. This never happened; you hear me? They made a mistake, had me confused with someone else." Dale wobbled over and sat on the hood of the Renault, "Please, don't mention this to anyone. I don't need any more problems."

"Don't worry, I won't say a word. Maybe I should take you to the hospital? The thin one sure gave you some bad kicks."

Dale lit a Marlboro was lit and sucked a ragged inhale and coughed. "I'll be all right. Take a break, and then we'll finish out the room."

"Come on Dale, you gotta be hurting. Call it a day."

"Can't, need the money and your father needs this finished." Dale dusted himself off and drank some water. His ribs were just beginning to ache. It was better he kept moving because once he stopped everything would be in pain. "Listen, Neal, really, I never met those people before and don't want to see them again. They made a mistake. That's all it was, a mistake."

Yes, they had mistaken him for a has-been, somebody to push around. Josef and Keith had also mistaken him for a dummy.

"Yeah, yeah, look, we really need to talk. You and Lucy are sailing. Isn't that nice? I'll see you in Coral Bay tomorrow evening," Dale ended the call as he walked into Josef's bar.

"Boss around?" He followed a pointed finger to the outside deck. "We need to talk," Dale interrupted Jo chatting with a customer. "Now!"

They retreated to the office. Dale closed the door. "Hey, it's stuffy enough with the humidity," Josef complained.

Lifting his shirt to show the bruises, "I guess you left out some details?"

Jo sank back in his chair. "You can't be angry with me? You asked me to talk with possible buyers. I mentioned it to the biggest movers. What happened?"

Slowly, Dale dropped into a chair. "I'll tell you what happened; they had me confused. You have me confused. I'm just the middleman here, same as you. I have seen nothing except one guy I know from years ago. Said the boat can't be fixed and doesn't have the cash to buy a next one. He wanted me to help move his stuff. Said he had a load, his words, a 'game-changing' load," he winced as he lit a cigarette.

"Wish you wouldn't do that in here, second-hand problems...."

"You want to talk about second-hand health problems?" He pulled hard and exhaled a cloud, "You're looking at a big problem. Never liked beatings or friends who went behind my back."

"You making threats?"

"No, not at all. Just stating the obvious. So, this Latino,

Juan, said my friend has his load. I know nothing about that. And you could have straightened that out easy enough without me taking licks."

Josef coughed, "Never liked tobacco smoke. Again, all I did was talk with potential buyers."

Dale inhaled again, releasing another cloud. "What's the answer to my question?"

"What?"

"How do we make money off both ends without getting hurt? That's your business: knowing who has and who needs, isn't it? It's a given; both sides are crazy with this white shit. I'm already in pain and that's gonna cost someone."

"What do you want me to do? What can I do?"

"Say I get maybe two keys and you and I move them in pieces. I think I can get my guy to go for that. All you got to do is keep it quiet. Can you do that?"

"Kind of difficult when everyone is watching and listening because the supply line has dried up. But I'll look into it. Give me a day or two. You trust me holding it 'til I move it?"

"Have to, right? No alternatives." He stuck out his hand and Josef gladly shook it. Dale turned to leave. "Nothing else you forgot to tell me? Who's this guy Juan?"

"Juan, I don't know who that is. The major player is a young Colombian, he has a pipeline to the source. His name is Carlos. His load went missing months ago, I guess. I'm really not privy to the details except that he owed some serious people serious cash. Seems they threw in upfront to get a lower cost and a purer product. The ship sailed, so to speak, but never reached. Look, Dale, I'm sorry. Maybe I should have known what to expect. Talking about a seven-digit profit for Carlos. I understand why he's hyper."

"Okay, let both ends have their deal and me and you have ours. Anything comes up, you got my number."

The police had ordered Eddie to move to a street less visible to the tourists, but still easily available to the locals who required his product. The Renault parked and Eddie approached Dale. "You need something?"

"Not in the mood," Dale winced as he pulled himself from the compact car.

"Got something that could improve your mood. I'll guarantee that!" was Eddie's quick reply.

"Come on, it's been a long day; like I said, not in the mood. Wait a minute, you're working out of my doorway?"

"Who says this is your door?" Eddie pulled up his shirt and showed the butt of his Beretta. "Now it's my government-sanctioned office. Got a problem with that?"

"Not really, what are you messing with, Ganja or dust?"

"Can get you most anything, rock mainly," Eddie palmed a few small plastic packets of crystal rock.

"Doesn't anyone snort lines anymore?" Dale asked.

"No one I know. Personally, I don't touch the stuff. Maybe a little taste to be sure of what I'm getting, but I leave that strung out shit for the street people. For an old white guy, you got a lot of questions."

"Been out of touch. Buy you a beer?"

Eddie glanced at his fake Rolex. "Almost time for my replacement. Let me pass along the work and yeah, I'll sip a few with you. You sure you wanna hang with me? People might get the wrong idea."

"Why? We're on a fucking island where the whites are what, maybe ten percent? Why can't I have a drink with a man of color?"

"Them rednecks and the 'Ricans see us as niggers." Eddie laughed, "You got a bit of red above your collar, and with all that beard and hair, you some sort of Confederate soldier?"

"I'm on the second floor. Knock." Dale grabbed his tool bag from the car and climbed the outside stairs.

Ten minutes later, they were drinking in front of a fan at Dale's open bay window. Yeah, mon, this place is heated. How come you ain't got A/C? I mean you one of the bosses making good cash. Should spend some on some comfort."

"How old are you? You make twenty yet? You should know by now, there's never enough money. I work day in, day out, and basically get nowhere."

"White man, I'm eighteen. I'm making my cash and soon... soon I'll have it all together." Eddie took a long pull on the beer and wiped his mouth, "I'll get my ride, and start..."

"Think you'll live that long? Son, you're in a very dangerous business. No one retires, unless someone or the system retires you."

"Do I look stupid?" Eddie was clear. "I know every part of this shit kills. Me, I'm planning on diversifying, you know, starting a business, buying real estate, houses, lying low behind a legal front."

"Then what? Think everyone on this rock doesn't know

who does or did what?" Dale replied as he handed a second beer.

"Sure, but nothing coming my way unless I make it. We don't get no breaks."

"What's your name?"

"Eddie."

"Eddie, this could be your lucky day, if you can keep your mouth shut."

"Hmm`? I'm not a talker, white man, I'm a doer. What you got?"

"Might have a friend who needs to move some high-quality dust. Can you do anything with it? You got any cash?"

"Why can't he move it himself? You setting me up?"

"Nah, my friend has some transportation problems. The dust wasn't for here, but now he's stuck. How much can you come up with?"

Eddie looked around, pursed his lips in thought. "How pure?"

"Pure-pure."

"I can bring ten grand."

"What do you expect for that?"

"At least a quarter el-bee. If the shit's as good as you say, then I'll make a pound out of it. If it's not, then we got problems. I figure white guys get the best of everything, from blow to blow jobs. Me, I just don't want to get fucked. Know what I mean, whitey?"

Dale grinned, "We can do some business. Can't say exactly when I'll have it. Give me a number where I can contact you?"

"Nah, no phone shit. I'm here every day until them in charge say I can go back up on the hill. You heard about the tourist couple killed up there on the steps? Well, that was my area. Now, it's smoking hot."

"Listen, don't come to me, I'll come to you within a week. Here, take another beer for the road. I got to shower and...."

Eddie interrupted. "Yeah, I know," he laughed, "you got a hot date. Okay, partner," he extended his hand and Dale shook it.

"Get a good scale, digital," were Dale's parting words.

It is not heroin or cocaine that makes one an addict,
it is the need to escape from a harsh reality.
Shirley Chisholm

CHAPTER FOURTEEN

Back in Coral Bay, they secured Starlet to the dock, and Lucy was again behind her bar. Keith carried a six-pack and met Dale on the bleachers at the ball field. Both scanned for spies.

"Dale, I'm sorry for what happened, but…"

"But, shit! Keith, your offer of financial freedom has dropped me back into the toilet I've been trying to climb out of. It just keeps getting worse. Here's the down-low; Josef, our old friend, can't be trusted. Can't blame him as he's facing the same goons as I am. Some skinny Latino-fuck named Carlos says what you got is his, and you stole it. He's lost a big chunk of change and isn't a happy camper." Dale pulled up his jersey and showed his bruises.

"Wait a minute, Carlos?" Keith buried his face in his hands for a quiet minute and then sat upright. "Carlos, thin? But there must be a lot of thin Spanish guys named Carlos."

"I can't describe him better than that. Why?"

"In Tortola, I just learned that my brother-in-law, Carlos, set me up for the divorce by paying some coke-head bitch to play me. All this time, I thought it was my stupidity; now I know it was a game. He and Maddy took me to the cleaners. Hard to believe a little squirt like him could move a load of blow."

"They from Colombia?"

"Yep."

"There's your answer."

Keith drained his second beer and stood up, wringing his hands. "Okay, so I've got his blow. I'll square with you. I found the shit on a yacht with everyone aboard dead, dead from greed. 'Rican DEA agents and the smugglers, a guy and a woman."

"And we might be next…"

"All I wanted was a payday for me… and you, break away money. Now I want payback. If you want out, I understand. It's okay."

"Out? How the fuck do I get out now? Keith, even if you'd told me the full story, I would have still jumped at the chance to make some serious cash. Who knew Josef was in with them? I mean, well, I don't know what I mean. I went to him because he knew the players, but I didn't expect this kind of hardball from the get-go. He's more in with them than with me. Now those guys know me and expect an answer, or I'm getting whacked. I do mean whacked 'cause the big guy likes to swing a cutlass. Tell me about these DEA?"

"All I know is the chief agent, Jeffers, tried to pin the killing of his agents out on the yacht on me."

"Jeffers, pot belly, shaved-head, dark as night? That's who framed me. They'd caught some younger guy with blow, but they wanted me because I wouldn't pay for insurance. Back then, insurance was like admitting to the law I was in the business. They had the patsy testify that I sold him the stuff; he walked, and I went down. Fuckers! What's Lucy know?"

"Nothing, and I'd like it to stay that way." "She might become collateral damage."

Keith chewed his lips. "Can't tell her. Not right now, anyway. Let's plan our strategy first. I want to hang Maddy and Carlos out to dry." He gave Dale the details about the phones and his calls from Tortola. "Jeffers showed up quick as shit. They were waiting for that phone. They traced the call, and I mean quick. They were on it in less than two hours. Two hours here is like a New York minute. And the other voice sounded familiar, but the hard-knock of the coke whore's tale muddied my mind, until now. Motherfuckers!" He screamed, "Motherfuckers!"

Dale sipped his beer and stared out at the bay until Keith regained his composure.

"Buddy, calm down. They're all fuckers. No sense blowing a gasket. Jeffers and his gang with badges aren't any better than the supposedly criminals they're hunting. Thanks to you, not giving me all the info, and I don't blame you; I would have done the exact same thing, but now there's no best way since that piece of shit Carlos knows about me. How about you give me a key and I spread it around? I know I can sell off at least a pound quick."

"Yeah, and word gets out, and you're dead."

"So? That's a given. For me, it's either go on the offensive or leave this rock. We get up some operating capital and burn these fucks."

"I might hate them all for what they did to me. I told you, Jeffers tried to pin the boat deaths on me. But I'm not killing anyone."

"Well," Dale rubbed his jaw, "what say, we let them kill each other. Thirty keys are enough to draw them all in."

"To where? And we got to be there, too. I don't want to get killed," Keith answered.

"Got to be a secure location, somewhere we can get out, ahead of all the confusion and mayhem," Dale replied.

"I don't follow."

"Okay, we got three groups, maybe four, or even five, now that I think about it. For starters, your ex and her bro, and DEA Jeffers. Then we got the local Rastas, who hate the spics for grabbing their market, and they're pitbull-mean and well-armed. There's the local corrupt police who don't like Jeffers or the spics as they can't get a cut of their action. The VI cops mainly protect the Rastas. Strength and violence protect the spics. Maybe, just maybe, we could enlist a few good police who could throw a net over the bunch."

"My friend," Keith threw his arm over Dale's shoulder and pulled him close. "You really think there's a straight cop anywhere in the Caribbean? Look, I'll give you two keys if you think you can off it without getting chopped to pieces. But I think you are on to something. We could pull them all together and they probably would kill each other. At the least, provide decent cover for our getaway with their dough. As far as an honest cop, our only hope with that is the FBI. They got an office on St. Croix. But we have to tell them that the DEA is dirty."

"Like they don't know?" Dale pulled a joint from his shirt pocket, took a long drag and coughed, and exhaled a stream of smoke. "Years ago, I found a place up on Mountain Top, bunkers from the Second World War. There had been a half-assed jewel heist in town. The crook rode off on a dirt bike. The police caught up with him, shot his ass dead, and never recovered the loot. Supposedly, he was at these bunkers. I checked them out, looking for the gems. Probably, the cops who shot him stole the loot. But the bunkers are so out of the way, I used them for a stash."

"I must be missing something; I'm not seeing how this would work for us?"

"There are two bunkers separated by a thick wall. Must have been huge gun emplacements. The place is still deep in the bush facing the harbor, just below the condos. I doubt very few locals, even old-timers, know they exist. Who wanders in the thick bush in this heat? Everything that grows wild on this rock seems to have thorns or needles."

"You did," Keith was smiling from the ganja.

"Yeah, well, that was years ago," Dale added. "Couldn't keep any shit around the wife and kid. Rather than rent a place that could be traced back to me, the bunkers worked well."

"You just left your shit laying there?"

"There's something, well, it's a drawer, a big drawer in the wall between the two rooms. Figured it must have been so they could shift ammo, the big shells, for the artillery. Do you remember the red Kawasaki I had? Well, that's why I had it. Throw everything into a backpack and hike back to the stash. Coming and going at night, coasting down the hill. No noise."

"How'd that work out for you?" Keith quipped.

"I didn't get grabbed with any drugs, just that rat-fucker's word against mine, and his stuck."

"What's your plan?" Keith asked.

"Don't have a plan except tell them all where the dust will be, get their money, and let them fight it out," Dale reasoned. "The last man standing gets the blow and we somehow get the cavalry, the FBI, to be there to protect and serve. I may not have paid taxes, but I paid my time. For once, let them bastards do something for me." He took another toke, "Okay, it's got to be fine-tuned, a hell of a lot of fine-tuning."

Keith inhaled the smoke deeply, holding it for several seconds before said, "Damn, weed's strong these days, huh? I remember the Thatch Bay Rastas ran the entire powder business a few years ago. You know anyone?"

"By chance, I just met one of their corner workers who wants to rise up the ladder. Figure I'll let him buy some and front him some more. He'll attract the Rastas selling out of turn, and they'll want to know his source. When we want him to, he'll lead them to the bunkers. With the phone numbers you have, we can give the same info to the Spics and Jeffers."

"Yeah, so how do we get money, a lot of money, and disappear without getting shot?" Keith asked. "All those you've mentioned like to shoot, stab, and hack. We know dead witnesses never testify."

"Let me explain these bunkers," Dale replied. "There are two entrances to two separate rooms, both facing the harbor. Bush covers the entrances on top. In fact, the jungle bush has grown over everything. I only used the east side. The drawer I spoke about slides both ways. The drawer top is open in each room. I guess if one side was out of ammo, they could pass more across to the other room. That kept the ammo divided, so a hit on the west shouldn't blow up the east side. Back in the day, I asked some older Frenchie guys about it. They said the cannons never fired any shots except to test the range and accuracy. That's as much as I know."

"All right, we got to record this deal somehow. Think we can hook up some closed-circuit cameras and record the DEA buying coke?"

"They'd just say it was a sting. But if you really want to, I was at Eglin with a guy who taught me some heavy-duty surveillance stuff. Little Pete Ricard knew his electronics. I can set something up to not only record, but also transmit. I'm positive of that."

"We'll consider the possibility of letting the world know who the bad guys really are," Keith posed. "So, you think they must work with Carlos and Maddy, or against?" Keith pondered, "If they shot the pair of mules on the boat, they're bandits."

"Yes, but if no one caught them," Dale reasoned, "Who'd know who stole the shit? If it would have been me, I'd have sunk the drug boat in deep water, opened the seacocks. The shit just disappeared. If Jeffers' gang got there before you, think they would have told anyone they found the drugs? Fuck no!"

"All of them have the money, and if we're selling 30 kilos, 66 pounds, at the going rate of twenty a pound for ultra-pure, and you certify this shit's never been whacked, that's over a million. Give or take what we sell to fund this operation. We offer it for half. We make four hundred large each. For that number, we gotta take some risks...."

"We'll figure out the math later. I guarantee it'll be worth the effort... but we got to minimize the risks. I don't want to die while trying to have my wife and her brother arrested for holding some blow," Keith calculated.

"Listen," Dale said, "we just started planning; this will take a lot of fine-tuning."

"Where'd you park?" "Behind Lucy's."

"Go get a beer at her place and I'll get you a sample and put it in your car," Keith instructed.

"So, what brings you back to beautiful Coral Bay, St. John?" Lucy smiled as she handed Dale a beer.

"We just returned from a sweet sail, but you know that."

"Yep," Dale nodded. "Just taking a break from heated Charlotte Amalie. Thought about you."

"And Keith. Never knew you two were that good of friends?"

"Old dogs, that's all. I don't know anyone in the present, only from the past. Seems safer. Anyway, enjoy listening to Keithy's survival tales, when I can pull some of it out of him. And that's only after several beers. But you know how that goes..." Dale gave her that grin, the stoned half-smile.

"Where is the boy?"

"I believe he went to your yacht for something."

<<<<<◇>>>><<<◇>>>>

"Si, tío Piedra, todo está bien. Encontré la carga faltante. Sí, creo...no, estoy seguro de que son nuestras cosas... Sí, tío, estoy trabajando para recuperarlo sin sangre. Sí, tío, te haré saber de cada movimiento. No te preocupes, todo está bien. Lo sé, sin sangre. Sí, tío trataré. No, lo haré." (*Yes, Uncle Piedra, everything is good. I found the missing load. Yes, I think...no I'm very certain it is our stuff... Yes, Uncle; I am working to get it back without blood... Yes, uncle, you will know every move. Don't worry, everything is good. I know, no blood. Yes, uncle, I will try. No, I will do it.*)

A deep sigh was Carlos' penitence. He was in a mess and the business was to not get messy. Messy people, even family, were replaced. There was no pension program. Those forced to retire, disappeared.

"This fucking Dale guy, he's who we gotta get, but we can't kill him until we find out where the load is." Carlos muttered to Hook, "All the grief these motherfuckers caused: me losing face with my uncle, stress on my sister, and the mother fucking money! The old fuck wants me to pay twice?! He'll pay, and pay, and pay. You keeping track of him, right?"

"Ah, jefe, ah, not quite. Lo siento, I'm sorry, boss, he wasn't at his dump when we got there. I put a streeter to watch his place. Saw Josef so he'd know to call if the man contacts him," Hook assured.

"Jesus Christ, the man admits he's got my thirty keys worth my six hundred grand and you don't know where he is? You fucking lost him?" Carlos was wrestling with his emotions. He wanted to scream, but that wouldn't be good for his image. Hook was a big part of his money machine, and he couldn't afford to hurt his feelings. "Okay, keep looking and get with me as soon as you hear anything? Entiendes?"

"Si," was whispered.

'Hitman' Meyers and Miles Faulkner were having lunch while chatting about Captain Breezewood's new car when Faulkner mentioned the same officer's new home addition. "Ever wonder how the other detectives make so much more money than we do? Does no one else see that? I know about the free money. Offered and refused. Yes, me-son, offered and refused. Same as you, same as you. We're the black sheep among the department's black sheep." He stated, "We're hired to be civil and to serve."

"Don't get your boxers twisted. That's life, to always want more. But we're doctors trying to burn out society's infection and our co-workers are germs, fucking germs. That was some bullshit in court today. Me and you bust that cruise ship purser dropping off five almost-pure keys," Meyers declared.

"The shit coke comes to court almost cut to ten percent and then half the weight. Fucking forensics had rats? The fucking perp walked away laughing. Fucking Judge throws it out because of the faulty evidence. Whew! I tell you; he walks away laughing at us. And our co- workers, who are supposed to have our backs, hang us out to dry."

"Laughing stock of the island. Channel 5 had its camera at the courthouse. Tomorrow everybody will think we took the powder. Detective Tom Meyers, clown." Hitman looked down at his food and just shook his head. "Pension, all for a fucking pension. You know that's why I became a cop, for the fucking pension. I've got to work twelve more years, twelve more fucking years, to get a pension that pays barely enough money to survive. No matter how hard me and you work dragging in the gutter rats, the gutter rats are gonna win. Then what? You and me get fucking old and this place is super dangerous because of the white powder."

"Yeah, I know what you mean." He pushed his uneaten fish sandwich to the center of the table, "Not hungry either. Yeah, these guys, our co-workers, buddies, think only about themselves, in this moment, not a thought about what type of criminals they're making for the future. St. Thomas is only twenty-eight square miles, a fucking rat cage, and we're letting them run wild; rats are getting ferocious."

"Not me and you," they fist-bumped, "not me and you, we ain't letting them do shit." Hitman's head shook up and down, "You remember how many times these small islands have been the murder capital of the U.S.A.? Per capita, five fucking times. More killing than South Chicago for the only hundred thousand plus the illegals we got here. Nobody cares. Few ever hear that, 'cause it's bad for tourism."

"What do you think, there's another five to ten thousand transient tourists per rock? They're the market for all the drugs. Then you got to add another fifty thousand illegals from the DR and Venezuela. Those refugees have no conscience."

"They the same as me and you, ducking and running, trying to live life."

"Yeah," Faulkner reached, grabbed Hitman's shirt and pulled him close, "We got to watch our own backs. We might be a joke to some, but I got a feeling we are a thorn in more than a few behinds. There's absolutely no one we can trust."

"The only way out of this is the FBI arrests every other copper on these rocks," Hitman surmised as they touched glasses. "Here's hoping they don't confuse us with the scum."

"Not all are rotten, but most. Remember back in '93 when the Dutch police came into St. Maarten and arrested four of their officials for corruption? Hell, they'd have to build a new prison for all the corrupt bosses here." Miles continued after they tapped their beers, "Our only hope is the FBI, 'cause they ain't barne here."

"Carlos, my amigo," Josef tried to hug, but the slim man shrugged him off, "What's wrong? You're gonna get your product returned."

"Hmm, that's still a problem. The old man doesn't have it, or so he says. Can't kill the messenger… as much as I want to," Carlos looked nervous and kept rolling his head as if it were stiff.

"Wait! Hold on, Dale? You can't be talking about snuffing my old friend?! He knows who has it. Live and let live, amigo. Live and let live," Josef said as he reached for a decanter of rum and poured two glasses.

"It's not that easy. The old man is saying the people who have it want to sell it back. I can't pay for it twice," Carlos contemplated. "Josef, you have been here, what, twenty years?"

"Thirty-seven."

"So, you know the ropes. I've been here three and change. Do you know the old man good? What would you predict?"

"Well…" He swigged his rum, "Dale is a stand-up guy. He got railroaded on a bad DEA rap and did all of five years. Refused to cooperate, even though it was all a set-up. If he would have cooperated with the DEA, he would have gotten off."

"You're saying he would never talk where the shit is?"

"No, I'm saying he didn't cooperate then because they framed him for not paying. Now, I'm saying he doesn't know where it is, if that's what he said. But come on, no one's giving you that back for nada." Josef poured another drink. Carlos pushed the bottle away. "Dale doesn't know. See, amigo, that's how it works here. Things are so small on St. Thomas, everyone who listens hears. Can't slide anything by on this rock without word getting out. These guys he met in prison show up with a pile they probably found, if it's yours."

"It's mine. My family has distribution people on every island waiting for someone to bring in a load. In Colombia, they know of loads going out, ten keys and bigger. No thirty key loads went out where they didn't know the people."

"Okay, but it's the old 'finders' keepers, losers' weepers.' Say their boat hadn't fucked up here, you'd never have heard of them selling it off to their own people in the US."

"We'd hear."

"If you say so, but it's the nature of the drug; cooler heads do not prevail." Josef declared and looked directly at Carlos, "Amigo, Dale is also my amigo, and I put you together. I don't want something to happen to him. You must expect that whoever has it, unless they are total asshole punks using the product, will try to stay invisible, get paid, and disappear."

"Josef, why can't you fucking say what you think...."

"Agree to pay and then hijack the money. You get everything and the people, the actual people... who ripped the load," Josef blurted, "without hurting other good people just trying to scrape the deal for a few bucks... like Dale. He's a good guy. You could work with him down the road."

"Josef, you're also a scraper."

"Everyone gets a little; then everyone smiles. You get everything for nothing, just like you want."

"What are you, the go-between?"

"No," Josef gave a slight shudder, "No, I'm not involved. Dale pays me part of whatever you pay him."

Carlos stared; his body cocked with his hands on his hips. "So, you say, get the Bens stacked, grab my merchandise, and then go gangland? That is excellent advice. I appreciate smart advice." He pointed at Josef and smiled. "I came here for what you just gave me. It is seldom I get what I want when I want it in St. Thomas. Everything is always wait, wait, wait, soon come." He patted Josef on the shoulders. "We can work together."

"And Dale?" Josef added.

"If he makes it through this first test, he's in. I can use dependable people. Yes. The downside, Josef, you get what Dale gets," Carlos smirked. "Dale gets a hot nine, you also get a hot nine. The downside of failing the first test is no more tests are possible."

"Ah, I don't see that. I'm cooperating; you had no idea where your shit was until I brought this to your attention. From the beginning, I told you I can't force Dale. I can call him, say you have the dough, and arrange a meeting."

"Do that!"

"Get the money, because he'll definitely check before he takes you to any meeting."

"You know, big-man, I talked with someone, not the old man; someone called me on a phone that was grabbed from the transport. That was after I met your friend. That's the main reason your friend is still breathing. I had friends at the police check and the location where the call originated was Tortola."

Josef sighed long and loudly, "All I know is what I've already told you. Dale is solid, he won't fuck you. You follow my plan and you may still have problems, but you knew upfront that big money mixed with your product can bring out the worst in people."

A chunk of a kilo was hidden under the Renault's spare tire. Dale calmly drove off the St. John ferry and took a right. The late afternoon was almost cool, with an easterly breeze blowing through his old car. Sapphire was the first resort he passed, then Paradise Point, then Sugar Bay, and the immense Wyndham. The road moved away, giving the hotels some privacy from passing traffic.

Traffic slowed as he hit Thatch Bay. It was the only village of old-style St. Thomas that remained on the East End. Everything else had succumbed to development. The rising real estate prices ended neighborhoods and spawned mini-marts, auto parts stores, and fried chicken restaurants.

Cresting the long hill at Old Tutu revealed the island's center with its first mall, Four Winds. When Dale had originally come to the island, behind the mall had been two lakes. A housing development and laundromat that drained phosphates had long ago filled those with weeds. Then the government installed a second mall. Excavating for the foundation, contractors found an ancient Amerindian settlement, which they quickly paved over for the parking lot.

Very little of the intrinsic island beauty remained. What he carried in his trunk helped no one to care. This island and all islands were now only about business. They sold themselves as vacation spots that tranquilized and temporarily healed everyone afflicted by the stress of surviving in the modern world. That stress transferred to the island's population, most living slightly above the poverty level.

Sure, what they were doing, selling a vicious drug, made

the territory more dangerous. Homes were robbed and some family members might disappear, but it was all business from the top of the government down to the welfare recipients. Dancing dust meant money from those who enjoyed being dazed and confused. That brought a smile to Dale's weathered face. Now everyone was in a daze, no longer dazzled. First, it was the exceptional beauty of the sea views melding into a perfect blue sky, followed by the magnetism of the leisurely lifestyle. Then the harsh reality of living on a small island became clear, surviving, living day to day in a location meant only for transients.

Everything was expensive except alcohol. Booze always flowed. Helped to forget that you paid enormous taxes and there were no public services. You didn't want to get sick because you feared the hospital. One time they connected the dialysis machine to dirty water and killed the patients. Firemen only arrived to watch buildings burn, schools were a battleground, and the police... the police are the same as everyone else... looking for a simple way to make money in the tropical sun.

"Well, I paid my dues. Now it's time to cash out and bid a fond, no, fuck fond, just good-fucking-bye to this place. I'll find another much more compatible and a hell of a lot safer place than St. T," Dale talked with himself. He again made a right turn, went across Skyline Drive, started down Mafoli Hill to his apartment before he caught himself. "No man, this is not a smart move bringing product to my place. Those fucking spics got to know where I sleep," he muttered as he made a U-turn.

In the glove box, he still had the keys to George's place where he had been painting. Dale sighed with relief. After the slight detour, he parked at the secluded house and just sat in his car enjoying the serenity. "Yes, I need a place like this, but with a fence and big, mean dogs." He laughed, "Uh-huh, someplace else is calling. Things are gonna get hot for me here real quick."

With Keith's gift properly stashed, the Renault headed back to town. As soon as he generated some money, a new mode of transport would be necessary. Dale chuckled; nah, nothing would be necessary. The Renault was faded white, but Dale had fixed some rust and used a yellow protective primer. Now it stood out on the roads as a mutated ladybug. There was no future for him on St. T. His aim was to escape the rock alive, that's all, and that might not be easy.

It was almost dark when the Renault found a parking spot. Dale watched the immediate area for suspicious people, then laughed, "Can't trust anyone." He cautiously looked over his shoulder and saw his new friend, Eddie, step from the shadows near the outside stairs.

As Dale approached, the young West Indian returned to the darkness and then burst out shouldering Dale's midsection. Dale's already tender ribs got another shot of pain as he reeled, and fell into the doorway. Eddie was on top of him, a pistol pointed at his head.

"What the…?" Dale stammered.

"Shut up! You being watched by that bum across the street. He already asked me about you. If you in trouble, you bring trouble to me, and I can't have none of that. Savvy? Let's make a show so they know I ain't working with you." With that, Eddie rose, gun still pointed, and watched Dale slowly stand. Eddie whispered, "You got my stuff?"

"No, please put the gun down."

Eddie got face-to-face so no one could hear. "I did my part; got the scratch and the scale. Are you fucking with me? Man, who are you fucking with? That street piece is from the DR. Them is soulless; cut your heart out for a dollar."

Straightening with painful groans, Dale looked, but couldn't discern any features of the individual across the street. He coughed and exchanged, "Mr. Ed, I am square business, but obviously we can't do business here."

"Figured so." With that, Eddie pushed a small package into Dale's stomach. "Grab the scale, double over like I just whaled on you. Now you know and I know you're smoking hot. This business is always big-time trouble. There's also a burner in the bag. Call me when you get your shit together. I mean tomorrow." H e shouted so the bum would hear, "Motherfucker, I told you this was my place. Get your white ass down the street." Eddie pushed him toward the Renault.

Visibly nodding with no more confrontation, Dale left. In the rearview mirror, he saw the shadow cross the street to speak with Eddie. Dale inhaled deeply and ached. "Never know where help's gonna come from. Glad the kid is on my side." Dale shook his head, "No, Eddie's only on his own side. Money motivates, only money."

He peeked into the bag at the stop sign and saw the small scale. It was maybe a half-inch thick. "The days of the accurate triple beam are gone forever. Got the first of a few burner phones we're going to need." Dale pushed the call button and in seconds, Eddie answered.

"I guess I must thank you for re-injuring my fucking ribs. It will take me a few hours to get your merchandise. Got any ideas for a safe place to meet?"

"Dump that fucking piece of shit car that says 'the white man is here.' I can get my cousin's ride. Pick you up at Drake's Seat, above Magens Bay, say eleven tonight. You can do that?"

"I'll try." Dale was pondering what it would take to get there without his car. "I'll try."

"Your old white ass better do more than try. We're talking my fortune here and your old ass better keep breathin'."

"I'll be there. Flash your lights."

I'm not addicted to cocaine. I just like the way it smells.
Richard Pryor

CHAPTER FIFTEEN

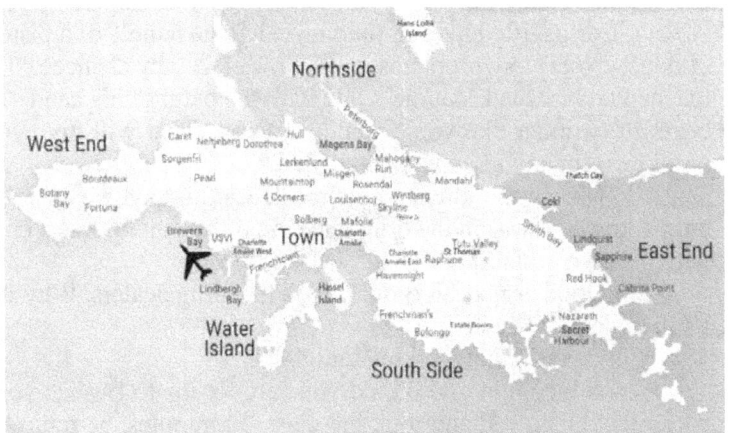

St. Thomas

   The night had cooled, and Maddie was sitting on the back patio. Everything was still, except for the sporadic appearance of bats against the horizon. Long ago she had become accustomed to the bats feeding in the early darkness. Keith told her, 'bats were the rats' Air Force.' She smiled, thinking of Keith and his way with words. He hadn't been such a rotten guy, and he'd provided a means to an end. She wished she could foresee the end of this business.

   "Why am I still here?" Maddie murmured to herself as she sipped a vodka. "I should leave Carlos, sell everything. Fuck it, let the lawyer sell it and send me the cash. Yeah, I'm leaving… this week. Let my brother handle his own mess." Perfectly timed with that thought, the screen door behind her clicked shut.

   "Sister, my beautiful sister," Carlos was almost singing it, "Where, oh, where, have you been my beautiful sister? You sit here talking to yourself? That is a dangerous sign."

   "You sound like you've started early."

   "And why not? We have reason to celebrate." Carlos replied. "I have located our lost load."

   "You have it?" Maddie exclaimed.

   "Not yet, but I know it's close, in St. Thomas. We will get it back. Already spoke to Uncle and by the end of next week, we should be in business again," Carlos paused, "and in Uncle's good favor."

   "Do you want to tell me, or is it all a big secret?"

"No secret. Josef sorted out a connection. It will take some coordination."

"Who has it? They stole it and killed our people? If they're that dangerous, will you be safe?" Maddie asked.

Carlos lifted his shirt and revealed the handle of a pistol. "I don't expect any problems, but I won't take any chances." He reached and cradled Maddie's jaw with the palm of his hand. "A beautiful woman like you shouldn't worry. That will give you wrinkles. Got any more vodka out here?"

"No, on the kitchen counter. Does this involve Josef? I didn't know he was in the drug business. I thought he was a chef with his own restaurant."

"Good drug dealers don't look like drug dealers. Why am I still a waiter?"

"So... you're not working tonight?"

"Took the night off. Would you care for me to freshen your cocktail?" he bowed and took the glass. In minutes, he returned with a bowl of ice and the bottle of vodka.

"The ice will melt, mi hermano."

"Drink fast, sister." He swirled the glass and gulped the clear liquor. "I will set this so right that everyone in ALL the fucking islands will know not to fuck with our family."

"Remember, our family does not like blood," Maddie asserted. "No, dear sister, our family does not like to bleed. Others will bleed..." he caught himself, "only if they do something stupid. But we are all reasonable. Everything will be all right." With that, he reclined on the lawn and hummed the Marley song, 'Everything's Gonna Be Alright.'

Suddenly he bolted upright, rubbing his legs, "Damn ants!"

"Yes, brother, little things have a way of biting."

"Shut up! Maddie, you have been zero help. I'm doing this alone. I will handle it." He brushed his legs, "No little or big thing is getting in my way."

"Our way," Maddie stood and hugged her brother. "I'm with you. I'm always with you. Family is family."

An island to the east, Keith was lying in bed enjoying watching Lucy undress.

"The way you are leering at me, maybe I should have a pole put up here and do some dances for you." She pranced naked toward him.

"Look at this tent." He pointed to the covers, "I've

already got a pole you can dance on. Lay here with me for a while."

"What, no wham-bam?" Lucy giggled.

"Never is wham-bam," he sounded offended. His arms encircled her and pulled her to the bed. "Always with passion." Changing the subject and attitude, "You ever think of leaving?"

Lucy rolled to his side of the bed. "So, that's it? Goodbye?"

"What? No, just asking if you ever feel fed up with everything? I've been burned out with the VI for a while, or rather it has burned me out. You're the only thing holding me here."

"Oh, oh, here it comes. Yeah, me, and your new best buddy Dale. So, you're getting itchy feet?"

"I guess so... but was wondering if you wanted to move along with me?"

She grabbed his shoulders and twisted Keith so they were looking eye to eye. "Who are you impersonating, Keith?" She pulled him close for a long kiss. "Sweetie, everything I have is here. You got a little more than a duffel. How are we going to exist at the next rest stop? Neither of us wants to go back to working for someone else."

Keith exhaled slowly, picking his words. "I have some money. And I think we can get by."

"Suddenly you have money? Working for me as a handyman made you wealthy?" She kissed him again and squeezed the tent pole under the covers. "You've been holding out on me?"

"No," he moved her hand. "Not really. I stashed some cash before Maddie's lawyer grabbed me. We," he stopped and kissed her, "we could travel for a while."

"And who will take care of my bar?"

"Sell it. You don't want to hang out with the last bastion of American hippies forever?" He cocked his head and gave her his best puppy look, "Come on, we get together real good. Time's passing us by. I've been saved, God, yes, God saved my ass. More money's coming when they publish my banana raft story."

Lucy pushed him prone on the bed and straddled him, slowly grinding her hips. "Holding out, huh?" She looked off for a few seconds. "I have been thinking I'm getting old... older. The VI is no place to grow old." She laughed, "I guess I am old, thinking about health care, crime, security. Yeah, this is kind of spur of the moment, but I could sell, probably tomorrow, if I had a mind to. A few of those stock-optioned millennials asked if I was interested in selling. For sure, they would fuck up the ambiance I've worked so hard to create." She slapped his shoulder, and they both laughed. "Where are you thinking of going?" she asked.

He pulled her to him and they settled into a long embrace. "Okay," he offered, "got something to tell you, but," he paused, "I can't tell you everything because that might make you an accessory before the fact."

Lucy sat upright again. She pulled open the end table's drawer, reached in, found, and lit a joint. "Uh-huh, here it comes; you *have* been holding out on poor little 'ole Lucy." She tried to tickle him before passing the joint. "Accessory, huh? What have you been up to with Dale? You plan to rob a bank?"

"No, just settle some scores. You heard that cunt in Tortola say my wife set me up."

"Her brother; she said Carlos set you up."

"And what did he get out of it? It was Maddie, Carlos isn't that smart. Well, I want what's due me."

"You ain't getting shit back, and if you're talking about getting violent, forget me."

"No violence. I have something they want. Something they lost and I, totally by accident, found. Just like bouncing into the waitress who spilled the beans."

"That was long after you spilled your shit inside of her." Lucy playfully punched Keith's shoulder, "Come on, let's make love and…"

"We'll get to that, I promise. But let's clear the air. What I found is contraband. Leave it at that. What you don't know can't hurt you. Dale's gonna market it."

"Big words: contraband… market." After some tokes, Lucy smiled and slowly nodded. "Like illegal contraband?"

"If it wasn't illegal, it wouldn't be contraband." They both laughed. "It's somewhat involved, but sort of big bucks. Serious breakaway money."

"Aha, that's why Dale's been here. He's broke-broke and looking for a ticket to Tomorrow-land," Lucy took another hit and passed the joint to Keith. After a long exhale, she asked, "And this contraband belongs to Carlos and Maddie? How's that work? You hire a detective?"

Keith reached *the* spot between her legs, "This is my ticket. You want to punch it?"

Lucy giggled, "Oh, aren't you sweet; tell me more."

"What I found definitely belongs to Carlos." Keith decided against adding how Carlos had strong-armed Dale. "How much you want for Starlet? I'll buy it so you know I'm sincere and have the dough."

"But if you buy my boat, what am I going to do? How would I leave this place? That yacht is my escape hatch."

"You keep the boat. I own it, you sail it. Haven't figured out everything yet, but if you help, that's all it would be; sail Starlet to St. Thomas and meet us."

"Where? When? I paid forty for the boat. You got that much?"

"Where and when, that's all still a gray area. All I want to tell you is, I'll commit to you. I'll give you eighty large and you hold the title."

Slipping into business mode, Lucy asked, "What, half now, half later?"

"No, all at once. You know me; I am not a trusting soul. But I trust you, and that is the best compliment I can give. In my book, it's even better than those three little troublesome words, I love you." "Do you love me?" Lucy interrupted.

Keith gulped and coughed. "Yes, I guess I do."

"You guess?" Another punch to his shoulder, "Aren't you the romantic!"

"Look, we're old-timers, or rather not old, but we started years ago, and this is where we've reached." His hands caressed her back, "I could give you words, but I would rather spend years, decades, forever, showing you how much I care about you."

Lucy wiggled atop Keith and joined them at their favorite places. Then she leaned down and savored a long kiss. "Well, partner, I guess that's what we are, partners. Can I take that as a proposal? No one's ever proposed to me."

"Yeah, you can consider it a proposal." He thrust as she ground her hips. "But don't start making wedding plans. I figure this will be a long engagement."

She pushed down, swiveling her hips, and reached out and pinched his nipples. "I don't mind if it is long, I like long," she ground her hips again. "But monogamous. Motherfucker, if I see you sticking something else, lawyers won't help you. A SWAT team won't help you! Special Forces won't help you!"

"Okay, okay, I get the point."

"Yes, but please don't keep your point to yourself, from now on." She was panting, "Come on Keith, finish me off." Lucy gasped and collapsed onto him. They were both sweating. Lucy laughed, "You fucking buy my boat, talk me into selling my bar, escaping with you after you commit some crime which shall remain unknown to me… all the while stuffing me with wood." She cradled his face with her hand. "Yes sir, Mr. Gardnar, you are some fucker."

"Hello, hello! Neal, you around?" Dale rapped again.

The door opened slowly. The powerful odor of high-grade marijuana escaped. After a cough, "Dale? Dale? What are you doing here? Please don't tell me there's an emergency and you need me," Neal begged.

"Not quite that. It is an emergency, but a personal one. Got friends coming in and would like to borrow your station wagon. My old Renault chose today to overheat and don't think I could fit two people with luggage into the old girl."

"Girl?"

"Oh, my Renault."

"You want to borrow my car? What will I use?"

"The Renault; I'll have yours back tomorrow evening. Promise."

"Sure, sure. I'm not going anywhere special. But you said your car was overheating? What's with that? I got to keep adding water, or what?" Neal turned and found his keys. "Dale, you feel okay? How're the ribs? When are we working again?"

"I'm all right, a few aches. Ribs will heal. We'll finish the house at the beginning of next week. Don't worry about my Renault. I filled her up with water. I'm just worried about her pulling three plus luggage up these hills. I'm kind of in a hurry; got to get back, clean up my place, and get ready. I'm not a big fan of company."

Neal coughed again. "Want to burn one?" He rolled his eyes and motioned with his head, as if that would lure Dale into his apartment.

"No, sorry, another time. Big thanks, Neal, I owe you one."

"Ah, don't worry about it. Next time, you've got to let me loose on anyone bothering you." Neal gave a slight kick, "I'm into karate big time."

"Sure, sure. I got to go. Like to chat. Another time. Smells like quality stuff."

Neal raised his head, revealing groggy eyes. "Yeah, fantastic. Later, Dale." Neal shut his door.

It was a quick run back to the out-of-town rental apartment. He unfolded week-old newspapers they'd used to mask when they were painting. He got the scale set and tested it with a pound of butter. Each stick registered an accurate one hundred and thirteen grams. Dale washed his face and hands. It had been an exhausting day and was not even close to being over. He slipped on plastic gloves and a dust mask. It was all working out fine, as if it had been pre-planned. Everything Dale required for the weigh-in came from their painting supplies.

Carefully, he took a box cutter and sliced the green plastic wrap on the quarter-brick of cocaine. Dale was tempted to taste it, but declined; tonight, he would need a clear head. Time enough to get blitzed in the weeks after they finished this deal. First, he weighed the Ziploc, 3 grams, and then filled it with a big spoon. He weighed out eight separate ounce bags and had almost a half-ounce extra.

Eddie had ordered a quarter pound. Dale assumed the young islander would be ecstatic with a chance for a windfall, but then, who could believe a white man bearing gifts? Dale laughed, "I'll do right by that kid and hope he makes it to a ripe old age, in his thirties, before someone offs him." That wasn't Dale's problem.

All divisions completed; Dale rinsed again. For ten large, Eddie was getting four ounces and two more ounces on the cuff for good intentions. Dale required Eddie's help, but couldn't let the West Indian know it. Better to pay upfront with Keith's dust.

Their project would need many things. Eddie wasn't exactly on the street, but his ear was stuck to it. Few were more aware of what was happening in St. Thomas' underworld than the street dealers. Keith and Dale required burner phones, closed-circuit sound, video recorders, emergency lights, and maybe a stolen ride. Protection? Guns? This West Indian kid could get it. More important, Eddie would be the face for it all. No one needed to see either Keith or Dale on a store camera. Let Eddie do it without having a clue what he was setting up.

Neal's wagon was almost as much rattle as roll. Dale pulled into the parking area below Drake's Seat early and sat on the wall, away from the car. The goods were in a shoulder bag at his side. He could easily drop it into the bushes fifty feet below if things started looking shaky.

Lights flashed, and Dale waved. Eddie walked over. "You alone?" Dale asked.

"No one needs to know this business," Eddie said.

"Let's talk," Dale almost sounded fatherly.

"Old man, you got my goods or what?"

Dale patted the shoulder bag. "Let's talk. What I'm doing requires some assistance. You could help me."

"What's my end?" Eddie asked.

"More dust. Can you get me eight burner phones?"

Eddie ran his fingertips through his close-cut hair. "No names, totally clean, never made a call. When you need them? What else?"

"As soon as possible with all this. Here's a list. Did you get the ten? There's two extra for your help. I'd like two motorbikes, dependable, and not red hot. I'll don't want them reported stolen for at least a week. Insurance or something? Understand?"

Eddie's phone illuminated the list. "What you gonna do with emergency lights and digital recording?"

"Not your business. I need that." Dale handed back a grand, "You get two ounces for your effort. Use this to buy the stuff. Pay who you have to. No mention of me. Got that?"

Dale thought and continued, "Use your head; don't smile for the store cameras. This ain't gonna be a big thing; my friend is going through a messy divorce. Wife's plugging his best friend. He wants to get it on video. It'll save him a bunch of money in court."

"Gotcha. A wife can clean you out." Eddie licked his lips. "How you want to do this? Where do I drop it off?"

"You got this burner number? Okay, I'll call you tomorrow. You know where to get this stuff?"

"Man... come on, St. Thomas got so many stores selling do-it- yourself home protection devices. Shit, I can probably walk into Kmart and get all this."

They shook hands. Eddie turned to Dale, "I don't know you, old man, but you the real deal. Keep your ass safe. You pissed off them spics."

"I know, I know."

"Who's this?" Keith asked.

"Who do you think it is? Your co-conspirator," Dale laughed. "New number?"

"Burner."

"What's up?"

"Things are moving fast; better get over here. I'm being watched, or rather looked for; I lost the tail. Got things moving; I need your help. What's new on your end?"

"Things are moving here. Told Lucy part of it. I guess I can be over there this evening. I'll take my dinghy around to Red Hook. Should be there about six. You can pick me up?"

"Sure thing. I'm not getting out and walking around anywhere in public now. I'll see you and blow the horn. Look in the upper mall parking lot. Gonna rent a ride. Don't know what it will be, probably a Suzuki Jeep."

"See ya."

Jeffers had taken a seat directly in the full flow of the air conditioner. The barroom was small. Only three other men sat around the table.

"The fucking guy hasn't called back." Agent Mazana remarked, "We found the phone, no prints, no other calls."

"I'll find him, if it takes years. He only got that phone by killing my brother. No way my brother lost his phone and his pistol without a fight." The smaller agent Luis stated, "Santiago was smart. They must have had a…"

"Hey, we'll get him and the drogas." Jeffers addressed them, "Word came down the pipeline that somebody else also got a phone call. Yeah, that boy Carlos has been talking big time, like he's the next Tony Montana." The agents laughed as Jeffers sniffed a few times. "Yeah, well, nothing funny about it. The boy doesn't feel he wants to play our way. Thinks he can get shit in without our help."

"That's what we were trying to do last time, boss, taking off the sailboat. Somehow, somebody else must have known we were going to…"

Jeffers Interrupted, "Pay attention to the forensics. They wiped the yacht clean." Jeffers belted his rum and wiped his mouth with the back of his hand. "It was a pro. I figure he was on the boat the entire trip from Cartagena. Protection provided by the family. Must have heard the shots and jumped our boys."

"But if he was working as security for the Colombians, how come they didn't get their shit delivered?" Luis asked.

Jeffers sneered as he spread his arms for effect, "Amigos, we are the security to protect the Estados Unidos, and what do we do? We go into business for ourselves. Cut out the middlemen, cut out paying for the product, make 100% profit. That's the American way, the ideal business. The government pays all our expenses." He leaned forward, "But we're out the money we took to the yacht for show and tell." He sniffed and wiped his nose. "Must be allergies. That was mucho dinero, a lot of fun times in someone else's pocket. This piece of shit calls back, tell him we'll deal."

"But boss," Luis whined.

"We'll deal... him a losing hand. Set the meeting wherever he wants. We're so strong... on land... that he won't be able to get away."

"We gonna flash the money again?" Mazana asked.

"It is important, we have to show... good intentions. But we'll have sniper rifles and shotguns. No one's getting away this time." Jeffers poured all the agents another drink for a toast. "To Santiago and Rivera, they were buenos hombres, buenos amigos." He grinned with a gold tooth flashing, "I'm looking after Rivera's wife... and kids."

He raised his glass, "To immortality and profit... and the great American way!"

The men cheered, "Immortality and profit!"

Keith had topped off the dinghy's fuel and concealed the coke and money the same way, tied to cement blocks, just in case. He looked at what he had. It wasn't much, but it was all trouble. He'd counted out eight stacks of ten grand each into a paper bag and then walked to where Lucy sat outside of her bar. He bent down and kissed her cheek. "Here, paid in full."

She opened the bag and looked, smiled, and said, "All this for last night?"

He kissed her again. "Just so you know, it wasn't shit talk. I meant what I said."

"Me too," she replied. "I've put the word out to a few of the stock- options up on the hill I'm selling. Said it discreetly, so I won't get too many comers."

"Look, ah, I got to go over to St. T, probably won't be coming back here."

Lucy reached up and pulled him into a tight embrace. "When are we going to catch up?"

"You're the getaway driver, at least for part of it."

"What's that mean? I'm still working."

"You know the north coast?"

"Sure," Lucy answered.

"Figure how long it would take to sail to Hull Bay, what, six hours?" Keith said.

"Give it at least eight, depending on the conditions."

"Smart girl; I know why I like you so much." Keith pulled her close for another kiss.

"Like me? Are we back in grade school? What happened to those three little words?" Lucy mused.

"Just be there and you'll hear those words whispered every day for the rest of our lives."

"Let's say, I'll hear them for many, many years. I like that better." She kissed him hard. The embrace broke, and he never looked back as he walked to the dock.

It was hot. Dale was soaked with perspiration. It had been before daybreak when he started clearing a path to the bunkers. He'd parked Neal's wagon in the condos' lot. Dale smiled; he had keys for a lot of places. Working for George had some benefits. Swinging a machete wasn't new to him, but it got old quick. He was wearing his only long sleeve shirt and gloves, but the thorny bushes had still scratched his arms.

By nine, he'd chopped a narrow path to the bunkers. It had been years since he'd climbed down inside. They were completely overgrown. None of the concrete walls were visible. This area, Mountain Top, was a small area that got more rain than any other section because of the elevation. It was a rainforest on a desert island.

"Just like the Mayan temples," Dale said, "the forest takes over. Let's see if I can get the hatches open." He'd brought a can of WD-40, but chuckled when he saw the first metal plate almost consumed by rust. With a few grunts, he strained his aching ribs and got the metal cover bent straight back. "Yeah, rust never sleeps, not in this climate. I'll get a piece of ply to cover this."

His flashlight lit the bunker's drab interior. The metal ladder seemed to have fared better than the hatch. He tried to shake it, but it remained rigid. Descending slowly, he searched the room with his light to avoid any surprises. It looked as if he'd been the last person to enter and that was over eight years ago.

Dale laughed, "No one walks in the bush in the Virgins, unless they're growing weed." Everything was drab, moldy white, and smelled musty of humus, a combination of humidity, fungus, and rot. Looking around, no one who entered on this side would know there was another 'sister' bunker adjoined. He sprayed the WD on the hinges of the metal door that was the sliding drawer between the two rooms. With a slight pry, it opened.

With a sigh of satisfaction and a few groans, Dale sat on

his haunches. "Okay, I've got gloves, no fingerprints. Throw these shoes away later, no footprints." He sighed loudly again. "This is the big show, our theater. Everything's got to be right. There's no dress rehearsal. I'll tie the lights to the struts over there and run a wire out the hatch. They ought to have enough emergency battery backup for an hour." He rubbed his chin, "Where, oh, where to put the digital camera? The recorder… hmm, yeah, I'll place a transmitter, high up one tree, run a direct wire, and send the shit straight to the newspaper. These mokes would never think we'd be so sophisticated." He laughed at the words, "Gonna smoke their asses. Just got to hope there are a few honest men still left on the local police force."

Carefully bending the bushes out of the way, since someone could notice chops, Dale slowly made his way down the east side and found the overgrown road that had been the supply route to the artillery during World Word II. He nodded, agreeing with himself. It was still possible to sneak a motorbike through the trees that had grown on the dirt lane.

The other bunker, the western half, needed attention. He scaled that side and found the other metal cover. These hinges still worked and with more grimaces, Dale swung the cover back and forth until it moved easily. The inside of the west bunker was better. Not much needed, only the product that would slide through the ammo drawer.

If everything went according to his plan, he'd be outside, holding the money, and Keith would be getting everyone's confession recorded before passing over the dust. Timed right, it would be then the feud should erupt. The DEA would get there first, pass the money, and confess their intentions to the world via wireless Internet.

"We must work on phrasing the questions so they can't say later that they were only on a raid," Dale kept talking to himself.

As soon as Keith got the money, he should be out of there. Dale wondered if they'd hear a motorbike from within the bunker. What difference would it make? The bad guys, all of them, would think there was only one way down the mountain. That's what everyone thought.

The DEA could fight it out with the Spanish. I'll bring up the Don Juan, fucking baby face Carlos, and the fat fuck, Hook, and lead them right to their stuff. The winner of that could deal with the Rastas further down the road. Dale clasped his hands as if he was praying. "Yes, sir, payback is a bitch," Dale's watch showed noon.

"One part's finished." As soon as he climbed out of the west bunker, the cell phone from Eddie rang.

"Where you been, motherfucker?" Eddie sounded impatient. "I've been calling you for an hour. Like I said, one-stop-shopping. I got everything at Kmart."

"Been sleeping, had the phone off. I still got to do a few things. Let me call you later," Dale realized the bunkers blocked cell service.

"Nah, nah, nah, don't want this shit in my cousin's car. Spools of wire, digital shit, man, this load is nothing but questions, and I don't have any answers."

"I'll meet you at Hull Bay," Dale reasoned.

"No. Old man, what you thinking?" Eddie roared, "Ain't no black men down there in Frenchy land. Hell, we'd be a show, everyone be thinking for sure it's got to be something bad going on between you and me. Catch my drift? And they be cheering for you."

The island is small; where could he hide? "Okay, you start work at one? I'll see you at the university parking lot, beyond the airport, as fast as I can get there."

Sometimes when I'm flying over the Alps I think,
'that's like all the cocaine I sniffed.'
Elton John

CHAPTER SIXTEEN

Neal walked out of the Soto Town mini-mart carrying a six-pack. The fat black man who'd beaten Dale was leaning against the Renault.

"Excuse me, I need to get in my car," Neal said politely.

"Your car?" Hook didn't move from against the driver's side door. "Where's the other white guy?"

"What other white guy?" Neal tried to get to the door handle. He looked around to see if the fat man had friends. "Excuse me." In a louder voice, "Ex-cuse me!"

Hook bounced Neal with his chest. "I asked you, where is the other white guy? I know this is Dale's car. Now tell me, or you *will* be sorry!"

"I'm already sorry." With that, Neal swung the bag with the six- pack and connected with Hook's jaw. There was a crunch and the big man dropped, sprawled onto the pavement. "Not as sorry as you." He kicked Hook in the groin. As the big man grabbed his vitals, Neal's shoe connected with the black man's face. Blood immediately erupted from his nose.

Never forgetting his priorities, Neal threw the beer in through the Renault's sunroof. Hook rolled as he winced in pain and twisted to reach the automatic he'd stuffed in his belt. Neal stepped hard onto Hook's hand, grabbed the pistol, cocked the hammer, and rested the barrel against the West Indian's broad forehead.

"I'm looking at you. Look at me." He pushed the pistol harder against the man's head until their eyes met. Tears were rolling from the edges of the black man's eyes. "You crying, big man? Here's the deal, that's my car, it's always been my car. Now, this is my gun. If you want it back, say so now. And I'll give it back to you, bullet by bullet. I'm not some punk. I know my martial arts, don't I?" He nudged the pistol against the man's head again. "Don't I?"

Hook nodded timidly in agreement.

"If I shoot you with your own gun, I'll get off. I took it from you after you tried to rob me. Yeah, you tried to carjack me. Tell that slimy little DR fuck you work for don't mess with us or I'll go Rambo on all your asses. Understand?"

Again, Hook nodded.

Neal got into the Renault and drove away. After driving three blocks, he pulled over and crossed himself. "Thank you, Jesus. You had my back on that one. Whew!" He grabbed a beer and twisted the cap, only to get soaked by the shaken brew.

"Okay, I deserved that." And he drove off.

"Yeah, hello, hello, uh-huh… this is Michael… yeah, the Frenchie." The policeman cleared his throat, "Thought you'd want to know, powder is hitting the street… Yeah, I know, you ain't selling it… yeah, you're welcome."

"A new player means more money for insurance." The policeman muttered, "Probably will be more work for the coroner, too." He took a last drag on the cigarette and flicked it into the street.

It was a beautiful dinghy ride from Coral Bay, around the giant stone cliffs on Ram's Head Point and along the south side of St. John. No matter the scenery, Keith seemed to have a continual private argument brewing inside his head. He had enough money, more money than he'd ever before had in a lump sum. Lucy was a dream woman. Now he had her, the sailboat, money, and everyone was smiling. So, why was he always thinking about revenge?

Carlos, probably with Maddie's knowledge and consent, had positively fucked him. No remorse. For what reason? That's what bugged Keith; why'd they do it? He flashed that their marriage had to have been only a sham. A chance for Maddie to get legal and… *fuck that bitch*… get rich off his sweat.

From Dale's info, Keith had their money and coke, but even that wasn't enough. That's why he was eating another two aspirins. His head was pounding. He had to pay them back, in triplicate. They'd played a game with him, and he'd lost, lost everything, and his self-esteem. That had been the first half of his own private Super Bowl… and he'd had no idea, or he'd have played better, smarter, and kept his dick in his pants.

This, the second half, was about to start with no spectacular half-time performance. Maddie and Carlos didn't realize, didn't know Keith was the culprit, the cause of their coke woes, and set to become the winning quarterback. It helped that

Carlos also royally pissed off Dale with an unnecessary beating. Josef should get some grief for setting Dale up.

Keith slowed the throttle on his outboard. His inflatable was in the middle of Pillsbury Sound between St. John and St. Thomas, looking north at the Cays, with Jost Van Dyke and the Tobagos behind. He fired a joint and inhaled deeply as the light wind swung the dinghy counter-clockwise. West was Cabrita Point with Great and Lessor St. James, then nothing but the blue Caribbean. Keith shuddered; he remembered floating. Instantly, he felt his temper flare.

"Fuckers, I would never have been out there, a fucking castaway, shark bait, if it hadn't been for my lovely wife and her brother." He stubbed out the joint. "Yeah, they deserve what's coming and so does my friend, that prick Agent Jeffers."

Dale was intent on driving when his regular cell phone rang. He didn't look and assumed it was Keith, but it was Carlos. "Hello, hello, anybody there?" Dale pulled to the roadside.

"Old man, you there?"

"I'm here."

"You got my packages?"

"Not yet. I won't ever have *your* packages. Don't you listen? Other people have it. I'm only the go-between. They've been in contact with me. When it's set, as I told you, I'd call," Dale replied.

"Can you blame me for worrying? There's a lot at stake... for both of us. And you disappeared. Where'd you go? Why? You afraid?" Carlos rattled.

"Just waiting for my ribs to heal. I didn't know I had to report to you?"

"Well, you do. Where are you now?" Carlos asked.

After a moment's thought, "I'm on St. Thomas. It'll be easier for me to find you." With a button press, he ended the conversation. "I'll enjoy this, you fucking piece of Colombian shit."

Ten minutes later, the station wagon wheeled into the university parking lot and he found Eddie leaning against a white panel van. Considering everything could be a trap, Dale was wary to approach until the side door slid open, showing several boxes. He backed close, got out, and opened the tailgate.

Eddie stuck out his hand to be shaken, "Got everything you wanted and more."

Dale checked the contents of every box: wire, lights, two digital recorders with cameras, digital transmitter, and microphones. One box had all the phones.

"Got you two fine scooters." "Scooters? They won't work."

"Nah, I mean cycles. Both are 350 Kawasakis. As long as you don't cut a bend the wrong way, no one's gonna catch you, no one in a car, anyway. You still need a car?"

"No, I don't think so. Where's the bikes?" Dale inquired.

"They'll be in Sib's Restaurant's parking lot when you want them there. Hey, check this thing out. I got the Bluetooth speaker you wanted and saw nothing like this voice-thing. What's a voice modulator? The guy in the electronics department said this is the only one he ever sold. Been on his shelf for four years. Wanted to know what I was going to use it for." "What did you say?"

"Kids, a birthday; everything was for a kid's birthday. Lights are real cool, just bulbs alone that hold a five-hour charge. Set them anywhere, and you got plenty of light. You got more of that merchandise?" Eddie asked.

"Sure, you sold it already?" Dale said.

"Sure-nuff, island's dry."

Dale felt around under the station wagon's driver's seat and pulled out his shoulder bag. He looked inside and then handed the bag to Eddie. "Take it all. You owe me ten more."

The young West Indian reached into the van's glove compartment and handed Dale a thick envelope. "Got more?"

"You're being discreet who you sell to?" Dale warned. "Dumb question, that's my business," the young black man replied.

"I mean, if you're the only man selling what everybody doesn't have, you're drawing attention to yourself."

Eddie lifted his shirt, again displaying the butt of his automatic. "So, let them ask me. I'm allowed to have my sources."

"I hope so," Dale replied, "I hope so." He half-hugged the shorter man, "Live long and prosper."

"Hey," Eddie pushed Dale away, "Don't go rainbow on me. I don't run that way." They both laughed. "I'll call you when I need more."

It took an hour of careful turns to sneak back to George's income property. Dale's brain tried to soak in every scene. He'd even stopped at two overlooks and taken photos of the lush views. He was certain; it would be a long, long time if he ever passed this way again. The last couple of years had been tough, but he was tougher, and that hadn't made an enjoyable combination. His thoughts turned to his ex-wife and son. The boy was eight. He'd like his son to get to know him as a father, not a drug-dealing, ex-prison convict. Those thoughts made Dale shudder.

The slammer had been an easy one, if doing time, anywhere is easy, but if this went south, fucking with the DEA and the local police, he'd be spending the rest of his life in Leavenworth. That's if they didn't execute him on the scene. He would have been resisting arrest. And with a nod, Dale assured himself that he would resist. No chance of getting pinned on this one.

After everything was delivered and hidden in the upstairs closet, he hit the bathroom. He deposited his beard in the sink. His bushy head of hair got a serious, ragged trim with a pair of scissors they'd used for masking.

Someone was looking out for him, and many more were looking for him. He looked in the mirror; it had been a lot of years since he'd had a clean face… a pale, clean face.

The first stop was the Wyndham and rent-a-car. He got a new, white Suzuki Jeep. There were many, almost identical, around the island. As he was leaving the rental car office, Dale asked for the hotel's off-season, local's rate.

"Sir, I need to see your driver's license. Okay, for you a queen or a double full? You have children?"

Dale nodded.

"Two full-sized will be $145 a night."

"Done. Three nights. No, just tonight. You're not pressed for space, in case we stay a few more nights?"

"Sir, you'll be half of the occupants."

Dale followed the desk clerk to check the room and then doubled back to the hotel's hairstylists. After they created his new coiffure, he purchased a few polo shirts that further boosted his image. Then, for pain relief, he soaked his ribs in a hot tub. It was almost time to meet Keith. He admired his new look in the mirror. Nodding, "If I make it, this new look stays. If I don't make it, be good for the police photos."

Keith was sitting in the shade of a portico at the upstairs entrance to the small group of stores at Red Hook Plaza. He never noticed the man approaching. "Let's go," Dale said.

"What? Who? Wow, what a change. You really improved your profile, Mr. GQ."

Looking at Keith's scruffy appearance, "Maybe you ought to think about it? Am I difficult to recognize? That's what I'm working toward. Got your brother-in-law and his guys on my ass. It seems like they're n e t w o r k e d everywhere. I changed the car," Dale pointed to the jeep. "We'll keep the top up. We're staying at the Wyndham."

"I guess you struck it rich. I brought these," Keith hefted the bricks in his duffel. He reasoned the best place to hide his money was on Starlet. If things went as planned, he'd have more money and was betting on Lucy to show up. He'd worked out a reasonable plan, but it depended on a tight time schedule. He felt the stubble on his face. "You know, I think you might have a point. It might be nice to look like a yuppie. Yeah, probably would be the smart move." He laughed and put his arm around clean-cut Dale, "Are you supposed to be a golfer? Ha-ha!"

Once inside the rental car, Dale went straight to business. "Buddy, things are red hot." They drove back to the hotel, taking turns explained the various stages of their separate plans. Once there, Keith underwent the scissors and even had his hair dyed darker. His mustache vanished.

After a sumptuous dinner, both soaked in the hot tub. "Wow, that punk really put a hurt on you," Keith noticed Dale's many bruises. "He'll get his. Who'd you off the stuff to? I know lawyers who…"

Dale cut in, "It's all sold to one guy. Let him worry about spreading it out. Before you ask, yes, I trust him. He's got us two sweet Kawasakis waiting. Tomorrow, early, we'll get the stuff and I'll show you the bunkers. It shouldn't take long to install and test everything. Truth, I'm nervous about being in the same room with that much dust."

"We're not getting drunk and going wild. In the old days, we'd have been cutting rails and licking tanned tits. Now, my belly's full, I've soaked for an hour; I'm just about in dreamland. You know, this is gonna work. I can't believe you knew about these bunkers. That's the game-changer. It probably couldn't work anywhere else. We couldn't escape. The bunkers are perfect."

"It's about time some things fall into place for both of us. It's not just the bunkers; Eddie, the young West Indian I'm selling the dust to, appears on my doorstep, literally on my fucking doorstep. Buys your stuff for cash. No hokey shit. Does me favors when he sees me about to be stretched over a barrel. Doesn't take advantage. And Georgie has an empty, secluded house. His son loaned me a car, right when I was in deep shit."

Keith stifled a yawn. "So, you made us some bucks?"

"Twenty large. Used two for what we needed and this place. Got the rest right here. Want it?"

"No, just wondering with all that loot, why you didn't get us separate rooms?" Keith laughed, "No problem, just wondering if you switched teams? Heard prison will do that to a man."

"Shaddup!"

Before seven in the morning, they'd stacked the boxes on the Suzuki's rear seat.

"Damn, I wanted to see the sunrise. I try to make it a habit; say my prayers," Keith said. "Got into praying when I went overboard. Every day I was awake, waiting for the sunrise, and solemnly prayed to be rescued. It worked. Been trying to keep up the practice. Missed a few, though, because of Lucy."

"Luscious Lucy, still luscious?"

"You'll never know. Yeah, a new brand of luscious, slightly subdued, mellowed with age. Just slightly, the way it's supposed to be. She called while you were in the shower, sold the bar. She should have the deal done tomorrow. When she sets sail over to here, that will start our clock ticking," Keith reported.

"What? Wait a minute; she's what? She's selling her bar? That's a shocker. What's she planning to do?" It surprised Dale.

"Sail off into the sunset with me, what else?" Keith grinned.

"Oh, you're smooth, really the original Mr. Smooth." Dale still winced from pain, raising his arm to mess Keith's new haircut. "Okay, here we are, almost to Mountain Top Condos. Grab a box and a backpack. Head in here," Dale pointed. "Be real careful when you enter. Try not to trample the grass down. Don't want any signs people might see; attract attention."

"Who the fuck are you, Hiawatha?" Keith joked as he carefully tiptoed off the road with his arms and back loaded. It took only a few minutes walking straight to realize that no one had been in the area. He put the box down and waited for Dale's signal so he could find the bunkers. A shrill whistle brought his eyes up as he tilted his head more and more. His partner was standing directly above him.

"Wow, talk about natural camo. I couldn't even see the concrete for all the vines and roots," Keith whispered.

"Come around, carefully," Dale replied. Keith cupped his ear to hear. Dale pointed and met him on the east side. "Here's the entrance. Put these gloves on. Don't scratch yourself, no DNA." He reached into the box he'd brought from the parking lot and switched on the bulbs they'd charged overnight in the hotel room. "Cool, huh? My man Eddie found them at Kmart. Can you fucking believe Kmart in St. T has these? No wires necessary." He pulled out a roll of duct tape. Take your time going down. Wait 'til you see the lights."

Keith concurred with a Phil Collins sing-song voice, "I've been waiting all my life."

Dale grinned as he taped one bulb under the top of the ladder. Then he stretched out and saddled another on one of the many pipes that ran along the ceiling. "Come and join me."

"Wow! Hard to believe these buildings are just rotting up here and no one has figured how to make a buck off them. Me, if I'd have known, I'd have bought them and built a house on top. Brick up the front gun slots and you'd have two big cisterns." He looked around and pried open the sliding drawer. It was a big steel box, eight feet long and two high, that slid on rails. He sprayed the tracks and worked it back and forth. "Wow again. Perfect. Steel on both sides so no one can shoot straight across, even if they pull the drawer out."

"Look," Dale pointed to a lever that locked the drawer from moving. "Push this and your side's sealed off. Figure they had to move artillery shells and couldn't afford both sides exploding and losing both guns if one side was hit. All right, let's get this show on the road."

They mounted the cameras on the floor, tilted up to view the room's center. Hard wired along the baseboard through the drawer, only about a foot of wire would be visible. If the DEA agents saw the wire by that time, the cameras will have already transmitted their performance. The local newspaper, probably their radio and television station, and the US Attorney's office would get every second through the all-powerful Net.

Instantly, it'd be sent to the cloud.

"Ever see the movie 'Enemy of the State' with Gene Hackman and Will Smith?" Dale asked.

"They blow the cover off a Washington scam? Lots of electronic stuff? Yeah, I vaguely remember it," Keith answered.

"My roomie for most of my time on government vacation

said he was the electronics coordinator. Petey Ricard taught me a lot. We can expose all these assholes who pretend to be crusaders and upright citizens. They're certified greedy fucks ruining everything under the guise of justice."

"Buddy, I think you're going a bit overboard," Keith offered. "Yeah, maybe, but we get paid while we give payback, our own justice... of sorts. We can put them on TV!" Dale exclaimed.

Dale's five-year stint had also been an internship of modern surveillance electronics. His professor, Little Pete Ricard, had caught the brunt of the system for designing a handheld device that could read home security codes. It was a mega improvement over Ricard's gas pump/ATM remote card reader. Little Petey had cost the system some serious money. He designed a new remote reader that made most home protection systems vulnerable to invasions. Middle America wanted Pete's blood. The insurance companies wanted him crucified. The court gave him life plus fifty as an accomplice in countless robberies, identity thefts, even a few murders. They didn't permit Pete in any room that had a computer, or near a cell phone. He was more than happy to explain how to beat a system he could no longer access.

Little Pete had taken to Dale. They were cellmates and Little Petey never shut up, talking, always talking. Dale was a practiced listener. Lots of diagrams later, he'd learned a lot. Old Dale may have been his moniker in the slammer, but he came out a new and improved version after learning a bundle about state-of-the-art criminal electronics from his roomie.

The hardest part now was climbing as high as possible on the brilliant red flamboyant tree to install the transmitter antenna. It was okay. Keith offered and took the thin cable up about forty feet. From the top branches, he could see the big, red roof of the Federal Building just below Bluebeard's huge white wall. Keith used tie wraps to hold the transmitter firm to the tree trunk. The plan was for Dale to continue setting up the recorder and transmitter. Keith would take the rental car into town and hopefully receive a transmitted message.

"Keith, it will take me half an hour to set up the batteries and inverter to power everything. What do you think? I'm wiring these lights to blink when I hit this," he pulled out a garage door opener. "Unless they clean out my pockets when they search me, and we know they'll search for weapons, I pop this and the lights flash so you know that I'm up here with Carlos' gang."

"Well, I think you're an evil genius," Keith gently tapped

Dale's shoulder. "No, buddy, this is about as good as we could make it. I'll stop and get burgers."

"Don't," Dale argued, "don't go anywhere you could be recognized. We can't take the chance. It's okay at the hotel 'cause we don't know anyone working there. You never know who you might come across at a burger joint."

"Speaking of which," Keith pulled out a long roach and fired it up. "Two tokes and I'm gone."

The electronics finished, Dale surveyed the scene, deciding how the foot traffic would flow on the day the deal went down. About midway from the road to the bunker was a sharp, spiny wild pineapple. He looked into the sack Keith had brought and found a plastic bag with an automatic pistol and a 'fucking' Uzi wrapped in oilcloth. He placed the 'surprise package' under the barbed leaves. It was a necessary insurance policy.

"Yep, everything worked like a charm, look," Keith said after meeting Dale in the Mountain Top parking lot. "It never dawned on me how cell phones, the new smartphones, make crime so easy. In the old days, we'd have had walkie-talkies." He lit the roach as soon as they ducked into the heavy bush at the roadside. The first five feet of their trail to the east bunker had not been cleared. Keith's untrained, and somewhat stoned, eyes couldn't find the entrance.

"Hey, watch it. Be careful, this is important. Don't trample anything; we don't want anyone to notice something out of the ordinary. Fucking condo owners walk their dogs down the road." Dale looked around and pulled Keith into the bush. "You got a good reading in town?"

"Here, look. You came across clear, with enough light. Wow, those tiny cameras are really something. And the mic picked you up, even talking low. It was a good sound check. If you feel this area's ready, what's next?"

Dale found the recorder and transmitter in the west bunker. Using his phone as the keyboard, he erased what they'd sent. Then, he typed in two Net addresses, the Island Guardian office and the U.S. Attorney's Office. Waving his phone, "All you do is hit this once and our enemies are all cooked. This is bigger than just the VI police, this is the fucking DEA."

"Remember when the Guardian did the series on corruption?" Keith mentioned.

"Yeah, easy to believe that got a Pulitzer about where all

the street guns came from. Not much has changed," Dale agreed.

"Remember the cocaine rats in forensics?" They both laughed, "Yeah, the rats were so smart they learned how to put a heavier cut on the confiscated dust."

"Yep, *they* guard and protect," Keith bantered.

"Only their own asses." Dale arranged the electronics and covered them with plastic, before heaping on some branches and leaves.

"You sure this will work?" Keith questioned.

"Yep, all you have to do is pull off the cover when you get here so it will accept the phone as a remote control. You must have the phone outside, at least at the opening, so it will connect. Don't forget that," Dale outlined.

"Better make a written checklist of all I gotta do," Keith replied.

"Just that and always try not to break down a path. We don't want anyone to know about the other bunker. I lead them here and send them down. You know they'll have one stay above to keep an eye on me and the money. It's a given, they're gonna try to rip me off and probably kill me," Dale sighed.

"So?"

"Can't let that happen," Dale returned. "I'm gonna have a pistol," he pulled the one Eddie had supplied from his belt, "Right here." And placed it close to the east opening. "We ain't playing, this is serious business, life and death stuff. The machine gun you brought is over there."

"Thanks for thinking ahead. Where's our escape route? Fucking hot day, huh?" Keith looked at his watch. "Past noon. Where we headed?"

He followed Dale carefully down the east side of the bunkers to a level that Keith recognized as once being a cut line, the road probably was used to build the bunkers. The trees that weren't bulldozed to make the road in the early 1940s had grown tall and produced enough shade to restrict the growth of competitive shrubs.

"We park your bike here," Dale pointed, "Mine's gonna be up top. I'll take my chances going down the paved road and around Four Corners, down to Hull Bay. You can coast quietly on this grade. Look, hardly anything except tall savannah grass."

"Where's this come out?"

"Keep following."

Keith walked cautiously to be certain there were no ditches, rocks, or fallen trees blocking the route. He timed the walk. The path opened to a driveway.

"Where's this?" It had taken them eight minutes of careful walking. On a bike, it would be half that."

"Upper Solberg. Come on, you know where you are. I know St. Thomas like the back of my hand. All you have to do is ride down and cut across. Traffic shouldn't present a problem to a cycle. We'll drive around and I'll show you. This is another of George's properties." Dale winked and slapped Keith on the shoulder. "Being the maintenance man has its unknown perks." He laughed, "But obviously not as good as floating around on a banana raft."

"Damn," Keith took a knee, "now we gotta hike back up."

"Thought you'd be in great shape after your survival drill and all the calisthenics Lucy must put you through," Dale laughed.

"How are we getting the cycles here?" Keith said as he rose and started walking.

"I told you, that's George's house. We park them there until that morning. I pick up one and ride it here and you follow with the car. Then you bring the one you'll use. That way we can see how good they are. Don't want them breaking down. Both will have full tanks."

"With that much fuel on this tiny rock we can go around, maybe four times," Keith guessed. "Let's hope there's no car chase. You got your exit planned?"

"Pretty much, go down through Soto Town and get into the Crown Bay area. If they're behind me in cars, the traffic at those lights will hold them back. I'm gonna hotwire a powerboat and take it near to Crown Bay, but not in the marina where it could be found. Thinking my dinghy would work, but if a bullet hits an inflatable pontoon, the chase is done. Here's what I'm thinking…"

They continued chatting and working out the details for the rest of the afternoon as they drove to various places around Charlotte Amalie Harbor. Even with their new, millennium yuppie look and spiffy tourist attire, they were very discreet in their movements.

There's no happy ending to cocaine.
You either die, you go to jail, or else you run out.
Sam Kinison

CHAPTER SEVENTEEN

"Do you really believe you'll get our load so easily, without paying for it?" Maddie asked as she reached for the bottle of vodka.

"Oh, it won't be easy or free for the motherfuckers who want to resell it to us. I'll show a good, smiling face and let them believe they'll be rich," Carlos lit another thin cigar. They were sitting around a table on the patio viewing the pristine, undeveloped island of Hans Lollik.

"Move your chair from here. You know I hate the smell of those shit sticks you smoke," Maddie ordered. "What will happen? You'll kill them? Then we will be murderers." She slugged her drink. "Why not just pay them and finish it? You know, the cost of doing business?"

"Yes, dear sister," he blew a smoke ring. "It is exactly that; they will pay dearly for doing business with our family, for trying to fucking rob us! We can't let them have a peso, not a fucking peso. Everyone will know and respect our family."

"So," Maddie stared at her brother, "your plan is to regain respect by killing them, so others must know. 'Others' means witnesses, means legal troubles. Are you so stupid to think this can't come back to us? Pay them, please, just pay them."

"Dear sister, lately you've been draining a lot of vodka bottles. Don't worry, leave everything to me. My men will dispose of the evidence. Without a body, how do they say it; without a body, there is no crime." Carlos' face tightened and his eyes didn't move from the horizon as he spoke. "I worked hard to set up the distribution. And, Maddie, you did your part, but this is not up for a vote. I am in control." He reached and gently clasped her hand. "Don't worry. Leave it to me. You're completely out of it. That's the way we have planned, and it has worked so far. Right? Come on, Maddie, smile."

"There will be no loose ropes or… strings, damn… whatever! I wish I was back teaching. Life had so little stress then." She refilled her glass with ice from the rapidly melting cubes in a bowl. As she lifted the vodka bottle to pour, Carlos grabbed her wrist.

"Sister, drinking this much, even a glass of vodka before noon, can be dangerous. Wait, this is number three? It may make you feel better now, but later, it could become a problem."

"Fuck you," she wrenched her arm away. The bottle slipped from her fist and shattered on the tile floor. "Damn you!" Maddie sobbed. "Life was so easy in Santa Marta until they talked us into this. Why don't you just pay? I don't want to be part of killing people. Bringing in drugs is bad enough."

"Calm down." Carlos rose, walked behind his sister, and began massaging her neck. He bent and came close to her ear and continued the massage. "It's easy. I've sorted everything out. There's one old guy who brought the deal to Josef. He's afraid of me. They are all afraid of me," Carlos paused and flicked away the butt of the cigar. "Since he's afraid, he will bring the men who stole it from the catamaran. Then they will all be quiet, very quiet."

Maddie was softly sobbing, "I don't know; don't you worry about your soul? Killing people? We were raised in the church." She slouched forward to the tabletop, still sobbed.

"A week from now, we will have our product. Maddie, please don't drink anymore. It's best to keep a clear mind." Carlos caressed her shoulders. "You are my sister; I won't permit anything to happen to you."

He continued, "Take a shower, no, soak in the tub. That should sober you. I'll be back this evening and we'll go out to dinner. Okay?"

Maddie made a semblance of agreed without raising her head from the table. Carlos looked at his phone as he walked to the driveway.

In Coral Bay, Lucy was sitting on the dock with dangling legs staring at her sailboat. She slowly sipped a rum punch as she chatted with her boat, "You know, Starlet, honey, this is what we've always planned for, dreamed about for years, busted my ass for, and finally, it's here. I got a decent man and a break-away chunk of change. Yeah, we can sail into the sunset, uh-huh, no more drunks to deal with, unless it's us. Girl," Lucy stroked her boat's teak cap-rail, "I'm done with smelling tobacco mixed with stale beer, mixed with sour sweat, and all the dumb shit conversations you gotta make to play nice."

She looked up at the blue sky and smiled, "Keith's a decent guy; I believe his eyes have finally stopped wandering. But me and him, we can wander the globe, you too, girl. You'll finally be the star of many a home movie," Lucy gave a tipsy giggle, "and not porn this time."

"Yeah, Keith must have quite a pocket full of fun, to dole out eighty big smackers for you. The tabloids must have really liked his survival story. Yes, my dear, he paid about twice your going rate, but you're worth every penny. Getaway money. I know you've been sitting, tied to this dock, patiently waiting for a handsome knight to sweep me off my feet and sail where the wind's blowing you. No destination known, until we find it."

Lucy took another sip and lay back on the dock, looking at the fluffy clouds. "I hear you, there's always a hitch. But we got our money and I still have you. No papers signed over. I must have either given him the best sack time, or he hasn't had any pussy in… well, forever. Ha!" She laughed, "Odd though, a guy like Keith, who took so many lumps from his bitch wife, just forks over stacks of crisp Franklins without a receipt." She wrinkled her face at the thought, but it broke into a grin. "Not my problem. You and me, girl. Tomorrow I'll have another chunk, almost half a mill, but if shit starts to stink, or the wrong stuff happens, we are gone. G-O-N- E, gone."

"Now, revenge is his prime motivation. The Colombian bitch and her brother deserve something for trying to crush a man like Keith. He'll dish it out and we'll disappear. The misfortune coming to them will be my good luck."

"He got you ready to go before he left. Tonight, I'm packing. Tomorrow, I sign some papers and hand over the keys. Let all these alcoholic, old tie-dyed flower children make their own drinks. Fuck them. Hey, that's a fantastic idea. I'll have a pour-your-own going away party. It'll be like the old Poor Man's Bar. Yeah, I'll just have ice and plastic cups. Let' em drink 'til their livers explode, or they finish my liquor stash."

Lucy laughed and then closed her eyes. "Yes, Starlet, this is our big break. We worked hard for it."

Eddie rounded the corner, headed to his doorway sales office when he saw the two Rastas get out of a white Escalade. He knew who they were, Thatch Bay Posse collectors.

"Fellas, what can I do you for?" Eddie held his hands up in friendship, and to let them know he would not pull a pistol. "Everything's good?"

The two dreads grabbed an arm each and dragged Eddie into the doorway. One turned away to watch the street while the other quietly stood looking at Eddie.

"What? What you got on your mind, bro? Everything's good; my money's up to date," Eddie rattled.

The Rasta smelled of high-quality skunk grass. He coughed, "Edward, it's always about the money. Word came to the boss; you selling more than he's supplying." The Rasta was tall, over six feet, and dwarfed Eddie. His dreadlocks draped to below his belt. "So, where's it coming from? You working a side job with the Spanish?"

"Not me, never," Eddie swallowed hard. "Hey, ah, a white man, living 'round here, saw me and laid a package on me. Fronted it. Couldn't say no."

The tall man shoved Eddie further into the corner. "Come on, nigger, ain't no white man gonna front shit to a little street dude like you."

"I ain't lying. I know it sounds strange, but he isn't the law. I checked him out. Old fucker paints houses. Says he found it. No shit, well... some friends of his found it... floating, I think. Can't fault me for making a few bucks. Wasn't enough to make any noise about."

The dread cut him off with a forearm pressed against his throat. "Everything makes noise, me-son, and we hear every fucking little peep that happens on the street. You sure he ain't Spanish? Doesn't matter, you owe the boss. Can't be selling shit on his corner and not pay the fucking rent, Eddie. You ought to know that!"

"Man, come on, give me a fucking break. I'm a lil' mouse just trying to make some cheese."

"Boss wants a grand. Be happy I ain't making an example out of ya."

"I don't carry that on me. I don't want no problems with you or the big man. I'll have it tomorrow."

"Now you sound like a Spico with that tomorrow shit, mañana, mañana. What you got now?"

Eddie pulled out a small wad and peeled off five hundreds, which the tall dude snatched. "Tell you what, Ed," the Rasta sniffed, "that white man's product good? Got any samples?

Heard you was selling powder, not rock. That's what got back to us. Boss knows what he's supplying."

"Sure, here, try this. People who ain't got rock, got no problem buying dust. 'Bout the same quality as Big Man's." Eddie took a deep breath, "I might set something up, move some of the white guy's stuff to the boss. Sounds like the old guy has nowhere to off it. And he might have a few keys."

"Keys?" The Rasta perked up. Still, with his arm against Eddie's throat, he tapped a bit of the white powder onto his thumbnail, bent, and vacuumed it up his nose. The tall dread closed his eyes. "Hmm," he sniffed again, "not bad. Where's the white guy's crib?"

"Don't bother, he ain't got it. He fronted me two ounces. Said that's a sample. I might be able to get him to bring more."

The dread relaxed and moved away. "Uh-huh, set something up. The boss been trying to find some. Don't know why, but shit drying up. Even the Spicos ain't got much. Maybe," the tall man laughed, "we can make a sweet deal. You'll get a piece and…" he backed out and nudged the other Rasta to the sidewalk, "we'll all be happy, 'cept the white guy. Have five more Bens tomorrow… with some info."

Eddie rubbed his face and neck. "You know me, anything I can do for the posse." He watched as they drove away. "Motherfucker! Can't make a fucking dollar. Fuck you, fuck Big Man, and fuck the posse! Fuck all of ya!" He saw a client stumbling toward him and he slipped back into the shadow at the doorway.

Transaction completed, he dialed the burner phone he'd given Dale, but got no answer. He left a simple message, "Got money for you."

The short West Indian looked at his surroundings. His eyes saw decaying old buildings, and his nose smelled more rot, the essence of the side streets of the tourist town of Charlotte Amalie. "See me," he quietly said, "see me, right fucking now, I'm moving up and out of here. Ya wanna rough up a number-one salesman, then you don't know how to run a business. Think I'll run some business right up all your asses."

The bathwater was as hot as Dale could take it. Adding to being roughed up, chopping the bush had caused more than a few sore muscles. He sipped a rum on the rocks as he chatted with Keith, who was resting on the balcony. "I could get used to this."

First, we got to detail this plan down to the minute. Lucy called while you had the door shut, taking a dump. She's selling the bar. Supposed to close tomorrow afternoon. That's super-fast. I believe I've motivated that woman. Figure she'll be royally hungover tomorrow night. On the next day, she deposits the money and one more to sail over here. We meet her and the clock starts," Keith outlined.

"Sounds reasonable. Think she can sail it over here alone?" Dale asked.

"Already checked. She says yes. But how about you helping her? That way, you two show up at Hull Bay and have a beer at Pierre's. Think anyone would remember you? You call me and I'll be there."

"Never know who's hanging around. They might know Lucy?" Dale answered.

"So, you're a couple. That's the other side of the island. We've almost got all the fine details worked out. It's a given Jeffers and Carlos are waiting and will jump as soon as they get the call. I'm sure they each have their plan worked out how they're gonna rob and murder me."

"And me, don't forget, I'm the visible one," Dale added. "You call Jeffers, I call Carlos, you call the local police, and I call the Thatch Bay Gang. Remember, gloves at all times. No cuts, no blood, no DNA. We got the cycles in place. My time to Hull Bay is fourteen minutes, screaming, careful on the turns, but screaming."

"Yeah, I'll leave the phones on... so even those dumb asses can track 'em. My time's nine to the Crown Mountain Road turnoff, but thinking I'm going to Lindberg Bay, by the airport. Found a nice twenty- four foot with a one-fifty horse motor. Watched the guy pull it into Yacht Haven Marina yesterday. Figure I'll grab it just before dawn on *the day*."

"D-Day?" Dale finished his rum and chuckled, "little trite, buddy."

"No, *the* day." Keith carried the rum bottle to the tub and refilled both of their glasses, "Ain't you styling, bubble bath and all." He closed the toilet lid and sat. "The only single point of failure for me is if someone grabs the boat. I figure it'll be there four hours at max. VIMP – Virgin Marine Police won't be awake yet. Too small of a deal for the Coasties, *and* the police… they don't look for shit that's outside their air conditioning. I'll be dragging ass when it is all over. It'll be a long day."

Dale clinked his glass against Keith's. "Partner, let's pray it is a long day and not the last day." He took a long swallow. "No problem, I'll help Lucy sail over. You want me to bring her here?"

"No way! Keep her on the boat. I don't want her associated with this at all. If things go sour, you have your set of cash. You know the plan. You'll get the ID from Fredrico?"

"Yeah, I'll meet him before he closes his bar. Says he's got a shirt and pants for me, too. I hope they fit. I gave him your sizes. He knows everybody on the cruise ships. Freddy lets them have a few drinks for free to help me out. I never mentioned you."

"Great, keep it that way. What else is on your agenda for tonight?" "My new West Indian best friend-dealer says he needs to chat. I'll sell him another two ounces. What do you think, let him know about the program tonight… or is that too soon?"

"Nah, don't fill him in; he only needs to know the story. You are middling the shit and will tell him where the meet is early that morning. If he's a greedy little fuck, he'll be ready to go."

"When you want me to go over to St. John? We still have a few things to complete."

"Tomorrow you and me will tie up as many loose ends as possible. The next day, I'll drive you to the ferry and then I'll come back and finish all I've got to do. I'll probably meet you at Hull and pick you up. Let Lucy stay alone on Starlet for that night."

"She got any idea what's going down?"

"Not really, she knows revenge is coming for Maddie and Carlos and she's all in for that. Should have seen her light up, red hot, when the waitress in Tortola told how she played her part. I thought Lucy was gonna cold-cock her." Keith smiled, "Lucy's one of the few good babes. Should have married her way-back-when."

"Could have, would have, should have; probably wouldn't have worked out… then. Now's the right time. You're tame, and so is she. The wildness has run out. Know what I mean?" Dale philosophized, "You'll both have enough cash, and be sort of on the same path."

"Sort of? What's that mean?"

"Keith, you have no idea where you two will go, just going together, and that's enough… same with me… I'm seeking a breather; you know, take a break. First, set the wife and kid up. I should have enough to move to some Spanish-speaking country, rent a piece of a beach, a boat, and a woman." Dale's voice changed, "Me, truthfully, I'm hoping to squeeze out a few more years in a country where it doesn't cost much to live in style."

They touched glasses. "Here, here! Get your ass out of that tub before you shrivel up like a prune. Let's get some dinner."

"Yeah," Dale rose as Keith took the bottle back to the balcony. "We'll keep running over the scenario."

"Sure thing, work out all the tiny, little bugs," Keith kidded, "Until we slur our words. Yeah, serious business; keep at it until there's no gray areas."

Dale was toweling, "Don't know about you, but I'm thinking of the two dark brown jug areas of that cute cocktail waitress."

Keith laughed, "Son, if that's what moves you, my advice, get a room, another room, so I don't have to listen to all the moaning."

It had been a long week for Miles Faulkner, and not enjoyable. They had called him and Meyers to investigate two shootings that indicated tensions were building between the local drug gangs. He sat at his desk rubbing some menthol cream into his temples while Meyers filled out reports.

"You know, Hit, if there wasn't cocaine, we probably wouldn't have shit to do. Three shot, one critically, and one dead. Two witnesses who might as well be blind." Miles wrung his hands as if trying to wash them of all the dirt he'd seen. "No one used to get killed over grass. Now, they all want to be gangsters, like in the movies. In fact, if it wasn't for those fucking movies, it would be a lot different."

"Miles, you're preaching to the choir. Fucking Hollywood; they probably sell bullets and automatics on the side. Now every dumbass wants to be a corner boy than pump gas. Oh, I forgot, that's all self-fucking-serve now. Get a gun and hustle, that's all they aspire to. No one wants a normal life anymore."

"You've lost track of the times, me-son, their normal is wiping up blood and bandaging relatives." Faulkner was exhausted, "None of these numbnuts make the right choices until they've had a near-death experience with a bullet or a cutlass, or one of their close friends bites it. Sad, but they all got hard heads."

"Look at the scene today: the whole family having a barbecue and out of nowhere comes a drive-by. POW, POW, POW! When we add it all up, this ain't no paradise; this is a war zone, no different from the Middle East." Hitman surmised, "Except, we ain't got no Army. Our boys in blue," he glanced around and dropped his voice, "can't even tell whose team some of these guys are playing on. They're here for the benefits and pension, but they're building houses and riding in fancy cars that someone else's paying for. And we... and we gotta watch our backs from both sides 'cause we ain't on *that* payroll."

Faulkner nodded his head at the Frenchie approaching. "Best we keep that to ourselves. Never know..." He turned, "Michael, how's every little thing?"

The short man in the bright blue polyester suit pulled the toothpick from his mouth and posed, leaning on Meyer's desk. "Some shit out there today, huh?" He removed his hat and scratched his head. "Damn, must have picked up a hundred 9mm casings. Figure they used an Uzi." He mopped his receding brow with a long handkerchief. "You guys heard about any new players in town?"

The detectives chuckled. Meyers answered, "Man, Michael, you're the player here. We are only yard dogs sniffing around, trying to pick up a trail. You're the street guy. Why? What's happening we should know about?"

The short man shrugged and leaned in, "Someone new got some good coke, not crack, but old-style powder, making the situation tense. My informants say it could explode. It's not the Dominican Reps, not the Ricans, and not the local crews. Thinking maybe you heard something? I know you got other sources...."

"And you and the boys ain't getting a piece of the new player yet?" Faulkner stated, "So, what can we do to assist in this matter of prime importance? Me and Hitman are here to help. You know, we're all on the same team." He nodded to his partner, who also nodded in agreement.

"Why you gotta make it out like that? I just want to keep the body count low. It's better to know who's out there."

"You think this drive-by was from the unknown guys?"

"No, looks like this one was retaliation for some domestic shit, you know, the wrong guy at the wrong house at the wrong time, wrong woman. That's how this one settles out. But with a new supplier, things could get really crazy, out of hand."

Hitman cut him off, "Like it ain't out of hand now? Twenty-two murders and it's just August? How many wounded; how many orphaned? Mikey, there's only 70,000 on this island. That's a lot of killing." He looked the Frenchie up and down. "You know all the big suppliers of dangerous drugs are fueling this violence and you don't shut them down. So, the wars continue."

"Come on," the short man stretched, "you know it's the laws that are fucking up the process. We can't just bust them, gotta have probable cause."

"Nah, Mikey," he was getting familiar with his most-distant coworker, "the fundamental law on this rock is supply and demand. We got ourselves one big-ass drug consumer here in tourist land. And we ain't making a dent, just keeping the coroner busy."

The Frenchie replaced his hat. "Just wanted to give you guys a heads up. Something's brewing and it could be bad. You might think things is just so-and-so, but you don't have the full picture. We, me and the drug squad, try to keep everybody happy, copasetic. We can only do so much. I know the streets are dangerous, but what we're doing is keeping it where it belongs, in the projects, and not affecting the tourist business. Okay, see you guys. Keep safe."

Both detectives smiled as the short man walked away. Miles uttered under his breath, "That Frenchie can bite me. He don't have a good bone in his body, but the way things swing around here, he might be our boss sooner than we think."

"Whew… what a horrible thought," Faulkner observed. "That drug squad should be renamed 'the drugged squad.' They pay people to supply them with clean piss for the mandatory monthly urine tests. Then, if they're dirty, they say it was something they *had* to do undercover on the job. What'd ya think, something brewing?"

"My friend, I say we sit low and watch. Dodge bullets and let them kill each other. Pray for the Feds to come in. Let's go for a ride; Mikey stunk up this place."

Eddie was waiting at the overlook above Magen's Bay. The view of the huge beach and offshore islands reflected the brilliant colors of the Caribbean evening sky. There were few tourists. Dale parked without a nod or a word and walked up to the concrete bench referred to as Drake's Seat. The younger West Indian scanned the area, cautious of any locals who might follow him for the Posse. He'd borrowed his cousin's car, parked it at the southern harbor overlook, and hiked the quarter-mile over the hump.

He pulled out his phone, pretending to take photos while meandering near to the older white man.

"You alone?" Dale whispered.

"You got that right. Watching my ass. My own people are beating me up 'bout your shit," Eddie replied.

"Why? It's good, isn't it?"

"Yeah, too good. My boss wants to know who, what, and where it's coming from. He wants a part of the action," the short, short man answered.

"That's up to you, if you want to let him in. I thought you were building your own bank account?" Dale asked.

"I am; motherfuckers are strong-arming me to get their cut. I'm supposed to talk you into selling to him direct," Eddie said, 'but that ain't gonna happen. They got no respect for a money maker like me. No respect at all!"

"Not so loud," Dale reminded. "Something's about to go down and you could be a part. Bring in anyone and everyone… if you want to."

"What's happening?"

"My friends with the stuff are gonna move the load in a few days. Be like maybe thirty keys. They got the Spanish waiting, but," Dale looked around, "if you had your head on straight, they could get their asses hijacked. Know what I mean?"

"Whoa, you talking gun stuff. I like to stay away from that. I bleed easy." Eddie nodded, "but, let's say the crew I work with got word that a transaction was taking place at so-and-so location. They ain't got no love for the Spicos. What's in it for me?"

Dale sniffed the fragrant frangipani bush. "Whatever you want because you can cut a deal with your guys. Oh yeah, blood's gonna flow, so be careful. I'm hoping to get a piece and then me and my friends will be the fuck out of there, hopefully before the lead starts flying. A smart fellow like you could pick up the pieces after the fireworks."

"Where?" Ed asked.

"Too soon, no set place yet," Dale lied. "Be a spur-of-the-moment thing, but I know it will be early in the morning, first light, a few days from now. You helped me when I needed help. That's mutual; I'm helping you, but be careful. Anything associated with the white dust is dangerous. The police, Feds, Spanish, and your own people, all want the shit to make big money."

"So, who don't know that?"

"Just saying, my friends are very careful; best you be, too. As soon as I know, I'll text you the location of the drop. Get ready to move fast. Got me? I have zero reason to screw you, but I'm telling you to be careful. This could turn into a mess, a real mess," Dale reminded and extended his hand. "Eddie, I like you. I don't like this business, but we know if you and I don't do it someone else will, and we might as well make the money. Agreed?"

Eddie nodded, "Whitey, what are you saying?"

"Stay back. Stay away from the action. And there will be lots of action. Keep your head low. Let your other guys do the wet work. Worse case, you get a pat on the back for giving your boss the info."

The islander pulled a small chrome-plated 38 from his pocket. "I'm always watching my back. There's no place that's safe anymore, no place. I know I'm selling shit that drives some people nuts. Can't trust a fucking soul."

"My friend, put that away. Keep it out of sight. Here, take this bag, like you're going to the beach," Dale passed the straw bag that showed a beach towel. "Got the cash?"

Ed discreetly passed a thick envelope. "It's all there. Count it, if you want. Now, you, a total stranger, are about the only person in the entire world who is helping me. Why?"

Dale chuckled and extended his hand again for help to get up from the ground. "Coincidences, me-son, coincidences. You were in the right place at the right time. Remember, I didn't go looking for you, you were on my doorstep. Eddie, in the last couple of days, you proved to be a valuable asset. I don't take that for granted. Listen to me, a lot of shit will happen fast, quick. Keep out of the line of fire." They shook hands and Dale parted with, "Keep safe."

At the hotel, Dale handed Keith the wad of cash. "Okay, I checked everything off my list. What else you got?"

Keith passed a glass of amber rum and then fanned the stack of bills. He handed Dale half. "Use this to get Lucy over here. Did you get a line on who's honest in the police?"

Dale replied, "Fredrico says there might be two police named Faulkner and Meyers who aren't on the take. He hears a lot of street talk from the delivery guys at his bar in Havensite. Everyone from the Health Department to the Girl Scouts has their hands out. Seems these two guys are college-educated and staying clean."

"Any idea why? They plan to run for governor?"

The older man laughed, "Hell no, if that was the case, they'd be grabbing all they could for their campaign like every other politician. Fredrico says he knows them from church. They all go to the Reformed Pentecostal and these guys work with the youth. Says he chatted with them a lot and they seem like they got a conscience." Dale showed his phone, "I got their numbers."

"Let's hope they aren't afraid," Keith said. "You call them from St. John tomorrow and let them know something's about to happen and they should be ready. Think they'll keep their mouths shut until it all goes down?"

Dale refilled and touched glasses. "Can't say for sure, but you're calling the Feds and we know they'll show. The Rican DEA, good and bad local police, the Feds. Seems like we got it covered, just hope they don't cover us," he paused, "with dirt."

"Okay, let's run through it one more time," Keith directed. "The escape bikes are in place, tanks full. We know they run good. We have the route down. I've decided on the boat I'll grab. We have our disguises. We planned our getaway with a few minutes to spare. We'll both be carrying money."

"Oh yeah, Fredrico included the ID. No idea how he got it, but he threw it in. I got the fireworks; what are you going to do with that? Celebrate our success with a show over the harbor? And the two sets of scuba gear in the back seat on top of a chunk of camo netting. That's a weird combination. Plus, the two dozen candles?"

"Ah, don't worry about it," Keith answered as he drained his glass. "I've got my little quirks, like everybody else. Where did you leave it all?"

"At the house with the bikes."

Crack is ruining the drug culture.
Hunter Thompson

CHAPTER EIGHTEEN

Driving to Red Hook the following morning, Keith got lost in his thoughts. It would be two hectic days until Dale sailed over with Lucy. The next part of the game had to get tricky. Time to be the mongoose and kill the snakes, all the snakes.

Dale nudged him when the light turned green. "Buddy, you're wearing a grim face. You worried?"

Keith shrugged, "Yeah, got to be. Making my to-do list and checking it twice."

"I still don't understand how you're getting out of the harbor. I mean, you have the uniform, but…"

"That's on a need-to-know basis and since you'll be on the other side of the island getting on a slow sailboat… no reason to know."

"Got you… trust issues," Dale reasoned. "I have them, too. Can't shed the old ways. Two people can't keep a secret unless one is dead."

"It isn't all that. I'm the loose end of this entire project. I've got to pull off some magic to disappear. Lucy and you will sail, and we'll meet if I make it out of the harbor. Otherwise, this island'll get tiny, quick." They shook hands and Dale walked the gangway onto the crowded ferry.

"Yeah, everything is on a need-to-know. Dale's a straight-shooter, but there's no need to tell him the details," Keith muttered to himself as he turned the car around to head to Georgie's rental house at Four Corners. The first job was to build three big smoke bombs from the fireworks. It was no problem, as he'd done it as a teenager. He took extra time melting candle wax to make them waterproof, in case it rained. The wax would also help everything burn once the long fuses were lit.

Next, he drove to his inflatable and transferred everything. It was easy now, since Dale had sold enough of the dust to buy whatever they wanted. He'd bought two of everything: two sets of masks and fins, two weight belts, two tanks and set up; the dive gear crowded the dinghy.

After topping off the fuel, he filled two extra containers with gas and motored to Charlotte Amalie Harbor, a broad, natural keyhole bay. The dinghy bounced along the wakes of the big inter-island ferry boats across the south side of St. Thomas to the edge of Hassel Island. Keeping track of his timing, Keith secured the dinghy to some scrub bushes and walked to the old Garrison Building. He hid the smoke bombs and gas bottles almost in plain sight beneath a rusting cannon. He was timing everything. He estimated when he was running, it would be in and out, eight minutes max.

He studied the scene, watching the beautiful Marriot Hotel across the harbor. A long sigh escaped. "Boy, what am I doing? All this to pay back a bitch of a wife and her shithead brother? Loads of risks, stupid risks; I've already got the money." He lit a joint, "This is where I wanted to finish my days. I loved St. Thomas, but it doesn't love me anymore." Keith took a long pull, held it, exhaled, and snubbed out the spliff. "Hmm, drugs are a way of life… and of death. Can't stop it. The appetite is too great."

The twenty-plus day charter sailboats were returning from the first half day at Buck Island. "That used to be me, taking tourists diving and fishing. It was a pleasant life. All I ever wanted. They played me to lose it all, for no reason other than misplaced love. Hmm," Keith laughed, "Maybe all love is misplaced. Me and Lucy might never be in love, better if we just stayed in lust."

Now came the tricky part. He put on scuba gear and checked his watch again before he dove in dragging the extra set. It was a clumsy, but short, seven-minute swim to the green channel marker buoy. The water was crystal clear, with at least fifty-foot visibility. Carefully, he used a slip knot to secure a yellow net bag with an extra set of fins, and a mask to one of the buoy's huge chain links.

The bright sun penetrated down through the surface to the sandy bottom twenty-eight feet below. With the compass in the regulator's console, he laid out a string of rocks pointing to Hassel Island. He shed his tank but kept breathing with the regulator extended as he also strapped it to the chain. Everything, two sets of scuba gear, would be ready when he'd need them. But there was always the 'if' that haunted his thoughts: if he made it this far.

Looking at the watch again, he pulled a long, last breath from the regulator and shut the valve on his tank. He'd held his breath for a full two minutes, swimming with powerful kicks, and made it most of the way back to Hassel Island underwater. Before he changed to dry clothes, Keith struggled to pull the inflatable up the shore behind some scrub bushes. It had to be there when he needed it.

Dinghies disappeared every day in every harbor of the world. If someone saw this one, they'd steal it. Quickly, he draped the camouflage netting over it and cut enough bushes to make it invisible. "This is the weakest link," he crossed his fingers and let out a long sigh, "but, it will work."

Finished with the exertions, he changed clothes, careful to pack everything into a shoulder bag. Keith walked along a trail until he came to the small set of shops that lined Careening Cove. He approached a young West Indian sitting on the old wooden wharf. "Hey buddy, you want a beer?" Keith asked.

The dark-skinned man slowly nodded.

"One hitch, I need a ride across the harbor. Buy you a beer and give you a twenty for your time. Got separated from my friends."

The local man nodded again, pointing to the small boat beneath his dangling legs.

Once off the dock, they skirted between the many anchored sailboats and the massive cruise ship dock.

Keith sipped his beer and was walking down the pier when he heard his name called. He walked on, slouching as if he were drunk. Someone grabbed his shoulder. It was Adil.

"What, Mr. Keith, you can't say hello to old friends?" The man extended his hand. "So very good to see you again. Heard lots of stories about you and a shipwreck. Are they true? What you back here for? Last time I saw you, hmm… well, you look better now. How's things? No more long hair, no mustache?"

"Things are okay." They hugged. Keith hardly expected a warm welcome. "Ah, just passing thru. Flying out tonight to the States." He sighed, "Yeah, good to see you, Adil. Been a while. Lots of shit in between."

"Come now, my friend, let me give you another beer and hear your tale first-hand."

"Can't now, but Adil, I'll try to come back before you close. My flight's not until eleven." Keith turned and walked through Yacht Haven Hotel, where he grabbed a taxi back to the rental car he'd parked at Red Hook.

He drove all the way back to the cruise ship area at Havensite. He parked at Wendy's and retrieved a bundle from the back seat.

With his ball cap pulled down and wearing shades, Keith

tried to be nondescript. Every tourist in the packed restaurant looked about the same. He finished his burger and walked to the restroom, carrying his package. That was the way it had to be because there were too many grab-n-go, small-time thieves. They frequented every St. Thomas restaurant, waiting for someone to be careless and leave something on the table. He wasn't protecting as much as hiding.

Once he locked the toilet door, he moved one of the suspended ceiling tiles, positioned the package, and then neatly replaced the tile. He splashed his face with cold water, staring into the mirror. "Okay, only one more thing to cross off my list." He shook his head and grinned. "In for a penny, in for a pound."

The stake bed truck-taxi that Virgin Islanders call safari buses, took forty-five minutes to straddle St. John from Cruz to Coral Bay. Loose Lucy's was empty except for two men with measuring tapes and notebooks.

"Sorry friend, the bar's closed. Under new management." The clean-cut, tan-less man smiled and spread his arms, "Great party last night. Think almost everything, but the kerosene for the hanging lanterns got drunk. Wait," he slid the covers of several stainless-steel coolers, "Here's one last Heineken. Take it, free, you're our first customer."

Dale raised the greenie and saluted, "Lucy around?"

"On her boat at the dock," the pale skin guy pointed, "She threw one hell of a bash. We weren't buying the stock, so she gave it away. Figure she's passed out."

"Keeping the name?" Dale inquired.

"No sir, this will become the Far Side, like the comic strip, plenty of funny characters."

"Good luck with that." Dale raised the beer again and headed to the dock where Starlet was resting. Lucy was sitting on deck wearing a brightly printed kimono, drinking coffee. She poured an extra cup when she saw the familiar face.

"Come aboard. Guess Keith figured I might get lost sailing across Pillsbury? What happened to you? Get hit with a lawnmower?"

"No, not at all. He's just worried about you. You know, everybody needs someone to worry about." Dale sipped the dark brew, "That guy's different now. Think he might have found religion after floating at sea…" He paused and made a clown face,

"Or something else got a hold of him... like a sweet woman named Lucy." They touched cups. "Like my makeover?"

"You look like those rich nerds who bought the bar. So, what's my man been up to? Anything I should worry about? I know he's working on something to screw over his ex and her bro."

Dale chose his words, "Yeah, he... we... got something cooking to fix those pricks. Keith said you ran into the woman who set him up for the divorce. That is some low-life stuff."

"Yes sir, good thing he held me back, or I'd probably be in Road Town's jail. The long-legged bitch sold him out to feed her nose. That's low, but plotting it, and paying for it, that's snake shit. Nobody deserves that. Keith and you were already here when I showed up. You dealt yourself some rotten luck. The shitheads..." she paused, looking for suitable words, "who robbed me and... I should have left, but I couldn't let them beat me."

"Time's supposed to heal everything. All of us, you, me, and Keith, lost a lot, but also, we made a lot: money, friends, and wonderful memories. Risk and reward, that's how we lived. Looks like we're headed for new times, better days," Dale said and they clinked cups again, "What else do we need to do to get out of here? I think these islands will look the best from over the stern."

"One trip to the bank. That's about all that's left. Figured I'd wait until I had a bodyguard. These wannabe gangsters like to harass me."

"Sweetheart, that's their form of sport," Dale laughed. "They love to harass everyone. Our worries are almost over. You shed your bar, and in another few days, me and Keith will finish what we have to do and be rid of the Virgins, finished with all this racial shit."

"Could never understand why they have such an attitude?" she posed. "Everything is rigged to help them, put in place by us, the mainland, and they still hate us."

"Not all of them," he thought of Eddie. "Some find respect when they're cut a break. But they kill each other over a few dollars and chase the tourists away from the islands. It's all a downward spiral. Crime, fewer tourists, fewer jobs, fewer tourists, less money, even fewer tourists, more crime, more violent crime. Then they only have each other to prey on. Nobody wins. Been going downhill for a lot of years, with a few hurricanes mixed in to help."

"Wow, and I thought I was cynical," Lucy remarked as they smacked a high five and laughed. "What a world we've enjoyed, huh?" Lucy refilled the cups. "I look to the friends I have back home in Wisconsin and couldn't do it. I couldn't take the boredom, especially the six dreary months of winter. Half a damn year cold and depressed." Lucy laughed, "To hell with skiing and ice fishing. I'll change clothes and let's get going."

Four hours later, Starlet rounded Privateer Point, the absolute farthest east part of the USA. The wind was blowing a brisk twenty out of the northeast. Lucy cranked in the main to close haul. Starlet leaped forward, cutting across the almost perfectly spaced swells.

Dale handled the wheel as Lucy trimmed the sails. "Man, oh man, I have missed this. Sailing... wow! What a great rush," Dale beamed. He could feel his luck changing.

Lucy took a photo and texted it to Keith followed by a call, "Hey sweetie, everything good? We're on the way, south of Frenchman's Key. The plan is to sweep outside and tack into Hull. We should be there about seven, with plenty of daylight. Coming to meet me? Great. What? Me, call who? Yeah, sure, no problem, I guess. Text me the number with the info and I'll make the call." Lucy puckered and kissed the phone.

Keith closed the phone. That was one more item crossed off his list. He chuckled at the thought of Lucy phoning Maddie. He wanted to see his house again. After this deal went down, he wouldn't be back. The house summed up his life in St. Thomas. It was filled with reminders, souvenirs of happier, better times. He wanted to take a few momentos to remember his successes... and failures.

If Maddie believed the phone message, she'd leave to meet her attorney Charles at his office in town. That would permit an hour to sit and enjoy the feel of his old nest. And he'd see his yellow Lab, Baron. Forced to leave his dog behind was one more time Maddie had stabbed him in his heart.

He stopped on Skyline Drive and looked down at his land. Keith liked to think of it as his 'estate.' Good, there were no cars in the driveway. He'd walled his place, and it backed on a steep hillside, looking to the north, over the small cays and bigger Hans Lollik. The house stood out; he had it painted pale yellow. Back then, he'd agreed with Maddie's color scheme; yellow supposedly represented happiness. One expects marriage to be bliss.

He laughed and muttered, "Now it should be dog shit brown. God help brother-in-law Carlos if he shows up while I'm knocking around. They'll get theirs soon enough."

The gate wasn't even shut. Maddie had rushed for her fake appointment. She must have something brewing with the attorney. Keith's smile broadened, "If I have my way, she'll be giving legal-eagle Charles plenty of business."

He didn't pull in but drove farther down the lane to where he knew there was a cut in the trees. A neighbor had excavated a driveway but got caught in the stock market slide and stopped. The rental car was hidden behind a canopy of bamboo. Keith knew his way, walked to the back edge of his wall, and crossed over into his yard. His yellow dog rushed from the shade of the bougainvillea, defending the territory.

"Baron! Baron! Buddy, it's me," Keith called, hoped it was just loud enough to cajole his dog into remembering his original master, but not enough to alert a neighbor. The loping dog stopped about twenty feet away to sniff the air. The dog's demeanor changed, but it charged again, leaping on his hind legs. Keith considered running, but knelt on one knee. The ninety-pound yellow Labrador bowled him over. Baron wasn't barking or biting, but wagging his tail while slurping his master's face.

"I know, pup, I know. I missed you, too. Good dog. Sorry, things got so fouled up. None of it was your fault. Turns out it wasn't even my fault." He hugged the dog. "Well, call it poor judgment, huh?" Keith rubbed the big head as Baron flung happy slobber everywhere. "Yeah buddy, you're a great dog. Bet you haven't been to the beach in a long while." At the word beach, Baron calmed and studied Keith's face. "We'll fix that. Got to go inside for a bit. Don't worry."

Keith made a split-second decision to take the dog along. "Maddie won't miss him; probably won't even realize he's gone for a few days and by then…"

She hadn't locked the back door. "Guess she believes you'll keep the thieves away." He took a deep breath and entered. The place had a delicate smell; jasmine from the front bushes drifted through the open windows. The kitchen hadn't changed. He nodded, knowing Maddie wasn't into cooking.

To the left was the spacious living room. Everything was the same as the day he'd grudgingly packed and left. Now it was obvious, Maddie was just putting in time until she sold the place. Maybe he could throw a wrench into her money-grabbing machine. He pulled a parcel from his shoulder bag, stabbed it with his knife, and tilted it making a small invisible trail of white powder on the couch cushions. Then he shook out the devil dust slowly across the room to the closet under the stairs. Keith wrinkled his nose at the waste, but he wasn't about to get any in his nervous system. This was only about evening the score with Maddie and Carlos once and for all.

The closet built beneath the stairway to the second-floor bedrooms had been one of his preferred stashes in his wilder days, before he'd married. At the rear of the large closet, Keith jiggled a baseboard until it popped free. He trailed the crystal powder into the hiding spot. He resealed the package, tossed it into the cubby hole, and then replaced the board. He froze when he heard the front door open and the screen door slam.

"Maldición!""Maldición!" Maddie exclaimed, "mierda, mierda, mierda. Dónde está el maldito teléfono? Maldito, Charles apurándome para una reunion. Esta maldita cosa siempre está perdida."

("*Damn! Shit! Shit! Shit! Where's my phone? Damn Charles, rushing me to a meeting! The fucking thing is always hiding*) Aha, there it is." The door slammed and seconds later the car spun in the gravel as she pulled away.

Keith whispered to himself, "Close, but no cigar!" He sighed, "Yeah, I'd have liked to have seen her one more time. Fuck it." He shrugged, checked the closet, and surveyed the living room again. From a shelf, he grabbed hand-carved, wooden models of his two boats. Fondling them between his fingers, he traced their lines. "Uh-huh, yep, and they say they can't take everything. That bitch took my heart and soul. I loved these boats, this house. Where she's going, she'll never miss these."

"Wasn't much I could do about it until now." He stared out the back window for a moment and caught sight of Starlet miles offshore.

Keith smiled, "Until now. In the next few days, this score's gonna get settled... in my favor. No fucking divorce court judgment, and I'm only sentenced to the time I've already served. Fuck 'em, fuck 'em all. I'm getting a pardon!"

He deposited the models into his backpack and grabbed a bag of dog chow from the kitchen cabinet. Baron was on the patio, waiting with his usual quizzical Lab look as if to say, 'Where are we going, boss?' Today, the lovable dog got his favorite answer.

"Let's go! Let's get out of here! We're going to the beach!"

Tail happily wagging, he followed his favorite master and bounded into the passenger seat as soon as the door opened.

"Yeah buddy, we're a team again, heading for the beach." With that, the big, yellow dog danced around on the seat. "Calm down, Baron, calm down. I know it's been a while, but luck has blessed us with a fresh start. Yahoo!" Keith shouted and scratched the dog's big head.

"This time, it's good luck!" He laughed and hugged the dog. "I've missed you. From now on, we're going everywhere together. You are my comfort dog. Lucy will love you, too. Don't worry; it'll be like the old days. Be on the boat for a while until we find the next place. You can handle that, can't ya?"

Baron continued fervently licking Keith's face until he was seat belted in. "I know, weird, but it's the law. Can't take the chance of getting pulled over."

"You didn't call me?" Maddie was irate. "Someone called and said Charles needed to see me as soon as possible."

"I'm sorry, Maddie, but it wasn't me," the secretary cowered.

"Is he in?" After the affirmative nod, Maddie opened the door and barged into the mahogany-paneled office.

"Maddie," Charles looked up from a stack of papers strewn over his desk. "What can I do for you?"

"Charles, someone called and told me you needed some papers signed. Que mierda?"

The attorney gave her a big-eyed look. "No, nothing new on the house sale. A couple from Connecticut is interested. They're on vacation looking for an investment property. I've done some transactions for them in the past. Looks promising, but nothing is in stone yet."

"Que mierda? I rushed here, hoping I'd finish with this fucking island." She lit a cigarette. "Drop another twenty thousand off the price."

"Maddie, please don't smoke in my office." He looked at the wall clock. "It's almost happy hour. Let me soothe your savage breasts, no, ah, beasts… you know what I mean. Over a few cocktails and we'll discuss how to proceed."

She cut him off. "Sé lo que quiera hacer, Sr. abogado, hazme el amor!" *(I know how you want to proceed, Mr. Lawyer. You want to jump my bones!")*

It was the lawyer's turn. "Calm down, Maddie, we make mistakes, no big deal. Speak English, my Spanish is so rusty, it's frozen." He grabbed her by the arm and led her from his office, bowed, and flashed his best lecherous smile. "Give me fifteen minutes to straighten this mess. For your trouble, I'll buy dinner and drinks."

Maddie shrugged and slumped onto his couch in his reception area, grabbed a magazine. "Quince minutos, no más." (*Fifteen minutes, no more.*)

He smiled at her stern look and replied, "Sí, madam. Seré rápido." (Yes, ma'am, I'll be quick.)

The yellow Lab burst from the car, dashed across the sand, and pranced into the clear water of Hull Bay. Keith grinned; it was all coming together. Everything would be again like old times. This was where he'd first lived shortly after arriving on the island. Pierre's Yard was a fixture for wandering international gypsies. He'd gotten a free ride south, helping to deliver a sailboat from Boston. Working only as a deckhand, to pull, heave, and watch the horizon, but it had carried him south.

Hull Bay didn't attract many tourists. It wasn't upscale, there were no nearby hotels. Today, only four couples were soaking in the Caribbean. This cove was a mainstay for locals. Coconut trees fringed the wide, white beach, but both ends were rocky. To the east was Tropaco Point, the separation from the world-famous Magens Bay. Among the immense boulders were a smattering of very expensive homes. Anyone who could afford to build among the stones had their own very private swimming pools, didn't frequent the beach, and were too glitzy for the basic island bar.

Pierre's old restaurant and tidy campground brought revived memories. "Didn't need much money back then," Keith whispered, petting the wet dog. Tourist rental cars packed the bar's lot; many jeeps were identical to his. "Got my first island piece of ass on this beach, Baron, a lovely northside Frenchie girl. Wonder what happened to Jackie? She probably has five kids by now. Should have hooked up with her and would have gotten a nice chunk of land from her family to build on." He wrinkled his face, "Ah, I'd still have ended up divorced. No one man can tame those Frenchie girls."

Baron bounded across the sand with a stick between his jaws, shaking water and wet sand. Keith threw the stick into the bay, knowing his dog seldom tired of this game. The scene choked Keith and a few tears hit his cheeks. This was the life he'd missed, forsaken for a stupid roll between the sheets. His dog, clear water, superb scenery, what else did he need?

As if on cue, Starlet nosed around Tropaco Point from the east. The sloop looked great, slicing through the waves with only the main and headsail. He watched Dale slowly work his way to the bow as Lucy brought her boat slightly off the wind to drop the sails. His partner pulled and folded the headsail, neatly lacing it to the starboard safety lines. Once finished, Starlet bore more east, caught the breeze again and rode into the shallows of the broad bay.

A deft move by an experienced captain, Lucy spun the wheel as Dale dropped the mainsail. Starlet's forward progress slowed while Dale tucked the sail into the boom's Lazy Jake cradle. Then he walked to the bow to ready the anchor. Baron sat at the edge of the water and watched the action with his resurrected owner. They both cocked their ears as Starlet's anchor chain rattled into the water. Lucy signaled Dale to tie off the chain. With a cloud of light blue smoke, she shifted into reverse, and set the hook into the sand bed.

Keith shed his shirt, dove into the cool water, and swam to the yacht with Baron easily following. He pulled himself into Lucy's inflatable and hauled up the dog.

"Really, Keith, a dog?"

"He's my old dog. Baron, meet Lucy. What she says goes, both captain and boss, a beautiful boss and captain, I might add."

"Bull," she knelt at the stern to kiss Keith.

"Permission to come aboard granted. Get your ass up here!" Lucy said and encircled her man into a groping kiss. Baron sat in the dinghy peacefully enjoying the motion of the waves.

"Uh, ahem," Dale coughed, "Need help to lift the hound?"

"I'm thinking," Lucy said, "Dale, ah, you want to take the dog to the shore and play with him?" She tugged Keith toward the hatch. "I'd like to drag this old dog below and play. What do you say?"

Without a word, Dale hopped into the dinghy and motored to the beach. On the return, he brought takeout barbecue and beers back to the yacht. Dale kept his mouth full and listened to the dialog rather than offer any opinions.

"So, how long will I be waiting here?" Lucy asked.

"If…" Keith caught himself, "things will go as planned. Dale will be here before eleven, the day after tomorrow. I'll see you both in Old San Juan, at the El Convento Hotel, at the bar.

Say about noon, three days from now."

"Sweetheart, are you sure you have to do this? Sounds crazy."

"Not crazy-crazy, just exciting-crazy." He flashed a toothy grin. "Look, babe, yes, I know it's stupid-risky, but they broke me…"

She cut him off, "Tried to break you. Hell, buying Starlet was your pocket change. You've got a second chance; leave with me, now. Forget this other crazy shit. Walk away."

"Can't, too many things in play." He stared at the sunset, "You know how long I was on that banana raft? Six days, six fucking days, thinking the end was gonna happen at any moment. I got the shit beat out of me twice 'cause of them. They took everything from me! The entire marriage was faked so she and her brother could sell coke. She never wanted to be Mrs. Gardnar; she used me like someone steals an identity. I'm positive now; this was all planned. They gotta pay; all the fuckers need to pay. They are paying me, and they're paying for their bad, bad karma."

"Aren't you afraid of bringing bad shit on you, on us, later? Come on, be reasonable; you don't need to do this."

"Look, Lucy, an argument will get us nowhere. All involved won't see it coming," Keith paused, "or me and Dale going." He grinned and hugged his woman. "We'll have some hairy moments, but it'll be over, short and sweet. Start early, done early. Believe me; you don't want to know any details. You're not involved."

"Fuck you! I sold my bar and my boat, heaved anchor like I'm already running. I won't lie," she said, pouring another round of rum. "I was ready to leave. The place got stagnant." She hugged him hard. "Listen to me, you assholes, keep safe."

They raised their glasses and chugged.

Dale coughed and spit a chicken bone over the side and began, "I need to do this; I need the cash. It seems almost everyone I knew from the old days shit on me, especially when I was down. Only Georgie came to my aid. Josef fucked me, Jeffers stole five years and my family," He winced tenderly, feeling his ribs, "and Carlos, well, that little Spanish prick will get what's due. I can promise that. Your boyfriend here, and me, we aren't dummies or punching bags."

"I agree, we could walk, maybe sail away, but it's eating at me and always will be unless…" Keith confessed. "They need to understand what they did to me and experience it to a greater degree." He grinned and raised his glass. "Like they always say, payback's a bitch."

"And, especially," Lucy started, "paying a bitch back after a divorce. If that doesn't get you a restraining order or a domestic beef, it's rare. You know I'm in with you, even if you aren't explaining anything except, 'I know it's dangerous.' Fucking with Colombians, coke dealers, corrupt police... what other dangerous low life is there?"

"The Rastas," Dale answered.

"Them, too? You are fucking nuts! Both of you! Hear me now, I'm no fucking nurse, get your asses chopped or shot and you're on your own. Go to the fucking hospital! I don't even like the sight of blood when I get my period." Her laugh was an infectious pressure release. "Okay, do what you want to do. Dale, if you aren't here by two, adios. I won't stick around to read about your bullet-riddled bodies in the Island Guardian."

Keith pulled her close. "He'll be here and I'll meet you where I said." They enjoyed a long kiss, while Baron rolled over to let Dale scratch his belly.

"What do I do with him, the dog?" she asked in between kisses.

"I'll give you his bag of chow when you take us in. He doesn't eat much, but you got to show him where to take a dump. He'll do his business now, with us, and in the morning, after he eats, run him ashore. Baron is smart and he can hold it for hours. Best to keep him tied in the cockpit when sailing, just in case a gull lands on the boat and he chases it overboard."

They kissed again. "I hope his master's chasing days are over?"

"They are, they are, guaranteed." Keith squeezed her hard and broke apart to get in the dinghy. "We'd better get going. Hate to, but we got another long day tomorrow."

"And another long, lonely night for me."

Keith smiled as Dale handed down Baron to the inflatable, "and that's why I brought you a pet."

Dale drove to the hotel. "Yeah, we're lunatics. Think this is gonna work?"

"Absolutely, but the timing is everything. Got to stagger our enemies' arrivals: DEA, Carlos' gang, Rastas, and corrupt police. Then the good police and FBI come and sweep up who's left. We've already disappeared."

"Why are you stealing the outboard? Why not just take the bike, or make it to another car?"

"Whoa, my guess is they'll follow me, and they can easily shut down this rock with roadblocks. I'll pull all the attention from you and Lucy. I make it to the beach and barrel out of the harbor. They can't get a copter up fast enough. Twenty minutes is all I need. The marine cops, you know, the VIMP, have the fast boats, but they'll probably still be sleeping that early in the morning. I've thought it through; I'm the criminal who leaves no trace. The way I have it planned; they'll be looking for a body for weeks."

"Oh, the way this will play out, I think they'll find plenty of bodies," Dale added. "I'm not contributing mine."

"Me neither," Keith laughed. "Me neither. Let's hit the bar and suck down a few rums?"

"And see some nubile, tanned tits," Dale added.

*Eventually, alas, I realized the main purpose
of buying cocaine is to run out of it.*

George Carlin

CHAPTER NINETEEN

Tourists packed the restaurant, wanting to squeeze in as many waking hours on their vacations as possible. Josef helped his bartender feed a steady supply of alcohol to the sunburned revelers.

"I'll have El Dorado 15 on the rocks," said an accented voice.

Josef looked up to see Carlos wearing a solemn face. "Amigo, I've heard nothing from you. Has your old friend returned? It's been days since…"

"Nope, nope, and nope. I have heard nothing from or about him. I don't believe he considers me on his side since you kicked the shit out of him." The bar owner growled while pouring the drink, "He'll still want to middle the product to you, if you didn't scare him off the island."

"Think he'll take it to my competitors, the fucking rug heads?"

"I would, but they're even less trustworthy. I doubt if he has any contacts on that side."

"Like you?"

"I was a good contact until you freaked out. I would have brought Dale straight to you; after all, he fucking came to me." Josef shook his head in frustration, "All the people you have on the streets and no one's seen that old Renault?"

"Disappeared," Carlos mumbled as he sipped the rum. "Don't understand how someone not in the business would know how to hide so good. Even got a banker checking if he uses credit cards."

"Carlos, Dale was a player, but got burned. I told you someone ratted him out. When that happened, by a strange twist of fate," Josef smiled, "my business expanded and I could distribute more, made more money. And that's why you and I are friends… the business kind of friends. How's Maddie? She hasn't been around in quite a while."

"This is stressing Maddie out, but not as bad as me. I've got to get our product back. My family is applying pressure everywhere, on every island, and on me. The old guy got the only extra dust. We know the load didn't sink; someone…" Carlos' voice became loud enough to be heard around the bar, "someone fucking stole it!" Carlos scanned the eyes of each person. Josef's patrons became silent.

"Quiet down. This is only *our* business, and there's no need to advertise *your* problem."

"Our business, but my problem? Listen, Josef, this could be a major problem for you if your friend doesn't reconnect. Perhaps you have already helped him sell my product?"

"Don't talk stupid, Carlos. I called you as soon as Dale approached me. Relax," Josef refilled the glass.

"So, now I'm stupido!" The Spanish rang through the bar. Two women grabbed their purses and started toward the door. Carlos turned to them with his arms spread, "Ladies, ladies, please sit. I regret my words." The women cautiously eyed the slim man. "Please permit me to buy you a drink. I did not mean to disturb your evening."

"I'll get you two of the same. Maureen, Jeannie, I'm so sorry for the commotion," Josef added his apologies and nodded. "I'll order you a plate of appetizers."

Josef turned to Carlos, "All is going on your tab. When my *old* friend calls me, you, my *new* friend, will be wealthy *again*. Please, no more loud outbursts, no angry words. In these times, people are afraid. Loud words can quickly escalate to loud bang, bang, bangs these days."

"Yes, *we* will be wealthy again," Carlos slugged the rum and extended his hand, which Josef gladly shook. "Keep in touch, my friend, keep in touch." He gave a semblance of a salute to the clientele and left.

Maureen, a willowy blonde, asked, "Who was that?"

"You don't want to know," the bar owner replied. "Ever see the movie Bad News Bears? Just drop the Bears."

The two men chatted until the bar closed and then crashed until after eight. While Dale showered, Keith compiled a list of phone calls. He showed it to his wet partner. "What do you think?"

"I think the cocktail waitress should have lived up to the cock and tail last evening. Oh, about this? Well, you've got everyone on there; you call Jeffers, the FBI, and the good police. I call fuck-stick Carlos, Josef, and my guy, Eddie. We tell them all the same thing; be ready to move fast, and be in town tomorrow morning by six, right?"

"Yep, let's hope they don't bounce into each other. What about the corrupt cops?" Keith asked.

"Seems logical that my guy would know them. I'll put it to him today, so he fully understands what's going down. He'll score some points for himself with the dirty cops. We know they're taking money from all the dealers to keep them *safe*," Dale explained. "He'll tell his Rasta brothers what's happening. I told you, both the dreads and the street police grabbed him asking where the powder came from. No one wants a new player in their game."

"But the police would welcome more payoffs."

"Another dealer syndicate would mean more violence taking over territory," Dale said. "The police don't need any more shootouts; that attracts too much stateside attention. All these jerks get paid with federal money. These islands are just enabled projects. The entire place is a welfare state and there's nothing well or fair."

"Let's get some coffee and breakfast specials," Keith called for room service. "Let's run through it one more time. Tomorrow, early-early, I take the outboard from Yacht Haven Marina. You pick me up at Lindberg Bay. I'll show you where today. There's a small pier for the college boats. I'm at the bunkers before dawn and will have everything ready. Then I call my numbers again from another new phone and leave it on. You meet with Carlos. Whew, sounds like a lot."

"I'll meet that prick at the fat prick Josef's joint. Check for the money. I'll make that perfectly clear when I talk with both those assholes today that I'll meet them at seven. They'll be anxious."

"Seven's good. I'll plan to have Jeffers' gang at Mountain Top at eight. I'll text you when they call me. I'm telling them to be at the parking lot and they'll get the next directions. You know they'll have an idea we're in a condo. You've got to be chauffeur again today. I'll make a few runs, quick stuff. It's Thursday, traffic will be the usual congestion." Keith answered the door and they wheeled breakfast in. "Figure to eat a lot of eggs; need the protein with my gal," he flashed his grin. "You can drop me off at Hull and go meet your guy. Pick me up when you're finished."

"How come you're getting relaxation therapy and not me?" Dale chuckled, sipping coffee. "Sure thing, I'll keep myself occupied for a few hours. Gonna sneak back to Georgie's place and load the gear I left there. It's already packed since I ran from the old apartment. I'll bring it to the boat when I pick you up.

Then I'm good to go."

The first chore took balls. Keith, neatly dressed, bought a new lock and a small pair of bolt cutters. With that, he walked boldly down the dock to where his escape boat was. He snapped the owner's lock off the steel cable and replaced it with his. No one questioned him. Changing the locks in broad daylight wasn't the act of a criminal. The boat would be easy to hot-wire the following morning.

They drove to Red Hook, where Dale called Josef and Carlos with the details. Keith phoned Jeffers using the voice distorter. "I know it's been a while. This conversation won't take long, so pay attention. I'll call with precise directions early tomorrow morning, about daybreak. Have the money ready. No tracking devices or exploding dye packs. You come alone, only you. I check the money before you see the product. When the transaction's finished, we go our separate ways."

He knew it wouldn't happen like that. Jeffers would have a squad and every trick he could devise. The payback mechanism began to churn a blend that would probably be bloody. Both groups had been eager for the calls and both said they would obey the rules. Most important, they had the money. Dale and Keith figured their opponents were readying their troops. They removed the batteries from the phones, so a trace wasn't possible.

The next route was to the west, as far as the Fortuna Road went, to the Stumpy Bay Bible School. Keith dialed the number for the FBI and was on hold for a few minutes. He attempted to imitate a West Indian voice, "Yes, sir, I want to tell you something big gonna happen tomorrow on St. Thomas. Yes, sir, big, gigantic. Yes, sir, cocaine. Lots and lots of cocaine, close to a hundred pounds. No, sir, I don't know where, but on St. Thomas tomorrow morning, early. Yes sir, no sir, you need not know my name. Best you come with just your own men, people you can trust, because local police are directly involved in this coke thing I'm calling about. If fact, I know, for sure, they're guarding the load. I'll call you tomorrow when I know exactly where it is going down. You be ready. Yes, sir, I'll keep you informed. Thank you, sir."

"That seemed to go well," Dale commented. "You almost sound like you 'barne here me-son.' A chance at a hundred pounds of dancing dust will get them off their asses. That size of a bust would get them a pay raise."

"Yeah, the guy I talked to, Agent Carusoe asked the right questions. He took me seriously. Let's hope he doesn't think it's a diversionary attempt. Don't believe the Fibbees get along with the DEA. No one trusts anyone outside their office, and sometimes not even that," Keith said as he dialed again, using the same accent.

"Officer Meyers, hello, you don't know me and need not know who this is. I'm a concerned citizen, tired of all the drugs and killings. Yes sir, yes sir, no, I won't give you my name. I don't want any reward money," Keith winked at Dale. "Wait, just listen, tomorrow there's gonna be a big score. Yes, sir, cocaine, more than a hundred pounds of cocaine. Why did I call you? I know you from church. Don't try to figure who I am, like I said, a concerned citizen. This deal will happen early Friday morning. It involves one of my relatives, a bad relative, terrible. I'll call you at this same number as soon as I find out the details. Yeah, my relative said police were guarding the shipment, so watch your behind," Keith ended the call.

"Okay, you did your civic duty," Dale said, as he patted his partner on the back. "Good job, enough to tantalize. Speaking of, you finished all the chores and are ready for Lucy?"

Keith stared at the beautiful view of Kalkun Cay and Savana Island. He nodded with a deep sigh, "In for a penny, in for a pound."

"More like forty pounds, buddy," Dale started the car singing Billy Joel's 'We Didn't Start the Fire.' "Where to now, boss?"

"Back to Lucy's boat. On the way, I'll show you the university dock where you need to meet me tomorrow."

In the morning, it would be a run for his life. The way they'd planned it, he felt he'd make it without being incriminated. After a short, one-beer-interlude at Hull Bay, the rental house was the next stop. Dale gathered his belongings and left a note thanking George for all his help with the excuse that the island's attitude had finally gotten to him. His replacement-in-waiting, Neal, would probably find the note that explained he'd caught a boat south. After the realtor's son had witnessed him taking a severe beating, only a few words were necessary.

His young West Indian contact parked at Magen's overlook. Dale used the phone to tell him to be cautious, follow the white Suzuki, and watch he wasn't being tailed. He stayed a hundred meters ahead and watched for any other vehicles. Before the road headed into Peterborg Point, Dale took a right and pulled over at the isolated Mandahl Salt Pond.

"Jesus, old man, where the hell you taking me? This is

my cousin's ride. Now I gotta wash off all this dust and mud. So, what's going down that needs all this spy secrecy?" Eddie asked.

"Tomorrow, the deal will happen and only you will know what, when, and where. My friends plan to unload their stuff to the Spanish."

The short West Indian cut Dale off. "What the fuck you talking about? The Spanish? I thought my posse would buy it…"

"Hey, just sit quiet and listen. You are about to become a major player and stop being a pawn."

"You calling me a prawn, a shrimp? I'm small but…"

Dale stopped him, "Never mind, not a prawn. Here's the plan: my friends are doing the deal and they don't like the Spanish. In fact, I'll lead the intended buyers from Frenchtown to the meeting. I'll text you where the meeting will be. All you have to do is hijack the load after we get our cash. Understand?"

The islander rubbed the stubble of his beard. "Real gangsta shit, huh? Them Spicos would do it to us in a heartbeat."

"If they knew where it was going down," Dale interrupted. "You, Eddie, will be the only person who'll have that info. Who you tell, well, that is up to you, but personally, it would be smarter to bring in your people rather than try to take these guys on alone. But I get my old white ass out of there first, you understand, before any shooting starts."

Eddie sighed, "Oh yeah, there'll be some lead flying. My boss hates that fucking Carlos motherfucker. The Spico's enforcer, Hook, put a real hurtin' on a few of our posse. Said they was outside *our* territory. How can those weasels claim any areas when they just arrive? We barne here! Mother fuckers! Okay, I'm listening; explain this shit to me."

"I meet Carlos early, maybe seven, and check that they have the money. I have to text my friends we're coming. Then he'll text you the location where you should wait for the load after the money's changed hands. The best bet is if you're waiting at Fairchild Park. I know this is going down somewhere on the north side, but my friends won't say where for their own safety. They aren't even telling me."

"Why's your friend gonna text me and help rip off the Spanish? You running a side game, old man? What else you ain't telling me?" "Oh, my young friend, there's plenty you will never know, but … Hook and Carlos gave me serious licks and one of my friends has a private score to settle with Carlos. There's nothing else, just be careful. If this plays right, and there's no reason for it not to, we all come out with a chunk of change." Dale continued, "Hang back and let the other guys be the soldiers. You gave them the deal, so that should make you a general."

"Hmm, general, huh, I like the sound of that, General Eddie. From here, I'm going directly to my boss. We'll be ready. You said Fairchild, right?"

"Right. Be careful and you'll grow old like me. Look, ah, you can't call me anymore. I'm tossing the phone. Just be patient. You have my word that my friend'll text you where the deal is."

"This is some crazy shit, meeting you and all. My people thought you was the man."

"I am the man; the man who's about to change your life." It was out of character, but Dale hugged his new buddy, silently hoped they'd both still be breathing at this same time the following day.

Josef's was Dale's next stop. This was the most important part of the scheme. Everyone had to be on the same page. He parked two blocks away in the Trade Winds Hotel parking lot, grabbed a new backpack from the car, and walked to the restaurant.

"Where the fuck have you been? These Spanish guys have been driving me nuts! They think you and I are working together against them," Josef blabbed. "And with a new clean-cut look, oh my, aren't we looking dapper."

"What, not even a 'hello, how are you'? How about a beer on the house?" Dale replied.

"Sure, sure, what information do you have for me? They want to hang me by my balls. You know how this shit makes everyone crazy. Big money, big worries," Josef reasoned.

"I know, and you know, I know," Dale stared at Josef, "We got to stick together and protect our own asses, partner."

"No, don't use that word, not even joking. We aren't partners." Josef looked around warily, "If someone hears that and reports it, I'll be shark food. Where and when?" Josef asked.

"Wow, you are shook up. Tomorrow morning, my friends will have the stuff at a location they pick." Dale said slowly, "I do not know where it'll be yet. First, Carlos shows me the money. Then, I call them, and the guys with the product say where. All I know is that it's not far and they want to do it early."

"Is it okay if I call him?" Josef requested and got a nod before dialing. "Hola, amigo, you know who you were waiting for, he's in my office. Okay, I'll ask him to wait for you." He ended the call. "He's coming."

Dale swallowed hard. He really didn't want to see Carlos, but it had to be. Leaving the bar without a tail would be the trick.

Josef brought beers, and they walked to the deck to watch the harbor activity. There wasn't much to chat about. Dale knew Josef's greed had spotted his own past, and no one's future plans were open for discussion.

Within five minutes, the gruff Colombian joined them. "Okay, let's hear the deal."

One more time, Dale explained the only way his friends would sell the dust. They picked the place and wouldn't tell him where until he guaranteed he'd seen all the money. Dale would ride with Carlos and direct him to the location, but only he would hold the money. If anything changed, the connection would be severed, and the dust is gone forever.

Carlos scoffed, "Old man, you think I am so stupid? Why would I give you my money without seeing the product?"

"Amigo, and I use that term loosely, I check the amount right here so there's no counterfeit, no shorts, no problems. I call my friends, give them the okay, and take you there. Put the money in this backpack. I hold the money and am with you until you get the product. I know you'll worry, because that's how you think about things. And, I have to say my friends are legit. They want to dump the load here, get the scratch, and disappear. Follow all my instructions; bring no more soldiers than your bodyguard. Don't try to rip off my friends and they won't rip you off. You have my word."

"Why should I trust you?" Carlos whispered.

"Because, you fucking have to!" Dale was losing patience. "The blow is untouched, as pure as it gets."

"Yeah, it's pure. It's my product!" Carlos shouted.

"No, it's not! They brought it to the island. If you want it, you gotta buy."

Carlos opened his leather jacket to reveal a small automatic pistol. "How about I take you and trade you for my stuff?"

Instantly, Dale whirled around and had his own pistol at the man's chest. All their antics were invisible to anyone in the establishment. "And you would do what, motherfucker? I could finish you now and sell it to the Rastas. Tell me something; did you just piss your pants? Huh? You sweating?" Dale released a pale, shaken Carlos and turned to the sea view.

"Gentlemen, gentlemen, calm down, we need cool heads." Josef took Carlos' pistol.

The Columbian was quiet for a few minutes, rubbing his face in deep thought. Dale broke the silence, "My way or I'm on the highway. I see and hold the cash; you meet my friends and get the blow. It's all very simple."

Always the negotiator, Josef offered a solution. "I know both of you. Let me stay with Dale. That way you have someone watching your money."

Dale shook his head 'no.' He'd already thought of this possibility and liked it, but didn't want to show any enthusiasm. "Nope, too many people. I don't think I can clear this change with my friends by tomorrow."

Carlos nodded to Josef. "The fat man comes along. Old man, you know him, I know him. Unfortunately, you and I got off to a poor start. That was my fault, but things would probably be the same. Seven hundred large is huge money. I have a big four-wheel-drive Pajero. My man, Hook, drives; you sit upfront with him and give directions, Josef holds the money in the back with me... or no go."

"I don't like you or anyone sitting behind me. I sit with Josef in the rear," Dale said, "and no guns tomorrow. Everybody frisks everyone before we start." He knew his words were wasted, but he had to said it; otherwise, he'd be condoning a shootout. They'd hide their weapons in the vehicle. He'd already hidden his.

"Si, señor, no problema. Then we agree. Josef, have coffee for us mañana, strong coffee. We will be here at seven as you require. No problems, no guns, y mucho dinero." Carlos extended his hand, Dale stared into his dark eyes as they shook, and what he saw was appalling over- confidence. This wouldn't end well for the Columbian, who foolishly believed he would outsmart everyone.

Dale hailed a taxi, knowing Carlos would try to follow. After many years fighting the choking traffic of Charlotte Amalie, Dale knew the side streets and shortcuts. Ordering the reluctant taxi man to make several t w i s t s and turns, he pressed a Ben Franklin into the driver's hand and told him to drive as fast as possible to the airport.

At the next side street, he tapped the driver to stop. He bailed, but left his ball cap visible on the back- w i n d o w ledge. It was an old trick, probably wouldn't confuse anyone intelligent, so it should work on this tail. A quick run through the Old Bourne Ice Plant brought him to his rental. Dale put on a long black wig Eddie had purchased. Slumped in the seat, just barely looking over the wheel, he wound through the back streets, up Mafoli Hill, and down to Hull Bay, satisfied no one knew his whereabouts.

There would be problems. The white dust always brought the devil with it.

On the boat, Lucy had been respectful and hadn't issued another a list of reasons not to do it. She realized they'd already had set their minds to do it. Keith spent a comfortable afternoon with his loves: Lucy and his Lab, Baron. Parting with a few tears, Dale drove his buddy to the hotel. On the way, they discussed everything that had transpired. After paying their tab in cash, they requested a five-a.m. wake-up call.

"One thing we got to do; something I forgot that could bite us later; the rental car," Dale said.

"What about the rental car?" Keith asked.

"The receipt, it's in my actual name, my VI driver's license."

Keith sighed, "Yeah, I can see that could make for a problem. What do you have in mind?"

"We look to rent another for you."

"Ah, I don't see how also giving them my ID will hide you?" Keith replied.

"Um, there's only one agent in the office. You get him to show you what's available and I'll cut the receipt out of his ledger book. Keep him out there for a few minutes and I'll erase it from the computer. It's worth a chance. Tomorrow, we're out of here. The car's wiped down and I'll leave it in Frenchtown, close to Jo's."

"Okay."

It was quiet, only a two-beer night. Both had a deep sleep, yet each awakened before the call. Keith showered while Dale made coffee with the Joe DiMaggio counter drip.

"Not bad," Keith tasted. "Good enough to get us off and running." "And running we will be," Dale added. "This will be a full day, plenty of exercise."

"Hey, we covered all the bases, crossed the Ts and dotted the Is."

"We think," Dale sighed.

"No time for doubts. Got to believe we did it all," was his partner's recourse.

They dressed, pulling jeans over bright tourist-style bathing trunks and long shirts over t-shirts. All the phones were charged and checked that all the necessary numbers were on speed dial. After they'd put on the clear surgical gloves under a pair of the soft cotton garden variety, they cleaned the room of all trash, and hopefully wiped everything of fingerprints. Each carried five pairs gloves, planning this to be a forensic nightmare.

On the way to Yacht Haven Marina, the duo checked and rechecked their schedule, especially the phone calls and texts. Keith had created texts for each law enforcement branch to accompany his verbal messages. All he had to do was push a few buttons. Dale had to only flash 'Yes' to Keith when everything was organized with Josef and Carlos.

They'd wiped clean every phone, SIM, and even the battery on the voice distorter. The hotel trash was dumped along with Keith's few extra clothes, in a roadside bin.

At minutes before six, the docks were empty. The key opened the lock on the outboard. Before undoing the bow and stern lines, Keith pressed a Ziploc with ten grand, more than double the boat's value, through the hasp and snapped the lock. He dropped the chain into the water so no passerby would see the cash. No sense in making a stranger pay. He sliced three wires, twisted two together, and touched them to the third to start the engine, and as quietly as possible, maneuvered out of the harbor. His course went west around both Hassel and Water Island. Past the airport, he calmly maneuvered to the University of the West Indies dock. He was securing the twenty-four-footer when Dale arrived. Walking toward the car, he suddenly remembered to leave a small bag on the boat.

"What's that?" Dale inquired.

"Nothing," Keith replied.

"They're already drinking coffee at Josef's. Saw their cars there when I passed."

"Cars? Thought you told them they should only have one?" Keith asked.

"We both knew they'd have a gang. Lots of money, lots of coke; no one follows directions…"

"Except you and me," Keith laughed nervously. He took a deep breath and exhaled a long, loud sigh. "It's all gonna be good. I love the feeling of adrenaline. That's the best drug."

"Probably the most expensive," Dale countered. "Consider all the shit it takes to wind us up enough to get our bodies to secrete it, the spirit of dilemmas."

"Doctor Dale," Keith muttered as they made the last turn at Four Corners and entered Georgie's driveway. "Okay, it's a go from here." Without further words, they shook hands. The rental pulled away and took the right turn, down through Solberg, into town.

Alright, send lawyers, guns, and money - Warren Zevon

CHAPTER TWENTY

The morning was fresh with just a hint of a sea breeze. The sky's early shade of blue almost continued into the ocean. Keith stood for a moment, gazing down at the tranquil harbor that had been an infamous home to the pirates for centuries. Not much had changed except the current 'gold' was now white powder. The island government was still being paid for protection and contraband, as it always had been, was one of the main economies. Crime paid well when almost everyone at the top got a piece of the lucrative action.

He started the motorcycles and let them warm up before pushing both uphill toward the bunkers. He left Dale's at the prearranged spot next to the sidewalk entrance to the condos. It looked as though it belonged to a resident. Each motorbike had a helmet strapped to the handlebars. No sense in being stupid and either getting injured in an accident or chased for a 'no-helmet' traffic citation.

The condo lot was full except for a half dozen spaces, more than enough to accommodate his expected visitors. Keith's cycle leaned against a tree on the old road below the bunkers. Once he placed the kilos in the west bunker, had the lights on, and made sure the tray rolled easily, he opened the hatch to the east side. Wearing his ski mask, Keith turned on the voice distorter, and did a check of the sound and video recording by sending a message to his smartphone.

After another adjustment, everything was ready to text the police, U.S. Attorney, and the newspaper who also owned a radio and TV station. That evening, after beaming the live-action video, the only people on the island who wouldn't know what happened in the next few hours would be the dead in the cemeteries.

He called Jeffers, who answered on the first ring. "Can't hear you; where's the meet? The time, when?" Jeffers was both stalling to get a fix and to hear a human sounding voice.

Keith replied distinctly with one word, 'text,' and knew they had his coordinates. The toughest part came next: waiting. He occupied the time by tying fluorescent red nylon strips to identify the trail from the road to the bunkers. He checked where they'd stashed the *just in case* guns, he'd removed from the boats off Anegada.

It was 6:50 when Dale entered Josef's parking lot. He tore off his surgical gloves, took a deep breath and surveyed who was watching. One burly Spanish man ushered him into the bar while another found nothing of interest after inspecting the rental car.

"Let's see the money," Dale casually said, "that's what we're here for. Once this is finished, we can get on with the rest of our day."

Josef offered a cup of coffee as Carlos unzipped the supplied backpack. Dale dumped the cash, fanned, and counted each of the seventy 'ten grand' stacks. He carefully felt the backpack to be certain they'd added nothing. All the while Carlos and his bodyguard, Hook, stood quietly. The other two Spanish had vanished, probably would join later to escort.

"It all looks good. If something's missing, it's only small money," Dale remarked before he sipped the coffee, but then decided against it in case they'd mixed in a slow-acting sedative or poison. No unnecessary chances.

"I'm not going to short you. Now, let's get moving," Carlos ordered.

"Not yet, my friends will call when they're in place."

"That's not what you said yesterday," Carlos impatiently whined.

"Yeah, I did, but you have a problem hearing." The wall clock was seven minutes faster than his 7:20.

Fifteen minutes later, a four-door pickup pulled to the rear of the Mountain Top Condo parking lot. Jeffers and Agent Luis got out and stood looking official in their DEA labeled bulletproof vests and ball caps. The driver's side rear door, invisible because of the nearby hedge, noiselessly opened and Agent Mazanas, wearing complete camo with a scoped automatic rifle, slid into the bush.

"What now, boss? I think we should barricade the road," Luis posed.

"I never care what you think," Jeffers tersely replied, obviously on edge. "I've got cars at the bottom of Crown Mountain ready if we need them. They'll clog every fucking thing if I call. They, no fucking body, needs to know what's happening up here… unless it gets out of control. That's why I'm here, to keep that from happening. But in the meantime, I want this quiet. If it's quiet, dumb fuck, we're able to sell this stuff and make a fortune. I figure these guys are amateurs. Who else would call us to a meeting at a condo with only one road in and out? We know they're here; phone GPS doesn't lie. That's another stupid amateur move. We grab the goods and the money, snuff these idiots, and have more for retirement. Entiendes?"

Keith watched intently, yet hadn't seen the man in camo, nor had the man seen him. He sent Jeffers another text telling him to walk along the road until he saw the red tags and to follow the trail. Once he saw the acknowledging movement, he withdrew deeper into the bush toward the bunkers, knowing the well-dressed DEA agents would move cautiously slow. From the top of the bunker, Keith made brief calls and texted Meyers and the FBI. Once he felt sure each group was underway, he texted Dale. It was all coming together.

On his side of the bunker, he plugged the phone into the antenna, sound system, and voice distorter. Everything was about timing. It was a given that each group would play by their own rules and try to fuck him.

He kept track of the minutes with his digital. Twelve minutes after the last text, he broadcast to Jeffers above and directed him to look for the bunch of red tape at the opening.

"What the fuck is this?" Jeffers was already soaked with sweat. "Where the fuck are you?" he said to an empty forest and then to Luis, "You know of anything below ground up here?"

"Nada, boss, could only be from World War II. Looks like the island forgot about it."

"Someone didn't," the DEA chief mumbled as they wandered around until they saw the last big fluorescent red strip tied to the rusty hatch. He pulled his pistol while the other agent slid the piece of plywood over and revealed a light below.

"Still think these guys are amateurs, boss?"

"Fuck you, get down there. I'll follow."

The invisible, distorted voice bellowed, "You alone, Agent Jeffers; stick with the plan."

The overweight man wiped his face and crossed himself. "I don't give a fuck; come down in five minutes. If you hear anything, come sooner. Got me?" His weight and the bulky vest slowed his descent and caused the ladder to creak. Jeffers coughed nervously from the dampness and exertion. The charged bulbs caused him to squint as he surveyed the dingy room.

Keith had flicked two switches; one turned on the transmitter and the other limited the sound to only within the bunker. Everything then became a live broadcast and should convince any jury these agents were corrupt. Few could immediately pinpoint the location. It would seem like they pre-empted the regular programming for a made-for-TV movie.

"You brought the money, Agent Jeffers?" The weird voice echoed.

"It's all here. Where are you? Can't hide much here. Help me out; who the fuck are you? Where the fuck are you?" Jeffers had his pistol aimed as he slowly turned, looking at every inch of the room, yet never seeing the small cameras at the base of the walls.

"I'm right here. I can see every move you make. You're scratching your nose. Like I'm gonna tell you who I am. Get real. I'm sure you remember your dead agents who tried to rip off this load of coke from the sailboat up Anegada way. I came along later and found them. The captain shot them when he figured your agents were banditos. Yeah, your boys had the money to buy, but it was all part of the scam. They shot back. Four people died when the DEA tried to rip off a load of coke."

"So what, who the fuck are you, the white knight who will sell me back what should have been mine? You think this buy will set things right? Provide a pension plan for the family of the not-so-lucky captain and crew? Enough talk; where are you?" Jeffers replied, fully believing he could say anything because he was talking with a soon-to-be-dead son of a bitch.

"Who do you work for besides the people who pay your wages? The West Indian and Spanish drug dealers?" Keith asked.

"Fellow, wherever you are, we are just like you, opportunists. Drug enforcement is the same everywhere; we show some of what we confiscate to make us look good, sell the rest to make money, and use some to make us feel good. We are in the middle of a dangerous business, but it's all business. Now, let's get down to it and do some business."

The drawer in the middle wall slid outward, causing the big agent to jump back. "Place the money in there. I count it and send you back the cocaine."

"You're fucking off-the-wall crazy! You want to rip me off. I wasn't born yesterday!"

"Do it, or I sell the cocaine to the Spanish who it originally owned it and tell them about your two attempted rip-offs, the one at their yacht and this one. I've got everyone on speed dial: the Spics, the Rastas, maybe even a few independent buyers from other islands. You'll never find me. Besides, you probably only signed a requisition for the cash. You're the boss of the local DEA, aren't you? I'm not doing business with a puppy, am I? Aren't you the top dog?" Keith chided his opponent and got the desired effect.

Jeffers took several deep breaths while he considered his

position. The perp was right; it wasn't his money. He'd get this prick and then kill him slowly. "Okay." He dropped the briefcase of money into the steel drawer and it creaked slowly closed.

Agent Luis stuck his head into the opening, "Everything okay, boss? Where's the perp?"

Jeffers put a single finger to his lips and waved his agent to come down the ladder.

Once Dale received Keith's text, they drove from Frenchtown, up Crown Mountain Road, and turned off at Scott Free. Carlos co-piloted from the passenger seat and kept prying at the destination only to get blank looks. Josef was visibly nervous; his white shirt soaked wet with sweat, but kept his right hand on one of the backpack straps while Dale gripped the other. It was a confusing, stressful situation for three of the four in the SUV. Hook drove in silence.

The guide to the load of dancing dust looked at the magnificent views and didn't say much, except 'slow' and 'turn,' until they reached the last road. Then it was obvious they were going to the condos.

"Amigos, aqui?" Carlos mumbled, smiled, believing they had them trapped in a dead-end location. "Bueno view up here. Which condo?" He asked as they parked in the lot.

It was minutes after eight and some condo tenants were heading down the road, either to work or taking children to school.

"Wait," was Dale's only response. He opened his door, tugged at the backpack, and Josef grudgingly released his grip. There was no obvious DEA visible. With the phone in his pocket, Dale fingered the buttons and hit the text button '1' and got an instant beep reply that meant, 'bring them.' "Follow me."

Then Dale hit button '2' and while leading the three off the road and into the bush, sent another prepared text to Eddie.

"What the fuck?" Carlos uttered. "I thought you said they were in a condo?"

"You said, not me," Dale replied as Josef caught up and again grabbed a strap of the backpack, not unnoticed by the Spanish. Hook pulled his pistol and was trailing, watchful of every step.

"Red tape, huh? You do this?" Carlos whispered, moving hunched over as if they were in a war zone, and perhaps they were. "Old man, you are full of tricks. I hope you didn't trick yourself."

"Just keep following the tape. Watch your step. Josef and

me will wait here. Your goods are over there."

"Where? I don't see anyone. Hook, watch them."

"Look around; there's a hole. They're waiting for you inside; climb down."

"Below? I don't understand what you mean, below?" asked bewildered Carlos.

"I see it, boss. Look over there, the big red ribbon," Hook pointed and shepherded the two holding the backpack.

"Okay, you go first. I'll follow," Carlos instructed his grim-faced assistant.

Hook's bottom was almost too big to fit in the opening, but he was agile for a large man.

Meanwhile, Jeffers' and Luis' attention was riveted to the drawer that'd opened, revealing bricks of cocaine. They bent over and counted.

"Twenty-six keys; hey, supposed to be forty! We had a deal!" Keith used the distorter one last time.

"Cost of doing business, fuckface."

The distorted voice frightened Hook, causing him to lose his grip on the ladder and fall six feet. His racket surprised the DEA agents, who turned and instantly fired. Multiple echoes were unbearable. The acrid smell of gunpowder didn't mix well with the unventilated mold. The bodyguard held onto his automatic and squeezed off more than a dozen shots before he succumbed as target practice for the agents. Hook had been lucky to hit Luis in his right thigh with two shots. Blood was pumping from the agent's femoral artery.

Carlos heard the shots, turned, and took a quick aim at Dale, who did a slick dive and vanished into the scrub bushes. One of the misplaced Spanish bullets hit a now-bawling Josef in the shoulder, knocking him to the ground.

Dale remembered being caught in a crossfire in Somalia. He rummaged through the dead leaves until his hand touched the oily rag wrapped around Keith's Uzi and pistol. A nervous voltage of satisfaction roared through his system. He lay prone, counted to ten to subdue his breathing, and then jumped up, spraying the area with 9mm lead. There wasn't much of Carlos visible because he was kneeling, looking down at the wounded fat man. Dale slung the backpack on and sprinted for his motorbike. He'd seen it where Keith had parked it.

As he darted between the cars in the lot, another automatic rifle burst windshields slightly ahead of him. Dale hit the asphalt and bellied over the broken glass. "Mother fuckers! We knew you'd be here and I'm ready." He loaded the extra clip

He'd taped to the small machine gun. "Now, it's all about firepower."

He had to clear twenty feet of open space from the cars to the cycle. Dale drew his legs up under him and assumed a sprinter's stance, stayed low as he hauled ass across the opening. Then he dove into a barrel roll as bullets chipped the blacktop. One burst thudded his back and pushed him into another tumble. He thought they'd hit him, but the cash in the backpack absorbed the lead. He looked up expecting to see Carlos, but it was an unknown wearing camo. Dale squeezed off a burst, driving the man to disappear behind a hedge.

The gunshots were better than any burglar alarm. Every current resident of St. Thomas heard them weekly. Sometimes they shot up in the air in stupid celebration, not expecting what went up could fall deadly.

Other times, it was a robbery or errant shots by police who never took time to aim. Everyone feared being collateral damage. Condo residents were busy dialing the police.

At a self-imposed roadblock less than a quarter mile below, the Thatch Bay boys also heard the shots. Eddie was riding literally shotgun with a sawed-off twelve gauge when Big Man ordered the two cars with his ten men up the hill.

Dale was unseen, laying behind his cycle, when the cars roared into the parking lot. The unknown camo-man took aim as the Rastas jumped out. Big Man sagged as two shots bounced off his 'well-purchased' Kevlar vest. Unfortunately, he didn't react well, and the slump made the top of his dreadlocks a successful target. His head exploded across the white hood of his Escalade. His still loyal posse rabidly attacked the location of the gunfire.

With the action and barrage of bullets drawing all the attention far to his left, Dale rose, quickly pushed the bike to the sloping roadway, hopped on, and silently coasted away from the mayhem. He deftly felt for the pistol in his belt before he tossed the Uzi into the bush.

Still silently coasting, he made it past the Four Corners intersection and swerved into a driveway as several sirens screamed by. He took only minutes to pull off his gloves, jeans and shirt, leaving only his red, printed 'Make America Great' t-shirt and swimsuit. A check of the backpack showed two bullet holes. Trembling, he kick-started the cycle and proceeded toward Hull Bay.

While the bullets thundered in the other bunker, Keith pulled himself up the ladder on his side and looked around. Pulling himself up the ladder on his side, he looked around but couldn't ssfigure out who was shooting above ground. Still, he felt they were safe. Nobody was aiming at him. Carefully, he picked each footstep down the hidden trail to his cycle.

His backpack in place, he noiselessly coasted down the overgrown road. The current battle was in the parking lot and he didn't give a damn who was shooting who. To him, they were all bad guys. He wasn't lily-lily white innocent, but he had the satisfaction that everything that had happened was now video evidence against the assholes. These were the true villains who'd spoiled a beautiful island with drugs for personal profit.

At the end of the overgrown road, he removed his ski mask, gloves, jeans, and shirt. He kept one phone and then tossed everything over an embankment. Donning the helmet, wearing a 'vote for' T-shirt and bright trunks, he looked the part of an older surfer trying to save gas, silently rolling down the many hills that now reverbrated with screaming squad cars.

Keith could hear cars coming up from Charlotte Amalie. He pulled over at the Solberg overlook and saw a gridlock of traffic. It was normal congestion, work and school traffic coupled with tourists. His watch read 9:37. Lucy said she'd wait until 2. Maybe he should forgo all the extra escape routes he'd prepared and just get to her anchorage. That's what he should have done.

Jeffers shot Hook again square in the forehead to be certain he was out of this game. Then he pulled Luis to a far corner and used his belt as a tourniquet to reduce the flow of blood. The bunker had muffled the other gunshots, but he assumed Mazanas had a battle ensuing above. He tried to call his troops but couldn't get a signal. *His* DEA were waiting if he could only call. The Puerto Rican's heart was pounding. He wasn't completely fucked yet. Stepping on Hook, Jeffers kept his pistol ready as he pulled himself up rung by rung. Near the top, he could hear the exchange better and knew Mazanas had a sharp, well-trained eye, plus the element of surprise. Two rungs before the surface, he got three bars of cell service.

"Jesus Christ, don't you guys monitor your radio? All Hell's breaking loose up here… Mountain Top… no, not the gift shops… yes, the condos. Leave one car with two guys at the Crown Bay intersection. Don't fuck around, get up here. Alert everyone; have VIMP get off their asses and patrol the harbor just in case. Stop everyone, check ID's. Luis' been shot; get an ambulance up here. Lock and load mother fuckers; this is war!"

Carlos was lying prone next to Josef, using the fat man for a shield. He heard other cars squeal into the parking lot, followed by a barrage of gunfire.

"Help me, help me, get me out of here," Josef begged.

"No can do, too dangerous," Carlos whispered. The younger man slid his pistol to the other man's head and pulled the trigger. "Now you're out of here. One less to testify. Where's that old fucker and my cash?"

The Spanish looked up at the billowing clouds, "Play with fire, get burned, mama always said. How will I get out of this? Got to be a way. Got to be." He phoned his two men who were supposed to be waiting. "Come to Mountain Top, no, not the gift shops, the condos; call everyone who wants a payday. Mucho dinero! Mucho! Come prepared to make these mother fuckers pay."

His eyes caught a movement at the bunker and saw Jeffers' head pop up, examining the area. "Madre de Dios, damn you, Jeffers, you're behind this! You ripped me! You set this up, working with the old fuck. I should have known. Cut me off for the Rastas! I'll ventilate your Puerto Rican ass!" Carlos aimed and fired, but Jeffers dropped out of sight.

At the Island Guardian News office, two blank monitors suddenly flashed a bright video of a room. No one paid attention until several gunshots were the accompanying soundtrack. "Hey, better get the editor in here. The boss is gonna want to see this."

"You're taping it, eh?"

"Absolutely, automatic, got it all! Somehow it's on the live news feed we use for all those idiots who send us stuff off their phones."

"What the shit, mon? Where's this coming from? How come we get it? This is a stable shot, not from a handheld phone that's wobbling."

"Who cares; might be another Pulitzer."

The cycle ride had been fourteen minutes, downhill almost all the way to Hull. It passed without incident or seeing anything that remotely looked like police. It had gone as planned, at least on his end. Dale saw Starlet's inflatable pulled up on the beach. The big yellow Lab came running to check him out, followed by a crying Lucy.

"Oh, Dale, I saw it on TV at the bar, everyone was..."

"Calm down, Lucy, calm down." He looked around to discern if she had attracted anyone's attention. "Don't draw any unnecessary interest. What'd you see?"

"People getting shot and killed... in a room... all about cocaine," she sobbed. "Is Keith okay?"

"I don't see why not; everything went like clockwork," Dale grinned.

"Are you sure?"

"Sweetie, neither of us can be sure until we see him walk into the bar in Old San Juan. Speaking of which, I'm kind of dry. Think you can hold it together while I see the news broadcast and grab a cold one?"

She swallowed. "I'd better wait here." Lucy dropped to the sand and held on to the Lab. Dale put the backpack in the dinghy.

Pierre's Bar had the usual local fishermen and a few tourist campers. The live-action glued everyone to the TV. The bartender had the radio blaring eyewitness reports.

"What's up?" Dale inquired after receiving and draining his first Heineken.

"Gunfight," a fisherman replied.

"Looks like a drug war to me," commented the bartender. "Radio says it's up at Mountain Top. The first part showed a big guy wearing a DEA bulletproof vest, talking about stealing back a load of coke. Must be in a condo, weird-looking place; see for yourself. They keep playing it back. Nothing new for a while."

"Probably editing it, so we only see what they want. You know how the Feds are," another fisherman added.

Dale drained the beer and paid for another to carry to the beach. "Crazy world," he said.

One tourist remarked, "Yeah, now even drug deals are on YouTube!"

Over the sound of the approaching sirens, Eddie's attention was drawn to a shot deeper in the bush, followed a few minutes later by two more. The rifleman, somewhere at the far end of the parking lot, had killed his boss and wounded two Rastas. The remaining six of the posse returned fire, and now it was quiet. He figured they'd probably hit the sniper and were reloading. Cops and reinforcements were on the way. This was not the place to be. He belly-crawled into the tall grass away from the condos.

"What the fuck are these red tags?" Eddie thought as he squirmed along the noticeable trail of trampled grass. He'd only fired twice at the invisible parking lot shooter. He took the time to replace those cartridges into his Remington 12. "Now I got the lucky seven. Seven shots of double ought!" he mouthed as he curled into a ball to catch a breather. "Not a bad rap line. Seven shots of double ought. This is some wicked shit. That old man really laid down some serious wet work. But where's his stash?"

The one-sided, whispered conversation continued. "No one could get out of here. Nobody passed by us except him. Ah, that old mother fucker had a backpack. Nah, it couldn't hold much dust. This killing shit is all about a *load* of dust. The road was blocked before and damn straight is gonna be blocked for hours to come." Eddie rolled over and saw the bright, Caribbean blue sky with billowing clouds. "This place ain't gonna be my end." He fondled the shotgun, "Nah man, this place is gonna be my beginning. Fuck'em all!"

The short West Indian got to his knees and carefully scanned the area. He spat and whispered, "Some stark, bloody shit, boy oh boy, Big Man bought it. Dude went down in an instant, looking at it head-on." There was movement off to his right, deeper inside the trees.

Bang! Bang! Bang! Afraid to be another target on the ladder, Carlos reached his arm down and fired. He heard a loud groan, but there was no way to tell if they faked it to lure him. It didn't matter; Eddie had sighted the Colombian and fired. The shot just grazed his right shoulder, but the force was enough to knock the thin man over the edge of the bunker into the tall savanna grass and bushes.

Eddie stood, racked in another cartridge, and with the shotgun raised, followed like a hunter. His shot had brought two more of the Rastas running. "What's up, lil' man?" The taller one yelled, "Where are they? Who ya shootin' at?"

Eddie signaled to be quiet and pointed to the hole.

"What de fuck is dis?" the taller one asked to no answer. He stuck his head down only to bounce out when pistols roared from below.

"I think that's where the powder is," Eddie answered, as a second well-armed posse member arrived. "Can't be many down there. I shot that Spanish fuck, Carlos, after he pumped shots down that tube."

"Sure, lil' man, den where is he? Well, dere's someone still 'live down there, shooting back! How far down you think it is? Can't be much, ten, twelve feet." The two Rastas ignored Ed and planned their strategy. "I'll drop while you shoot to keep dem ducking. Den you drop. Many shots as we heard, dere can't be any dat ain't bleeding."

The two checked their automatic pistols, straightened their protective vests, grasped hands, and said a quick prayer to Jah. Pushing Ed away from the opening, one straddled it, and as soon as he dropped, the other roared gunfire into the hole.

A lucky shot from Carlos had hit Jeffers in his right shoulder. He'd wedged himself behind the immobile Luis. Both were severely wounded, yet still cognizant. The first dread man dropped, accompanied by too many pistol shots to count. Luis took careful aim and extinguished the island boy who'd fallen into this inferno, seconds before a second dreadlock dropped onto two bodies. A shot finished the younger DEA agent with a hit in his throat. Jeffers kept still, listening to the last gasps of his amigo, waiting for a clean shot. His only hope was reinforcements.

Eddie watched from above as the second dread slowly straightened, stupidly confident his lanky body was fully shielded behind his vest. Ed saw his friend get hit twice and bounce back, but the tall dread emptied two full pistols before crumpling.

Follow or flee was the short West Indian's indecision as gun smoke waved up from the square opening. Through the haze, he could see three still bodies. It was all about the dust. He forgot about chasing the Spanish gang leader, Carlos. "Now or never, if I want my Beemer!"

Squad cars and ambulances packed the entrance road, haphazardly parked behind the two Rasta Escalades. Two carloads of misplaced Colombians made their worst, bad-timing mistake. Even though it was logical that more law enforcement was following, they continued winding up the hill until blocked by empty cars. It didn't take brains to be a gang member. Loyalty or greed, their purpose didn't matter since it had trapped them. More firepower was their response.

Two unfortunate DEA, directed by Jeffers, pulled into the driveway and immediately succumbed from a torrent of Colombian machine guns.

Most of the regular St. Thomas Police, who'd arrived, dove from their four squad cars into the dense roadside bushes, along with two pairs of EMTs. Frenchie Detective Michael was *accidentally* in the second car to arrive after the Rastas. This was accidental because he had no intention of ever shooting or being shot at. His 'protect and serve' was directed only at his own well-being. He shrunk below the dashboard after the windshield exploded when two dreads opened up shredding his partner. He fingered his pearl-handled, chrome-plated 38 snub nose revolver, came out of his daze, and radioed for backup.

"Back up from who, Mikey? We got everyone headed up there. Protect yourself! Shoot the bad guys! Part of this thing is on TV."

"What?"

"Yeah, mon, no shit, looks like the Rican DEA was buying a load when it went sideways," replied the radio dispatcher. "It's on TV, Channel 6, it's still playing out; got to be somewhere near where you are. Otherwise, why they shooting everybody up there?"

"Me no know?" finished the conversation as horrendous gunfire then erupted from behind, down the hill, and burst the car's remaining windows. He never realized he was trapped between the Rastas, the Colombians, and a DEA sharpshooter. He tried to make himself as small as possible, dodging the shards of glass. Bullets were flying in all directions.

"Hmm, what to do, what to do?" With his foot, he deftly opened the driver's side door and shoved out his partner's body. Sal had been a righteous guy, an excellent partner for many years, but was deader than a doornail now. Mikey squeezed under the steering wheel, slid out the door using his partner's body for a screen. His only view was from under the cars. No way would he stand up and be a target for flying bullets.

Ahead, beside, and behind, the Frenchie could see legs moving, well, only feet. Some were wearing hard, shiny, police issues, but from the condo area, just ahead, the feet he saw approaching were dark and wearing sandals. Mikey carefully fired and watched a cursing Rasta drop. He hadn't seen the other pair of sandals and couldn't react in time before his life ended with a 9mm rhythm.

It was a multi-sided battle. The few, still healthy Rastas held the higher ground, bewildered police patrolmen and women were flanking along the roadsides. Colombians owned the rear, murdering the two DEA. Myers and Faulkner became the unlucky participants at the tail of all the lodged cars. They pulled up behind the riddled DEA pickup.

They'd been listening to a duel play-by-play from their dispatch desk and on the island's key radio station.

"It's total, bloody confusion, the kind only cocaine creates. Your source wasn't joking, must be a huge load," Faulkner confided. "What you wanna do?"

Meyer checked his pistol, counted an extra clip on his holster, and shared the two he grabbed from the glove box. He nervously smiled, "Collect our pensions." He removed his easy-target white shirt and pinned his badge to his dark blue police vest. Faulkner did the same. "No sense wearing a bullseye." Pointing to the bullhorn, "This'll draw enough attention."

Just before the last turn, they stopped, got out, and advanced on foot. Carefully, weaving only twenty meters, they could see several men who were not law enforcement, firing indiscriminately. Faulkner and Meyers took careful aim, semi-protected by trees, and shouted, "Police, hold your fire! Drop your weapons!"

The men, no longer shielded by their cars, spun and opened up in their direction. The two experienced police had already taken aim and popped off four of them. Two more tried to run to either side of the driveway, but they were cut down by several shots from within the dense hedge along the roadside.
Again, Meyers used the bullhorn to little effect. The gunfire now was echoing from the condo parking lot. The air force arrived with the FBI in a helicopter bellowed their own amplified, "Put your weapons down!"

That met with more bullets. The copter swung, shielded by the condos, and heavily armed men in black uniforms rappelled down ropes, encircling the firefight. One FBI found DEA sniper Mazanas fatally wounded. He'd probably killed and been killed by the two Rastas crumpled nearby.

The FBI cautiously swept the condo and parking area. Meyers, with Faulkner, rallied the few not critically wounded police and slowly moved uphill. The Rastas were undaunted, continually firing at the few remaining Colombians who tried to defend all sides. The bad guys made a vicious last stand. The only two mobile dreads fired a barrage as they backed into the bush near the red trail markers.

"No boss, I don't know what happened. We either lost the video feed or something's blocking the cameras. Me, I think a body fell on it. It's war up there. Lots getting shot and killed. I think we've seen five so far."

"Run the last few minutes again. Yeah, broadcast it all again. We'll broadcast it all day," The Island Guardian News editor barked. "The entire world will see this!"

"Wait, wait, just listen," the technician directed.

Eddie shivered from the blaring gunfight. He figured it was curtains for the Thatch Bay Posse, and probably him, too. He easily fit, dropped, and landed with a thud. He twisted and rolled into a crevice between the dead. The small man gagged from soggy, bloody bodies, the stench of death and gun powder, combined with faint moans. He readied his shotgun and bellied toward the only thing slightly different in the grimy room, the metal drawer.

From a corner came, "Yo, kid, help me. Help me out of here. Yo, kid, I'll make it worth it to you. Help me!"

Keeping the gun leveled with his finger on the trigger, Eddie turned, but couldn't see who was talking. Looking around the room, he'd bounced down on the big guy he knew had been Carlos' guard. Two of his posse were strewn at angles close to the ladder. Wedged in the corner was a half-propped, sagging, bloody body wearing a DEA vest.

"Help me, have mercy, my friend," came again as he looked into the drawer and saw his dreams coming true. There lay the kilos, dumped out of a knapsack. The old white guy hadn't lied.

"Don't touch that!" The voice again, "I'm DEA and this is a sting operation." The definitely dead DEA agent seemed to stir.

"Move again and I'll bust seven double-ought in your dead-looking Rican ass," Eddie mouthed.

"That's mine!" Jeffers gasped, "All mine!"

Frightened by the dead man talking, Eddie thudded against the metal drawer and it moved. Just then, a familiar head appeared at the hatch, "Yo, lil' bro, what's down there?" It was one of the remaining posse.

"Only the dust we came for and a DEA guarding it."

A hand clenching a pistol rose from behind Luis as the Rasta descended the ladder. Jeffers could have been aiming at Eddie, it didn't matter. Eddie popped off one deafening shot and jumped into the drawer, leaving the other two to fight it out. He was small enough to fit and smart enough to use the upper dividing wall for leverage to push the drawer closed.

In the dark, on the other side of the bunker, Eddie heard threats, curses, amid several rounds thundering like it was a war movie, but he paid little attention. He felt invisible, moved quickly, busied himself feeling around the drawer, and stuffing the keys to his future back into the duffel bag. The only light was a cylinder of blue with a ladder attached. "Fuck all of you. It's now *me* cuttin' the deals."

He mounted the ladder, feeling like the bird about to fly away from its cage. Desperately, he peeked over the edge, and warily scanned the area. Off to his left, the 'whoop-whoop-whoop' of a copter accompanied by gunfire and shouts from a bullhorn. Eddie wiped sweat and perhaps some tears from his eyes.

"Adios, all you sorry-assed motherfuckers," he mouthed.

Fifty-plus pounds of dust on his back was almost half his body weight. He'd tried to be graceful, but the heavy backpack twisted him when he missed a step at the unseen, bush-covered edge of the bunker. First, he slipped sideways, the load of drugs swung higher on his back, and pushed him head-over-heels, noisily into the tall grass. The fall had separated him from the sawed-off. He still had his pistol. Eddie stayed motionless, fearing a bullet from an enemy would find him. Now, they were all enemies. Carrying his future, he had no friends.

If the battle was over there, then his route was in the opposite direction. His only thought was to get as far as possible, as quickly as possible, from this danger zone. It took less than a minute, after catching the harbor view, to get his bearings; it was simple; get down off this so- called mountain. Not so simple was how to do it without getting grabbed or worse, shot, and robbed of his fortune. He could see some flattened grass, not much, but enough to make an impression of a path. "I don't give a fuck if this leads to a goat pen; it's going downhill and so am I" The short man muttered, constantly watching to make sure he wasn't being followed.

Keith rode to Hull Bay, but Starlet had already gone. If he hadn't started down toward town and instead headed directly, he would have made it. Dale's Kawasaki was leaning against a sea grape tree on the beach. They hadn't waited. There was no one to blame but himself. He would have done the same thing; followed the original plan. He had a phone, the one he'd used to call Meyers and the FBI. If he used it to call Lucy, that could implicate her. Once this settled down, the federal and local forces would go over every bit of evidence. The phone still had one more part to play.

He checked and knew he had enough gas to make it to the college dock. The big question was, did he have enough luck?

FBI agent Carusoe was surrounded by his men in black. They'd climbed down ropes and now the copter surveyed the area from above. His six men arrested the two wounded Rastas. The Colombians had lost the fight to the VIPD. No DEA remained. The body count was sad.

"Lots of youth wasted here," Faulkner said to Carusoe. "It's a shame."

"Guess I'm gonna pull rank here and take charge. What do you know about this? Why this war?"

"No problem for us, boss. Take control; just tell us what you want done. My partner, Meyers, got a call yesterday saying there was gonna be a big buy. This morning, we got a call followed by a text with the where and when. By the time we got here, it was World War III."

"Exactly the same for me, calls and a text. I didn't believe it, but had the copter ready, anyway. Minutes from the airport to here," Carusoe sighed heavily. "Wow, lots and lots of blood. I was in Iraq, two tours, and never saw this much blood." He pointed, "Over there's a bunker. Got any idea what it's about? Five dead and two wounded inside it. No drugs or money. Two are DEA. From ID, one's the head honcho."

"This was a gun emplacement guarding the harbor during the Second World War. I came up here only once when I was starting as a patrolman. Followed somebody, supposedly stole a load of jewelry from a store downtown. That was in the late nineties. Never much thought about it again. Sort of figured it had become part of the condos," Meyers mentioned as he walked up.

"Gonna keep the undertakers busy. It will be one hell of a funeral. We got dead DEA, VIPD, dreadlocks, and South

Americans, about thirty in all. You know any of these guys?" Carusoe asked.

Meyers answered, "Faulkner and me, well, we're not in the drugs unit, but we knew most of the big players on this small rock. Hard not to." The policeman started lifting the sheets placed by the EMTs keeping the flies away. "Our main drug guys, well that's them over there under those sheets, Mike and Sal. The local island boys are all part of the Thatch Bay Posse. That's what they called themselves. This here was their boss, Big Man, Rashad Degannes. He's originally from St. John and pulled this gang together, mostly convicts, experienced strong-arm men, getting their supply from down island. You know probably better than us how the white death powder moves up the Caribbean chain."

"Our intel had them being supplied from Jamaica," Carusoe added. "These other guys are the new gang out of Santa Marta, bringing in more of the white." He pointed, "Don't see anyone here who looks like a boss. From what we'd heard, they were struggling for control of the supply; then their supply suddenly dried up."

"Now the blood's drying. How about we secure the perimeter until the coroner and the ambulances get everyone hauled out of here? You gonna have your own forensics?" Faulkner asked.

"Yep, yep, and yep," the FBI agent sighed. "It's gonna take a while."

A drug is not bad. A drug is a chemical compound.
The problem comes in when people who take drugs
treat them like a license to behave like an asshole.
Frank Zappa

CHAPTER TWENTY- ONE

He'd always been a pampered city boy, never one for hiking the countryside near his home in Santa Marta. Carlos spent his teenage years on the white sand beaches, luring lovely continental college babes for his satisfying evenings. There was an upside; it was nearly impossible to get lost on small St. Thomas in the daylight since the ocean was always in view. His Rolex read 10:22.

The shoulder wound was bleeding, but not badly, after being winged by the little black fucker. It could have been considerably worse, but he'd been lucky enough to dive away almost simultaneously with the blast. The wound could still identify him as part of the horrendous chaos on the mountain. Jacket off, he stripped his shirt to look at the damage.

There was only one cut, a quarter-inch deep on the outside of his shoulder, where the bullet had grazed. First, he ripped the sleeves off his shirt, folded one to cover the cut, and secured it by wrapping with the other. He rubbed some spit using leaves and removed most of the blood from the outside of his jacket. It looked good enough not to draw immediate attention.

Carlos sat to collect his energies. Everything had gone to shit because of the old white fuck. He assumed they'd killed Dale during the battle, and that provided some satisfaction. There wasn't much else to be happy about. More money had disappeared, and he still had no product. Who could he phone? Did any of his men escape? Who wasn't dead or arrested? The positive side was he was still alive and free.

What would be his destination now? St. Thomas would be red hot for many, many months. He had to get off the rock. Flying would be impossible; TSA at the airport would look for him. A boat was the only answer.

Maddie, yes, he had to get in contact with his sister, but once she knew about all the bad shit that had gone down, she'd go ballistic. But they were family, and so was Uncle Piedra. He'd help if only to make his nephew work and work to pay back all the product and the lost money. Carlos would have to content himself with being a soldier in Piedra's army for many years to come. That would be okay, as long as his uncle helped him escape.

His sister wasn't picking up. Where could she be? There's no way they could implicate her in this mess. He left a quick message: "Sister, call, I need you."

A combination sigh-moan formed as he rose and started walking through the trees, moving east. The crest of the island was a rainforest. The trees not only provided shade but also cover from the helicopters that he could hear. The young man watched every step. If he was lucky, he'd make it to his sister's house after dark. Carlos knew he shouldn't take a chance on hitchhiking.

"It'll all work out. Damn straight, it would have been easier if I'd have ridden directly to Hull Bay rather than over-thinking this. But I didn't know if I could trust any of them, even Lucy and Dale. Guess that makes me the asshole." Keith had probably left Mountain Top several minutes after his partner. The extra twenty-five minutes he'd wasted going down Solberg and then retracing his route had cost him a free ride.

It was a hot eleven and sirens still whizzed around. He saw two helicopters working slowly across the ridge of the island. Again, coasting down Solberg Hill, Keith saw the first roadblock, a fire truck barred traffic. Men, he supposed were National Guard, inspected cars. He took a deep breath and proceeded.

Two green uniforms blocked him as he tried to make his own lane. "Hey, need some ID," one shouted.

"Oh man, just coming from the beach, didn't bother to grab my wallet. What's up with all this?" Keith asked.

"Yo! You're what's up! Shut it down! Show us your hands!" Both soldiers tried to block him. One grabbed his arm and Keith jerked it away. He cracked the throttle and sped off, squealing a wheelie.

Roaring down Back Street, dodging traffic, this was what Keith had expected. Guessed the gunfight, that he hadn't seen and heard very little of, turned out to be bigger than anything that had ever happened on St. Thomas. He'd never considered that the National Guard would turn out in only a few hours. Hell, it usually took the VI government weeks to pry them out of their own homes following hurricanes.

There was another blockade waiting for him at the Crown Mountain intersection. Instead, he took the low road as if he were going to the marinas, but sped up on the short straight-away. The bike almost slid out when it hit the gravel on the small side street. This took him up and over, behind the WAPA power station, between the island's big water tanks, then down to the airport. No one was following him close. Guess they all decided it wasn't their job.

Only one SUV with a flashing blue light, siren wailing, was far behind him. They were moving too fast to take aim. Keith caught glimpses in the bike's mirror. He slid lower, almost prone, on the seat. This was the race for his life. A slight grin of excitement formed. Once he crested the knoll, he could see two more cars with green uniforms blocking the wide entrance to the airport.

It was a dumb possibility that the people fleeing the chaos at Mountain Top would try to escape by air. Since there were no long bridges to the next islands, the getaway choices were by plane or boat. Or they could always just sit tight. They secured the airport junction by two SUVs pulled nose to nose. Five men checked the entering cars. They weren't set up to inspect people coming out from the terminal. That's exactly where everyone figured the fugitives would head. In the two minutes it took to make his approach, he saw men standing, ready, with pistols aimed. Motorcycles weren't new to Keith, but dodging bullets was.

A rusty Honda 250 had been his only transport, aside from his thumb, the first two years on St. Thomas. He'd never forgotten the roads, the sharp bends, and the many, many close calls. On a bright morning, rolling out of bed in the tropics, no one could have expected something like this, manning roadblocks to stop desperate, escaping felons. The guys in green imagined Keith was a career criminal, a killer. At that early hour, no one knew what had happened, only what was on the radio news, and that was all full of exaggeration and exclamation points.

Now, he could see himself as part of the wild Mad Max movies and swung his weight side-to-side, weaving the cycle. He saw barrel flashes from two of the four guns. He couldn't hear over the bike's motor, and thankfully, he felt no hits. One of the green uniforms made a move to block the bike to the left as Keith pointed that way. He successfully faked, cranked it up, veered to the right, but then saw the center open.

Another shot at him, but it whizzed by and blew out a parked SUV's windshield. The rest of the National Guard flattened to the ground, afraid of getting hit by friendly crossfire. As he slid between the two cars, his rear wheel spun out, but completed the left turn. The SUV that had been tailing him squealed the brakes, slid, and smashed into the roadblock.

The motorcycle skidded as he leaned into the turn. It fishtailed a few times and almost slid off the road before he regained control. He pushed on the right grip to make the bike lean dangerously over that same direction. Keith kept it that way to make a harder target. Hell, everything was out of control. This was some seriously dumb shit when he could have been riding his babe's slow sailboat to who-knows-where.

This was the last lap, the road to the college dock. He roared, weaving between the two lanes. Keith somehow relaxed and prayed the boat was still there. It was. He jumped the curb, stopped the bike, and his limbs were shaking. There was no one around. Quick thinking, he pushed the bike down the dock and splashed it into the water. The outboard's hot wire worked again. He shoved off and motored away, appearing to be a mature fisherman, still wearing the black backpack. He pressed off another prepared text, watched it click 'delivered,' and then tossed the phone into the sea.

In five minutes, he had the boat around the airport runway and headed into Elephant Bay. He spied one of VIMP's go-fast boats moving through the anchorage. Their fleet comprised sleek, high-powered watercraft confiscated from convicted drug smugglers.

Keith made a slow, wide loop to the north and dodged into Krum Bay. It was horrible luck that he'd drawn their attention. He pushed the throttle down and the 150 Johnson coughed, but brought the small boat up on a plane. In a close arc, he cleared the brown cliffs at the west point of Water Island with no other boats in sight. The outboard roared across the broad turquoise expanse of Limestone Bay, but it was a momentary relief.

As he made it around that island and passed the entrance to Gregory Channel, he saw the law speeding toward him. It would be only minutes to his goal on the east side of Hassel Island, or until the pursuers were alongside. Keith reached for the bag he'd left on board just for this occasion.

He steered the boat to the south, parallel to Frenchman's Reef Hotel as if he were heading to St. Croix. That caused his followers to make a wider arc, trying to cut him off. They headed directly south. About midway to Buck Island, Keith changed direction, cut back on the throttle, and watched the police chase boat over-compensate. He spun the wheel; his outboard plowed back to the main harbor. Keith slowed, knelt, and lit the fuse. The VIMP crew made a wide circle and followed, but were now a quarter-mile off his stern. He took a deep breath, lashed the wheel all the way to the right. That would keep it circling. He placed the small bomb he'd created from the fireworks between the two big red plastic gas tanks. He dove away as the outboard spun around the green channel buoy.

One quick last look, Keith popped up to gulp a huge breath and got his direction. He hadn't realized how much the backpack filled with cash would weigh him down. Underwater, he heard the explosion as he swam hard, searching for the big chain that anchored the navigation marker for the harbor entrance. With no mask, he was as calm as any hunted man could be; he breast-stroked above the white sand bottom.

Positive he'd never altered his course; his lungs were aching when he finally glimpsed the dark vertical outline of his goal. It hadn't been far, maybe twenty meters, usually an easy swim, but almost twenty pounds of Ben Franklins on his back made a difference. There were the huge chain links with his two sets of scuba gear still attached. Quickly, he opened the valve on the top tank and sucked in a long breath, another, and another, finally relaxing to sit on the bottom.

The knack of putting on dive gear underwater is one of the first lessons of a scuba course. Keith did it, matter of fact. He unfastened the net bag, got a mask, and cleared it of water. With clear vision again, he checked his watch; it was just approaching noon. As he put on the fins, he heard several high-powered boats moving to the center of the channel.

This was a day St. Thomas would remember. Hopefully, in years to come, he'd be around to reminisce about it with Lucy. Ah, Lucy, where was Starlet now? After several more deep breaths, Keith looked at the compass next to the air gauge on the regulator and began a leisurely kick toward Hassel Island. It took a bit of experimenting with the buoyancy vest to keep him off the bottom. Combined, the weight belt and the backpack had him crawling along, bouncing the stones he'd placed as markers. He couldn't pop up to the surface too soon.

Ten minutes later, he saw the bottom rise. Keith kept swimming to the north, following the slope. He estimated he was close to his destination and made for the shallows. Cautiously he raised his head, first looking to where he'd come from. A half dozen government vessels surrounded the smoking mess that had been his escape boat. The Coast Guard cutter was meandering out of the harbor to add more Homeland Security. VIMP inadequately tried to fight the gasoline fire-slick with small foam extinguishers.

The burning wreck held everyone's eyes. Keith forced

the air from his vest, unbuckled, and shed the gear. He wrapped the weight belt through the deflated vest so it would sink and pushed it away from the shore. They shouldn't find any of his gear for a long time.

Wary not to be seen, he bolted from the water and hid in the nearby bushes. On land again, Keith sat and regained control. It was 12:30 with lots of activity in the harbor. He found the inflatable still well- hidden, pushed it into the water, and tied it off. Then, he became a tourist climbing over the ruins of the Hassel Island Battery. And best of all, it looked as though he was the only one who'd made the trek that day. He found the gas bottles and his bombs stowed under the cannon. Stashing one in his 'money' backpack, he lit the long fuse for the other and made his way down to the dinghy. It started on the second pull, and Keith slowly followed Hassel Island's shoreline farther into the harbor.

Near the stores in Careening Cove, the dinghy swung clockwise and crossed the harbor. He was close to Yacht Haven when another explosion erupted behind him. Plenty of smoke with shooting flames brought a self-knowing nod and smile. He glided to the dock with the last bomb in the damp backpack and slid into the deck shoes he'd left in the inflatable a few days before. Only a few more moves and he'd be home free. Dale was right, this was much too much-complicated shit. It would have been wiser to get on the boat in Hull, but this was between him and Maddie and her fucking brother. The rest of them deserved what the white powder brought.

Down the dock, he was tempted to have one last beer at the infamous Bilge Bar, but decided against it. He had to fight the cocky feeling that had undermined more than a few of his past efforts on this island. No familiar faces passed him, but paranoia made all weathered boat bums, wealthy skippers, and bikini'd crew look familiar.

Out through the hotel's gate, he went to Wendy's. Keith bought a burger with fries, sat next to the front windows, and watched the room and the street. With four cruise ships at the West Indian Company Dock, everything was busy. Tourists lugging liquor and souvenirs back to their ship clogged the sidewalks. Official vehicles with sirens fought to get through the usual traffic mess. The hospital was a mile up the street and the National Guard had set up housekeeping at Mandela Circle, the main roundabout.

It was past two. He chewed his burger slowly, listening to the blabbering wall TV while eavesdropping on the customer's conversations. Couples wearing Pittsburgh Steelers' jerseys loudly feared this was a terror attack, yet didn't want to forego a greasy taste of home. The TV loop told everyone to remain calm. The authorities had everything under control, and that no violence had happened near Charlotte Amalie. Photos that must have been from the news helicopter revealed damaged police cars in unnamed locations, the smoldering slick from a burning boat outside the harbor, and a fire in the scrub of Hassel Island. The footage was tagged that nothing connected the incidents.

Looking at his small table, he'd only taken a few bites and already had indigestion. It was time. Keith waited for the bathroom to clear, entered, and locked the door. This was the first time he'd removed the backpack. He sat on the toilet and washed off the accumulated salt and grime with damp paper towels. The toilet was his necessary stool to move the ceiling tiles.

The damp shirt and shorts went up as the wrapped bundle came down. He pulled on a white shirt, pants, and socks. With the supplied proper ID hanging around his neck, he became a crew member of the Oceanic Emerald, an assistant purser. He slicked his hair, closed the ceiling, and walked out with an official cap under his arm. Shades in place, he carried the backpack as a shoulder bag. After purchasing more burgers and fries, he marched to the cruise ship dock.

The main entrance to the Havensite Shopping Mall was a zoo of people. Four cruise ships contributed over ten thousand extra people to the mass of hustling locals. Shopkeepers and taxi drivers made money in the dock area. This was a familiar layout. In past years, Keith had pulled his dive boat to the dock and picked up tourists for his two-tank special. The first dive was the wreck of the Cartanza on Buck Island and the second was off the same island's south side, at the wreck of the Wye. Six divers netted him an easy $800 for a day after commissions. So far, today looked good, and he wouldn't have to pay any kickbacks.

At Ricardo's Perfume and Liquor Warehouse, he purchased two bottles of 151 proof Bacardi and two more of his favorite Cruzan Estate Rum. Now it was three on a scorching, tropical afternoon and definitely his third and final act. Keith was feeling antsy, but he took the time to arrange his purchases. The two bottles of Cruzan and the burgers went in the backpack with the loot. The homemade bomb went with the Bacardi.

A park bench beckoned, and he took a deserved breather to study the area. The increased security was all local, unarmed, and barely trained. Tourists still bustled, pushed, and argued for bargains. Keith saw a large trash dumpster near to the security gate for the passengers. After that, only the ship's gangway presented an obstacle. He felt 100% positive that the distraction and his ID would get him aboard.

A flick, the long fuse lit, and he tossed the bag with the strong Puerto Rican rum into a corner of the big bin. Cardboard liquor boxes from the many stores covered it. That would contain the exploding glass and shouldn't injure any passersby. Keith leisurely walked to the perimeter security gate. After a slight glance at his ID, the guard waved him through. Sunburned, boozed-up tourists lined at the entrance to the Oceanic Emerald. As a crew member, he waited at the gangway, permitting appreciative guests to board.

BABOOM! The steel walls of the dumpster reverberated the blast.

Every head turned toward the direction of the sound and saw the smoke and flames. The dock area instantly became total chaos. Tourists ran for their ships. It was a madhouse. Keith reached to assist an elderly couple to board. Not prepared for the sudden rush of passengers, the cruise ship's security welcomed his 'official' help. They'd let him carry the backpack with the visible Wendy's bags and rum bottles on board without inspection. He *was* part of the crew.

The ship's entrance quickly clogged with frightened people pushing and shoving their bulky bags of souvenir purchases. Confusion amid loud complaints echoed across the dockside. Every cruise ship blasted horns as a call for passengers and crew to return immediately to their ship.

His watch read 3:54 and knew the regular departure time was 5. The crews were hectic, pressed into action by intercom instructions. This was not a drill; the loudspeakers kept repeating. The crews had practiced, yet expected nothing like this. The Emerald opened another gangway to accommodate more frightened passengers.

A grin formed as he slowly, subtly retreated to the elevators where he soothed the demanding, worried Midwesterners, New Englanders, and Californians. All pressed into the small elevators. For a few minutes, Keith cajoled and joked that it was all an island prank. Nothing to worry about; and displayed his bottles of rum, prescribing a strong, soothing cocktail.

That's all the guests saw from within his ever-present black backpack.

At 4:30, there were more incessant horn blasts and he could feel the engine vibrations. After many carefully packed elevator loads, the herd reduced in size; however, the noisy demands to get to safety increased.

Keith politely, but 'officially' inquired with the Filipino security team at the gangway if they could handle it without him, and he assisted a wheelchair guest up to the pool deck. He beamed, making casual conversation to ease the fears of the old man and his younger nurse companion. After more long horn blasts, the ship's bow thrusters pushed the floating hotel away from the dock.

From the top decks, Keith could see the two pumper trucks that had responded to the explosion. Several firemen were crawling around inside the dumpster. "Indeed, the public was served well today," he muttered.

Looking responsible, wearing his hat, he informed many tourists that they could relax; cruises were the safest vacations. Off the starboard, he pointed out that they'd extinguished the fire on Hassel Island. Crossing to the port side, he saw the Coast Guard cutter with divers searching for bodies and winching up the charred remains of the outboard.

It was time to change identities again. Keith walked along the interior mezzanine using the ruse of making certain the ships' on-board shops had reopened to placate the passengers. At one, he bought a pair of sweatpants and at another, a hooded jersey with two beach towels, all emblazoned with the ship's logo. After changing in a public restroom, and packing the uniform in the shops' bags, he became a passenger.

Because of the turmoil ashore, the Emerald extended its happy hour to regain the festive vacation mood. Keith carried one margarita, reclined on a relatively secluded deck chair, and enjoyed the cold burgers. The backpack was his pillow and the beach towels were blankets; he spent an uninterrupted night.

The fire department blocked the entrance to Mountain Top when they received another alert; a boat had exploded in the harbor. The VIFD had no fire-fighting vessel and instead watched the efforts of the Coast Guard and VIMP. They saw another flash and smoke at the south end of Hassel, but again, they had no way to get over there. The day had exhausted their supplies and the personnel. No excuses. All available were ordered to Havensite after the last explosion occurred.

Miles Faulkner remained in the parking lot as liaison with the FBI boys to secure the crime scene and keep the residents from ruining evidence. It would take days, maybe a week, to gather all the bits and pieces. FBI Agent Carusoe rode down the hills with Meyers and they compared the texts they'd received a few hours earlier with only the words: Dust 4-D Estate Charlotte Amalie, Skyline Drive.

"What do you think?" Meyers inquired as he looked and saw his passenger had his eyes closed.

"I know I'm damn tired," Carusoe sighed. "Haven't had a day like this since we attacked Saddam. Luckily, none of my guys were hit. DEA lost honorable men; too many mothers lost sons."

"Too many greedy guys forgot most of the 'Thou shall nots,'" Meyers added. "VIPD lost a few. Hate to say it, but none they can't do without. Personally, I'm hoping this is a wake-up call, or maybe a call to arms. Get the residents, neighbors, friends to fight and take the island back from this damn drug culture."

"Don't know what to tell you there, bro, but it's bad everywhere," Carusoe replied. "Maybe you, me, your buddy, and only a handful of others in important places on these rocks called 'The Virgins,' aren't taking a piece of the pie to stay quiet. It's the same everywhere. This is an actual war on our mother country, where we were born, and raised our children. Doesn't matter if it's here, Miami, St. Louis, Chicago, or Detroit, everyone is fighting and dying over drug money."

"But what makes them want it so bad, to spend every cent to get high? Kill their brother or neighbor, pimp their sisters?" Meyers asked.

"That is the billion-dollar question, buddy, maybe the trillion-dollar question."

"Me, I see it like them rats that run and dive off the cliffs up there in Iceland: lemmings. Got food, companions, but suddenly some switch throws inside their brains and they know this world ain't enough," Meyers offered.

The patrol car's radio interrupted, "Incident at Havensite secured, repeat, Havensite secured. Return to normal duty."

"Hmm, ain't gonna be no normal duty for a long while. Lots of funerals and lots more hospital visits. Only a few, by my count two, lived to get arrested? Nah, nothing will be normal here on St. Thomas for a long while." Meyers continued, "So what do you think, Mr. FBI, about this text? My phone says it came from the same number that sent the others directing us to the gun battle."

"Between us, tomorrow isn't gonna be any better than today. Let's get some coffee on the way to the airport."

"Airport?"

"Yeah, going to need some sniffer dogs and their handlers," the FBI responded. "I'll have four of my men meet us. After this morning, we need to be equipped with the necessary capability. I'm not taking any chances of getting caught in a trap, and I don't want to wait until tomorrow. The perps might be at that address, licking their wounds and ready to disappear."

"Roger on that," Meyers answered. "I'll call and get the Attorney General to issue a search warrant. I figure today everybody's standing by."

It'd been a non-stop day and his short legs ached from walking. Eddie trudged in the intense afternoon heat through thorny scrub bushes. He'd found a ravine where cast-iron pipes carried water up to one of the condominium projects on Crown Mountain. At one connection joint, there was a slow leak. He cupped his hands and drank. In the small pool that the leak had created, his reflection shocked him.

"Jeez-Louise, wow, I ain't never looked this bad," Eddie said as he splashed water and rubbed the dried blood from scrapes on his face. "Can't go much farther this way, 'cause it leads to Soto Town, Spanish and Rican territory. Sure nuff, with what happened today, they'd be happy to shoot my black ass."

Eddie struggled to heft the duffle and slowly edged up the side of the ravine. "Never expected my future to be so damn heavy! Man, I got to come across another road here somewhere." The sun was sinking in the west, creating shadows. His watch read 5:30 and his body felt like it was past midnight.

Ahead, he heard children and moved up higher on the hill. No reason for anyone to see him carrying a sack after what went down today. He knew he was somewhere below the Scott Free Road. After crawling up another steep embankment, he ran into Crown Mountain Road, and he sat on the low side weighing his limited strategies.

He still had his pistol. If someone wanted to take him off, he'd fight. He pulled a wad of cash from his hip pocket. The old white man had done right by him for sure. He stood, brushed himself off, and climbed to the roadside. "Up or down, does it matter where I get a ride to? Need a good excuse to be sittin' here," Eddie mumbled as he heard a truck downshift for the steep grade. He waved his arms as a van came into view. It slowed and then pulled away.

"Fuck you, too!" he exclaimed. "Can't blame you, looking the way I do, and what you've probably heard about today's shit. Place ain't safe no more, not at all."

A pair of lights appeared, headed up the hill. It was an open jeep, probably tourists. The Suzuki with two couples stopped. "What's up, friend?" They said, feeling they and the stranger were part of the islander 'Jah-Love' thing.

"Trying to make it home after a hard day," Ed replied.

For once, his compact size was a plus. The pair in the back seat squeezed over and gave him a place.

"Where's home?"

"Where you going?" Eddie asked.

"Looking for a place to get some prime sunset photos. Where do you suggest?"

"I know just the place," and directed them to the Magen's Bay overlook.

That morning about ten, at Bluebeard's hair salon, Maddie first heard about the gunfight. She knew it involved her brother. Her first stop was to her attorney, but Charles was in court. She went to the bank and withdrew ten grand. That with her credit cards should get her on the first plane south, back to Colombia.

The airport had been sealed off before noon. She listened to the voice mail from Carlos, and that made her want to disappear even more. He was an asshole. They were all assholes with this macho-male shit. Their mentality was to kill everyone who slightly offended their dignity. *Damn it,* she thought, snarled in traffic. It would take hours to get home, pack, and find a place to hide.

Wait, maybe she shouldn't go home? Her mind was whirling. Was she a suspect? Would they discover she'd been part of it? There was a slim bit of consolation. No, she was only a sister; he'd never told her anything. She was living off her divorce settlement. Yes, they'd believe her; they had to. They always believed attractive women. They'd believed her against Keith.

After too many minutes in stagnant traffic, Maddie lifted her buzzing phone, "Where are you? Where? How do you NOT know where you are? No… no… don't say anything over the phone! No! Don't come to my house. No! Absolutely not! I'll call you later."

Her nerves kicked in. She stared blankly ahead, intently squeezing the steering wheel. A honking horn shook her from the daze. Her dumb fucking brother had ruined everything. She'd escaped from boring Santa Marta the same way as most attractive Colombian women, by first learning English. Her uncles had helped by putting her through school after her father had been arrested. It was all planned in the family drug business.

Later, Maddie had to play a part to pay them back.

With dumb-fuck, always horny Keith, she'd made her play and won, won big. House and island lady status, she couldn't do much better than that. For only screwing the gringo, she finally screwed him out of everything. Now, her dumb-fuck brother had screwed her out of the same house and the same status. Maddie was seething.

Maybe Josef could help her out. The fat man would try to do anything for her if she let him sniff her crotch. All men were the same. Money and pussy, pussy and money; money bought pussy, and that's how the world revolved. Sex, that's what drove them, and she was ready to ride along, out of here with anyone. She'd gladly spread her legs for a boat ride south, north, east, or west. She was a survivor.

"No, Josef's not here. Haven't seen him all day."

Another dead end, Maddie tried her attorney again. He still wasn't in. She saw an opening, turned, and followed a side road up through Mafoli Estates. Sib's Country Bar was open, and she needed a cocktail.

"Yes, miss, what'll it be?" a young waitress asked.

"Vodka gimlet, make it a double," Maddie replied, staring off into the lush foliage.

"Say, don't I know you?" the waitress asked when she brought the drink. "Aren't you Carlos' sister? Haven't seen him in here, or anywhere, for weeks."

"No, I don't know who you're speaking about. Leave me alone, okay, leave me the fuck alone!" Maddie yelled.

She avoided everyone's eyes and finally relax after two gimlets. With a slight buzz, she drove over the island's hump and the traffic problems vanished, but *her* problems remained. There were no cars at her house. The dumb dog didn't even come bounding up to slobber on her. The place, her place, was quiet, and that was good, what she needed. It was 2:30; Maddie threw some clothes in a bag, took a Valium, lay on the bed, and passed out.

<<<<<◇>>>><<<<◇>>>>

At 11:15, Starlet passed Cockroach Key, heeled over on her port side. They'd pulled anchor and split in record time. Dale was eager to get out of St. Thomas and put both his distant and recent pasts behind him. His adrenaline was still pumping as he twisted to watch the entire seascape. No boats were following.

The breeze was perfect, blowing about fifteen out of the southeast. It was a cool day with a brilliant blue sky. The only sounds were the occasional snap of a sail and the constant panting of Baron, the Lab. His big yellow head was on Lucy's lap while she blankly stared at the approaching blue water.

"Guess my heart's okay," Dale finally broke the silence. "If there was ever a time I should have had a heart attack, it was this morning."

"Huh?" It snapped Lucy from her trance. "Yeah, okay. I guess that's good, huh? What's our heading?"

"Yeah, that's good. Damn good. I'm still vertical, sucking in air, and not bleeding. Felt like I was twenty again. Oh, we're going 270, due west. What's the ETA on the GPS?"

"Oh, I didn't set it. I know where we're going and we got plenty of time to get there," Lucy shuddered with a slight sob, "I hope Keith meets us."

"He will; not to worry, babe, Keith is a very smart guy," Dale cleared his throat. "Worrying doesn't do anyone any good. Believe me, we had it all clocked."

"Then why didn't he come with us?" Lucy's eyes were red. "Because he loves you and wanted to draw all the attention to the south side of St. Thomas. Out here, we're on a leisurely sail. He knew what he was doing," Dale answered. "He told me you were not to be an accessory."

"Fuck you and him! What's the difference if you're here with your bunch of cash and we get boarded and searched?"

"Lucy, that's all part of Keithy's scheme; the boat police are looking on the south. I didn't figure it out 'til a while ago. Personally, I thought he was nuts, but now I realize, he's just *nuts* about you."

"What *was* his plan?"

"Never really told me, trust issues. I got him a few things and knew he had a boat ride involved in it, but he kept his cards close. This kind of thing, I did my stuff, and he did his, *but* it was all *his* thing. You got me? He had a score to settle." Dale continued, "He could have done it easier; it got done and we

245

didn't dirty our hands. We didn't hurt anyone, they hurt each other. Anyway, that's how I look at it. Keith was scoring big points on that fucking Carlos and his wife. Me, I wanted the Feds and everyone to see how corrupt this place is. Girl, Keith got stripped by his piece of shit wife and I got stripped by a bunch of badge-wearing bandits."

Lucy sighed, petting a very contented dog. "You guys, what is it that makes everything a game? Macho fucking macho, huh? You have to always outscore the other guys; I'll never understand it."

"No, you won't. It's all about time," Dale hunched over the yacht's wheel. "Time is the most valuable, non-renewable resource each of us has. Sure, we all take some hits during our lives, but when we get blindsided for someone else's profit, that's fucked! And they deserve to get fucked back!"

"I got robbed and raped," Lucy blurted, "but I didn't hunt them down!"

"Tell me you wouldn't have loved to?"

She cut him off, "Sure, but where would that have got me? I'd probably be worse off." Lucy's eyes teared up again. "Dale, those times were horrible for me. They robbed me of everything, my dignity, my self- esteem, and the least of it, my savings. Now, I carry a pistol."

"Lucy, I'd have probably collapsed dead with a paintbrush in my hand if Keith hadn't come along with this deal. Be proud you could continue on; that's what I had to do after my bust. Those fucking corrupt cops… sure I was breaking the law, but they didn't want to enforce, they only wanted a cut. If they would have played by the rules…"

"Here's what I don't understand; you work around the legal system and expect the system to stand up for you when you need it?" Lucy exclaimed.

"That's the American way, babe. That's all I can say. Now, all them fuckers who could have kept a sweet place sweet, instead soured it with greed. I'm not saying I'm gonna ride a white horse off into the sunset, but," Dale smiled, "I am sailing into it. Hey, you got another cold one?"

"Yeah, okay, but I'll never comprehend why all the risks," Lucy replied, as she pushed Baron's head away and went below. After a few minutes, she climbed out with two beers. "I set the electronics. GPS says we'll get to San Juan around midnight."

<<<<<<>>>>><<<<>>>>>

His sister's house was dark. It was 7:30. Her car was there.

Carlos watched from above on Skyline Drive. She'd told him not to come, but where else could he go? He'd hiked the entire distance, many miserable miles through that damn forest and along the roads with his jacket slung over his damaged shoulder. He'd been too afraid to hitch a ride. All he thought about was what was coming next.

Maddie wasn't happy and who could blame her, but he believed she was exaggerating her problems. There was no way they could connect with her. He'd escape from the island and then they could blame him. So what, they'd never be able to extradite him from his homeland.

"Oh, fuck!" Carlos whispered as he saw two unmarked panel vans and a car turn into her driveway. It was dusk and the streetlight at the front of her house came on. Six men with two dogs got out of the vans. They looked like the worst possible news.

"Oh, fuck! Oh, fuck! Oh, fuck!" Carlos muttered. His heart raced. "Not to worry. Nothing to worry about. We've never done any coke there. There should be no traces to excite the dogs. Whatever Maddie had couldn't be enough to draw attention."

"Inside, inside!" Agent Carusoe banged on the screen door and rang the bell. "We have a search warrant for these premises. Hello! We're coming in."

As they entered, Maddie was at the top of the stairs rubbing her eyes. "What? Who the fuck are you breaking into my house?"

"Not breaking in, ma'am. Are you the owner or resident of this address: 4-D Estate Charlotte Amalie? We have a search warrant issued by the Assistant US Attorney General to search for drugs and drug paraphernalia." Carusoe handed Maddie the warrant as she folded and sat on the stairs.

"Ma'am, I'd like to ask you to sit in that chair, over there, in your living room. Please do not impede our search," the FBI agent barked.

Bewildered and groggy, Maddie held the warrant and staggered to the chair. Two FBI agents, wearing intimidating black jumpsuits, stood beside her.

As soon as the dogs entered, they perked up, bouncing and yipping, signaling they had sniffed something good. One danced on the couch, whining, with its tail wagging.

"Got something, boss, definitely got some happy dust,"

one handler remarked.

"Can't be," Maddie objected, "No way, I don't have drugs here, I don't do drugs." The tranquilizer, coupled with the vodka, slurred her words.

The other dog pushed open the door beneath the stairs and started incessantly barking. "Something big here." That handler directed another agent to continued the search as he struggled to pull the 'happy' dog away.

Minutes later, the FBI man reappeared with a wrapped package. He opened the bag and displayed a half a kilo, licked a wet finger and exclaimed, "Wow, my tongue's gonna be numb all night! This shit is pure."

"It's not mine," Maddie mumbled. "I never saw that before. I have no idea how it got there. Someone must have planted it!"

Meyers sighed as he walked outside and opened a bottle of water. "Wish I had a dollar for every time I heard that."

Carlos sat in the darkness of the roadside bushes until he saw two men lead his handcuffed sister to the car. Both were wearing bullet-proof vests; one was stenciled FBI and the other VIPD.

At Magen's Overlook, the tourists were so satisfied with their accidental guide; they gave him a ride home.

"Where're we going?" The driver asked.

"Stay straight, we going east," Eddie yawned.

The girl beside Eddie giggled, "Stay straight? That's kind of difficult, we're on vacation." She passed beers from the cooler to everyone except the driver. "Yeah, they even condone drinking and driving here, don't they?"

"Best not to be too obvious," Eddie advised to watch the road ahead. "Cops can be pricks when they want to… especially if they see a chance for some money in it for themselves. They say we got a law here, DWW, driving while white, if you catch the drift."

"You mean you can bribe cops here out of a DUI? That really makes this America's Paradise," the driver joked. laughed.

"No, you didn't get the meaning; you get pulled over because you aren't a local, driving while white. Then they figure out something to charge you with. The cops want you to pay them cash immediately, right then and there. Buy your way out of almost anything on this and every other island, from what I hear," the short man reflected. "Money talks on these saltwater rocks. Hey, up ahead, take that right."

"What's this place called?" asked the girl in the front seat.

"Tutu, new Tutu, look over there at those old white high rises, that's Old Tutu, projects."

"Toot-toot?" the driver asked.

"Yeah, but T-U-T-U. You're right though, what my dad told me, this valley is where they kept the slaves when they grew sugar cane on St. Thomas. The toot-toot was the sound of the wake-up horn they blew every morning to get the niggers up and moving." Ed's voice dropped. "Lots of a new kind of slaves now."

"Really? Hey buddy, thanks," the driver said as they pulled off the road. He reached to give Eddie some money. "Come on, man, we'd never have seen that great sunset if it wasn't for you."

"Nah, man, keep your cash. You'll never know what a huge favor you did for me with this ride; it was a real lifesaver. Seems white people treating me good these days, fantastic."

Eddie waved goodbye and walked into his parents' home lugging the duffle. "Hi, mom, what ya got cooking? I'm hungry. Been a hell of a day."

"Watch your mouth, you know the Lord rules in this house," Ed's mother proclaimed. "Stewed chicken and rice with peas. My God, you're a mess; best you bathe before sitting down to eat."

"Ya know, mom, I'll go to church with you on Sunday. I got a lot to say thanks for; you and pops been good to me. Thinking might buy a taxi with some money I saved by living here with you. Me and pops could run it," Eddie hugged his mother.

"Lord be blessed, Jesus hallelujah!" his mother exclaimed. "We was hoping you'd quit that awful street business. My lord, the news today is all about death, doom, and destruction. I was praying you wasn't involved," the woman said as she closed her eyes and tilted her head, "my prayers been answered."

They were still hugging, and Ed said smiled, "Mom, God willing; today was the last of my street days. Thinking we'll start a taxi business, maybe upscale, yeah, have the only BMW taxi service on St. Thomas."

"Make us proud son; you'll make us proud.

If you got bad news, you want to kick them blues, cocaine
When your day is done and you got to run, cocaine
JJ Cale

CHAPTER TWENTY–TWO

The moon rose and Carlos sat in shock after witnessing his sister get hauled off by the FBI. He'd seen that the local police were in on the bust, but this was going federal. It didn't look like Uncle Piedra could spread enough cash around to buy Maddie out of this. Carlos' thoughts dwelled on his own problems as cars passed on the road just above him on the hill. He ran through his phone contacts. Where could he hide and for how long?

Then Carlos remembered Elizabeth, big tits Betsey, the waitress from the Red Hook bar, Pillsbury Sounds. She had a secluded apartment out on Cabrita Point in the East End, and he knew she liked him. He dialed her and was pleasantly surprised she was waitressing nearby at Sib's restaurant. No problem, she'd believe his lies, that his apartment building was being tented to exterminate termites.

The restaurant was relatively close, and he knew the parking lot was dark. "Good, I'll only have to backtrack about a mile," he muttered with a loud sigh. "I'm beat, totally worn out. Fuck all of you! I've scrambled through the woods with my bad shoulder." He shuddered. "Everything's gone, everything's fucking gone." The only slight consolation, he knew his situation could have been worse. He wasn't dead, badly wounded, or arrested. The ending of the Mountain Top scenario was a mystery. Where was the coke and the money? He knew Josef didn't get it; he was permanently on a cold slab.

"Damn, I wished I'd have killed that old fuck, Dale," Carlos thought out loud. "He probably caught at least one bullet during that crossfire. Fucker set me up, him and fucking Jeffers. That fat-assed Puerto Rican must have got his. It'll take a lot of work to get this operation back on track, but Uncle will help me." The cops still had a van in the driveway. That erased any chance of sneaking in to clean up. He took a deep breath and turned back the way he'd come.

Sib's was a perfect place to hide. It always had lots of people. On the crest of the island, above the city to the south and close to Magens Bay on the north; it was the intersection watering hole for locals and tourists.

It was a dark, moonless nine o'clock when he stumbled into the bar. Carlos checked the lot and saw Betsey's Jeep parked in the back row. He dialed her number again. She didn't pick up, and he left a voicemail, "I'm not very presentable and would rather take a siesta in your back seat until you finish work. It's locked; when you get this, could you come out? Gracias, hermosa mujer."

Carlos smoked in the dark, pondering his options while swatting mosquitoes. Half an hour passed before Betsey arrived.

"What? Why don't you want to come in? You don't look that bad," she said as they embraced. "Come on, we can have dinner together. I'm almost at the end of my shift."

He wrinkled his face in a negative. "No, senorita, estoy muy cansado. Ha sido un largo día." *(I'm very tired. It has been a long day.)* Carlos sighed and passionately kissed her.

"Okay, okay, I don't know Spanish," she unlocked her car. "I'll bring some burgers and beers. Should finish in another hour. Are you sure you'll be comfortable?" She hugged him and he winced. "What happened? Are you hurt?"

"Ah, well, sort of... fell off my bike, yeah, fell off and scraped my shoulder. Yeah, that's why I don't feel presentable," he forced a laugh. "You know me, I always want to look my best. This day has been something else; I got run off the road by a police car. Who can I complain to?"

Elizabeth held the Jeep's door open and said, "You must have heard the news, a huge gunfight; a boat blew up in the harbor. Then bombs went off on Hassel Island and around the cruise ship dock. Charlotte Amalie is locked down. You probably couldn't get to your house anyway... if it wasn't being fumigated. Don't worry, shouldn't be any problem getting to my place."

"Really? All that happened on this small island today?" He was getting better at faking surprise, "I've been out riding since early. I never think of using my phone to get news."

"Get some rest. You can shower and we'll have a nice meal," she kissed him and shut her door.

Betsey wasn't the smartest, but it didn't take her long to see through Carlos' story. A glimpse of the shoulder wound when he came out of the shower wrapped in a towel started her questions.

"Carlos, that doesn't look like anything that happened in a bicycle accident. What is it you're not telling me?" she asked.

He'd been thinking of what to said, "Maybe better, I tell

you nada? Entiendes?" He rifled through his pants pockets and handed her several hundred-dollar bills. "Rent, I need a place to stay for a few days. I don't know exactly how long. If I tell you nada, then you can honestly say you aren't involved."

"But… but I can see you were…"

He interrupted her with a kiss, "Tranquilo, relax, I've got a few minor problems and don't know anyone else I can depend on." His arm ached as he pulled her close, "It's best if you trust me; let me stay, and you continue with your schedule. I'll keep out of sight until I," he swallowed hard, "… until I decide what to do? Should only take a few days and I'll disappear."

"Carlos, there's a thousand dollars here, for only a few days? How big are your problems? I saw your sister; she came into the restaurant earlier today. Wasn't in a very good mood, why don't you want to stay with her?"

"Relájate, entiendes? (Relax, understand?) Forget the questions. Accept the dinero, por favor, my sister and I aren't getting along."

"Look, I'm not stupid!" Betsey shouted, "I figure you're involved in the shit that went down at Mountain Top today. I don't want to get tangled in some mess. You and I had a few good times, but it's been weeks since you called me." She threw the money at him and sobbed.

"Okay, just tonight, I need a place to crash." Carlos groaned as he picked up the bills.

"Tonight's all right. Tomorrow we'll think of something. Come on, we better eat these sandwiches before they get cold," Betsey conceded.

Close to the pool on the cruise ship's upper deck, Keith reclined on a lounge chair. He was in his sweats, covered with beach towels; his knapsack close, stowed under the chair. Keith looked like the tourist he planned to become. Still too wired to sleep, he sipped some rum.

The money could still be a problem, he thought, if it's marked somehow or has consecutive serial numbers. He fanned a few stacks and laughed; the bills weren't sequential.

"How's everything tonight, sir?" asked a crew member. "Huh, what? Oh, everything's cool, I guess," Keith replied, pushing the money back into the bag.

"Don't you want to go to your cabin?" the crewman looked at his watch, "2:37."

"Well, ah, actually I slept earlier. Had some drinks in the last port before all the excitement. I came back, laid down, and conked out. Was anyone hurt? Anyway, thought I might see the sunrise. What time do we get into San Juan?"

"Please stay away from the rail in the dark. We should be at the dock about seven and be disembarking about 8. Let's see," the crewman looked at his phone. "Sunrise will be 6:33 this morning. We should still be outside the harbor, but you'll get a great view. You won't have that much company enjoying the sunrise. Have a pleasant night. Remember what I told you about staying away from the rail."

"Thanks," Keith muttered and curled up. He knew Lucy would also sail past tonight. "Yes, sir," he smiled, "ships passing in the night."

"You told me you'd go. Only one day, *please*, is what you said," Betsey droned. "You see the news, Christ, it's on the TV and radio, over and over. Five DEA agents are dead! Just that alone makes you one of the ten most wanted. Fucking twenty-one dead and another seven wounded."

"I know, babe, I know. I'm working on getting out of here." Carlos tried to stay calm.

"And you've been using my phone. If they track the numbers you called, I'm gonna get screwed."

Carlos rose, hugged her, and licked her neck. "Honey, Betsey- baby, how about you getting screwed now?" He squeezed her pantied butt. "It'll only be a day or two more. Come on, be good, huh? That wasn't my fault. Those guys probably don't even know I was there. I didn't shoot anyone. As soon as I could, I got away from there. It was all those crazy local guys, Rasta druggies."

"Look, the paper lists six Spanish names who they say were soldiers for a Colombian drug gang," Betsey continued.

"Well," Carlos turned and looked at the sea view. "I know nothing about that. Fucking Josef drags me to a meeting."

"Yeah," she interrupted, "The man who owned the Casablanca, Josef, is dead!"

"No lo sé. *(I don't know)* That fat bastard was still breathing when I ran. I swear I didn't know what was going down."

"Carlos, I like you, but you got to leave," Betsey ordered as she slammed the bathroom door.

He grabbed her phone and dialed. It rang 9 times before he connected, "Sí, entiendo. Sé que la situación en todas partes está al rojo vivo. Pero tío, por favor, sácame de aquí. Estaré allá mañana." *(Yes, I understand. I know everywhere is red hot now. But Uncle, please get me out of here. I'll be there tomorrow,)*

"Okay, Elizabeth, my Queen Elizabeth, I'll be out of here tomorrow night," he said through the door. "So, babe, how about you call off work and get us a delicious dinner tonight? We'll watch the stars and..."

She opened the door, "You promise? You promise only one more day? Because I can't take this stress. I'm so afraid they're coming after you."

"Bets-baby, the only person coming after me is family, my family. They know how the law always pegs us Colombians as drug dealers. I did nothing, but how do they say that; guilt by association." Carlos grinned, "Racial profiling. They've watched too many movies. Family is always family. Come on, here, take this," he handed her some money, "Get some steaks and what you need to make some margaritas. I'll grill."

"Okay, but after tomorrow, you gotta go," she kissed him, "I'll miss you."

"Queen Elizabeth, for your help, I'll send you a plane ticket to visit Colombia. You'll stay at our ranch in Santa Marta."

Two cups of strong espresso from the ship's coffee shop re-energized Keith. The rum had relaxed him enough to doze for two hours. Getting off the cruise ship had been no problem. They hadn't asked for any identification. If you were already aboard, you must belong. He'd kept the brim of his ball cap down, trying to seem hungover. Didn't matter, they probably weren't looking, but taking no chances, he hurried away from the port area and caught a taxi into town.

It was just after nine and they'd meet at noon. Keith needed a new wardrobe. Everything he owned was on Starlet: two pairs of shorts, and three jerseys.

He shrugged, walking down the street, "Yeah, I've been living like Mister Meager. Time to get some fresh duds."

The first clothing store he encountered got all his business. "Okay, señor, I need some styling duds." The salesman took Keith at his word. "No, I don't think I'd do well in a white linen suit. How about three shirts, and two, no, three crew necks, and a pair of walking shoes. Plan on doing a lot of sightseeing."

Spiffed up, Keith could have been a model for Panama Jack. Another Taxi took him and his bags to the El Convento Hotel in Old San Juan. It was his favorite place in Puerto Rico. His affection had something to with it housing nuns for 250 years and now with a great bar and restaurant. As he walked up the steps, "I'll bet a lot of virgins who lived their lives here are twisting in their tombs while lots of women are twisting on the beds upstairs. I definitely know one who will be!" It was a few minutes past noon and it shocked him that Lucy and Dale weren't already there.

"A rum and soda," he said to the barman and took a comfortable chair in the rear of the bar, watching both the door and the wall clock. Into his second drink; it was past one. "What could have broken on the boat?" he was thinking when they finally waltzed in.

"Lucy," he said as he rushed her, and between kisses, "what kept you?"

Dale ordered at the bar, waited for the couple to take a breather, and gave his buddy a long hug, "Good to see you, bro, great! Didn't know we had to clear customs in the VI before coming to PR."

"They check the boat?" Keith questioned.

"Nope, just paperwork," Lucy answered. "Now, I'm ready to sail anywhere. Only have to sign you on as crew. But I will work you hard; you hear! And I had to locate a kennel to put Baron in for the night. Didn't know how long this was gonna take."

Keith lifted her by the waist and danced her around, "Whatever you say, skipper, whatever you say."

The drinks delivered, Dale said, "Weird, we didn't have to clear in," he shrugged, "just clear out, and that sounds good to me. Been thinking I'll follow your plan, buy a sailboat here and head up to Florida. Walked around while Lucy was pushing the pencil for Customs; lots of boats for sale on the docks."

The three touched their glasses. "Better days ahead."

"How'd it go?" Lucy asked, "Well, I guess you don't have to give me any details *now*, I mean, you're here safe and sound. But one of these days, you know you will tell me what all went down." She kissed him again. "This fucking old bastard wouldn't say a word." Lucy slapped Dale on his back.

"What you don't know shouldn't hurt you," Dale said, raising his hand to ordered another drink. He nodded to Keith, "Good to see you, buddy. I never doubted you. Thanks for this breakaway."

Keith and Dale clasped hands. "We're unknowns, like DB Cooper, and we'll keep it that way. Think Lucy and me will get a room here; no sense rocking the boat."

Dale sniffed the air, "I think tonight I might just find a nice, lady friend." He got close to Keith, "Feel I got an excellent reason to celebrate, about seven hundred large reasons. Whew, that's more than I figured on."'

"You earned it."

Lucy looked at the clock and stood, "You boys can hug it up later, but I haven't had any loving in days." She pulled Keith from the chair, "Take me upstairs and make a dishonest woman out of me!"

"Can't argue with that."

That evening there was a pleasant, cool breeze out of the northeast. Betsey drove a very nervous Carlos to Sapphire Marina and stopped outside the gates. "Please, get out here. I don't want anyone to see us together. If you don't get on that boat tonight, forget about me," she said, and then they kissed. "I'm not a gangster's girlfriend. Too fucking dangerous."

"Dulce, Elizabeth," Carlos crooned in a heavy Latin accent as he pulled her close. "Sweetie, you saved my life. I will never forget that. I'll take care of you."

"Carlos," she pushed him away, reached, and opened his door, "take care of yourself. Be careful, now, good-bye." She drove off into the dark.

He braced himself and started cautiously toward the docks. A catamaran from the Moorings fleet was tied to the visitors' pier with two people on deck. One waved to him as he approached, "Carlos, venaquí *(come here)*, we have been waiting for you."

"They told me to be here at eleven. Here I am," Carlos answered, and climbed aboard.

"No one following you? I'm Remy, the captain," The man said as he started the motors. "No reason to stay here."

"Where are we going?" Carlos asked to no reply.

The only other person on deck was a slight woman who undid the dock lines and shoved the bow away from the pier. She walked to the cockpit and instructed Carlos to go below.

Waiting in the cat's salon was a shocker, his Uncle Piedra. Carlos froze, looking at his father's brother. The fifty-year-old man could pass for thirty: slim, trim, and muscular.

"Ah, mi sobrino, está todo bien? *(My nephew, is everything okay?)* The older man put his arms around Carlos. "Your eyes, you haven't been sleeping well? I can imagine the stress of this situation. Have a drink." The uncle poured two rums. They clinked glasses, but Carlos waited for his uncle to drink first.

He wasn't certain of what to expect.

"Muchos gracias, tío, I had to get off St. Thomas," Carlos drank and refilled their glasses. "Shit went bad."

"I know, I know," Uncle Piedra was understanding. "You've had a lot of problems. Try to get some sleep. We'll talk about it in the morning."

"Where are we heading?"

"I'm catching a plane in St. Maarten," his uncle replied and moved to his cabin. Carlos had another glass of rum and slept on the salon's sofa.

The smell of coffee woke him. Carlos poured a cup, climbed to the cockpit, and found his uncle enjoying the brisk morning.

"Nephew, come, sit, enjoy this view of nothing but sea and sky, no land in sight. Coffee's good? Would you like another cup?"

"I'm fine, gracias," he replied. "Un buen dia." Carlos sat across from his uncle, behind the captain at the wheel.

"You met Remy last night. He's the new delivery captain. We are changing the process. From now on we will rent yachts that will meet other rented yachts at different islands. No more, how do they say it, all our fish in one barrel."

"Piedra," Carlos leaned toward his uncle, 'I'm sorry; I'll work with you any way I can to make up for these problems. How can I help?"

"Oh, Carlos," the older man laughed as he rested his coffee cup on the deck, "I think you've done enough. Look around, there is nothing, no land. Okay, that's what you've left our St. Thomas operation with, nada, not a fucking thing. In fact, less than nothing, you owe, and owe big."

"I know, I understand, whatever I can do to make it up," Carlos whined.

The uncle nudged the captain. "Remy, go below and check our course. Please compute how many more hours until St. Maarten."

"Probably about midway now, boss, twelve more hours. We're doing about eight knots. Get there tonight."

"Go check that thing you have anyway, the J-pass?"

"Okay, the GPS," the skipper nodded and went below.

"You see, Carlos, I need to make a point. I gave you a business before your time; that is obvious now, long before you were ready. But you are my brother's son, family."

Carlos rubbed his face with his hands as if trying to cleanse it. "Uncle, it wasn't my fault. Those fucking Puerto Rican DEA tried to steal that load."

"But boy, how did they know where and when to meet our boat? Someone had to tell them."

"I don't know, Uncle, I don't know."

"It wasn't the Captain or the crew because they died protecting our product. The information about where and when had to come from your end."

Carlos was thinking, shaking his head while rubbing his jaw, "Only I knew; they called me from St. Barths..."

Piedra interrupted. "On what phone? You see, nephew, you should have used several phones so they couldn't trace the calls. We, my men, steal information about other operations. We have a simple antenna. What do you think the US government gives the DEA to intercept smugglers? The very best electronics!"

"Uncle!"

"You fucked up. This is your fault. Our load is lost. Our money is lost, and your sister's in prison."

Carlos hung his head and wrung his hands. "Lo siento!" he shouted, "I'm sorry!"

"I will give you another chance. Tú eres familia. You are family; otherwise, you would have been already dead. Look at me!" He pointed an automatic pistol at Carlos. "I'm giving you a chance, only because you are family. Get up! I said get up! Your stupidity cost a fortune! Now you must pay! Jump overboard!"

"What?! No, uncle, you can't, please give me a chance," he pleaded.

"What can I do with you? Carlos, your sister will be in prison for years. She did nothing except listen to you. You don't know how many times she called and warned me that you, her own brother, was taking stupid risks. So, what can I do? Someone's got to pay; be the example. Even in the familia, there must be control." He backed Carlos to the stern.

"But you said you would give me another chance?" Carlos begged. "I might... I can make it right. What do you want?"

"I want you to jump. I do not want to shoot you."

"Uncle!"

"You are family," he handed the younger man a life ring.

"Here, take this and jump in the water. If you make it… to land… then, well, you made it and God smiled on you. This is your chance, your only chance. Jump and I'll throw it to you. Jump!"

Carlos snatched the red life ring and jumped. His uncle waved as the sailboat quickly moved away, and muttered, "Buena suerte, mi estúpido amigo!" *(Good luck, my stupid friend.)*

In Old San Juan, the next morning a new chapter opened for Lucy and Keith. The couple slept past nine and enjoyed a leisurely breakfast before they freed a very excited Baron from the kennel. The big, yellow dog sprayed his scent on every light pole as he happily dragged them back to Starlet.

Dale had gathered his gear and was waiting under the awning shade in the yacht's cockpit. Lucy went below to make coffee.

"I listened to a lot of news reports. No mention of anyone getting away," Dale smiled. "Local islanders fighting for turf against Colombian drug lords."

"We listened at breakfast. Big news. They think the boat explosion erased me," Keith chuckled. "Yeah, that guy's erased, gone for good. The best part, the Virgin Island Marine Police, VIMP, is taking credit. They say their sharpshooter hit a fuel tank on the outboard. The tide must have carried the body out to sea. What jokers!"

Dale snickered, "They're trying to paint the DEA as fallen heroes. They fell all right, straight to hell. Hard to deny the videos. Went immediately on YouTube. The world loves reality blood and violence."

"Any idea what happened to your West Indian friend? I hope he got away."

"Nah, hope so, but no way of knowing. We never exchanged names and addresses," he grinned, "won't be any sending postcards. He's a smart kid. St. Thomas will be red hot for months, but if he keeps a low profile and sits on his stash, like us, he's set for life."

Keith leaned back against the cushion and scratched Baron's ears, "Took a few more years than expected, but like they say, every dog has his day."

"Well, buddy, this has been great," Dale put his arm around Keith. "We took a chance, a big chance, and it paid off. I can never thank you enough for giving me a second lease on life."

"Come on, Dale, I could never have pulled this off alone."

Lucy brought three cups. "Hey, you two are getting very touchy-feely with all this hugging. Something you want to tell me?" she laughed.

"Just thanks," Dale hugged her. Then he stooped to pet Baron before he grabbed his backpack. "I think I'll get a room where you stayed last night and spend the week looking for a good boat." He stepped off Starlet, turned, and with a big grin, saluted, "I'm off to find newer places and faces. Y'all keep safe and smiling; and don't take no wooden nickels."

Lucy snuggled against her man and asked, "Where you want to sail to?"

"Let's stop at Dominica on the way south. Got some friends there I'd like to see again."

NOT THE END

ONLY A NEXT BEGINNING

ABOUT RALPH TROUT

I was born lucky to be the only son of a Pennsylvania family. More good fortune was being raised on a beautiful farm twenty miles northeast of Pittsburgh along the Allegheny River. This was post-WWII, and my mother's parents were gracious to have my family live in an upstairs bedroom. Perhaps gracious isn't the best word because the upstairs bedrooms had no heat. I never forgot how cold it was in that house.

A degree from Pitt during the unsettling decade of the steel mills imploding meant little, except that construction paid better, and you had to find work somewhere other than Pittsburgh. As soon as I could, I moved to the warm tropics. I tried Hawaii, but didn't care to exist as a 'haole.' A move to St. Thomas, USVI and taking over construction for a realtor, made the Caribbean my home for thirty years. In the domino effect, I got hooked on sailing, scuba diving, fishing, rum, and all other types of fun under the tropical sun. Tank diving evolved from lobsters to sunken wrecks and treasure. Fishing grew from a weekend day to two years dragging baits from my trawler around nearly every island in the Caribbean chain.

Jimmy Buffett sang it in a Pirate Looks At Forty, *'the cannons don't thunder, nothing to plunder, I'm an over forty victim of fate.'* Living and working throughout the Caribbean in the '80s and '90s was fantastic surrounded by gorgeous women, countless boozers, smugglers, white-collar criminals, and know-it-all cruisers. Late summer and autumn, when the leaves were changing in colder climates, the storms blew through. In retrospect, the islands were the losers to unrestrained development. Tourism is a fickle monster.

The salty-life wasn't for everyone; you had to be a hearty sort. Plenty of couples split up; islands are incredibly hard on women. But the small saltwater rocks suited me. My tropical tales are convoluted memories enhanced as each year passes. My good friend, Rocky Mountain Earl, professes to never let facts stall a good story.

The Caribbean Compass first took my stories. My fiction Caribbean tales include The Wreck, Soucouyant – The Caribbean Vampire, Something Fishy, Soon Come – Divorce Caribbean Style. When I learned the intricacies necessary to plant a tropical veggie garden I shared the info in: The Caribbean Home Garden Guide. My greatest adventure is Road Trip: Huautla – The Mushroom Cult. All my books are available on Amazon.

S